The Caves of Etretat

Book One of Four

By
Matt Chatelain

The Caves of Etretat by Matt Chatelain
Copyright © 2011 by Matt Chatelain
ISBN 978-0-9878330-0-6

Cover design by CreateSpace

Original art by Matt Chatelain

Published by Matt Chatelain.
For further information, go to mattchatelain.com.
To contact, send email to matt@mattchatelain.com.

The Caves of Etretat

To Mom

Matt Chatelain

Foreword

I have been led to certain knowledge and this has caused me to re-evaluate everything that I believed about the world. The knowledge did not come easily. I was manipulated into walking a trail, never knowing what I was to find until it was upon me.

In light of what I now know, my last task before I leave this world will be to write a chronicle, these four books, so that I may reveal how this began.

A whole series of events were occurring in step with my journey. Others had happened before I was born. I have inserted various journals at key points in this chronicle to clarify the multitude of connections leading me forward.

The beginning of any path rarely indicates where it will end. Now I know that the answer was within me from the very start. I couldn't see it, not until I had walked the entire way. After all, that is the purpose of the path.

Paul Sirenne

Matt Chatelain

CHAPTER 1
Murdered!

I had a feeling something was wrong before I even opened my front door. The three men standing on my porch, flashing their badges, did nothing to dispel my concerns. Behind them, I noticed a badly parked car with a rotating red light stuck on its dash. The tallest man spoke softly.

"Good evening. Sorry to disturb you at this late hour. We are looking for a man named Sirenne... Paul Sirenne."

"That would be me. What is this about?"

"Mr Sirenne? My name is Detective Harris. This is my partner, Detective Stafford and this is Inspector Norton from Interpol, who is here strictly as an observer... I'm afraid that I have some bad news. I was wondering if we might come in for a few minutes?"

Worried, I stepped aside and allowed them in. The two detectives entered, followed by the grimy-looking Inspector who walked in quickly, his shifty eyes darting nervously left and right. The men accompanied me to the study, where several easy chairs served as a setting for the conversation.

Sitting down, Detective Harris pulled out a small tape recorder, placing it on the coffee table between us. Detective Stafford excused himself, asking directions to the kitchen, claiming to be thirsty. I didn't believe him. The Interpol Inspector remained standing, looking at me intensely with his beady eyes.

"Sorry about the tape recorder. My memory is terrible and I can't take field notes, not legible ones anyway... It's always so difficult in these cases. I never know exactly how to proceed. However, experience has taught me that being direct is always the lesser of two evils. I'd like you to prepare yourself for a shock, Mr Sirenne, a bad shock..."

Detective Harris shifted in his chair, waiting for my reaction. I felt a hard knot in my stomach, replacing the butterflies that had previously fluttered there. I nodded to him bracing myself.

"Mr Sirenne, your parents have been murdered."

"What?... That's impossible, Detective... I just saw my father and his wife three days ago... they were fine," I protested, choking up.

"I'm terribly sorry, Mr Sirenne, but we are positive of our facts. Their identity was confirmed through fingerprinting. Your father and his wife, identified as Paul and Darlene Sirenne, were killed two nights ago, shortly after midnight."

"What happened? Was it robbery?" I asked, my voice trembling.

"No, I'm afraid it's nothing that easy, Mr Sirenne. They were murdered, then mutilated. Nothing was stolen, as far as we can tell..."

I felt flushed. My mind was spinning.

"But why? They never did anything to anyone. Who would want to hurt them?"

Inspector Norton answered me.

"Detective Harris doesn't know why, Mr Sirenne, nobody does... But I think I know who... I'm not from here, you see... I'm not even supposed to be on this case... Did you know the police knew about this from the moment it happened? Someone called it in. Curious, isn't it?... As soon as I heard about the murders, I knew they matched the pattern of a serial killer I call the Shadow-Killer. By chance, I was right here, in town for a convention. Lucky for you and for the local police... I've been investigating the Shadow-Killer for many years now, spending every hour of my spare time... He is the most elusive monster I have ever encountered, responsible for at least forty-five murders, most of them in Europe. I now believe that he has come here, to Canada... to Ottawa, to kill your parents."

"I want to see them."

Detective Harris jumped in, trying to take back control of the conversation.

"I'd suggest you don't, Mr Sirenne. He left a grisly scene. It's better if you remember them the way you last saw them."

"I don't care..."

"I know how you feel, believe me, but you should give this some time. Anyway, the bodies have already been removed and taken to our forensics lab..."

Norton interrupted Harris again.

"... For all the good it will do... The Shadow-Killer never leaves a speck of dust behind... You'd know that, Detective, if you'd seen what I've seen..."

Ignoring him, Detective Harris continued.

"... Anyway, listen, how about we talk a bit more and after that, if you still want to see them, we'll take you down to the morgue... It's the best that I can offer right now."

Detective Stafford came back into the study, holding a glass of water, when Norton interrupted Harris yet again.

"... Mr Sirenne, I am convinced your parents were selected, *chosen*, by the Shadow-Killer for some reason. If I am right, this might be the break I have been waiting for... Detective Harris was right not to want you to see their bodies. The Shadow-Killer's *modus operandi* is brutal. He is inhuman when killing people. Seeing what he leaves behind is hard, even for seasoned officers. But what he did with your parents... it is truly horrible..."

I felt numb from the assault of these revelations. Norton continued his rapid-fire delivery, disregarding the looks from Detective Harris.

"... It seems as if the killer wanted to leave a message for someone. He staged the bodies, placing them in such a way that they would... uhm... look like two letters- an H and an N... Does that mean anything to you?"

My mind was a blank. I could hardly think, let alone reason.

"An H and an N?... HN?... No, I'm sorry it doesn't, Inspector..."

A disturbing question came to me: how could a human body be positioned to look like an N? The H seemed easy enough, but the N baffled me. How could anyone position a body to look like a proper N? Detective Harris interrupted my train of thought.

"Mr Sirenne, don't go down that road... I know what you're thinking... Norton, how could you blurt it out like that?... Listen to me, Mr Sirenne, just let it go..."

My mind kept working at it, ignoring his advice, bending an imaginary stick figure this way, that way, desperately trying to make it fit the shape of an N. I kept failing.

"Tell me how he did it," I asked in a low voice.

"You don't want to know, Mr Sirenne, don't ask me that," Harris retorted, looking increasingly ill at ease.

I remembered what he had said: my parents had been mutilated.

"Tell me!" I insisted, daring him to look away.

"I'll tell him, Detective, if you're too squeamish..."

"Norton, no. You're just an observer here."

"Give me a break with those stupid rules. He needs to know. He's got to understand what he's facing... I'm going to tell him and you're not going to stop me."

Norton sat down in a chair, next to the scowling Detective Harris, and looked me straight in the eyes.

"He placed your father in the shape of an H by opening up his arms and legs, his body acting as the centre bar. I believe the legs wouldn't take the right position so he... uhm... he cut the tendons. That way he could place both legs in a straight line... then he cut off the head to finish the job."

His words burned an image in my brain, etching it there like acid on a copper plate.

"What about Darlene?"

Norton continued with his description, his voice tightly controlled, his eyes never leaving mine.

"The N was harder. Again, he used the body as the angled bar in the centre of the letter. After removing the head, he placed the shoulders at the top and dropped the right arm as the first bar of the 'N'. I suppose he didn't like the short length of the arm... The proportions probably seemed wrong to him. No matter why, he removed the left arm from her body and placed it below the right one, clasping the hands, to make that bar as long as the legs, the other vertical bar of the N. He then placed both heads on the ground, one after each body... I think he was trying to make sure we knew that the letters represented full words, although I have no idea what those words might be... I had hoped you would know?..."

He stopped speaking, sitting there in silence, chewing his lower lip strongly enough to leave marks.

My head felt as if it was about to explode.

"Inspector Norton, Detectives, perhaps we could continue this later. I don't think I can handle any more right now."

Norton's eyes took on an odd look. Slowly, his mouth softened into an insincere smile. Detective Harris cut off whatever he was going to say.

"We understand. You need some time to recover from the shock of all this. However, we will need to meet again soon. We'd like you to come down to the station and make an official statement, at some point in the next few days."

He rose, picking up his tape recorder, directing Norton to follow him. The Interpol Inspector headed out of the study, a sullen look on his face. As the three men reached the front door, I asked one final question.

"Has my father's house been released by the police?"

Detective Stafford replied:

"Yes, Sir, it has. That was one of the reasons we came to see you in the first place. I guess we forgot to mention it with everything going on. The Forensics Department finished with it a few hours ago... See you down at the station, Mr Sirenne."

They left the house and returned to their car. They were talking to each other. It seemed to me as if they were arguing with Norton. I couldn't blame them. I had found him abrasive. Still in shock, I stood on the front porch, watching them leave. Only one thought made it through the numbness:

I needed to go to my father's house.

Located in the Glebe area of Ottawa, it had been my birthplace and my home until I moved into my own house ten years ago. Now, I would have to go there to face the end of my family. I didn't feel ready.

While I drove toward my father's place, my rear view mirror allowed me the occasional glimpse of a familiar vehicle and its driver, Norton. His companions were nowhere to be seen. Perhaps he was intent on protecting me but I doubted it. His comments had seemed disjointed to me, despite the circumstances. Everything he said had come across insincere, as if he were following another agenda. I resolved to ignore him for the time being. Let him do his watching.

To some, police protection might seem comforting. To me, it felt like an irritant. I preferred to mind my own business and for others to do the same, even in dire circumstances. That way I hurt no one and no one got hurt. I almost changed my opinion when I arrived at my father's house. Even Norton's company would have been preferable to that of my own thoughts. I hurried up the entrance staircase and stopped in front of the door, taking a deep breath. I felt frozen in place, unable to open it.

Breaking the spell and forcing myself to move, I removed the police tape with a trembling hand and entered, closing the door behind me. I looked around the entrance hallway. Everything looked normal but it felt wrong, empty, too quiet. I walked into the living room and there it was: the bloody outline of the H and the N. I was horrified by the bloodstained dots after each gruesome letter, knowing what had left those imprints.

Seized by a sudden, irresistible impulse, I ran to the kitchen, filled a large bucket with hot water and picked up a heavy bristle brush.

Those stains had to go!

I returned to the living room, trying to stay calm, to think nothing about what the stains *represented*. I knelt down, splashed some water on the floor, and began scrubbing the dark stains. I didn't care if I scratched the wood. At some point, I started crying in great, wracking sobs, the tears streaming down my cheeks, dripping onto the bloodstains on the floor.

By the time I was done, my tears had dried, evaporated by a burning resolve unlike any I had before. I did not know how, I did not know when, but I would catch that monstrous killer. He would pay for what he had done.

***

I returned home and collapsed on my bed, falling into a fitful sleep. Next morning, feeling somewhat more settled, I made a few phone calls. I informed my lawyer about what had happened and he began doing what was necessary to wrap up my father's affairs. I also dropped down to the police station, as requested, to make a statement. I ended up talking to Detective Harris again, who seemed to have developed the same dislike for Inspector Norton as I had.

He informed me that Norton was a loose cannon, acting pretty much how he pleased. The local police were in charge of the investigation and Norton had done nothing but slow things down. I made my statement, after which the detective assured me that I had been eliminated as a serious suspect. He promised to keep me informed of any progress in the case, particularly where Norton was concerned.

I had not been home five minutes, when the doorbell rang. A delivery truck was parked in front, the driver waiting at the door with a package.

"Who's it from?"

The driver looked at his clipboard.

"...Uhm... Ah, here we are: it was a sent by Mr Sirenne, three days ago, with instructions to be delivered today."

My father had mailed this to me just before he died.

I signed for it hurriedly and he handed me a thick, cardboard envelope. Closing the door in the driver's face in my haste, I ripped the package open, pulling out a large hardcover book. It was *The Hollow Needle* by Maurice Leblanc... the letters HN!   .

If the Shadow-Killer wanted my attention, he had it now.

I opened the front cover of the book and found a small note, readily identifying the almost illegible scrawl as my father's handwriting:

Son,

After all this time, I have decided to send you this book for safekeeping. It is the key to an incredible secret and riches beyond belief. Our family has been keeping this secret, waiting for the time when you will rediscover it.

Someone has been watching me, Paul. A man with a European accent. I was planning to give you this book in six months, on your thirty-fifth birthday. His presence has changed all that. There is no more time to waste, son. You must begin the Hunt now.

Read the book, Son. Only by looking beyond its words will you succeed. The fate of the world depends on it.

Remember: secrets of this nature have a tendency to attract trouble. No matter what you do, keep your research discreet. I know you will need help. Organize a small team but choose only your most trusted friends to help you.

Good luck. Call me as soon as you can.

Your Father.

A knock at the front door interrupted me. I closed the book, putting it down. Norton was there, looking for more information. Norton with a European accent. I did not let him in this time, forcing him to talk from the front porch.

"Ah, Mr Sirenne. I hope you are calmer today, so that we can finish our conversation."

"I'm not sure we have a conversation to finish, Inspector. It seems the police do not completely recognize your involvement in this case..."

He interrupted me, taking on an aggressive tone.

"Mr Sirenne, no matter what they have told you, I am the only one who knows what we are dealing with here. The man who did this is unlike any other serial killer you might have heard of... This one is in a class of his own... Usually his murders have a certain twisted logic to them, one that means something only to him... In the case of your parents, he departed from his long-established pattern and left the clearest of messages, HN. These two simple letters are very important in the scheme of things, since they have convinced me that the Shadow-Killer specifically chose your parents. I'm positive he watched them for at least two weeks before moving in for the kill, you know... He meant for this message to be seen by someone and I am having trouble thinking of anyone else but you... By the way, what did that truck just deliver to you?"

His voice dropped and his gaze sharpened. He left the question hanging in the air, saying nothing else, pressuring me for an answer. It was an obvious ploy but it placed me in a quandary. What was I going to tell him?

I had little choice. My father's warning had been crystal clear.

"I own an antique bookstore, Inspector. The package was a book I had ordered, nothing more... As for those letters, you asked me about them before and I gave you my answer. Nothing has changed since then. I still have no idea what those letters might mean."

He brushed aside my statement as if I hadn't even spoken.

"... Look at it from my viewpoint, Sirenne: the Shadow-Killer doesn't play around. I know this more than anyone else... Either he left this message for you or he just killed your parents as a lark, leaving you to inherit all their money, which, according to my research, is a considerable sum, is it not?"

I found his words offensive.

"Inspector, I think this 'talk' is over."

His demeanour changed instantly.

"Fine. I understand. You are still... upset. I will leave now. But you would do well to remember my words. In all the years I have chased this murderer, he has never left a message as clear as this. The Shadow-Killer has an agenda and I am convinced you are part of it, willing or not. You had better be careful. You really don't want to get on his bad side... nor on mine, for that matter. I think he will get in touch with you and I *will* be there when he does."

"I admire your tenacity, Inspector but you have misjudged me in this situation. I have nothing to do with the Shadow-Killer. My father and Darlene have just been killed and I am trying to come to terms with that. It is making it very difficult to know how to react, a fact which you seem to be taking advantage of. I need some time to reflect... and grieve."

Norton's eyes stopped their incessant movement and focused directly on me. He stepped closer abruptly, bringing his unshaven face within inches of mine, keeping his voice low and threatening.

"I've been chasing this monster for fifteen years... I've seen the bodies he's left behind, checked every detail, talked to every witness... Let me tell you, in all those years, he has *never* left a *single* clue to anyone but me... except for this time. This is my best chance to catch him. Either you hired him or he left you a message. I don't care which it is. Just as long as it leads me to *him*... and you're not going to stand in my way, playing your stupid games!"

He was either crazy or he was trying to goad me. Either way, he seemed obsessed. It was time for this to end. I pulled away, distancing my face from his stinking breath.

"Listen, Inspector, surely you recognise that I want the murderer found as much as you do. Stop wasting your time with pointless accusations and get back to the real job, of catching the killer."

"Fine, Mr Sirenne. Have it your way... But don't think this is over, because it's not," he raged, heading back down the stairs, muttering to himself.

I didn't know if I had done the right thing, of lying to him, but it was too late now.

Keeping others in the dark was not a new thing for me. I was born with a predisposition for secrecy and solitude. My father had reinforced this secretive approach to life through frequent games of strategy and planning. I had learned to keep my own counsel, to do things my way. I hated it when someone told me what to do. Dealing with the law was no different. In any case, I didn't like Norton and I didn't like the way he was shadowing me. I would involve him when I was ready and not a minute before.

When my mother was killed in a car accident three years ago, my father and I had drawn closer to each other. He had later remarried but I had never gotten close to Darlene. Now they were both gone, taken from me by that murderer. Nothing would stop me from solving the mystery that lay hidden within the pages of the book my father had sent me. It was his final wish. He had thought it important enough to mail the book, aware of the looming threat. He had stressed the importance of secrecy. The Shadow-Killer was probably not far behind, looking for the very same book and the clues it contained.

I returned to my study, where I examined the book more closely. It seemed like a good quality, leather-bound hardcover. There was nothing particularly remarkable about it, except that it was in perfect condition. The Hollow Needle, by Maurice Leblanc, had originally been published in 1909, although this copy was printed in 1955.

I recalled that I had seen another book similar to this one, many years ago, a gift from my father on my ninth birthday. I remembered that it too had come with a cryptic message but I could no longer recall what it was. I would have to look for it.

I wondered what my father had been trying to tell me. This was not a new process between my father and me. Nothing had ever been simple with him. It was always a puzzle or a mystery, never a straight answer. *'Keeps your mind active and alert, ready for anything'*, he would say.

As a child, I had grown to love the little challenges he frequently prepared for me. My keen mind eagerly ferreted out every clue, every hint. I would rarely fail in my efforts, anxious to see the smile in his eyes and feel the pressure of his hand on my shoulder when he congratulated me.

Every now and then, he would present me with a masterpiece puzzle, every exquisite detail worked out perfectly. He called these exercises *hunts*. Once I had solved a hunt, he would invariably organize another one in short order. I could see him now, pointing the way to the start of a new trail, calling out to me:

'The hunt is on, Paul. The hunt is on! What waits for you at the end? You'll never know unless you begin.'

This book had to be the first clue leading to such a hunt. If so, this would be the last one I would get from my father.

I wondered where I had placed the other copy of The Hollow Needle. I wanted to read the note it contained. Vaguely remembering seeing it in my bedroom, I headed up the stairs, almost running, feeling a tinge of excitement.

I had never understood why my father created these intricate puzzle-and-clue-based adventures. Looking at the situation I now found myself in, I wondered if perhaps, he had been training me all along, preparing me for this very task.

Entering my room, I approached the small shelf above my bed. I scanned the titles, finding the book easily, to my relief. Removing it from the shelf, I opened it from the back, finding my father's original note, an old piece of Vellum paper. The tape holding it in place had dried out and yellowed, the glue having become crusty over time. I wondered why my father had done that, knowing we held the same reverence for books.

The thought slipped away when I read the note he had written so long ago:

Dear Paul:

On the occasion of your ninth birthday, I give you the same book my father gave to me when I was nine. It's a wonderful story but it is also so much more.

It is the beginning...

The beginning and the end,
Follow the circle, it bends.
The end and the beginning
The answer in the connecting
                                    Your Father

PS:
A real story ends near Etretat
Lost until Paul infers new ideas subtly
You ought understand responsibility,
Necessarily after moiling Etretat

When I had read this note at age nine, I had not grasped my father's true intent. Today, it seemed obvious that he was signalling the start of a hunt. Something was going on in the town of Etretat and it was connected with this book.

It was time to read the Hollow Needle again, with fresh eyes and a new purpose, forced upon me by a killer and an ancient family legacy. I returned downstairs to the study, placing the two copies next to each other on the coffee table. They were virtually identical. I chose one at random, sat back in the recliner, a cup of coffee on the side table, prepared to re-discover what I had long considered to be Leblanc's finest novel.

The Hollow Needle had been *the* phenomenal book of its time. It was a story full of historical mystery and treasure, with no less than the venerable Sherlock Holmes making an appearance. Filled with charm, respect and a proper code of ethics, it brought me back to another era, when even villains had morals.

Its main character was a man named Arsene Lupin, developed by Leblanc as a French counterpart to the immensely popular Sherlock Holmes in Britain. Lupin, a gentleman-thief, was a likeable rogue, able to steal your heart and your paintings at the same time. He was possessed of the same clarity of thinking as his British alter ego, making him a perfect adversary for Holmes.

At the story's core was a fantastic concept. In France, off the chalk cliffs of the small town of Etretat, a hundred metre pillar of rock projected mightily from the salt waters of the English Channel. According to Leblanc, the needle of rock was hollow, a secret held for centuries by the many kings and queens of France. Used as a stronghold and a repository for treasure, knowledge of its existence had been lost during the upheaval of the French Revolution. Of course, gentleman-thief Arsene Lupin rediscovered it. The most interesting part of the mystery involved the Fort of Frefosse, found on top of the southern cliff overlooking Etretat. It was at the base of this fort that the secret entrance to the Needle was located.

At the bottom of one page in the book, I noticed a clever note from the editors, probably added to convince the reader of the validity of these assertions:

'A few years after this book was originally released to the public, the army was commissioned to alter the fort because of undue attention since the book's publication.'

Very convincing indeed!

So convincing that I found myself half-believing the Needle was truly hollow. Having finished the book, I got up from the recliner and went to my desk, turning the computer on. I called up a search engine on the internet, entering the name 'Etretat'. I was surprised to find that it was a real place. I found several pictures of the Needle. Encouraged, I tried search queries, such as 'treasure', 'hollow', etc. This landed me in a website where I found the following statement:

'Etretat, a popular tourist destination, often attracts treasure hunters looking for the famous entrance to the hollow Needle. Well folks, the Needle is indeed there, however, it is, without a doubt, completely solid.'

I felt as if I had hit a brick wall. Luckily, this was not my first time on a hunt. There were always obstacles and pitfalls along the way. Treasure was an incredibly elusive prey, far rarer than one would think. Many of them had already been found or plundered, while others had been proven to be wild goose chases, such as the Oak Island mystery.

I was far more compelled by the challenge of solving my father's hunt. Treasure was almost incidental.

One thing was certain: whatever this Hollow Needle mystery was, it was not about a hollow needle!

***

I was moving at great speed. Looking down, I could see landscape flying by, forests, fields, tilled land, then more woods... I was puzzled... What was I doing here? Where was I? With sudden clarity, I became aware that I was in a lucid dream. I seemed to be flying, although I was not in command of my direction of flight. The landscape changed. I was now moving past farms and roads, with the odd house here and there. I could hear the sound of waves crashing somewhere ahead.

I approached a cliff with a number of strangely shaped patches of grass on it. A golf course. I slowed down until I was hovering over a big building. Just beyond it, I saw a couple walking along a path, their arms linked together. They were approaching a squat, cement structure, an old bunker. An intense yellowish light was emanating from its every opening. For a brief moment, the man looked up, his face illuminated by the bright glow, before turning back towards the bunker opening, walking in with the raven-haired woman.

He had looked like me!

The surf was crashing heavily below. I flew towards the edge of the cliff, almost colliding with it before coming to a full stop. Without any warning, I dropped into a vertiginous descent towards the water below. It felt more like falling than flying. Panic gripped me, my eyes locked on the rapidly approaching water.

I was going to hit it hard!

I woke up with a start, my arms and legs flailing, screaming out, unable to stop myself. I was drenched in sweat. It took me almost fifteen minutes to slow my heartbeat and calm my nerves. I realised that I had fallen asleep in the recliner after I finished reading the Hollow Needle. I could neither figure out what had brought on the vivid dream, which still disturbed me with its odd intensity, nor explain what it could possibly mean. The man entering the bunker had looked like me. How could he be me? Who was the woman with him?

I was baffled.

A new thought intruded - a thought about the book. I vocalised it to give it form.

"What about that quote about the fort? Why did the army change the fort, if the story about the hollow Needle is false?"

"Because the quote about changing the fort is false, that's why," I answered.

"But how do I know that? Why even place such a comment in the book? It's so easy to verify... Anyway, the editors wrote that remark, not Leblanc, and my copy of that book was published in 1955, years after Leblanc died. Why would the editors care?" I continued.

By now, I was sitting up in the recliner, any hope for sleep completely gone. First the dream and now this. I wouldn't be able to rest until I had some sort of answer. Sighing, I got up and went back to my computer. I typed 'Fort of Frefosse' into the search engine. A single photo of a tattered postcard showing a blurry picture of the fort, circa 1900, came up. That was it.

Not exactly satisfying results.

Trying different search engines, I came across another picture, dated November 28 1911, showing several people posing in front of the fort area. Coincidentally, the angle was similar to that in the postcard photo. The fort's outline was radically different, the main structure having been completely destroyed, leaving a deep pit surrounded by a jumble of broken stones. All that remained of the fort were a few crumbling walls. This photo dovetailed nicely with the editor's note in the Hollow Needle but was it related to my father's hunt? Why was the fort destroyed?

I found an online reference to Leblanc's Villa in Etretat. Originally purchased by an estate, it was later taken over by Leblanc's surviving granddaughter. She had renovated it into a bed and breakfast themed around the Hollow Needle mystery.

Still searching, I located an internet site with something of substance. Maintained by a French caver, most of the site was about various cave systems but one page had a summary of a most interesting book:

The Secret of the Kings of France

or

The True Identity of Arsene Lupin

by Valere Catogan

Etretat is a small, nondescript town situated on the coast of the ancient Gaulish territory. What could have attracted emperors, kings and queens to this tiny village, lost in a small valley, nestled between two of the tallest chalk cliffs in the country? Historically, Etretat was previously known as *Esttretat*, as referenced in the 1628 Gerard Mercator Atlas. However, if one examines the map of the King's Navy (1534, Maritime Archives), one will be surprised to read:

'*Ici est tr. Etat*' (translation: Here is tr. State)

Could 'tr.' stand for treasure? Treasure of the State?

Here are a few historical facts, relating to Etretat's mystery:

1) In 1300, the Hundred Year War began. One century later, after a brief cessation of hostilities, Henry the Fifth landed in Normandy with his troops somewhere on the Gaulish coast, on what was quite likely the site of Etretat itself. How did Henry the Fifth reach the top of the precipitous cliffs with his troops without anyone witnessing the invasion?

2) Alexander Dumas' novel of the Three Musketeers was based on historical facts: The Duke of Buckingham actually fell in love with Anne d'Autriche and he did receive the famous pearl necklace from her. However, one mystery remains concerning these historical events: how did the Duke succeed in evading the vigilance of the Cardinal of Richelieu and manage to enter several times into France when there were increased patrols along the coast?

3) In 1670, a secret treaty was signed by Charles the Second and Louis the Fourteenth, having been negotiated by the Duchess of Orleans. How did she leave France to reach England? Where did Jacques the Second, escaping from Guillaume d'Orange in 1688, land secretly on the Normandy Coast?

4) Napoleon Bonaparte ordered plans to be drawn for the construction of a port of war in Etretat. This project was brought to a standstill by the insistence of Talleyrand. Fouchet noted that Talleyrand had never previously concerned himself with naval affairs. A few days prior to his sudden concern, Talleyrand had received a visit from the Baron of Bellevert, later pronounced an English spy. For years, Talleyrand did everything possible to distance Napoleon and his engineers from this small beach.

5) Why, after the 1830, 1848 and 1870 revolutions, did the de-throned kings head for the roads of the Seine, instead of others, in particular those towards Calais, or Boulogne? Most likely, it was to reach the mysterious Etretat.

Could these events be connected to the secret held within Etretat's cliffs?

What secret could this little town be hiding? Certainly not the hollow needle as suggested by Maurice Leblanc in his Arsene Lupin story. Etretat's great secret was in fact a camouflaged docking point, hidden below the massive cliffs, invisible from above and inaccessible on foot from surrounding beaches. One could only reach the hidden dock thanks to a tunnel that pierced the cliff itself. This tunnel made it possible to leave France for England discreetly, or vice-versa.

Who dug these tunnels? History does not reveal its secrets on this matter. No matter its origins, the elite kept the secret of the kings of France during many long centuries. During the early part of the 19th century, they took new precautions to ensure that secrecy was maintained. Rich families purchased key neighbouring properties. A tunnel, which once connected the hidden docks to a small valley, was lengthened to reach into Etretat's *Donjon*, then later, to the *Villa Le Petit Val* and finally, to the *Villa des Oeuillets*. Mr Beaugrand, jeweller for the Queen, owned this last villa, by seeming pure coincidence.

Today, this secret is no more. Some tunnels were rediscovered by local fishermen but the majority of the tunnels no longer exist. Access to the eight hundred metre long main passageway is completely forbidden. The ancient dock was eroded long ago by the tide and the collapsing cliffs have buried its few remains. The *Villa des Roches* tunnel has been walled up, although one can still see its entrance point to the left of the stairs leading up the Amont cliff.

Etretat has not yet revealed all its secrets. During the Occupation, the Germans made many discoveries. Unfortunately, all documents pertaining to these discoveries were destroyed at the end of the war during an allied bombing run that destroyed ninety percent of the city of Havre.

(This text is a partial summary of a document written by Valere Catogan, a nom de plume used by Raymond Lindon, who researched the history of Etretat, aided by Maurice Leblanc.)

End of document.

The text was referring to a secret backed by historical facts, something much more plausible than a supposed hollow needle. The author, Raymond Lindon, had sought to hide his identity, writing under the pseudonym of Valere Catogan. I could not help but wonder why. In addition, the article mentioned that Leblanc had helped Lindon with the book.

Leblanc appeared to be in the middle of it all. His story of the Hollow Needle, while admittedly fictitious, seemed intended to attract attention to Etretat. In my case, it had succeeded. Another fact struck me: it was now 5:00AM and I was exhausted. I went to bed, my head brimming over with tunnels, treasures, and secrets.

***

The next few days were very busy for me. I took an indefinite leave of absence from my business, a successful antique bookstore that had been in the family for generations. I left it in the capable hands of my manager, until I could sort out what I was going to do. The police had agreed to release my father and Darlene's remains within a few days and I struggled to find the time to complete the funeral arrangements and attend the reading of the will.

I was the only one present.

Norton had been right about one thing: my parents had left me a veritable fortune, more than fifty million dollars. I had never known that they had such wealth. It had certainly never been apparent in our daily life and my father had never whispered a word of his fortune to me. I almost felt betrayed. Where had these riches come from? How had I ended up with a family secret hidden in a book? Who was the one who had brought it into our family? My grandfather? My great-grandfather?

Normally, when I had such questions to contend with, I would turn to my father for help. I was now forever deprived of his calm advice. Yet, he was not completely gone. I could still imagine his voice, as if he were right next to me:

'You won't solve anything in that state, son. First, you have to calm down, get a bit of perspective on things. Take some time and think things through.'

I found solace in following his advice, allowing my stronger emotions to settle. I felt much anger and sadness but, gradually, these feelings cooled. Logic and planning took their place.

The killer seemed to be running circles around both Norton and the police. I had no confidence either of them would find the killer or solve the deeper mysteries surrounding the case. I also had to be realistic. I was no detective. I had no experience in these worldly matters. I had never been the physical type, always being more cerebral in my pursuits and shunning public activities.

I was confident that I would be up to the task given time but time was exactly the thing I did not have. A killer out there had resorted to a flagrant act, attracting unwanted interest from the police, in order to get *my* attention. It could be no coincidence that my father sent that book to me shortly before being killed. He was being watched and had decided to act.

I faced a crucial choice: keep the book safe and do nothing or take up the hunt and unveil the secret before anyone else. If I did nothing, it would mean that I allowed the death of my father and Darlene to go un-avenged. I would be a sitting duck, waiting for the killer to pay me an unwelcome visit. There was really no choice. I had to solve the mystery before the killer did. Unfortunately, he was already well ahead of me. I was playing catch-up.

I needed help.

My father had understood this. He had known that I would not have time to cover all the bases. He had suggested that I would need to assemble a team. Sharing the secret was risky but necessary. Thanks to my father's will, I now had ample resources to fund the assembly of such a team.

All that inheritance money implied something else: the treasure I was seeking had to be something else than mere wealth.

CHAPTER 2
Assembling the Team

Selecting anyone to assist me in this dangerous venture was a difficult task. After much deliberation, I chose three of my closest friends, Jonathan Briar, Fabian Coulter and Liam O'Flanahan. I contacted them to arrange a preliminary meeting. A date was set for the day after the funeral.

On that day, I woke at 8:00AM, got up, showered, placed both Hollow Needle copies in my satchel, and headed out on foot to *The Top Nut*, a small coffee bar. Inspector Norton was still following me in his car. I evaded him by walking through several mini-malls in quick succession.

Ducking into the coffee shop, I stood in the doorway for a moment, looking around for my friends.

"Hey, Paul, we're over here!"

Turning in the direction of the voice, my eyes fell on Fabian Coulter. I had selected him for his amazing skills with everything computer. He was a world-class hacker who had earned his repute in the highest circles. A computer security consultant for the government, there was nothing he could not access. This thin, pasty man, a perpetual night owl, was my closest friend. We had known each other for more than twenty-five years and I trusted him with my life. His wiry strength and keen intellect would serve us well in our search.

Seated next to him was Jonathan Briar. Tall, fit and bald, the head of the history department at the University of Ottawa was an expert on ancient history. He had been my unofficial mentor for the past ten years. It was partly thanks to him that the Dead Sea Scroll deception had been uncovered. His specialty, however, was Roman history. We had worked together many times before. Our most recent foray had been about a year ago, focusing on the legend of the San Saba Silver Mines. I had always been impressed by Briar's ability to quickly collate masses of research into pertinent information. In his mid-fifties, he was still an energetic man, neither afraid of confrontation, nor of hard work.

Finally, there was Liam O'Flanahan. Short and overweight, O'Flanahan was a publisher of unusual books and a self-admitted expert on mysteries, conspiracies and the bizarre. He was the one who had convinced me to waste two years of my life, and no small sum of money, on the Oak Island mystery, his personal obsession. This Irish, red-haired man believed that, to convince anyone of his 'theories', he simply had to speak louder or perhaps a lot louder. Abrasive and irritating, O'Flanahan would never rest until answers were found. I knew I could trust him.

These three men, if they agreed to my proposal, would become my compatriots in an odd partnership. We had investigated countless mysteries before, spending evening after evening engaged in conversation about lost treasure and forgotten history. We were amateurs to be sure but, as a team, I was convinced there would be little we could not figure out.

"How was the funeral yesterday?" asked Briar "I'm so sorry I could not attend."

I sat down as Bridget, the waitress, brought me a cup of coffee.

"It was a funeral. It went as well as it could have. I still felt emotional when I got home. I had a pretty rough night... Anyway, I'm glad you all decided to come. You may not believe this but I think that my father sent me a lead to another hunt just before he... before he was murdered," I explained.

"Is the hunt connected to your father's death?" O'Flanahan asked, his nose already sniffing out a possible conspiracy.

They all knew about my father's hunts. Briar had even accompanied me on several occasions. He had been impressed at the twists and turns required to solve the devious puzzles.

"Yes it is, Liam... Gentlemen, I called you here because I need your help. You know that a monster, who has already claimed at least forty-five victims, murdered my father and Darlene. According to Norton, an Interpol inspector, this monster killed them to send a message: the letters H and N..."

My mind flashed briefly on the bloody scene in my parent's house. I tried to banish the image back to where it came from.

"In all confidence, I must admit that, when questioned by Norton, I held back a key piece of evidence. I would like to share that evidence with the three of you. I can only do that if you agree to join me in a hunt that could prove both dangerous and lucrative... Don't make this decision lightly, gentlemen. There is a killer involved in this and he is already on the job. I doubt that he would hesitate to murder anyone who stood in his way. Unlike any previous adventure we have worked on together, this one will likely be fraught with real danger. While making your decision, keep two facts in mind. One, I am convinced that I cannot succeed without your help... and two, I am willing to pay you each a hundred thousand dollars if you say yes."

Coulter was the first to take the bait.

"Paul, you don't even have to offer a single penny. I'd help you for nothing..."

I was touched by his friendship.

"... But if you're offering the money anyway, I won't object too strenuously," he continued.

O'Flanahan exploded into a loud guffaw.

"That's the spirit, Coulter... As for me, Paul, I'm all in. I mean, how can I not be? I live for conspiracies and you're giving me a hundred thousand bucks to get in on the ground floor... plus there's danger... Who could resist that? Sounds like a hoot."

Looking considerably more restrained, Briar was the last one to speak. He was independently wealthy, so money would not be a serious enticement for him.

"Paul, this offer certainly comes as a surprise, especially so soon after the double murder. I admire your courage in taking up the fight so quickly. Consider me in. As for your money, keep it! We'll use it in your father's hunt. I have no need of it... However, you now have us all exceedingly curious. It is time for you to reveal what you held back from Norton and why."

I pulled out my father's copy of The Hollow Needle, placing it on the table along with the note that had accompanied it.

"This note is what prevented me from revealing everything to Norton. The more I think about it, the more certain I am that it was the right thing to do. The authorities would only slow things down and I am convinced that time is of the essence. My father's murder was the starting gun and we haven't even started running yet. We must hurry if we are to have the slightest chance of wrestling the prize from the killer."

"You think that the killer knows about the Hollow Needle?" asked Briar, looking curious.

"I do. The killing of my father and Darlene seems to have one important feature. Norton said that leaving clues is out of character for this killer. What made him do it then? Why did my father send me the book just before the killer broke into his house?" I said, jabbing at the book's title. "He had to be trying to prevent the killer from getting it."

"This is getting good, Paul. I can see what you're getting at. The killer has got to know something and not just about that book. He knows something about the secret your dad was talking about in that note of his," O'Flanahan added excitedly.

"... And my father outsmarted him, sending me the book before the killer could find it. Perhaps sending it is the very thing that got him murdered...We are dealing with a ruthless man, one who holds many more cards than we do."

"Well, what are we wasting time for, then? Let's get on with some facts," prodded an incensed O'Flanahan.

"Very well... let's start with this: the book he sent me is, in fact, an exact duplicate of another he gave me when I was nine years old, leading me to believe that this was my not my father's last hunt, but rather, his *original one*."

Removing the second copy from my satchel, I dropped it on top of the first. O'Flanahan picked them up, looking them over closely, a keen interest in his eyes.

"I grew to understand your father quite well in the ten years I knew him, Paul," Briar said. "He always seemed purposeful and deliberate in his actions. What could he possibly have been trying to teach you, back then, when you were so young?"

"I'm not sure it's like that, Jonathan. I don't believe that he intended for me to start on this particular hunt, at least not until the time was right. I think the second copy was intended to spur me on to remember the first. I found another note in the original copy, which led me to re-read the book. Prodded by a curious little comment from the editor, I searched on the Internet and was led to an internet page that suggests Etretat may be at the centre of a forgotten historical mystery... The way I see it now, all previous hunts were intended to prepare me for this original hunt... Gentlemen, I believe my father was about to reveal what he knew but was killed before he had the chance..." I explained.

"Are you sure you're not reading more into this than is really there? We've all done that before..." Coulter asked, playing the devil's advocate.

"I am convinced that this is a real trail and I think we should follow it. I need you to help me confirm that I'm not deluding myself," I finished, looking for support.

"What do you want us to do, Paul?" Coulter responded.

"I believe this warrants a little more armchair detective work despite the pressure of time. I was wondering if you could each spend a couple of days doing some research individually and then we could compare notes on Thursday evening..." I did not get the chance to say any more.

"Paul, you know I live to investigate forgotten history..." Briar said "Seems to me like my skills could be of some use. I will search out what information I can about that area of France. Did you perhaps bring any pictures of that fort you mentioned?"

"Yes, I have a couple..."

I fished for them in my satchel and placed them on the table. The before-and-after pictures had the desired effect.

"The fort is completely destroyed in this later picture. Who did that and why?" questioned Coulter.

"It certainly is strange." agreed O'Flanahan, "Look at the extent of the damage. It suggests an explosion. What else would cause that kind of destruction?"

"Don't forget about the editor's note. It states that the army was involved. What's that about? Why were they involved?" I added.

"I might be able to help with that. Most cities have converted their documents to electronic format. I can hack into those sites in my sleep. I'll see what I can turn up. Might clear this whole thing up. Might be nothing," suggested Coulter.

"Might be *something*, though," interjected O'Flanahan strongly. "I'll go through my contacts and my files. I've never heard about this interesting tunnel stuff. Perhaps I might find something that will help."

My friends got up, eager to begin their research. I emptied my coffee cup, ordering a refill while I watched them prepare to leave. I felt a bittersweet excitement at the thought of a new hunt, coming from a gift my father had given me more than twenty-five years ago.

"So Thursday evening then? I'll arrange for supper and we can review our findings."

They nodded their heads in agreement. Each took the time to offer some well-meant condolences before leaving but somehow I felt they weren't necessary. My father was still right here next to me. I sat back down, drank my coffee, and spent a few minutes with him in silence.

CHAPTER 3
A Decision Is Reached

I ordered a few pizzas while my friends seated themselves around the dining room table. I reflected on how different we were from each other. Coulter, in his late twenties, dark-haired and short, was a generally quiet man. O'Flanahan, in his early thirties, was loud, obnoxious and never stopped talking. Finally, Briar, with his ageless face, taller than average, was a garrulous man who viewed almost everyone as a student. As for me, nearing thirty-five and slightly overweight, I was an average man whose only quality was a keen mind.

They had each brought some material with them and appeared anxious to share it. I had previously set up a dry-erase board on an easel at the head of the table.

"First, I want to say thanks to all of you for coming in through the back..."

"You kidding? Outsmarting that Interpol cop was the most fun I've had this week," O'Flanahan commented and Coulter snickered in agreement.

"... Well, I appreciate it. The less attention from him the better. Anyway, from the look of those folders, it seems that each of you have found some information. Where should we start?" I asked.

"How about the origins of the fort? After all, that's what started this whole thing," suggested Briar, half expecting an objection. When none came, he cleared his throat and began a scholarly presentation.

"... As you might know, historically, Etretat was primarily a fishing village. During the eighteenth century, an oyster bed was added at the Queen's request. Long before all that, Etretat was a natural port. While the water near the shore is too shallow to allow ships to moor today, there were once deep trenches in the marine floor that allowed ships to anchor within the safe confines of the cove. These trenches, most of which have filled up with rubble over the centuries, extended right under the current location of the town of Etretat. I also believe that under Etretat's famous beach are the remnants of a shipyard, a Roman shipyard. Allow me to illustrate this for you."

Briar walked over to the dry-erase board and, picking up a black marker, drew a quick outline of Etretat's beachfront, a rough semi-circular shape with two huge cliffs, one on each side. Before Briar could continue his discourse, Coulter had a comment to make.

"Sorry to jump in so soon, Jonathan, but the cliffs don't seem to extend into the sea sufficiently to protect ships of any significant size."

Briar smiled briefly. He had been expecting the objection.

"While that may be true today, it is important to make note of the geology of the area. Those cliffs are composed primarily of chalk, Turonian chalk to be more precise...There are also protrusions of Cenomanian chalk. These have a different rate of erosion, the Cenomanian chalk being generally more crumbly and nodular than Turonian. Of more importance is the average rate of erosion of chalk cliffs, which is approximately twenty centimetres per year. Geologically speaking, that's pretty fast. Romans occupied this area perhaps as early as 50 AD. A quick calculation informs us that, back then, the cliffs advanced into the channel almost four hundred metres further than they do now. That would have provided significant protection for a very large fleet indeed. As an interesting aside, this does imply that the famous Needle of Etretat would have been deep inside the cliff back then."

Briar, drawing another map, connected a line from Etretat to an area near the Seine River.

"I located, on an eighteenth century Guillaume Deslisle map, a reference to an ancient Roman road linking Etretat and Lillebonne, or *Juliobonna*, as it was known by the Romans. Lillebonne was located near the Seine and was an active trading town. The Romans obviously felt that it was worthwhile to build a road between these two towns. Therefore something important was going on in Etretat back then. This is the curious thing, though: to build a road and a shipyard and for these facts to remain largely unknown, historically-speaking, is a very difficult thing to achieve. Someone must have kept things very quiet back then. Today, there's almost nothing left except for a few remnants of the roman road, a metre below ground, and some ruins on the north side of town," Briar wrapped up.

He had barely seated himself when Liam O'Flanahan stood up, a wide smile on his face. He walked up to the easel, seeming excited to tell us about his own research.

"That was real interesting, Briar, but I think you missed the point. Sure we're looking to get some history but what we're really looking for is TREASURE! And I think I found it. Let's forget all that Roman nonsense and instead, focus on King Francis the First, who took over the fort, in the early 1500's. He renovated it and installed at least one cannon, which is still on display at the Museum of Rouen. He used the fort to protect the coast but also, I suspect, to blackmail ships passing within reach of his cannons. That was point One!"

The doorbell rang, interrupting O'Flanahan's discourse. There ensued a brief interruption, during which pizza was received, the driver was paid and drinks were served. Eventually we found ourselves back at the table, munching in time with O'Flanahan's speech.

"Francis the First was France's original Renaissance monarch. He was well educated, interested in culture, architecture, and artists, which is mainly what he spent his money on, apart from his incessant wars. Francis convinced Da Vinci to come to France, who spent the last few years of his life there. Think of what that could mean. Da Vinci himself!..." he said, his eyes far away. An exaggerated cough from Briar snapped O'Flanahan back to reality.

"Hum... Yes, anyway, another area of interest was exploration. Francis funded Jacques Cartier on at least three expeditions to Canada, to search for gold and diamonds. Cartier's first voyage was in 1534. That was point Two."

By now, he was speaking loudly. I had started feeling uneasy the moment he had mentioned Cartier, the name sparking a distant memory. O'Flanahan was up to something. He continued, increasing the volume of his voice even more:

"On Monday, Paul mentioned something about an internet page involving tunnels. I looked the page up and found an interesting mention of Etretat in 1534, on the ancient 'King's Maritime Map'. The King it refers to can only be Francis the First. A coincidence?... I think not, if you note that the date of the map was 1534, the same year as Cartier's first expedition. On that map, Etretat's original spelling might be seen as a clue, if one accepts the 'tr.' as an abbreviation for 'treasure'... I believe that, on his first trip to Canada, Jacques Cartier did find treasure, contrary to recorded history..."

Incensed, I stood up, shoving my chair back with a screech, intent on preventing him from saying what I was sure he was going to say:

"Don't you dare, O'Flanahan..." I started but he was too far gone, ignoring me completely and increasing the volume by several decibels, getting it out before I could stop him.

"... Found in Canada, I say, TREASURE that he brought back and hid in the Fort of Frefosse. But, you ask, what treasure did he bring back? Isn't it obvious?..."

"Stop, don't say it..." I shouted, getting angrier by the second.

"He brought back the OAK ISLAND TREASURE, that's what!" Liam O'Flanahan concluded, screaming at the top of his lungs.

O'Flanahan had done it again. He had managed to link my murdered father's hunt to his time-wasting Oak Island Treasure. How dare he?... I had to admit something though. O'Flanahan was tenacious. Also, Briar and Coulter were laughing at me, so I sat back down, my eyes still glaring.

"All right, O'Flanahan, although I'm sure you did that just to bother me, go ahead and try to logically justify this... this nonsense!" I said through clenched teeth.

"Come on, Paul, take it easy. We're just talking here. I know you think the Oak Island Treasure is fictitious but really, it makes sense this time. Listen to the facts, no nonsense here, just what we know about Oak Island. The first point is that something went on there... Even you have to admit that. The 'money-pit', as they called it, was covered with large heavy flagstones. There were heavy oak platforms every three meters, to a depth of nearly thirty-six metres. On different levels, they found charcoal, putty, coconut fibre. Thirty metres down, they found an inscribed stone, complete with cryptic clue. Most importantly, let's not forget how the designers of this incredible site rebuilt two entire beaches. Using flat rocks, eel grass and coconut fibre, they successfully hid two flood tunnels, hundreds of meters long, connecting no less than five feeder drains into each of those flood tunnels. This absolutely ensured flooding, should someone dig down past thirty metres. Someone wanted to keep his treasure in there, even at the expense of an invader's life."

"But no treasure was ever found. You know that, Liam," I pinpointed.

"In this case, I think that's a good point. Look, guys, no one knows who put it there or when but it *was* there at some point and somebody went through a whole lot of effort making sure it stayed hidden. The likeliest theory is that it was used to store gold intended to pay Indians and soldiers garrisoned in Quebec and Montreal, although some people insist the Oak Island was connected to Templar treasure. No one really knows, so your guess is as good as mine. We do know that, officially, Cartier never found anything. What if he arrived at Oak Island and saw the gold being hidden? What if he sneaked in and stole the treasure? Would he admit to it? Who would he tell? One thing is for sure: Francis financed a second trip, so the news from the first trip must have been good in some respect."

Coulter was nodding his head.

"You make some sense, Liam but it's just theory. Little proof there, I'm afraid. We can't forget the basic rules of treasure hunting. Until we have enough solid facts, our conjectures will never amount to more than a Thursday night chat. I, on the other hand, unlike the two of you, came armed with real facts. Facts that are pertinent to the changes in the Fort of Frefosse!"

Our ears perked up. We knew that Coulter was never one to exaggerate.

"As I said during our prior meeting, I have easy access to restricted documents. This allowed me to delve right into Etretat's records. I downloaded everything I could find from 1900 to 1920. After a sleepless night poring over old documents, I came up with this."

He held up an official looking piece of paper.

"This, gentlemen, is an accident report, dated November 13, 1911. It identifies a fellow named Old Man Vallin, if you can believe that. He had offered to carry out some minor road repairs to facilitate militia travel. There is reference to the poor character of Old Man Vallin and to his reputation for drunkenness. On October 26 1911, Vallin managed to acquire several sticks of dynamite, purportedly to remove a rather obstinate boulder on one of these roads. He also purchased several bottles of wine for the trip. He reported taking a wrong turn and ending up on the trail to the Fort of Frefosse. By the time he arrived at the fort, he was hopelessly lost and drunk. Mistaking a dynamite stick for a candle, he nearly blew himself up. In a state of panic, he tossed all the sticks towards the fort's entrance. The resulting explosion destroyed the old fort. The town was in a furor. I also found reference to a court summons for the unfortunate Vallin. Strangely, the case never went to trial. Vallin was declared innocent of wrongdoing and the incident was labelled an accident. The land on which the fort stood was sold within days and a golf course was opened on the site," Coulter put the sheet down on the table. Then he pulled another from his folder.

"I might have been satisfied with that, if it weren't for this document. It shows various outstanding taxes in Etretat in mid-1911. Here, you will note Old Man Vallin's large tax debt. So large in fact, that it was likely that Vallin's home and land would be repossessed by the town. Not a rich man, our Vallin. Yet, on Nov 20 1911, just a few days after the explosion, Vallin paid his taxes in full, with cash, according to the notes in the ledger. Where did all this money come from? Who gave it to him and for what? Too many questions and too many coincidences," Coulter concluded, tossing the second sheet on the table, satisfied that he had out-done the others.

We broke into conversation, congratulating Coulter on his excellent contribution. Even if we tried to ascribe innocent explanations to these facts, their number was growing beyond what coincidence could easily allow. Eventually my friends quieted down and looked at me. They knew it was now my turn to talk about my findings. Retrieving the two copies of The Hollow Needle from a nearby shelf, I placed them in the centre of the table.

"I thought that I would go at this from a different direction. I have to admit that while this mystery about Etretat and its fort is utterly fascinating, I found myself more captivated by these two identical books. Perhaps a natural inclination, since I am in the book business. Another factor influenced my choice between the books and Etretat: the books were *here,* in my hands while Etretat was not. So, I examined them more closely. The first oddity I noted was this..." I opened both books to the page opposite the list of chapters, containing the printing history. "... These books, printed in 1955, are from a limited private edition and are individually numbered. The original copy, the one my father gave me when I was nine, is stamped number one in a limited printing of four and one, whatever that means..."

"Could it mean five?" interrupted O'Flanahan. "... After all four and one makes five, doesn't it?"

Briar jumped in, irritated by O'Flanahan's comment.

"Why say it that way then? Surely it means something less... obvious... than that."

O'Flanahan, offended by Briar's insinuation, barked a reply.

"Tell me what it means then?"

"Come on, guys, let Paul finish what he was saying. We can figure that out later," interjected Coulter in a low voice. O'Flanahan looked sheepish for a moment, then smiled and sat back in his chair. I took this as my cue and continued.

"... My point was that, if you examined the copy my father sent to me before his murder, you would note that it is *also* number one in a limited printing of four and one. By logical conclusion, one of these books must be a counterfeit copy. Stranger than this, they are both signed by Maurice Leblanc, apparently genuine signatures, yet Leblanc died in 1939, well before these books were printed."

I paused for a second, noting that my audience seemed in shock at my revelations. The best was yet to come:

"I examined both for the slightest material difference. The paper, the ink, the typeset, the font, absolutely everything was identical and all in perfect condition. If one was a counterfeit copy, it had to be the best work I had ever seen. I kept returning to the note from my father at the back of the original book. The note and, more specifically, the dried-out tape that kept it in place. Once applied, tape will almost invariably damage a book. Over time, the glue can stain the book, or stick to the pages, as you can see here, where my father's note is taped to the book..." I opened the book from the back, revealing the dried glue residue. "...My problem with this was that my father simply would not do this. Not ever. So why did he do it here?" I stopped, waiting for one of them to come up with an answer. Coulter was the first to suggest a possibility:

"To call attention to it! He *wanted* you to look at it and wonder about it," he affirmed.

Liam O'Flanahan jumped in, his curiosity getting the better of him.

"So, tell us, did you find out anything after that?"

"Actually, I waited for the three of you to come here, so we could discover together what my father might have been trying to tell me. If we are to be in this together, what better place to begin can there be? The trail is right here. What should we do?" I asked, looking around.

"Take the note and the tape right off and let's look at everything carefully. That's my suggestion," O'Flanahan answered, going for the direct route.

Nods from the other two carried the motion. Using a pair of fine tweezers, I tightly pinched the note and tape together then lifted. It all came off easily, with a slight zipping noise, the dried glue flaking off the page, its adherence long gone. Pulling out a magnifying glass, I bent over the book and scrutinized the area that had been covered by the note and the tape.

I was looking at the edge of a leather covering, wrapped over from the outside onto the inside surface of the cover. I could see stitches but some looked odd. Examining them more closely, I realised that what looked like stitches, across an area of about eight centimetres, were in fact *white ink* drawn to look like stitches. On either side of the strip, the stitches were real.

"There is a hidden pocket here."

"What? Are you sure?" asked Briar, looking stunned.

"Yes. Watch..."

Lifting the revealed flap with the tweezers, I peered inside, seeing a folded piece of paper. Reaching in, I pinched the paper and pulled it out, unfolding it carefully. I read it aloud.

Paul:

If you have found this note, you have discovered the Great Hunt. My father taught me the way of the Hunt, and gave me specific instructions to teach you. You in turn will teach your son, preparing him. He is the one who must solve the mystery of the Great Hunt.

It will be his duty to regain our lost heritage. I know that part of the trail to our past is in this book. There's something curious about the Fort of Frefosse, I am sure of it. Good Luck, Paul. Prepare your Son. He must regain what our family has lost.

PS: A real story ends near Etretat,
Lost until Paul infers new ideas subtly.
You ought understand responsibility,
Necessarily after moiling Etretat.

Your Father

Each of us sat back down in our chairs, reflecting about what I had just read. There was something about that bothered me.

"There's a problem with that note. It's not my father's writing..."

"... Do you think it's a counterfeit?" O'Flanahan asked.

"No. That's not what I meant. It's not my father's writing; it's my grandfather's..."

"Are you telling me that your grandfather was also named Paul Sirenne, like your father and you after him? Isn't that odd?" observed Briar.

I nodded my head in agreement. It *was* very odd. My father had never explained that to me satisfactorily, even though I had asked him about it on several occasions. There were many secrets in my family's history. Briar continued:

"If this note was written by your grandfather to your father, then the note is referring to you. The Great Hunt was intended to be *your* task from the very beginning."

"Wouldn't that date the Great Hunt back to the time of the story in The Hollow Needle?" Coulter asked excitedly.

"Yes!... Yes, it would," I answered. "I have to say that I am getting overwhelmed by all of this. Let's have a coffee break."

"Excellent idea," Coulter said without hesitation. "Perfect timing!"

Coulter followed me into the kitchen, while Briar and O'Flanahan stayed in the dining room, looking over the files. Within moments, they were arguing about something again. What was it with those two? Meanwhile, I was having difficulty accepting what the note implied.

It seemed as if nothing was accidental about any of this!

My father had known that I was meant to begin this hunt. Perhaps he had not known about the killer at all. This was part of a decades-long plan, held secretly in my family, each father teaching his son, waiting for the appropriate time to begin the Great Hunt. Luckily, he had sent me the book and, as a result, the killer's attempt to rob me of my heritage had failed.

My train of thought was interrupted when Briar came running into the kitchen, holding a sheaf of papers.

"Coulter, where did you get these?"

"Those? Didn't I tell you? I guess I forgot. When I was searching for financial details, I did a random search and got some Francis the First financial records dated from 1525 onward. There were several folders there, along with the financial stuff, so I downloaded all of them. I printed some random sections to bring here."

"I think I found something... I couldn't help looking, you know how much I love these old documents... I found a sheet dated 1530, which drew my attention. It's a letter from the College de France's administrator, Guillaume Bude, addressed to Francis the First. It summarizes a search for documents concerning the Fort of Frefosse and refers to additional documents, perhaps plans or drawings of some sort, but they are not with the page. Do you have more of this file? We might be able to get an architectural drawing of the fort from back then," Briar asked, his breathing shallow and rapid.

"Yes, there is more to the folder where that page came from. I brought my laptop, so we could check it out," assured Coulter.

Excited, we headed to the dining table only to realize that Coulter had not accompanied us. He peered at us from the kitchen, a determined look on his face.

"After the coffee is done, of course!"

We finally found ourselves standing around his laptop while he punched a few keys and called up the folder. After a moment or two, a frustrated Coulter muttered.

"It's not there. I can't find it but look at this. I think it *was* there at some point."

He pointed at two files. The file Coulter had printed was numbered 'F1-3-1530-73' and the following file was 'F1-3-1530-75'.

There was a file missing!

Coulter called up the folder index and found some notes.

"It says here that the document 'F1-3-1530-74' was not found in the file folder when the files were scanned into computer. It was assumed lost."

"Can you search for it in other folders? Maybe it was misfiled," suggested O'Flanahan.

Coulter's fingers flew over the keyboard. A page of results popped up and we began perusing them. With four of us looking, few details were likely to be missed. Just after Coulter's second cup of coffee, we found it. It had been filed in a folder containing castle drawings and engineering plans. O'Flanahan, his expertise in conspiracy showing, said:

"If you wanted to hide this document, there could not be a better place than this folder. It actually looks as if it belongs here. Someone placed this here intentionally."

"Why didn't they simply steal it?" Briar asked.

"Perhaps they were unable to. The physical documents were housed in the Royal library. Not an easy place to steal documents from... It would have been much easier to misfile them deliberately," Coulter suggested.

We connected the laptop to my network and soon had a page printing. We placed it on the table, sweeping the rest of the papers out of the way. I was leaning over to examine it when O'Flanahan seized the paper, pulling it to his face and examining a small section of the dungeon drawing closely. A strange tremor ran through his body, the hand holding the paper flopped to his side and he collapsed backwards into his chair.

"I've... I've seen th... those before..." he stuttered, gasping for breath. Suddenly, he jumped up, full of energy and screamed at the top of his lungs:

"I'VE SEEN THOSE BEFORE HA-HA!"

He did a weird little jig, looking utterly ridiculous, and then ran frenetically to his coat, pulling out an old tattered paperback from a side pocket. I recognized it instantly.

The Oak Island Mystery!

"No-no-no..." I shouted. O'Flanahan ran back, slipped on a loose area rug and almost fell but caught himself and kept going, limping a little while swearing under his breath. He slammed the book on the table, opening it to the page showing the inscription found on the tablet from the money pit.

"There!" he said. "Look at that and tell me that those aren't the same symbols," he challenged.

He pulled out the page showing the dungeon layout and pointed to its centre where identical geometric symbols, a circle, a rectangle and a triangle had been pencilled in. I had to admit that those symbols *were* similar to several of the symbols found on the inscription tablet of Oak Island. For a moment, it seemed as if O'Flanahan had actually found, impossibly, a link between Oak Island and our Etretat Mystery!

Luckily, I also remembered that 'mysterious' Oak Island code. After all, I had spent a fair bit of time on that 'mystery' myself:

"Hold your horses, Liam. I believe the stone with the original inscription was lost in the early 1900's. I also believe it was discovered that the tablet 'inscription' as we know it today, was the work of a company trying to sell shares in their newly registered Oak Island Mining Company. Using a very simple transposition of symbols with English letters, that cipher was easily translated to the phrase: 'Forty feet below two million pounds are buried'. That inscription is a fake!" I concluded.

Liam O'Flanahan looked discomfited, which, admittedly, made me feel better but his discomfort only lasted for a few moments. He shrugged it off as if nothing had happened.

"You're right, of course, Paul. I forgot that part in my excitement. But, if it's a fake, how come the symbols are on those plans?" he rallied back.

Jonathan Briar, ever the professor, pounced on that one.

"Actually, O'Flanahan, when you think about it, the symbols in that inscription are not particularly rare. Circles, rectangles and triangles are all common geometric symbols. The Romans certainly used them. So did the French. Perhaps it is just a coincidence?"

We were in danger of veering off-track, so I pulled the group back into focus.

"I think it is time to summarize what we have found and decide what our next move should be. This evening has been very productive, much more so than we had any right to expect, really. So, where should we start?" I asked.

Briar jumped in immediately.

"I think that we have to start with the geological information. Leblanc's book implies that the Needle of Etretat is hollow, a statement we know to be false. However, its premise is generally accurate. A crumbly material at best, chalk is easily eroded by the elements, waves and tidal currents. It is prone to cave formation, in particular, vertical pipes, following along cracks or weaknesses. These cracks often widen into large caves. For example, there is the Beachy Head cave system, which is more than four hundred metres in length. Therefore, Leblanc's premise in The Hollow Needle is essentially plausible, if not factual. Those cliffs are like Swiss cheese. If you ask me, I would stake my reputation on the probability of secret tunnels and caves being involved, even if the needle itself is solid," Briar stopped speaking for a second, cleared his throat and continued. "Finally, the port of Etretat was both a boon and a danger. Enemy ships could approach as easily as local ships. The Romans probably built a road to Etretat to simplify access to the shipyard. Then, they erected a badly positioned fort to protect themselves from pirates. Later, because of the fall of the Roman Empire, activity ended and all of this was somehow lost to history. Fishermen took over the area, oyster beds were built and life went on. The next step is up to you, O'Flanahan."

"Thanks, Briar. Although I did get a wee bit carried away with the Oak Island connection, there are still some powerful facts to consider. The fort fell into ruin over the centuries. It attracted the attention of Francis the First in 1530, or perhaps even earlier. Possibly, it has something to do with those mysterious tunnels and hidden beaches mentioned in Raymond Lindon's book," stated O'Flanahan.

"Don't forget that Leblanc assisted Lindon with that book. How much is from Lindon and how much from Leblanc?" I added.

"Right. Well, at some point before 1530, Francis commissioned a rebuild of the fort. Perhaps it was to protect the coast, as Briar suggests, but it could have been the presence of those tunnels that motivated Francis to rebuild. Following this, he sent Jacques Cartier to Canada, in search of gold and treasure. Possibly, he returned with more than history says he did, although I am not sure why he would hide his success," O'Flanahan said.

Fabian Coulter continued the review:

"The facts are that Francis rebuilt the fort and he used it often. That's it. Then the fort seems to have dropped from sight until the early 1900's when it caught Leblanc's attention and was featured in his famous story. Soon after that, Old Man Vallin blew it up, at the request of someone, whose identity remains unknown," Coulter concluded.

"I just want to add a few points to what we've put together. The first is that we have barely touched the surface about the tunnel business. Today, the tunnels to the beach are still there, so there must be some substance to these stories. The second point is Leblanc himself. He is at the centre of all this. He found Etretat as a young man and he kept coming back to it. He rented a summerhouse there and later bought it. It is certain that he became fascinated with the small town and was instrumental in drawing much attention to it through his books, both fiction and non-fiction. All this attention bothered someone enough to pay Old Man Vallin to blow the fort up and perhaps, also, to hide its architectural drawings. Finally, we cannot forget what the two Hollow Needle books and their notes imply. That may be the most telling point of all," I finished.

Silence ensued while each of us reflected on what had just been presented. Finally, Briar spoke for the entire team:

"I am convinced *something* is going on. Historically speaking, Etretat has drawn far more attention than a small fishing town deserves. Yet today all is forgotten, which, in itself, is odd. However, when Leblanc revives interest in this quaint little town, the Fort of Frefosse is coincidentally destroyed. Something is happening, or rather has happened, and I think the fort is the focal point of these events."

"I concur," supported Coulter.

"It's got my vote," O'Flanahan agreed.

"Gentleman, this is a solemn moment," I exclaimed. "From the slightest of clues, we have found a path to follow. The Great Hunt has begun."

"May we beat the killer to the goal," added Coulter sombrely.

Our exhilaration turned to trepidation. Coulter's comment had reminded us of the dangers inherent in our pursuit.

"The question is: what do we do about it?" O'Flanahan asked, getting directly to the heart of the matter again.

"I believe that some of us have to go to France, to Etretat, and continue the investigation on site. The rest can stay behind and continue with the research. We can communicate by...uh..."

"Don't worry about communications, Paul. I've got that covered," stated Coulter. "I think it would be best if I stayed behind for a while to set that up and do a bit more searching on the Internet."

"Me too, Paul," added O'Flanahan. "As you know, I'm in the publishing business. I cannot just stop that machinery. It will take me at least a week to reorganize. I've already taken steps in that direction. In the meantime, I am positive that I can touch base with my contacts and turn up some useful information."

Jonathan Briar was nodding his head and looking sad at the same time.

"I would also love to go but the finals are beginning and I have papers to grade. Once that is done, I will be completely available."

This was not what I wanted. I wanted us to work as a team. I knew that we could succeed in our search but we had to work together. Phone calls would simply not be enough and I said as much to them. Coulter assured me that the problem was easy to solve. He was convinced that we could remain in communication via the Internet. With that problem resolved, it was agreed.

I was going to Etretat!

CHAPTER 4

Travelling to France

I peered out of the plane window and looked at the water below. I placed my laptop on my knees. Selected specifically for the occasion of this trip by Coulter, it had been the first purchase in his plan to keep us in contact with each other. With my overstuffed bank account footing the bill, he had bought without restraint. For several days, delivery trucks had dropped off dozens of boxes filled with high-tech toys.

The laptop had come with a satellite uplink and an extended-life battery. It also had solar panels imbedded in its cover to increase battery life. Along with all this came a very special pair of glasses. Wirelessly connected to my laptop, the techno-glasses contained miniaturised cameras as well as viewing screens projected on the inside of the lenses. Microphones and headphones were built into the arms of the glasses. The cameras had a zoom function so powerful, they could double as a pair of rudimentary binoculars. I could also view scenes in either infrared or ultraviolet.

The point of these expensive toys was to keep me connected to the net. After Coulter had cobbled some software together to make it all work, my team could receive the sound and video from my glasses while sitting in comfort at home. They could talk to me and I to them. They could send information to me and it would be displayed on the miniature screens. While the projected screen image was no more than a few centimetres across, the impression was of a translucent sixty-centimetre screen, floating about half a metre in front of my eyes.

The only problem with this incredible technology was that I had to speak aloud for my three teammates to hear me. Unfortunately, no one could hear *them!* This created the impression that I was talking to myself. The airline stewardess came by and asked:

"Would you like something from the bar, or would you prefer a complimentary orange juice?"

"A glass of juice would be fine, thank you."

While she served me, I heard O'Flanahan's voice in my ear.

"Hey Paul, how's it going?"

"Good."

"Say, this techno gizmo that you and Coulter put together is incredible. I can see everything around you as if I was there."

"Thank you," I answered to both O'Flanahan and the stewardess who was handing me a glass. This was disconcerting.

"What do you want, Liam?" I whispered.

"I was wondering if you could do me a wee bit of a favour?" he begged me in an unctuous voice.

"Such as?" I asked.

"Could you turn your head to the right seventy-five degrees? I wish to settle an argument with Coulter," he explained.

I automatically turned my head, feeling like a remote control camera. My eyes now rested upon a pretty, raven-haired, bosomy woman, sitting across the aisle.

"Now that's more like it. A much better sight than that boring window view of yours. I was right, Coulter was wrong," he affirmed with a laugh.

Having noticed my momentary stare, the dark-haired woman smiled at me briefly then looked away, causing me to feel slightly embarrassed.

"Are you interrupting my thoughts for anything more than this?" I asked, trying to keep my voice low.

"Of course... What sort of person do you think I am? I was just letting you know that your reservation at the Villa Leblanc has been confirmed," he replied glibly.

"Why don't you try to find some more info about that court case with Old Man Vallin. Why did it get dropped? Who was the prosecutor? Do some digging."

"Right you are, Paul. I'll get on it. See ya," O'Flanahan disconnected, causing a loud popping noise in my ear.

I decided to get up and stretch my legs. I made my way to the forward cabin, scanning the passengers and wondering what they would think if they knew what had happened to me. Returning to my seat, I reflected about Leblanc. He held a central role in all this and it made me all the more curious about him. Leblanc had previously been a writer of some literary note but, after the creation of his Lupin character, he became the biggest celebrity of his time. Arsene Lupin was adored by all of France, with the exception of the police, who were often ridiculed in Leblanc's stories.

What role did Leblanc have in Etretat's real mystery?

Leblanc bought a summer Villa there, in 1917. He was forced to abandon it in the late 1930's when the Germans invaded Etretat. He and his two daughters escaped to Perpignan, a town in the southeast of France. Leblanc died in Perpignan while in exile from his beloved home. His death was soon followed by that of his youngest granddaughter. A trust, set up by Leblanc, managed his Villa after the war. After the trust completed renovations, Leblanc's surviving granddaughter, Victoire, had taken over its management, operating it as both museum and a bed & breakfast.

I had also been thinking more about the Fort of Frefosse. It had been built fifteen hundred to two thousand years ago. If Briar's geological information was accurate, the cliff had extended about four hundred metres further into the channel at that time. When we looked at the few pictures we had of the fort, we had assumed that it was built to protect the shipyard below. It would have been incredibly distant from the cliff edge two thousand years ago, making it useless as a defence against naval attack. So why was this location chosen? There *had* to be some other factor involved. I suspected it might be the other feature Briar had mentioned in his geology class:

Tunnels. Tunnels and caves.

He had said that this type of chalk cliff was prone to having vertical pipes and large cavern systems. What if such a vertical pipe had been found on top of the cliff? Could a fort have been built over the pipe to conceal access to a cave system below? Would that have been motive enough to build the fort in such a disadvantageous location? My thoughts were interrupted by the captain, announcing that we were about to begin our descent. I heard a crackle in my ear. It was Coulter.

"Hey, Paul, I came up with something *really* interesting! You won't believe it."

"Hi, Fabian. What did you find?"

"I downloaded a whole pile of French newspapers and started scanning for stories that might relate to our search. I did a random search for Vallin, the name of the guy who blew up the fort," he continued.

"What about him?"

"He was killed a few months after the explosion. Guess where he died?" he taunted.

"Just tell me," I asked.

"He died at the fort. Nobody knows what happened. His body was found by a couple of local boys. He might have been beaten but it was hard to say because 'he fell from a good height into the jagged rocks' according to the report."

Coulter signed off soon after. The plane landed and I made ready to leave, collecting my carry-on luggage. The woman from across the aisle stood up, glancing at me briefly and smiling once more. I smiled back, taken in by her natural beauty. There was something about her. However, my mind was stuck on Coulter's latest revelation, that Vallin had been killed. Someone hadn't been happy about the fort being blown up. That someone had a conversation, a final conversation, with Old Man Vallin.

Had we uncovered a murder in Etretat, another connection in a series of events that culminated, almost a century later, with my father's own murder in Canada?

***

I got off the plane, carrying my overfull satchel. I had brought no other luggage, sure that I could buy whatever I needed on the way. I arranged for the rental of a Porsche, which was conveniently equipped with a GPS. It suggested various routes from Paris to Etretat. I selected the first one and, following its prompts, navigated through the streets of Paris, until I reached the A13 towards *Rouen-Caen*, continuing on towards *Le Havre-Pont de Tancarville*.

After the bridge, I headed towards *Bolbec*, on the D910. I heard a beep from the glasses and the monitor came on. Briar's head appeared a meter in front of my face. It was very distracting, so I had him turn off his laptop camera.

"It is quite odd to be conversing this way, my boy. I can see the scenery you are looking at. I hear the vehicle sounds in stereo. I could almost swear I am in the car with you. A capital idea, these techno-glasses," Briar stated.

"Thanks. But they have disadvantages," I added.

"I have heard about some of them. O'Flanahan is often unstoppable, as are you, my friend... I did call you to discuss something of interest, however. I have been researching since our last meeting. That is why I have not been in contact. I must even admit to ignoring some grading of papers, a thing I rarely do..." Briar confessed.

"You seem to have 'the bug' pretty bad, Jonathan," I commented.

"You are correct. This Etretat thing is very odd indeed. At first, with O'Flanahan's Oak Island nonsense, the Great Hunt seemed like poppycock but every time I turn around, something else pops up, yet another bizarre fact," he continued.

"What have you found now?" I asked him.

"I decided to read some of the Leblanc stories, in order to get a better feel for what he was like as a writer. I came across a biography of him. Apparently, he was a sickly man. He supported his sometimes-actress sister for much of her life," Briar filled in. He was on a roll. "...The one thing he was not, was an adventurer. He was neither into politics, nor public affairs, shunning most publicity, except when promoting his novels. I felt quite confident of this version of his life, until I came across a curious book, entitled *Filatures*, published by the University Press of Grenoble in France in 1980, dealing with the 'sum of Leblanc's writings'."

"The sum of his writing?" I asked.

"I kid you not. Unbelievable, I tell you. The book, subtitled 'A Walk through the Cycles of Lupin and Rouletabille' claimed a very strange thing, that Leblanc's writing, when analysed, showed two distinct writing 'styles'. Some storylines, words and names were thought to have been chosen for some deliberate reason beyond the needs of the story. The purpose of this work is extremely nebulous and I found it quite bizarre that someone would have thought of doing this analysis in the first place. By the way, another place where you can find a similar type of dual writing is in coded letters," Briar pointed out.

"In coded letters? Do you mean to tell me that Leblanc was hiding codes in his books?" I asked.

"It is quite possible, if you believe the conclusions of this author," he answered.

"Codes about what?" I wondered.

"Indeed! I thought back to his biography, which held no place for a man hiding codes in his books... What was he trying to say and to whom was he saying it? I came to the inevitable conclusion that, either 'Filatures' was contrived statistical nonsense, or that Leblanc's biography was falsified in order to hide certain key facts. Something in this business is askew," he commented.

"Codes or not, Leblanc seems to be right in the middle of it again."

Briar signed off only to be replaced within moments by an overly excited O'Flanahan.

"Listen, Paul, Do you remember the name Raymond Lindon?"

"Yes. That was the author who wrote about the tunnels in Etretat, as Valere Catogan."

"You got it, boyo. I've been doing some research about him. First thing was, I learnt he became the *Avocat-General* of France, their version of Attorney-

General. Then I figured out that the name 'Valere Catogan' is an anagram of Avocat-General, which explains his pseudonym. He was also elected Mayor of Etretat at some point. So Lindon, assisted by Leblanc, wrote a book linking Etretat to treasure and historical mystery. The very same book whose title presents Lupin as a real person, not a fictional character. Finally, an absolute clincher this one, provided to me by Coulter just a few minutes ago, a young Raymond Lindon was the assistant to the attorney who was going to prosecute Old Man Vallin, before dropping the charges. More wood for the fire, wouldn't you say?" O'Flanahan said, sounding proud of himself.

"Almost too much," I added.

"It seems to me that there are a lot of people involved: Leblanc, Lindon, Lupin... and we can't forget that killer of yours, or the books your dad sent you. I can smell a conspiracy all over this mess. But that's okay, I love that smell, he-he... You're not still upset at me for that stunt I pulled on the plane, are you?"

"No, Liam I'm not. God knows, I needed a laugh. Everything has been so serious lately and it doesn't seem as if it's letting up. I managed to evade Norton at the airport... At least I think I did."

"I don't think he knows about the three of us yet. That gives us an edge and I intend to keep it. We can do a heck of a lot behind the scenes," supported O'Flanahan.

"Thanks, Liam. I appreciate that, I really do. Listen, I'm getting into a bit of heavy traffic here. How about we touch base again once I'm settled in?"

"Right-o. See you then."

I arrived in Etretat near nightfall. The drive had gone well but I was exhausted and suffering from jet lag. I found the *Rue Guy de Maupassant #15* and, moments later, drove into the parking lot of the Villa Leblanc. The Villa was as impressive as I had imagined. The gabled roof, its imposing garden, complete with Roman statues, and the inviting entrance were more than I had expected.

The front door opened and an older woman, white haired and matriarchal, walked out, smiling at me.

"Welcome to the Villa Leblanc. My name is Victoire Leblanc," she stated in a strong, clear voice.

"Thank you. I am so glad to meet you. My name is Paul Sirenne. I have a reservation," I answered.

"Ah, Monsieur Sirenne. I remember taking your reservation. Please come in. You must be exhausted. You drove directly from Paris after your plane trip, yes?" she asked me.

"Yes, I did. I am a bit tired, I must admit... Also somewhat hungry..." I added, noting my empty stomach.

"Well then, let us not waste any more time. We will get you signed in and I believe our cook may be able to put something together for you. While you settle in, I will arrange to have some food sent to your room, perhaps with some white wine?" she suggested.

"That sounds wonderful," I agreed, following her in. The villa's interior was beautiful. It had been carefully restored with exquisite attention to detail. One section was roped off and signs informed me that this was the entrance to the famous Hollow Needle Museum.

I knew what I was doing tomorrow.

Signing in was mercifully quick and I was directed to my room. I lay down in the sumptuous bed only to be roused shortly after by a knock at the door. It was a maid, bringing me a seafood platter and a half litre of white wine. I inhaled the shrimp first, my personal weakness, then quickly took care of the rest. I dropped back onto the bed and, without further objection from my stomach, fell asleep.

Matt Chatelain

CHAPTER 5

The Needle of Etretat

The aroma of coffee awakened me. Next to my bed was a small table, upon which a single cup coffee machine, connected to an antique timer, was busy percolating. I jumped in the shower adjoining to my room, and then had the coffee in lieu of breakfast, my stomach unsettled from the long trip and the late night meal. I headed downstairs and went out to the garden at the back of the Villa. I wanted to go see the Needle but had decided to delay doing that until later in the afternoon, after the Arsene Lupin / Hollow Needle museum tour.

I wandered the path, enjoying the garden. Leblanc's villa was far bigger than I had anticipated. I came across a stone bench and sat down, feeling the morning sun warming my face. A cool breeze was blowing and I felt refreshed. I heard a car door slam and saw a taxi driving away. A familiar-looking raven-haired woman was walking up the entrance stairs of the villa, meeting up with Mrs Leblanc.

I heard voices talking excitedly but they faded away in the wind. I returned to my reflections, closing my eyes for a few moments.

***

After the museum tour, I was ready to go see the Needle. I put on my techno-glasses and started a recording of the walk for my friends, knowing they were still deep in slumber. I headed down Rue de Maupassant, enjoying the clear blue sky and refreshing sea air. I took a left on Brindejont, which turned into Rue Prosper. Eventually I arrived at Etretat's renowned black pebble beach. To my right, I saw the magnificent Amont cliff with its incredible 'elephant trunk' arch. Turning my head, I peered through the Aval arch.

There it was: the famous Needle!

I headed left, arriving quickly at the *Terrasse Guy de Maupassant*. Continuing on, I clambered up a tourist trail, heading up the Aval cliff. Along the way, I noted the mysterious 'door in the cliff' and wondered what was behind it. About halfway up, I stopped for a break. After a brief rest, I stood up and finished the marathon climb. It would have been more inspiring had I been in better shape.

Arriving at the top was a letdown. The view of Etretat and its beach was excellent but I could see nothing of the Needle. Following the posted signs, I approached the edge of the cliff and was finally able to see the Needle in its entirety. I'd examined pictures of it but nothing compared to the reality of being here, of seeing the Needle in its full splendour, surrounded by the swelling and crashing of the channel water. It was incredible. I finally understood the fascination with the possibility of it being hollow and, better still, filled with treasure.

Moving away from the edge, I followed another trail, skirting the golf course, which now covered the Fort of Frefosse area. In the distance, I noticed a worn structure, a bunker. It was exactly like the one in my dream. My attention was drawn to the small trail in front of me, leading me to the *'Chambre des Demoiselles',* a small chamber carved into the edge of the cliff. In Leblanc's story, it had been the key to the puzzle that led Lupin to find the hidden entrance in the Fort of Frefosse's foundation.

There was a small bridge leading to the chamber's rectangular entrance. I entered into it, noting the carved letters 'D' and 'F' projecting from the floor below the small rectangular window, exactly as described in Leblanc's book. Stepping up onto them, I was elevated roughly to the window's height. There, on the left bottom corner, I saw a quartz crystal sticking out, shaped roughly like an eagle's talon. Looking through the crystal was supposed to reveal the special brick that opened the secret tunnel. Closing one eye, I could indeed see a moss covered brick wall, all that remained of the Fort of Frefosse's foundation. To my surprise, I noted a small white cross, intersecting my gaze through the eagle's talon.

My excitement could hardly be contained. I rushed out and ran back across the bridge, scrambling down a small path, nearly slipping off the precipitous edge of the cliff in the process. It led me to the fort's old brick foundation. I reached the exact location I had seen from the Chambre des Demoiselles but, to my disappointment, could not move any of the bricks, no matter how hard I tried.

After a while, I calmed down. I already *knew* the secret tunnel into the hollow needle was fiction, made up by Leblanc's fertile mind. Yet here I was, pushing and prodding every brick within reach, like a treasure-chasing *amateur.*

Still, it had been exciting, if only for a few moments!

It was reaching mid-afternoon and I was tired, still suffering from jet lag. I spied the large golf club building, a few hundred yards away, and decided to head there to sit down and get a drink. I was walking through the parking lot when a car horn sounded twice, attracting my attention.

It was Inspector Norton.

He motioned for me to get in. Curiosity gained the upper hand over apprehension. If he'd wanted to arrest me, he would have done it already. I had barely seated myself in the passenger's seat when he took off briskly, his leaded foot seeming to express anger.

"Well, well, well. What a surprise. Running into each other on a completely different continent. I can barely explain it. Can you?"

He was toying with me. I stayed on my guard.

"There is nothing to explain, Inspector. The police said I wasn't a suspect."

"Do you take me for a fool, Sirenne? I knew what you were up to from the beginning. Did you seriously believe that you could evade me so easily?" his face was getting animated. "...I don't know what you think is going on here, Mr Sirenne, but let me assure you that this is not a game..."

"Someone has murdered my father and his wife. I know how serious this is."

"And you think that impresses me? I have personally seen seventeen of the Shadow-Killer's victims, including my beloved sister..." he stopped abruptly, perhaps having told me more than he wanted. Now I knew why Norton was so vehemently obsessed with this killer. He had a personal vendetta. Looking at the man again, I tried to sympathise with him.

I failed.

His eyes prevented me. They were shifty, scanning the horizon without cease, never settling on anything. He seemed almost unhinged. He watched him take a deep breath, visibly trying to contain his emotions. He drove to the beach area and parked on the side of the street, near a bistro.

"I just want to have a quick drink with you and talk quietly for a while. The situation has changed. There are things you must be made aware of..."

He was making an effort of some sort and I nodded my agreement. We exited the car and I followed him. He wove his way between the outside tables in front of the bistro, walking to the very back and sitting down, his back against the wall. His eyes continued roving all around while he placed his order with the waitress. I added mine and listened to him explain the reason for his presence.

"Do you know a man named Harry Styles?"

"No."

"No matter, I didn't expect you to. He was the manager of a car dealership in Ottawa. He was on the same flight that you were on..."

"...Okay..." I responded noncommittally. Where was he going with this?

"... There's a big problem with him having been on that plane... He was killed twenty-four hours earlier!"

"What?"

"You heard me. Killed. That's right. Dead as a doornail, yet he got on the plane... or rather, someone using his ticket got on. I've got some news for you, Sirenne. The Shadow-Killer is right here, right now!"

As he said this, his eyes darted madly in every direction. He looked haunted... or perhaps, *hunted*!

"Look, Sirenne, I don't know what you think you're doing here but you've got to know that you are a really small fish in a very big pond. I'll tell you something else. I'm convinced you lied to me, back there, at your house, when we spoke that second time, maybe something about that package you received... No matter. You know something and you're not telling. The killer left a message and you got it all right. Since then, you've been spending money all over the place, big money. Then you disappear, or at least you try to. These are not the actions of an innocent man. These are the actions of a man with something to hide..."

"Inspector..."

"No, let me finish. You must hear me out. I don't care what you're doing here. I don't even care that you lied to me. I just care about getting that killer. You go ahead and keep your little secrets, it doesn't matter. I'll find out about them eventually... No, Sirenne, all I care about is that this is the first real chance I've had to get close to that murdering monster. I can *feel* it. You can't imagine how frustrating this has been, how all-consuming it has become. Yet, no matter how hard I try, I always come up empty-handed. Not a single shred of physical evidence has ever been left behind. No hair, no dead skin cells, no saliva, nothing! In order to do that, he would have to be wearing a damn body-condom!... And, of course, there are never any witnesses, nothing out of the usual. Even this last murder, surely done on the spur of the moment in order to obtain that plane ticket, was perfect. He didn't bother with any of his usual games, mind you. It was a clean kill..."

He shuddered then sat up straighter and continued.

"... That murder and the murder of your parents have spoken to me. The killer was acting hastily, almost rashly, not caring about the consequences, about the attention these murders might attract. I believe this is totally out of character for him. He knows something, something about you, Mr Sirenne..."

"Me?"

He was starting to get to me. I knew he was right.

"Yes you... and I can tell you this: not much frightens me anymore but I am frightened now... and so should you be. The killer is here because of you and I am convinced he is watching your every move, waiting to pounce when the time is right. He could be anywhere, he could be anyone. Your only value to him is that you have not given him what he wants. When he gets it, it will be over for you... and the only thing between you and him... will be me!... Perhaps you'll start singing a different tune then, Mr Sirenne?"

He laughed, too loudly and off key. His assurances of protection gave me little faith. This man was no longer in his right mind. He was obsessed with the Shadow-Killer. Yet, it was important that I consider his warning. I was not sufficiently prepared for this situation. All I had was my ability to think and my father's training to keep me alive.

Would it be enough?

Norton left the bistro, warning that he would be watching me. I had recorded the whole thing with my glasses for my friends. Even if the Shadow-Killer had murdered another man to come here incognito, my task remained unchanged. I had to understand what was going on, or else I would end up in the killer's wake, a dangerous place to be.

Leaving the bistro, I decided to head to Etretat's City Hall, known locally as the 'Mairie', to examine their older records. It was possible Coulter had missed something. According to my tourist map it was located on *Place Maurice Guillard*. It was only a few blocks away and I was rested after my short break. I hurried down the narrow street.

Arriving at the building, I entered and walked up to a long counter, which blocked access to most of the rooms. I approached it and a man stood up from the other side. He was thin and small, wearing a half-cap, an unlit cigarette, a *Gitane,* hanging precariously from his mouth. He had armbands around his upper arms, his cuffs folded up. Despite being shorter than me, he somehow managed to look down at me.

"Yes. What do you want?" he asked abruptly.

"I was wondering if I might look at some of your older records?"

He looked at me more piercingly than before.

"You're not from around here," he stated flatly, "why do you want to examine our older records? What records?" he asked, looking at me suspiciously, demanding an answer with his eyes.

"I'm looking for records from the early 1900's, hopefully around 1911. Court documents, newspapers, that sort of thing," I rattled on, hoping to find a receptive ear. Instead, his attitude became less and less pleasant.

"No. Absolutely not. You're not allowed. We don't keep these documents here anyway. You'd need a form 1138-G and those are only issued with approval from the mayor and he's away this week and next week," he shot back at me, with a finality to his tone that would not be brooked. He turned away from me, walking to his chair and sitting down, studiously ignoring me.

I stood at the counter for a while, looking at his back. Getting impatient, I tried again.

"Excuse me but why are you ignoring me? My request is not unreasonable. I would like an explanation."

Without looking at me, he responded brusquely.

"I have already answered your request. I don't know you. It is time for you to leave. I must close."

He pulled out a set of keys from a desk drawer. Standing up, he lifted a section of the counter, dropping it back down after walking through it.

"Come on, let's go. I must close. Summer hours," he stated, gesturing at me with his arms. I was literally pushed out of the building. He quickly locked the door, after which he headed off behind the building. Feeling frustrated, I started walking back to the Villa Leblanc.

I began having the impression of being followed. Not sure why I felt this way, I turned around and saw a man walking on the sidewalk some distance from me. I pressed the tiny button on my glasses, activating the binocular mode. The screen came on in front of my eyes, displaying an enlarged view of what I was looking at. Tapping the button a couple of times, I increased the magnification. The screen revealed the man from City Hall.

I turned around and shut the binocular mode off. He was following me, no doubt about it. The question was why? He couldn't be the killer, the coincidence would be too great. Leblanc's adventures happened almost one hundred years ago. How would that man even know about any of that? There was nothing I could do about being followed, so I ignored him and kept walking.

I would've broken out into a fast run but I was exhausted and my feet were tired.

***

Arriving at the Villa, I found Mrs Leblanc at the counter. She smiled as she saw me approach.

"Ah, Monsieur Sirenne. How are you? Did you have a good walk?" she asked, noticing my sweaty, dirty clothes. A sympathetic look appeared in her eyes. "But what am I doing, talking on, while you are so obviously tired? Why don't you head on up to your room and I will have some hot water and salts brought up to you, for soaking your feet."

A feeling of relief washed over me.

"Thank you, Mrs Leblanc. That is exactly what I need. You have read my mind," I replied.

I headed up to my room. Once in, I sat down at my bed, taking off my shoes and socks. After a moment of rest, I opened my laptop on the bedside table, starting it up. I checked to confirm that it had recorded my walk and my meeting with Inspector Norton and the man from the Mairie who had followed me. I saved it all and sent it to the team in Ottawa. As I finished, I heard a knock at the door. I stood up stiffly, walking slowly to it. Mrs Leblanc was there, a big bowl in hand.

"I'm sorry monsieur Sirenne but my maid has gone home for the day. My daughter has recently arrived but she is still busy unpacking, so I came with the water, if you do not mind," she apologised.

"Nonsense. I am embarrassed to put you to so much trouble," I answered, grateful for the attention. She came in, motioning me to the chair by the desk. Bending down, she placed the flat-bottomed bowl by my feet. I slipped them into the warm water and she opened a packet of salts, pouring them into the steaming liquid. A relaxing herbal smell wafted up from the bowl. She handed me a small towel and stood up.

"There you are. Soon you will be back to normal. You did too much today, your first day here..."

That was an understatement.

"... You must learn to pace yourself," she paused, looking at me curiously. "Did you enjoy our tour?"

"Yes, very much. I was told that you had a hand in creating it. It was fantastic. I'm afraid it is what inspired me to walk. I had to go see the Needle right after the tour," I exclaimed, avoiding mention of the other encounters.

She laughed out loud.

"You must be looking for the treasure of the Hollow Needle, like all the others who come here. Fooled by my grandfather's books," she said.

"Not exactly like all the others. My father gave me a copy of The Hollow Needle when I was nine. I've dreamed of coming here since then," I explained.

Her look softened in understanding.

"Yes, the trip brings you closer to your father, does it not? The memories and the adventure all together," she empathised.

"Yes, you have it exactly. Leblanc and Lupin were the heroes of my youth. My father was the one who introduced me to those heroes," I said, my mind flashing on many memories.

A conspiratorial gleam appeared in her eyes.

"Would you like to see Grand-Papa's office? The place where he wrote so many of his books?" she suggested. "It is closed to the public but I could make an exception for you. I think you would appreciate it much more than just the average tourist, don't you?"

She had hardly finished speaking before I had lifted my feet from the steaming water and started drying them off. Selecting some clean socks and my glasses, I slipped on my shoes and followed her to another section of the Villa.

We arrived at a door on the first floor. Before opening it, she cautioned me.

"Please do not touch anything. It is being prepared for an upcoming presentation and many items have been placed specifically for this."

"Don't worry, I'll just look," I replied, thinking of the recording cameras in my glasses. Looking was all I needed to do. She opened the door and ushered me in.

The room was light beige, complimenting the polished furniture. Leblanc's desk was simple enough, letters strewn over one side, a few reference books on the other. Behind his desk, an impressive built-in library rose from a drawer unit to the top of the wall. A few pictures were artfully placed on the ledge at the bottom of the bookcases. I walked around, examining everything avidly.

"I must return to the front desk. Perhaps we can come back another time?" Mrs Leblanc informed me after a few minutes. Before we could leave the room, I heard a voice, coming from the hallway.

"Maman? Where are you? Maman?"

Mrs Leblanc opened the door and called out.

"Here, my dear, I am in Grand-Papa's office with Mr Sirenne" she answered.

I was standing deep in the office and could not see Mrs Leblanc's daughter from my vantage point. As soon as she entered however, there was no mistaking it.

It was the raven-haired woman from the plane!

"This is my daughter, Raymonde, Mr Sirenne."

"I think we have seen each other before, Mr Sirenne..." she exclaimed with a twinkle in her deep hazel eyes.

"Yes, I am sure we have..." I replied, an embarrassed smile breaking out on my face.

She smiled back instantly, turning to look at her mother.

"We are needed at the front desk, Maman. The large group has just arrived."

With a sigh, Mrs Leblanc followed the both of us out and locked the door. After saying a few parting words, they headed down the hall, towards the front desk. Both of them were walking away, my attention drawn to the daughter. Without being able to explain why I felt this way, it seemed to me as if a deep connection already existed between us.

I returned upstairs to my room and sat down on the edge of the bed, wondering why I was feeling this way. Suddenly I was looking at Coulter and O'Flanahan on the techno-glasses' screen. They had been along for the ride for a while and had seen everything

"Hi guys, what's up?" I asked, seeing the concerned look on both their faces.

O'Flanahan took the lead.

"Well, while we were enjoying your tour of Leblanc's office, we noticed something. Do you recall the point when you walked by the desk?"

"Yes, there were some letters and a few books," I remembered.

"Right. Well, we can't be exactly sure but this letter here caught my eye," O'Flanahan's face disappeared, replaced by a still image of a letter, angled sideways on the desk. "As I said, we're not absolutely positive, but take a look at the handwriting on that letter," he continued.

I turned my head sideways, trying to straighten the letter out. This accomplished nothing because the image I was looking at was inside my glasses and moved with my head. Feeling a bit silly, I straightened my head. No matter what orientation it had, the image was just too blurry.

"Sorry, can't make it out. What about it?" I asked.

"Do you remember about four years ago, the little book I published about the conspiracy theory that Hitler didn't die in the bunker? The one that claimed he had escaped in a submarine convoy?" O'Flanahan asked me, changing the subject completely.

I couldn't see where he was going with this.

"What about it?"

"Well, I had to do a fair bit of research during that period and ended up working with some copies of Hitler's letters and orders. I got pretty familiar with them. That letter seems to be in the same handwriting," O'Flanahan dead-panned. Next to him, Coulter was shaking his head up and down.

"I think he's right, Paul. This isn't nonsense. Even Briar agrees," he confirmed.

I was dumbfounded... Hitler?... What was Hitler, of all people, doing writing letters to Leblanc?

"Hold on, you can't be serious... You said you weren't sure. And anyway, Mrs Leblanc said that she had placed all sorts of things in the office for an upcoming event. Maybe it's not even related to Leblanc," I scrambled, trying to find some reasonable way out of this.

"Those were our exact thoughts, Paul. We're not completely sure because it's too blurry in the video. But we can see the date just fine, January twelfth, 1910. That's just before the events with Old Man Vallin. Hitler or not, I'm convinced we need to get a closer look at it. We need you to sneak in there and get that letter," O'Flanahan stated with conviction.

"WHAT? You want me to break into Leblanc's office?" I exclaimed.

"Calm down Paul. We just want to look at the letter, not steal it. Just go borrow it and bring it up to your room. We'll examine it, and you can return it later on, when everyone is sleeping," Coulter oversimplified, adding: "... Anyway, your glasses can see in the ultraviolet and infrared range."

I was lost.

"So?" I asked.

"We think we can use them to help you pick the lock on the door," Coulter said, in a plain matter-of-fact tone.

They were both serious. I had to admit that, if Hitler was involved, I wanted to know about it as quickly as possible. I agreed to do it, as they both knew I would. Secrecy was still paramount in our minds. Breaking in seemed like the most viable option. I had a few small tools for my computer, in a little pouch. I could use them to pick the lock. I had never done it before but I was familiar the principle. It should be fairly easy.

I waited a few hours to let everyone settle in at the Villa Leblanc. Eventually, I decided the time was right and opened my door slightly, looking down the hallway.

No-one around!

I sneaked out, tip-toeing down the corridor and staircase, quietly finding my way back to Leblanc's office. I knelt down quietly by the door, pulling out my tools, while looking nervously around.

"Stop looking around like that. I can't focus on the doorknob" Coulter's voice blared in my ear, scaring the heck out of me. He sounded just as nervous as I was.

Keeping my head still, a screen appeared in front of my eyes. The view of the doorknob changed suddenly to a green monochrome when Coulter altered the visual range to infrared. However, it did little to reveal the actual locking mechanism, hidden within the now green doorknob.

"That's not very helpful," I stated as I knelt there, *in flagrante delicto.*

Coulter switched the cameras to ultraviolet. The door colours changed into a bright red with a luminescent yellow border, the doorknob now totally black. Very psychedelic, but equally useless. Increasingly exasperated, I grabbed my tools and tried to pick the lock. I slipped a small screwdriver into the key hole and jiggled it along the top, trying to 'scrub' the pins, not even sure where the pins were or what 'scrubbing pins' actually meant. Meanwhile, Coulter kept shifting from infrared to ultraviolet, flashing psychedelic and monochromatic green tones. It was giving me a headache. I was about to voice some sort of protest, when O'Flanahan exclaimed.

"Wait, Paul, look at the edge of the door, by the doorknob."

I immediately saw what he was looking at. The metal flange, holding the door closed tight, was missing. I pushed my screwdriver in between the door and the jamb. The door instantly snapped open and slammed loudly against the side wall. I knelt there, listening for any reaction, frozen.

"GO, GO, GO, what are you waiting for? Grab the letter and get out of there," O'Flanahan blasted.

His scream galvanised me into action and, my heart hammering in my chest, I jumped up, ran to the desk and snatched the letter. I ran back out, slamming the door behind me. I then walked nonchalantly down the hall and up the stairs, trying to pretend nothing was going on while I tried to catch my breath and calm my racing heart.

Meanwhile, O'Flanahan and Coulter were laughing nonstop.

"Listen to his breathing. Sounds like a train or something. That was funny. Did you see him go, go, go, when you said it? Ha-ha-ha," howled Coulter. O'Flanahan could say nothing. He was laughing too hard.

"Be quiet, both of you," I urged them, to no avail.

***

Moments later, we sat in my room examining the letter closely. It was written in German, so Coulter used a translation program, providing us with an English version:

January 12, 1910

Sir,

I have recently read your book, The Hollow Needle. I found it quite revealing and interesting. Allow me to come to the point. I have long been fascinated by certain historical mysteries and treasures, both mystical and real, particularly those evidenced in architectural detail.

During my studies, I came across a reference to the mystery and treasure to which your book alludes. Not in the exact same manner to be sure, but close enough to warrant further research. I may be able to arrange for a short visit to Etretat in the near future, when I am visiting my sister in England.

I would like to discuss certain matters that might be of interest to us both.

I await your reply anxiously.

Johann Hister.

If this was indeed Hitler's handwriting, the whole Etretat thing had suddenly taken another turn for the unexpected. The name Hister sounded familiar. It came to me quickly: I had seen it in books about Nostradamus. Several of his quatrains were believed to have used the name 'Hister' to represent Hitler. I told my friends about the connection.

"I remember that too, now that you mention it, Paul..." replied O'Flanahan.

A tired-looking face appeared suddenly on the screen. It was Briar. He had been listening in.

"Hold everything, gentlemen. I just had confirmation from my very excited friend in Nuremberg, a specialist in World War 2 history. That handwriting is indeed Hitler's. Best of all, Hitler *was* in England for a brief period of time, quite early on in his life, visiting his sister, exactly what the letter asserts. It has to be him!" Briar rambled on jubilantly.

"What does this mean? Could Hitler really have come to Etretat?... Before World War 1?" Coulter asked, incredulous.

"We don't know yet. It seems to me that Hitler knew *something* concerning what Leblanc was writing about. Perhaps, like us, he recognised certain inconsistencies in the whole story. He was obviously driven to contact Leblanc. Let's not forget that this is a young Hitler, during his formative years in Vienna. He had not yet written '*Mein Kampf.*'... So, the whole thing is quite possible. In addition, even if he was rather poor at the time, Hitler's sister had a few coins to rub together. Not much, but certainly enough to pay for the odd trip across the channel, directly to Etretat. The distance was short enough," Briar surmised.

"I could agree with that theory..." supported O'Flanahan. "...But if he did come here, it was certainly done discretely and has remained a secret ever since, not a simple feat to achieve, let me tell you. Unfortunately, this letter is not enough to prove that he visited Leblanc... And even if he did visit Etretat, what occurred during that visit? Both are dead now. We will never know..."

"We must keep searching. I don't think I could stop myself now, too much is happening.

My father' murder has to be connected to these events of a hundred years ago. I want to know what Leblanc did back then," I affirmed.

"How? What else can we do?" Coulter asked.

"For now, each of you continue digging. Review the videos of Inspector Norton and that man from the Mairie. Try to find more connections between the past and the present. As for me, I have to return the letter and get some sleep. Tomorrow, we can figure out our next step."

My friends logged off and I removed my glasses, turning them off. Connecting them to my battery charger, I selected the European power setting, and plugged t in. My eyes wandered the room, settling on Hitler's letter. I picked it up and held it carefully, the faded paper feeling almost crumbly. I had to return it soon. It was nearing 12:30 AM.

This was probably as good a time as any to do the deed.

I sneaked down the hall again, arriving at the office without incident. I knelt down in front of the door, leaning on it slightly, intent on using the screwdriver again. The weak latch gave way unexpectedly under the slight pressure of my shoulder and the door fell open, banging loudly against the wall again. Losing my support, I fell, rolling forward into an unintentional summersault, ending up flat on my back, the wind completely knocked out of me.

From my crippled vantage point on the ground, my left hand still holding Hitler's letter, I could see the top of the doorway. In the middle of this area, I made out a misty dark area, moving slightly. Bending my head back, my gaze slid down onto Raymonde, Mrs Leblanc's daughter!

I scrambled around, ending up in a cross-legged sitting position on the floor, facing her.

"Er...hello there, Raymonde, how are you, this fine evening?" I stammered, frantically trying to think of a way to explain this.

"What are you doing here? Why are you in Grand-Papa's room? You were stealing his papers! That is it," she questioned, then accused.

"No, I wasn't stealing it, I was... er... I was returning it," I explained weakly.

It didn't even sound believable to me.

"And you think that makes it right? You broke in here to return stolen papers? And who stole them if it wasn't you? Tell me that, you... you liar," she continued. How had I allowed myself to get into this?

"Wait please. You are right. I did take the letter. But I am also returning it. At least let me explain, then you can call the police if you want," I begged, bringing my hands together, the letter in them not helping my plea. I returned the letter to the table, tapping it down, smoothing away the wrinkles as best as possible. "I know this looks bad but I swear this is truly important."

She glared at me for a while, trying to look serious, but finally a smile began working against her frown.

"No thief could look as pitiful as that. Get up and explain yourself... No wait, I have a better idea. Meet me for breakfast downstairs, tomorrow morning. You can explain yourself then and it had better be good. Now back to your room," she stated, motioning me with her hands. She followed me, not saying another word. I went into my room, looking at her one last time.

"Thank you for believing me," I said.

"Don't thank me yet. We will wait for tomorrow to see if thanks are due or not," she returned, and then closed the door, double-locking it from the outside.

Matt Chatelain

CHAPTER 6
Raymonde Leblanc

It was about 7:30 in the morning. The sound of a key in my door had woken me.

"Be down in fifteen minutes. I'll be waiting for your explanation," Raymonde Leblanc stated through the door.

I showered, dressed rapidly and hurried downstairs, joining her at the corner table in the dining room.

Time to face the executioner.

"I have already ordered breakfast for you. Your story had better be good," she said.

With a sigh, I sat down, looking at her. Her hazel eyes were luminous, accentuated by laughter lines. She seemed to be in her mid-thirties. A shock of raven-black hair was barely held in check by a colourful ribbon tied behind her back. A few freckles adorned her cheeks. It made her look somehow mischievous. Her nose was small and pert. A wide smile and perfect teeth.

She was beautiful.

"Thank you, uhm... Raymonde, for giving me a chance last night. I know we didn't start off well but it is all a big misunderstanding..." her disbelieving look interrupted me. "No, I mean it. It really is. But I have to go back a bit in order to explain why I am here," I began.

"Fine. I will listen," she returned.

I started by explaining about the murders, the Shadow-Killer and Norton.

"You poor man. To lose your parents like that..." she sympathised. "... And so brave to take up the chase for answers, willing to face all the dangers."

"The dangers will be there no matter what I do. The serial killer is out there and it doesn't seem like anyone has a chance of stopping him any time soon. I have to do this. Bravery has little to do with it."

Raymonde reached out and patted my arm in sympathy. I finished my explanation by talking about the book my father had sent me:

"... When I re-read your great-grandfather's Hollow Needle book, something in it made me question what he was really writing about... I asked a few friends to help me do some research. We discovered some things that convinced us that there might be a forgotten mystery, here in Etretat, which began with the murder of Old Man Vallin. There is a direct link between my family and your great-grandfather and the Fort of Frefosse is right at the centre of it all," I continued.

She was surprised when I mentioned the fort but let me continue:

"... We decided that coming here was the next logical step and, because of... certain circumstances, I was selected as the one to do the travelling. My friends remained at home for the time being and we decided to... uh... to stay in close communication throughout the trip. I would do the physical investigation, they would do the research and together, we would figure out what, if anything, was going on in Etretat."

I stopped, interrupted by the waitress bringing our breakfast. I had omitted mentioning the techno-glasses because it would lead us right back into that plane cabin and how we met, thanks to O'Flanahan. She would know that it wasn't just me looking at her, she would ask more questions and things would get messy. I just couldn't take that chance. I would explain later, when it would be easier to laugh about it.

There was another reason I had kept quiet about the glasses.

From the moment I had seen Raymonde, I had felt attracted to her. The feelings were out of place but they were there nonetheless. I could not tell if she reciprocated my feelings but, after being caught stealing that letter, I didn't want to make any further mistakes and risk losing her burgeoning trust.

I noticed a thin man sitting at a table near us, turning his head away when I looked at him. I recognised him as the unpleasant clerk from the Mairie.

My heart jumped.

Had he followed me here and slept the night? He was listening to our every word. Was he working for the Shadow-Killer?

A bead of sweat broke over my brow and I felt butterflies in my stomach.

"Are you all right? You just stopped talking? You have gone all pale," Raymonde said, concerned.

"No... uh... It's my stomach... It's cramping like crazy. I must return to my room. Can you help me there?" I asked getting up, holding myself slightly bent over.

Raymonde looked suspicious but helped me out of the restaurant. I felt her warm, shapely body press against mine in the narrow hallway leading out of the restaurant. Before we could get to the stairs, I straightened out and leaned against her, whispering in her ear:

"I'm fine. Not sick. Sorry about that, trust me, I'll explain in a few minutes. However, we must leave here now. Let's go to my car."

I steered her towards the exit and the parking lot. We walked quickly, hurrying to the Porsche. Slowing down, Raymonde questioned me:

"What is going on?"

"I am being followed. That man sitting next to us. I met him yesterday, at the Mairie, where I was trying to get information about old records. He was inexplicably rude and refused to grant me access. Then, he followed me here. Suddenly, this morning, I notice him, sitting there at the next table, listening to our every word. Do you know him?" I asked.

"No, I'm afraid not. I haven't been here for years. But we should not have too much trouble finding out who he is. If he slept here, his name will be on the register. Maman will probably know him. She knows everybody around here. Where are we going?" she asked.

"I don't know. I just want to get away from him. How about we drive to the Needle and sit on a bench and talk there," I suggested.

"And what of breakfast? We walked away from our meal. I am still hungry," she argued, pouting a little.

"How about we stop and order a take-out meal on the way?" I counter-offered.

"*Non*," she flatly refused. "I want to sit down for my breakfast. I will not sit on a cement bench, eating on my knees. There is a restaurant at the golf club, near the Needle. We can have breakfast there."

"Fine," I agreed, trying to keep the peace. She certainly was temperamental. Personally, I was fine with coffee for breakfast. I opened the car door for her and she got in. I was about to get in when I saw the clerk from the Mairie watching us through the restaurant window.

Incapable of resisting, I waved at him with what I hoped was an insolent smile and got in. Starting the powerful engine, I slammed it into gear and pushed my foot down hard. The wheels spun with a sharp screeching sound and we took off like a bullet, the back end of the car sliding sideways, nearly out of control. I almost hit a street sign when we shot out of the parking lot, narrowly avoiding an oncoming truck.

"What are you doing? Why are you going so fast? You nearly hit that truck, back there," screamed Raymonde.

"Sorry, rented car. Not used to it yet..." I explained weakly. I had not expected such a burst of acceleration from the sports car.

"That was scary..." she continued. I noticed her fast breathing and its effect on her chest, unable to help myself.

"...And keep your eyes on the road. Get that foot off the gas and turn left over there," she ordered.

We reached the golf club restaurant quickly, thanks to her expert directions. We were seated at a table overlooking the Aval cliff and ordered breakfast from a tall, balding waiter, whose shiny head made me think of Briar. When he left, Raymonde leaned back in her chair, looking a bit amused.

"Well, now that we are here and all alone, perhaps you can finish your story?"

"Yes. I'm sorry for acting so suspiciously but, believe me, knowing what I have found out, I would want no-one else overhearing," I said.

"Unless that someone was going to call the police about a thief," she teased.

"We both know the time has passed for that," I shot back, calling her bluff. Her hazel eyes jumped to mine.

"Well, you *do* have some backbone in you after all. Yes, you are right. I will not call the police. I don't like involving them anyway. I must admit that I know something about this mystery... I will explain to you after you have told me the rest of your story. But be quick and to the point," she added.

What was this? She had something to tell me? I reached in my jacket pocket and pulled out my glasses, pausing before putting them on. I had not worn them last night, when returning the paper to Leblanc's office, so my friends in Ottawa knew nothing of my 'chance' meeting with Raymonde, an event best left unexplained in my opinion. However, if Raymonde had some information that was connected to this mystery, I simply had to record it. I was in a difficult position. Balancing long-term benefit against short-term embarrassment, I activated the techno-glasses and put them on.

"Why did you put those on? Do you have a problem with your eyes?" she asked right away.

"Yes, the glasses.. uh.. help me see better," I said lamely. And farther. And in the dark. And record everything I see.

"Next time, pick a better style. Something lighter, not as black or heavy looking. You look like, how do you Canadians say it?... like a 'dork'. Is that the word?" she stated rudely.

Feeling insulted, I was about to reply, when I noted a look in her eyes. She was taunting me.

"Thank you for the suggestion. How about I tell you the rest of my story?" I said, avoiding any facial expression.

"Go ahead, Mr Sirenne," she agreed.

Yes! In her eyes, she was laughing!

"Paul, please. As I said, I arrived in Paris, obtained a car and drove directly here. My focus was on the Fort of Frefosse. You see, your grandfather... hold on there, he's not really your grandfather is he? More like your great-grandfather isn't he?" I asked her.

"Yes, of course you are right, but it is so awkward to say that. At home, Maman always called him Grand-Papa and so did I," she explained.

"Oh... Well, as you may know, the Fort of Frefosse was blown up in 1911, supposedly by the army. The only problem was, our information revealed something different. Someone called Old Man Vallin blew it up. Furthermore, an unknown person paid him to do it. Then, two months later, someone killed Vallin by throwing him in the crater left from the fort's destruction. The actual events do not match the historical version. So, I came here, looking for clues to help me discover what Old Man Vallin was up to and who had killed him. I went to the Mairie and met that little man who followed me and spied on us. That evening, your mother showed me your great-grandfather's office. While there, they... uh... I saw a letter..."

Raymonde interrupted me.

"... That letter in your hand. I have seen it before, long ago. Maman showed it to me. It was from Grand-Papa's papers. Maman must have put it on the desk for the presentation coming up," she added.

"Yes, well, I thought I had seen the handwriting before. I did not have time to check it out because you came in, if you remember. That was why I went back later to *borrow* the letter, so I could check more closely and see if I was right about the writing," I explained.

"Who had written the letter? Tell me," she demanded, a fierce look in her eyes.

"Wait, here comes breakfast. We can't let the waiter overhear us," I said.

Raymonde was flustered but kept silent. The waiter served us and left. The moment he was out of hearing distance, she pounced.

"Now, you will tell me who wrote that letter. No more delays. I will eat and you will speak," she insisted.

"Fine, if you put it like that," I said, watching her attack the breakfast ravenously. "We, uh, I believe that the letter was written by Adolf Hitler."

The look in her eyes was worth all the delaying tactics.

"Hitler? That is impossible. Are you positive?" she asked as a formality, not really doubting me. I was gaining her trust.

"Yes... A specialist from Nuremberg confirmed it. Not only that, Hitler was living across the Channel with his sister, when that letter was written. He could easily have travelled to Etretat. We don't know if he did, we don't know if your great-grandfather met him but the letter said some very interesting things. It implied that the Hollow Needle mystery might not be complete fiction..." I found it impossible to stop. I had to tell her the rest. After all, she had a right to know. "... There is more about the Fort of Frefosse. We believe it might have been built over a tunnel leading to a huge cave. We think that the Aval cliff is hollow and that your grandfather knew it. Thanks to that letter, we have learned that Hitler may also have known of it," I explained. She had cleaned her plate in the time it took me to tell her about Hitler.

She grew thoughtful.

"I too have my questions about Grand-Papa. I'm sure you know that Maman was with him when the Germans invaded our poor little town. She has never forgotten those events, although she rarely talks about them. That is the time when she lost her sister and her father. Her mother had died when she was born. Relatives took her in after Grand-Papa died. Gone or not, Grand-Papa's spirit was always with us, haunting us. When Maman re-opened the Villa and asked me to return, I decided that I was going to find answers to all my questions about Grand-Papa, if only to be done with it, with him... to finally be able to get on with my life and maybe help Maman get on with hers... Something else happened instead... You happened!" she said, her eyes probing deep into mine.

"Me? What about me?" I asked, keeping my eyes wide open and guileless.

"Don't play the innocent with me. From the moment I saw you looking at me on that plane, I haven't been able to stop thinking about you. You are certainly the strangest man I have ever met. You come here with information and wild ideas that seem to fit into everything that I suspect of Grand-Papa," she added hesitantly, as if she wanted to say more but didn't dare to.

Nodding her head to herself, she continued:

"The thing is that, even with all your antics and your lack of respect, I like you... I feel that I can trust you. I think that we need to work together on Grand-Papa's mystery. Together we will solve this thing and catch that murderer who killed your parents... And I think that we need to talk to Maman about all this. I will need your help with that," she admitted, looking at me earnestly.

She liked me! I glanced at her, a smile on my lips.

"Let's go right now," I agreed, eager to return to the Great Hunt but she shook her head:

"No, not right now, later. We will wait for that man to go away. Today, we will walk to the Needle and you can tell me everything you know."

She stood up and walked over to the waiter.

"Hand him the bill," she commanded, pointing at me with her finger, then left the restaurant, disappearing from view.

Paying the waiter and giving him a good tip, remembering his excellent timing, I hurried out of the restaurant, catching sight of her walking onto the trail to the edge of the cliff, by the Needle. I hurried down and joined her.

We walked in silence, next to each other. I felt her body so close to mine and could think of little else. I wondered what I was doing, thinking of a relationship, with so many dangers and challenges facing me. The problem was that I couldn't stop looking at her. She seemed so full of life, so radiant.

I couldn't explain *why now* or *why here* but I knew I was falling in love!

I moved nearer to her. She didn't shift away, her warm body brushing against mine tantalisingly. She turned her head towards me, smiling shyly. I looked deep into her eyes and slid my hand into her waiting fingers. She entwined her arm into mine, pulling me tight against her. I could feel her every movement against me. I felt thrilled, my thoughts and emotions running wild.

Walking along, a brisk wind stirred up. Something about the whole scene felt vaguely familiar, like a *déjà-vu*. I tried to dispel the feeling but it only grew stronger when she started speaking.

"I used to come up here, as a little girl. I wandered the countryside but this was my favourite place. When you mentioned the tunnels and caves, it made me think of that time... Tell me, Paul, have you ever heard of Jean Auel?" she asked me.

"Jean Auel? Yes, of course, she wrote the book 'Clan of the Cave Bear'," I answered.

"I was fascinated by her description of the Neanderthals and how they lived in their caves... Well, those caves, they are here, in France," she said.

I understood where she was going with this. She continued:

"I have gone to some of them because I wanted to see the wall paintings. France has thousands of caves and people have been living in them for more than twenty-five thousand years. Considering that, it seems very possible that there is a cave here too, right under our feet. Who knows for how long it has been here?" she said, stopping abruptly and looking down.

I wondered why she was looking at her feet. It dawned on me that we were standing where the Fort of Frefosse had been. If a cave was here, we were standing right above its entrance, buried below thousands of tons of concrete, sand traps and landscaping. I noticed a large, familiar-looking, structure near us.

The déjà-vu feeling was back.

"What is that?" I asked.

"That is the first bunker built in Etretat by the Germans," she answered, leaving me dumbfounded.

"You mean to tell me that the first bunker they built was right over the ancient Fort of Frefosse. Doesn't that seem odd to you?" I queried.

"Yes, now that you mention it like that. Let's go in and look around," she suggested.

It was a crumbling affair, a bad mix of cement and local sand. The bunker was a stark reminder that sixty years ago, this small peaceful town had seen horrible destruction and upheaval at the hands of the German army.

I was walking closer to the bunker when a powerful feeling swept over me, as if I were being watched from somewhere nearby. Was the Shadow-Killer here? Had the man from the Mairie found us? I looked around in a panic trying to see who was there. I looked up in the sky behind me and it struck me that this was the scene from my strange dream, the one after my father's death. I could not explain to myself how I could have dreamt about this exact moment. Remembering another aspect of the dream, the strong light coming from the bunker, I turned back towards it and looked closely at its every opening.

They were dark and lifeless.

Raymonde felt my tension and her arm tightened on mine when we entered the bare doorway, leading us into a simple room. The cement was crumbling away everywhere except for the floor. It was in better condition, having been poured from a later batch. I saw Raymonde frowning. We were both wondering the same thing: why would they have re-cemented the floor, if not to fill in or hide something? Apart from that, there was no other point of interest, nothing unusual at all. Perhaps that dream had only been a dream. We went outside, heading back onto the path.

She caught my arm again, pulling me against her side.

I stood silent, feeling her pressing against me, and thought about Maurice Leblanc, about what he had been up to and how it had led me here, to Raymonde, his great-granddaughter.

I thought about my father, about what he had said to me so long ago, a phrase vividly remembered:

"Son, one day, you will be thinking about how life has brought you full circle, when the end has brought you back to the beginning. That is when the real mystery will begin to be exposed. That is when you will begin to know why I have given you this book."

In a way, my father's end had led me to this beginning with Raymonde. I wondered if my father had been trying to tell me something about the circle of life, something I had not understood until now, until today. Perhaps the real mystery had nothing to do with treasure. Perhaps the treasure was not what I thought it was.

Smiling to myself, I pulled Raymonde very close to me, and kissed her.

I forgot all about my father after that.

Matt Chatelain

TOP SECRET

ADOLF HITLER'S EYES ONLY

FROM OBERSLEUTENANT WEISSMULLER

2ND OF FEBRUARY, 1937

This is to be my final report about the Etretat research project. I have succeeded in our original goals a full two years ahead of schedule. I believe the result to be exactly what we desired.

All specialists, historians and archaeologists who did research on Etretat have been eliminated. No trace of them, or their research, will ever be found. In some instances, this required drastic measures, all of which were successfully conducted in complete secrecy. I was able to remove all key documents from the universities involved without any major incidents.

As a result, I can now categorically state that only the two of us are aware of the secrets which lie below the cliffs of Etretat. Of course this leaves whatever our opponents in Etretat might know. They and their cursed town have unfortunately remained inaccessible, resisting my most strenuous efforts. They are well protected. Luckily, it seems their desire for secrecy is as great as ours since they have remained completely silent about what is hidden within their midst.

We can therefore conclude that we are safe to begin the next phase. I have already begun to make preparations for this. My appointment to this post in your army will help in this regard. No matter what our opponents may attempt to do to repel us, this time they will not succeed. We will be victorious and the caves will be ours.

I have attached to this document a brief summary of the pertinent research for your examination. I believe that once I have access to the caves themselves, an even clearer picture will emerge.

Matt Chatelain

Summary Report

1) The Creation of the Caves.

The Caves are believed to have been formed by the impact of a meteorite into a shallow seabed, about sixty-five million years ago. Through natural geological processes, the cracked seabed raised up, until it became an imposing limestone plateau, towering more than one hundred meters over the retreating waters. Four hundred and fifty thousand years ago, the Weald-Artois Anticline ridge, in the Doggerland region, failed, causing a massive flood, releasing more than a million cubic meters of water per minute. Lasting several months, this flood carved out the core of the English Channel.

During the flood, the cracked area of the seabed around the meteorite was exposed to hyper-erosion, the flood gouging out the cracks into much larger holes before receding. The process concluded one hundred and eighty thousand years ago when the Weald-Artois Anticline ridge failed again, this time causing a flood of unimaginable proportion, which finished digging out the English Channel and the caves.

2) The Formation of the Rift in the Cliff (Location: Present-day Etretat)

The Weald-Artois flood created many new lakes in surrounding valleys. An inland fresh water sea was formed on the mainland, not far away from the buried caves. Over the years, several tributaries developed, emptying the inland sea waters into the new English Channel. One such tributary eventually became the Seine River.

Over time, a small offshoot of this river dug a narrow path in the chalk bed, passing by the buried meteorite. Finding a weakness in the rock, the water dug downward. Breaking through at the edge of the cliff, the water began pouring out into the channel. Over the years the tributary grew, eroding the opening into a long narrow valley, its floor gradually lowering to the level of the channel waters.

The inland sea slowly drained over thousands of years, leaving an alluvial plain of incredible scope in the center of France. When the inland sea's level dropped, gravel was deposited on the tributary beds, gradually filling the smaller rivers completely with fine gravel. The small river emptying itself into the newly created port of Etretat stopped flowing on the surface, becoming an underground river. Plants encroached on the dry river bed until it vanished completely, hiding all evidence of the water still flowing below.

3) The Roman period of Occupation

By 54 BC, the caves lay deep in Belgica, a Gaulish territory, near the town of Caleti. The Gallic Wars had begun years before. Caesar was developing serious plans to deal with the bothersome Gauls, who had been harassing the Romans for almost three hundred years by that time. Unfortunately for the Gauls, Caesar's decision to commit most of the Roman military resources to the Gallic Wars was the turning point, setting the stage for the final confrontation.

Vercingetorix, chief of the Averni tribe of Central Gaul, incited by the brutal Roman attacks, managed to successfully unite the Gauls against the Romans. The inhabitants of Caleti, learning of Vercingetorix's rallying cry, sent ten thousand men to join the growing army, seriously depleting their ranks at home. Caesar captured the town of Avaricum, exterminating the local Gaul population. Caesar suffered a defeat at Gergovia but finally cornered and defeated Vercingetorix at Alesia, effectively marking the end of the Gallic Wars.

It was at this point that the small port in Caleti was taken over by the Romans. Shortly after, construction of a road linking the port with Juliobonna was begun. During this period, two Roman structures were built, one on each cliff. One of these was a Roman garrison, while the other was a fort, designed for private use.

This fort, known today as Frefosse, is believed to have been built over the cave entrance. It seems a deliberate act because efforts were made to keep the caves secret. The port remained in use until the end of the Roman period. By 300 AD, it had collapsed into ruins.

The caves were re-discovered by Francis the First, during his rebuilding of the Frefosse fort. He chose to keep their existence hidden, using them as his private repository for gold and other valuables. It is surmised that knowledge of the caves was lost during the turmoil of the French Revolution and they remained undisturbed until Leblanc's amateurish efforts brought attention to them once again.

End of Summary

Matt Chatelain

CHAPTER 7
Talking to Mrs Leblanc

We arrived back at the Villa Leblanc around five pm. We had spent the rest of the afternoon, walking slowly along the paths, talking about each other, about who we were. It gave me the opportunity to explain about some of my other reasons for believing that there was a mystery in Etretat. I told her about my father and his hunts. I explained about the note found hidden inside the book. Yet, all through it, I breathed not a single word about my techno-glasses, ending the afternoon feeling as if my opportunity had come and gone.

I would find an opening when the time was right.

Apart from my one omission, what I told her convinced her that working together was the right thing to do. We would join forces, trying to ferret out the connection between my family and hers. We agreed that the next step was to talk to her mother about her grandfather, specifically about the period when they had escaped from the Germans and left Etretat, in 1939.

We knew that Hitler had sent Leblanc a letter in 1911 but, if Leblanc's biography were to be believed, Leblanc had never met with him, either publicly or privately. Raymonde's mother, who had accompanied Leblanc in his escape from the invading German army, might reveal a link between them. Leblanc had died shortly after his escape from Etretat. We hoped that Mrs Leblanc would be able to shed a bit of light on his final days. However, Raymonde had warned me about this issue. The topic we wanted to raise was taboo around the house. It was going to be difficult to broach and we had to proceed delicately.

We parked in the lot and got out of the Porsche, walking hand in hand. Her mother was at the counter when we entered Leblanc's Villa. She looked relieved.

"Well, well, well. My missing daughter is finally here to take over the desk."

Mrs Leblanc came around the front desk and hugged Raymonde tightly.

"I was worried. You were gone so long, without even leaving a note," Mrs Leblanc said tenderly, then released her. She turned to me, a knowing look in her eyes. "Young man, if you are to be with my daughter, I must welcome you to our family properly. Come here," she stated, accepting no alternative. I approached her, not knowing what to expect. To my surprise, she held my face with both of her steady hands, then leaned over and kissed me once on each cheek, both of which reddened immediately. She moved away and said:

"Welcome to our home, Paul Sirenne."

I leant over, kissing both her cheeks.

"Thank you," I answered, adding "I will keep an eye on her for you."

"You had better. Just remember that *I* will be keeping my eyes on the *both* of you. Now, you can tell me what happened... No, actually, both of you go on up to my private room. I will finish here and be up in five minutes. Off you go," she ordered.

We went up the stairs and down the hall to the left. At the very end was a door with a sign that read 'Private', which Raymonde opened. We walked into a spacious sitting room. Off to the left was a large bedroom and on the right, was a tiny bathroom. We sat down on a small love seat. I was suddenly pressed up against Raymonde.

"I like this sofa, don't you?" she said innocently.

"Yes. It's very... uh... very cozy," I answered, feeling warmer all of a sudden.

"That is what I thought too. Cozy," she said, her eyes smouldering.

"Do you think your mother will be up soon?" I asked, trying to dampen the mood. She slapped me lightly, a fleeting smile on her lips.

"Spoilsport."

While I smiled back at her, a realization hit me.

Her mother might well reveal some key information and I just couldn't conceive of not recording it. My only worry was that I had not been in contact with my friends at all for more than a day. I knew it was only a question of time before one of them tried to contact me, possibly interrupting me while in conversation with Raymonde and her mother. Unfortunately, I could not control the events unfolding around me. I would simply have to take my chances. I pulled out my glasses once more, trying to slip them on surreptitiously.

I failed.

"Why are you putting on those ugly glasses again?" Raymonde questioned immediately.

"I... uh... need them to see your mother clearly..."

Noticing her disapproving look, I continued.

"What's the problem? They don't look that bad, do they?"

Shaking her head, she replied:

"I'm sorry to say this, Paul, but it's for your own good. You don't look good in those glasses. Not at all..." she stated.

I was realising that the idea of keeping the camera-in-the-eyeglasses thing a secret might not have been a good one. At least, my friends hadn't tried to connect as soon as the glasses were turned on.

"I understand, Raymonde, but I think it's really important that I not miss anything, not a single nuance of your mother's expressions," I explained, hopefully in a very sincere tone. She maintained a doubtful look but was prevented from arguing further by her mother, who came in through the door, another case of excellent timing. I was learning that Raymonde was very shrewd. It was difficult to get any deception past her.

"Sorry my dears, it took longer than expected" she apologized. She seated herself in a comfortable-looking red chair facing us, her eyes briefly glancing at my glasses. "Now let's start at the beginning. What happened this morning?"

Mrs Leblanc had lost no time and gone right for the jugular. I looked at Raymonde to see who was going to explain. She took on the task.

"You remember last night, when you first introduced me to Paul? Yes? Well, a little later, I went out of my room and... I found him just coming out of his. He was bothered by something. He explained about a letter he had seen on the desk, when he was in Grand-Papa's office with you. He thought he knew who the real author of that letter was, so I brought him back to the office to look at it again. We confirmed that he was right about it and decided to talk about it over breakfast."

Mrs Leblanc's face took on an odd look when she asked us:

"Who wrote the letter?"

I jumped in, nearly bursting with the news.

"It was Adolf Hitler, Mrs Leblanc."

If I had been expecting a big reaction, I was disappointed.

"Adolf Hitler?... How interesting. What happened after that?"

"...While we were eating, Paul noticed a man eating at a table next to ours. This man, who works at the Mairie, was spying on us. He had followed Paul here, after refusing him access to old town documents. We became worried and left quickly. That was when I forgot to leave you a note," Raymonde finished.

"I know who you're talking about. It's Jacques Vallin," Mrs Leblanc stated.

"Excuse me, but did you say Vallin?" I asked, my heart beating faster.

"Yes, one of two, unfortunately. And not a thought between the both of them. Two brothers, one small, the other large, neither exactly honest," she answered. "I wondered why he rented a room here last night. After all, he lives just down the road."

What was a Vallin doing following me? Why had he been so uncooperative? Was he on the killer's payroll? At the very least, this descendant of Old Man Vallin, aware of what had happened long ago, had placed himself in the exact position to effect his own research, while at the same time being able to frustrate others with the same goal.

"This Vallin name is familiar to me. It is one of the reasons I have come here. In 1911, someone killed his ancestor, Old Man Vallin. It cannot be coincidence that today, almost a hundred years later, his great-grandson seems to be actively pursuing his own quest to uncover the Etretat mystery. That is why we thought it important to ask you what happened back then when the Germans invaded Etretat and you were forced to escape with your grandfather," I asked.

Raymonde looked a little nervous when I broached the subject so directly but her mother took it calmly.

"It is all right, Raymonde. I know that you tread lightly where certain topics are concerned. However, I am not as fragile as you might think. For many years, I have reviewed those dreadful events that happened to me so long ago. You must understand, I was very young and don't remember anything clearly. I do know that before it happened, I was aware of something bad going on. The way everybody was acting. People were scared, angry! Papa was gone, had been gone for a while, and Grand-Papa was taking care of my sister and me. Then, one day, Grand-Papa was there with a small valise for himself and an even smaller one for both of us. We threw in a few things, my favourite blanket, my sister's teddy bear, and some clothes. Grand-papa was crying and trying to hide it. My sister and I were very scared. We stayed quiet and did what we were told. Grand-papa took us outside, where a man was waiting with a horse and wagon. I didn't know his name, but I had seen him before," her voice became steadier as the memories grew clearer.

"We got on the wagon. *'We are going on a little trip to visit with some friends'*, Grand-papa said to us. He gave us some cookies to eat and a little bit of goat milk. Along the road, we saw hundreds of people walking, carrying everything they owned on their shoulders, in their bags, their suitcases, their boxes. Many were crying openly. I remember feeling very sad and thinking that this was no ordinary trip but rather the end of something. Grand-papa hugged us a lot and tried to make us feel better. No fires were allowed at night and we often travelled in the dark.

"We travelled for many days, staying on narrow roads in forested areas. I heard some bombs far away once, and, on another occasion, a plane swooped right over us, having come up on us from behind. Eventually, there were fewer people on the road with us. Finally, after many days we arrived in Perpignan. Grand-papa shook the driver's hand for a long time, saying a few words to him. They both looked very serious. I never saw the driver again. We walked the rest of the way, Grand-Papa leading us by the hand until we arrived at a tall house on the outskirts of Perpignan.

"That is where we stayed... until he... until he died!" she hesitated, her eyes far away. "He was unwell, you see, and the long trip had taken its toll. He hid it well, kept up a brave front for his 'little girls'. A few days before the end, he got better, or seemed to. He left us in the care of our friends and went out for the day. He left with a small leather satchel, a bit like the one you have, Paul. When he came back later, he looked very tired. He did not have the satchel with him anymore. That night was the last time he had me come and sit with him, by the fireplace in our small apartment. He looked sad and I could tell that he was worried. He said many things, talking for a long time. He was not making sense to me, not to my five-year-old mind anyway. I do remember a few things. He talked about someone, someone who worried him very much. He also thought something was his fault then said that he had tried to fix it. I have one other clear memory of that night.

"He took me upon his knee and, holding my two small hand in his, taught me a little song. He asked me to always remember it and to tell it to my children when the time was right. I guess this must be that time. It is a silly song, really, more of a ditty":

'The beginning and the end. Follow the circle, it bends.
The end and the beginning. The answer in the connecting'

"We sang it many times. He told me that, one day, the song would mean something more," she finished, her voice fading away.

Her story had exposed something that I could not accept.

Her little ditty, the song taught to her by her grandfather was *exactly the same message* from my own father. How had these identical verses travelled the continents, over a century ago, ending up with both our families? It could not be coincidence.

"We need to go to Perpignan."

"Why do you say that, Paul?" asked Raymonde.

"It's the ditty, the song. It says that the beginning is the end. Well, Maurice Leblanc's end was in Perpignan and that is where we have to go. To the place of his end, to see if any clues were left. I'm very curious about what he could have done during the day that he disappeared. What was in that satchel that he took with him? Why did he choose Perpignan as a destination? These questions are all important at this point. Perhaps Perpignan holds the answer to some of them," I explained.

I did not know how to broach the subject of Maurice Leblanc's ditty and their connection to the one from my own family. I feared it might be too much for Mrs Leblanc to deal with, so I avoided the topic for the time being. Mrs Leblanc had yet more to reveal:

"I believe that I might shed some light on a few of those questions of yours, Paul. During that time, everything was chaos. There were few places safe from the invading Germans. Perpignan was close to Spain and was relatively unimportant strategically. So was Etretat, for that matter. Perpignan was also home to a few of Grand-papa's old friends. I think on the day he left, he may have gone to visit one of them, for the express purpose of giving him the satchel. I believe that it contained a journal of some sort. I have a few memories, during our travel, of Grand-Papa leaning over a sheaf of papers, by the dim light of a candle. I do not know whom he could have gone to visit, unfortunately. I only know the address where we lived in Perpignan," she explained, picking up a pad of notepaper and jotting down an address. "I think there is a chance that someone there may remember him. He was famous enough in his time. Now I am afraid that I will have to bid you both a good night. I am feeling a bit tired," she admitted, her voice shaky again. She hugged us both tightly and we agreed to meet for breakfast in the morning.

Walking along the hallway, it was apparent that Raymonde was leading me to her room. My glasses suddenly squeaked and I was looking at Fabian Coulter.

"Hey, Paul, where have you been? We've been trying to connect with you... Say, who's that walking ahead of you? She looks familiar..."

I reached up and turned the techno-glasses off without saying a single word. The situation was complicated enough. I removed the glasses and slipped them back into my pocket before Raymonde opened the door to her room. It was similar to my own, with a large bed against the wall to the left of the door. On the far side of the bed, an alcove with large windows nestled two chairs and a small coffee table. We sat down there, looking at each other in silence for a moment.

"This has certainly been an eventful day," I said.

She smiled at me, her whole face lighting up.

"I'll say. I feel as if I am in a whirlwind. Things are happening almost too fast. But that is the way I like it... and the way I like you," she added, her hand reaching out to hold mine. "I must ask you something..." she looked questioningly into my eyes and I nodded at her. "... When Maman told us about Grand-Papa's little song, it seemed to me that you were holding something back. Were you?"

Her ability to pick up so much about what I was thinking impressed me once more. Several times today, I had been near potential disaster because of her quickness of thought and her no-nonsense way of speaking about it.

"Yes, I did hold something back. If you remember, I explained to you about my father and the copy of the Hollow Needle he gave me when I was nine. It had a note from him, which started me on this hunt. What I may not have told you was the exact wording of that note. Don`t worry, I don't have to tell you, because your mother just told us the exact same words!..." I paused, seeing the stunned look in Raymonde's eyes. "That's right... impossibly, Raymonde, that little puzzle found its way into our two separate families, almost a hundred years ago. Our grandfathers have both left us the same clue, intent on leading us directly to this forgotten mystery... When you and I were walking together at the Fort of Frefosse site, I believed that my father's gift had led me here so that I would discover treasure can be found in unexpected places... like in you..." I explained, seeing her smile at my comment. "But, now, I'm not so sure. How could that ditty have come to be in both our families?... I didn't want to burden your mother with that question. It would have been too much. She already looked shaken up."

Raymonde stood up, walking around the small table, and pulled me into her waiting arms. We kissed, a long lingering kiss, filled with passion. She drew her face away from mine for a second.

"That was a nice thing to do. I had to say thank you somehow," she whispered.

She led me to her bed, where she sat down, leaning back into the pillows. I felt excited and so did she, judging from the smouldering look in her eyes.

"You weren't thinking of going back to your room right away, were you?" she asked innocently.

"..Uhm, uh, no, not at all. I was hoping I might stay a little longer, in fact," I answered, feeling like there was no turning back. I saw eagerness in her, which I could not help but feel as well.

No, there was no going back!

I lay down on the bed, my body close to hers. I leaned on my right arm, looking down at her, then bent down and kissed her again, with a yearning that was growing by the second. No matter what else might come, I had already found my true treasure.

***

I woke next morning, vivid flashes of the entire night still running through my mind. I felt completely rested, although I had not had many hours of sleep. Next to me, Raymonde was lying in bed, still sleeping. I couldn't believe that I had ended up here, with her. She stirred, waking up. Pulling an arm out from under the sheet, she touched my leg tenderly.

"Good morning," she said, a bit shyly. "I'm glad you stayed the night."

"I'm not sure that I had any choice. You were irresistible. I certainly didn't expect for things to develop this quickly but I am happy they did," I said.

"Me too. I have never been attracted to anyone so rapidly before. You are not the type of man I am used to seeing around here. You are very odd, you know. You seem to have answers for some of my deepest questions. I don't know where this is going between us..." she said but I interrupted her.

"...don't worry about that, Raymonde. How about we simply focus on this mystery? Let's not make it too complicated. I know that I am extremely happy being here with you. I want to spend as much time with you as possible. What better way can there be to do that than searching for answers which will mean so much to both of us?"

"I couldn't have said it better, Paul. Now let's get up and get showered, we have to meet Maman downstairs soon."

Raymonde slid out from the sheets, slipping a bathrobe over her slim shoulders, and headed for the shower. I collected my clothes, intent on putting them on and going to my room, to update my friends on the Internet. Her voice stopped me when I passed by the bathroom.

"And just where do you think you are going? Aren't you coming in for a shower?"

On second thought, perhaps I could leave my Internet friends to stew in their ignorance a little longer.

***

We had our breakfast a little while later. Raymonde's mother joined us for coffee, having been delayed by work at the front desk. Her knowing eye noticed our little looks and touches and she drew the obvious conclusion. After breakfast, it was time to leave for Perpignan. We said our good-byes and headed off.

The real problem was that I still had not found a single moment to update my friends back home on my progress. Things were moving fast and I had been without any privacy since last night. I wasn't complaining; these were the facts. However, my three nosy friends were likely to be full of time-taking comments and questions, time I did not have. They would simply have to wait. I would connect with them as soon as I could. Additionally, it seemed to me that Raymonde was getting highly suspicious of my glasses. Her comments about my 'dorky' appearance didn't fool me for a second. She knew something was up and I had to be extremely careful not to be found out. This tiny little deception was producing some seriously unanticipated complications. Now, all I could do was to follow through and hope for the best.

Somehow though, following through was starting to feel like a noose tightening around my neck!

We took off down the Rue de Maupassant, setting the GPS destination to *Orleans*, planning to travel directly through France towards Perpignan. I set the cruise control at a leisurely hundred and ten kilometre an hour, following the directions on the screen. While we were travelling, Raymonde's conversation drifted from small talk to a more serious topic.

"I feel so strange, travelling with you, a man I did not know a few days ago... now my lover... heading toward the very thing I came back to confront. Everything feels like it is changing. I am a little afraid of the coming changes but not enough to stop myself from going on."

"I know what you mean. For me, it started a few weeks ago, when my father and Darlene were murdered. Since then, my entire life has been turned upside down. I must admit that before this, I have been an armchair sort of person, thinking and reading about the world rather than going out and touching it. All my life I've felt as if I were hiding in a cave. Only now am I beginning to discover how much I have missed in the real world," I said, looking at her for a second and returning my eyes to the road.

Her hand tenderly touched my shoulder.

"I am glad you waited until now. I would surely have missed you otherwise. Still, the whole situation is a little strange, do you not think? There are so many mysteries surrounding us, it is difficult to see the situation clearly," she worried.

"With every step we take, I become more convinced that this is just a glimpse of what is really going on. I can only hope that the little ditty holds the key to this mystery."

While talking, I reached down and pulled out my glasses. This conversation was important. I squinted at the road when I put them on, pressing the record button at the same time. I noticed her frown and a slight biting of her lower lip but she remained uncharacteristically quiet about the glasses. My squinting must have been better than I thought. I breathed an internal sigh of relief.

Unfortunately, I had forgotten about Coulter's programming skills. He had left a monitoring program running that alerted him as soon as I turned the glasses on. His dishevelled face suddenly appeared on a screen in front of my eyes, causing me to swerve sharply. I corrected quickly but not quickly enough to evade Raymonde's sharp sarcasm.

"Apparently, the glasses do not improve your driving. Is everything all right?" she asked coyly. I wasn't fooled, not for a second.

Coulter chose this moment to begin talking.

"Finally, you're online. The others will be on in a sec, I've just flagged them. We need to talk."

I froze for a moment. I had just been asked two questions at the same time. I had to try to answer both without letting on that I was doing exactly that.

"Uh, everything's fine, thanks..." I coughed a bit, trying to sound hoarse. "Can't, uh, can't talk right now..." I hoped that Raymonde would think my throat was dry and that Coulter would recognise that I was in a delicate situation.

Jonathan Briar came online, complicating the situation even more. The screen split automatically into two smaller images, another display improvement by Coulter. Briar looked irritated. Raymonde chose this moment to reply.

"Would you like some water?"

I nodded silently, desperately. The moment she leaned back, reaching for a bag on the minuscule back seat, Briar began talking.

"Finally, my boy, you are online. It's been a while. We have much to review and little time to do it in. You have provided us with such excellent material and we haven't had the chance to..." Briar stopped in mid-sentence, having just seen me look into the rear view mirror and slice my hand across my throat, the international symbol that meant *stop talking right now*. In a smooth, deft motion, I slid my hand up to my hair, finger-combing it, when Raymonde turned back to the front of the car, bag in hand, fishing for a water bottle. Briar's face got all red as he understood my gesture, made all the plainer when Coulter jumped in with an inflammatory comment:

"Hey, Briar, glad to see you. Paul seems to be in a bind and wants us to be quiet," I could have strangled Coulter at that very moment. Instead, I quietly accepted the water bottle from Raymonde and drank a gulp, taking my time swallowing. I needed a few moments to think. Meanwhile, Briar was unhappy and getting vocal about it.

"He WHAT? This will simply not do..."

The screen changed into an oval, splitting into three equal sections, with a sleepy O'Flanahan appearing in the top section. I was finding it difficult to keep my eyes on the road.

"What's going on? This darn computer won't stop buzzing. What's the emergency?"

I drank another slow gulp of water. By now, Raymonde was looking at me eagle-eyed, knowing something was up. Briar took control of the conversation.

"Enough of this. My boy, listen to me... this ridiculous situation has gone on long enough. We are grown men, trying to solve a complex mystery, egged on by a brutal killer, who murdered your parents let us not forget, a common goal requiring our valuable time and serious expense. But are we solving our mystery? No, we are not. Instead, we are STAYING QUIET, because one of us..."

"He means you, Paul."

"Be quiet, Coulter, don't interrupt me... because YOU..." Briar pointed right at the camera when he said it, "... You have elected to keep this a secret in an elaborate attempt to turn this crucial collaboration into a total FARCE..." Briar's face was apoplectic when he screamed this last word. I was sorely tempted to reply, stopped only by the fact that I was sitting in a car, supposedly alone with Raymonde.

"Paul, you seem a little distant? Are you all right?" she asked.

O'Flanahan had begun laughing at Briar's last explosion.

"Come on, Briar, give Paul a break..," he said facetiously.

"No Sir. It is time to end this. Either Mister Sirenne speaks now or I leave this idiotic group and go on to more productive pursuits..."

"Aw, come on, you don't mean that!..." Coulter said.

"Paul? Are you going to answer me?" Raymonde asked again.

By this point, I was getting seriously confused.

I had four people talking directly at me and I was trying to drive, not to mention drinking a lot of water. I was still trying to find a way to answer everyone at the same time and keep the deception going. I thought I had the perfect comment that would satisfy everybody.

"Just a second, I'm busy..." I said, in a slightly exasperated tone.

As soon as I uttered the words, I wished I could pull them out of the air and pop them right back into my mouth. What had sounded reasonable, only an instant before, now seemed completely inappropriate, probably because it was. Several things happened all at once. Briar stopped talking, stunned into silence by my comment. Raymonde's face grew red, her eyes flashing and O'Flanahan gasped aloud:

"He blew it... Paul blew it with the dame. Be quiet everybody, I want to hear what happens next."

The worse thing about this was not being able to tell my friends anything while they rambled on and on, messing everything up. Raymonde's mouth tightened and she said, in a neutral tone:

"What do you mean 'you are busy'? Doing what? What is keeping you so busy?"

I felt a tightening in my stomach. O'Flanahan laughed some more.

"Yes, I know, but, I meant something else... uh..." I said weakly, trying to look into her eyes and failing, feeling incredibly guilty. Moments stretched into eternity while she looked at me. Me and my glasses. It was during this endless moment, as I wallowed in my guilt, that I saw something enter into her eyes, a glimmer of understanding.

I was caught!

She spoke quietly but clearly:

"Stop this car."

"Right here? Don't you think we should..." I tried stalling, to no avail.

"Stop the car, right now. Park right over there," she ordered pointing at a wide shoulder coming up. I had no choice but to obey, dreading her next statement.

"Ever since we met, I have felt that there was something odd about you. It has taken a little while to figure it out but now it has become clear to me... That's right, pull up right here... I would have to say that I first became suspicious when you put your glasses on when we went to talk with Maman. No matter what you said to me, I knew you had some other reason for putting on those ridiculous glasses. People wear glasses to see far or to see close. I have just figured out that you put them on for both of those reasons. Therefore, you do not wear your glasses to see better, you wear them for some other reason. The reason you looked distracted and were too '*busy*', is that you *were* distracted and busy... Get out of the car," she ordered flatly. She got out herself and stood there waiting, her arms crossed. Superimposed over her, I could see the faces of my three friends, all hanging on her every word, as if they were watching the best of soap operas.

"Good Luck, Paul," Coulter said in sympathy.

"Yeah, good luck. You're going to need it, pal, he-he-he..." O'Flanahan added, chuckling.

"About time, I would say. Just rewards and all that, my boy," Briar said, waxing the moral authority.

"Thanks for everything guys," I whispered, trying to inject, in those simple words, as much sarcasm as was humanly possible. I opened my door and walked around the car, coming to a stop in front of Raymonde, looking at her sheepishly while she held her hand out:

"Give me your glasses right now."

"What? You can't be..." I protested. She cut me short.

"Be quiet and give me your glasses."

I could no longer avoid it.

I took off my glasses, catching a last glimpse of a grinning O'Flanahan waving goodbye to me, and handed them to her. She took them gingerly, surprised by their weight. She examined them from all angles, finally catching sight of the miniature view screen projected on the inside of the glasses. She could not stop herself from smiling, having finally been proven right. She looked at me in victory and put the glasses on. I noticed that their thick, blocky shape made her look different, perhaps a bit less... educated.

She stood there for a second, looking somewhat bemused, until finally, she spoke:

"...Uhm, hello?"

She fell quiet, listening to the three traitors. She nodded her head and smiled, then laughed aloud. I realised that the glasses were now pointed directly at me. The guys probably had a full frontal view of me in my abject misery.

"Well, my name's Raymonde. Yes, I am the daughter of Victoire Leblanc... and you are?" she continued her one-sided conversation and walked away from me, leaving me to my own thoughts.

At least this entire nonsensical situation was over.

Why I had allowed myself to lie in the first place? I realised that I wasn't being fair to myself. I was under a lot of stress. My decisions were made without reflection, something I usually avoided.

No matter the reasons, the deed was done.

I looked at Raymonde from where I stood. She looked so vibrant, so alive. Looking at her, I realised that I truly loved her. For whatever reason, I had been led to this incredible woman and I was not going to lose her, not for something as ridiculous as a pair of glasses. I resolved to do everything I could to make things right.

She had finished her conversation with my team and was walking back towards me, taking off the glasses. She looked much better without them. She also looked upset. I could stand the suspense no longer and stepped forward to take my punishment.

"Raymonde... Before you say anything, could you please listen to me for a second? I know I lied to you. It was a big mistake. It started with O'Flanahan and... and the airplane thing... I just couldn't explain that..." her nostrils flared. "The point is, it happened by accident. Because of that, I was dishonest with you. At first, I couldn't tell you for fear that you might not even listen to me and then later, I just couldn't find the right moment to explain..."

She held up her hand, motioning me into silence.

"Enough! Stop these excuses. What you did was wrong. You lied to me and things got complicated after that but it's because you lied in the first place. I hate being lied to."

I looked down and dejectedly kicked at the gravel with my left foot, then looked back up at her.

"I am really sorry. I know I made excuses. I admit that I made the wrong choice... However, I promise I won't make that type of choice again. I don't want to lose you... I... I can't lose you..." I explained, my voice catching a bit. Her eyes stayed hard for a moment then softened and she allowed the smallest of smiles to grace her lips.

"All right then. We have wasted enough time on this. It seems your friends have information to share but that will have to wait until later. For now, I want you to show me how to turn these off..." she asked, lifting the glasses in the air.

I pointed at the small button, which she pressed. The miniature screen faded away. Then she put them in her handbag.

"I'm keeping these for now. I want you to stop in Orleans for a bit. I'll direct you when we get there. Now, before we go..." she gave me a long kiss, holding me tight against her. I held her as close as I could. After what seemed forever, we separated, both feeling much better.

When I got into the car, I noticed far behind us, another stopped vehicle, an old beat up truck. Two men, one tall, one short, appeared to be working on the engine. The short one looked familiar. Ignoring them, I drove off towards Orleans. I decided to connect to the A13 and cross the Seine near Lillebonne, since we had come across that small town in our research. For a while we drove in silence along the river, reflecting on the challenges ahead. After the Ferry crossing, the road followed a meandering river, which would veer away from us and then return at some later point.

We kept going until the road cut into the side of a rocky hill. I noticed the old beat-up truck again, coming up fast behind us. It approached close enough for me to see, in my rear-view mirror, the faces of the two people in the cab. My eyes were drawn to the shorter one again, the driver.

"Raymonde, we're being followed. I think it's the Vallin brothers."

She turned and looked behind while the truck edged closer and closer. I could hear some type of whining noise.

"Can't you go any faster in this thing?" she asked.

I pressed on the gas and the Porsche accelerated easily. We moved away from them, outdistancing them quickly. They were having trouble keeping up. I saw the driver put his arm out of the window. He was holding something.

It was a gun.

A shot rang out, almost sounding like an explosion, quickly followed by another, and my side mirror blew off its mount. The exploding glass shards shot into the back of my hand. It jerked sideways from the pain, exactly when I was accelerating madly. I lost control of the Porsche, veering sharply to the right, the car careening dangerously close to the cliff wall. I jerked the steering back to the left, the car fishtailed and, despite my strenuous efforts to regain control, drove right off the road.

Sliding onto the gravel shoulder, going very fast, the car careened straight down the bank of a steep, rocky hill. A wire fence, no match for the bulk of our speeding vehicle, snapped apart instantly with a screeching sound. Everything was rattling in the car. Raymonde held on for dear life while I desperately tried to steer, feeling like some insane slalom skier. I could see several boulders directly ahead that would finish us for sure. I pulled on the emergency brake, sending the back wheels into a slide. Turning left with the steering wheel, making the car start to spin sideways, I released the brake, flooring the accelerator, and we shot forward, left of the boulders, missing them by centimetres.

I could now see a narrow bend in the river, directly in front of us, and a dirt road beyond. I frantically estimated that we might just make it over the narrowest part of the river, if we went faster. I pushed the gas pedal to the floor. The car jumped forward, flew up a small bump, sending us flying most of the way over the river. Hitting the surface, we skimmed over the last section of the river. The wheels hit the bank, finding traction. A final burst of acceleration gave us enough momentum to leave the water behind and reach the dirt road. I hit the emergency brakes and we skidded sideways, until, finally, we rocked to a standstill!

Dust was all around us. Little clicks and clacks could be heard coming from the engine. I turned it off. It turned over two more times then, rattled to a stop. Raymonde was gulping in great big breaths, trying to regain control of her senses. Her hands were still tightly clasped to the edges of her seat.

"Wow. I take it all back. That was incredible driving. How did you know there was a road down here?"

I managed to stop my finger from trembling and pointed at the GPS display.

"Nothing to it, my dear. All in a day's work," I said, hoping that I was projecting an unflappable appearance. I opened my door and got out on shaky legs. I hurried to the other side of the car and helped Raymonde out. Holding on to her, I turned and looked up the slope. I couldn't believe that we had made it down alive. I could see the skid marks in the grass and gravel. I had somehow taken the only path possible for us to survive. We had been very lucky. Peering at the top of the hill, I saw the edge of the road, where two men stood, looking down at us.

Instinctively, I waved at them and smiled, dusting off my arms and legs, my meaning plain. Those boys would get no satisfaction from me. I was sure that we were out of firing range anyway.

I examined the car. It certainly wasn't pretty. At least, it still seemed functional. I didn't think the frame of the car was bent and the engine was still in running order. I had to admit that the rental company might not be too happy but who cared about them at this point? We were still alive and that was much more important. We got back into the car and, successfully starting it up again, headed off down the dirt road. I checked the GPS and found a way back to Orleans. I stuck to back roads, in an attempt to avoid our would-be followers.

The Vallins had just shot at us and I had no idea why they might want us dead. The developing relationship with Raymonde had made me forget how dangerous this pursuit of ours really was. I vowed to myself that I would be more careful from now on.

Arriving in Orleans, I drove to an electronics store, as directed by Raymonde. She had me wait outside for a while, after asking for my credit card. She would not explain anything. When she was done with her mystery shopping, my credit card safely back in my pocket, she insisted that we go out to supper. We ended up at a small bistro. The candlelit place was very romantic.

She ordered some trout for both of us. The waiter came back with our wine and I made a fuss, insisting to be the one to sniff the cork and fill her glass. I sat down, my social duty done, and suggested a toast.

"To our future. May there be less excitement in it."

She laughed and clinked her glass against mine, adding simply:

"To us."

After our meal, feeling anxious and tired, we rented a room in a small *Pension*, near the bistro. Collapsing into bed, we fell asleep within moments. I woke at some point in the night, feeling her body moving against me. Her hazel eyes were open, looking deeply into mine. She opened herself and we made love slowly, with the strongest passion I had ever felt.

Then we fell asleep again, this time in each other's arms.

CHAPTER 8

Leblanc's Hidden Message

Next morning, we sat at the small breakfast table in our room, sipping some coffee. We both felt determined to be more cautious this time. She got up and returned with two things. A bag and my glasses. She could not stop herself from smiling when she sat down, trying to impose a frown on her face and failing. Picking up my glasses, she held them up in front of me.

"This is for lying to me." she said, snapping my glasses in two.

My heart jumped. My glasses! She had broken my glasses! She reached out and patted my hand.

"There, there, now you've learned your lesson. It's all over. Now for the surprise."

Pulling out two gift-wrapped packages from the bag, she handed one to me.

"This is for you."

I opened the wrapped box while she explained.

"Your friend Fabian Coulter helped me with this. They were very supportive of you when I talked to them, you know. They explained what had been going on and told me some of the things they were discovering. I realised right away that we both needed to work with your friends if we were truly serious about figuring this thing out, and there was no way that I was going to wear those ugly glasses for one more second than necessary. So I had your friend check online for the closest place where I could buy some better looking glasses, in a matching style, of course."

Wrapping paper finally removed, I opened my box, pulling out a brand new pair of glasses. They were incredibly sleek. Raymonde had a pair that looked almost the same, except more feminine. She put them on and I understood that style made a difference after all. She looked great. When I put on mine, she nodded her head.

"Much better, Paul..." she laughed. "...Much better!"

I got up and looked at myself in the mirror. At least the 'dork' look was gone. I thanked her for the gift. She had taught me a lesson and I had paid the price - literally.

We were soon underway and this time, the miles flew by. We stayed on the main road, certain that we were not being followed. While I drove, we each put on our glasses and activated them. Within moments, the guys connected, all of them smiling.

"Gentlemen, you are all on time," said Raymonde. She had planned everything!

Jonathan Briar was the first to speak. He could never resist the opportunity to pontificate.

"It is an honour for us to finally talk with you officially, my dear. I must say that your presence has us all excited..."

O'Flanahan tactlessly interrupted him:

"Why is your side-view mirror broken?"

I briefly explained yesterday's events. Although concerned, O'Flanahan's main regret was that I had not been recording with the glasses when I went over the hill. We all agreed that things were becoming serious and that we should give the situation the respect that it deserved. After that, we began discussing in earnest, Coulter leading the fray.

"I have to show you some video for a second... hold on while I call it up... here it is..."

The screen changed to a moving video of someone walking along in an airplane. It was me. This was the video from my flight to France, when I returned from stretching my legs. The video froze at the moment I had been looking to the rear of the cabin, a few seats behind Raymonde. Coulter's voice reached my ears, explaining what we should be looking at.

"I'm sure you all remember this scene. Let me paste this picture next to it. It's from a car commercial. The man you see in it, the announcer, is Harry Stiles..."

The image showed a thick man, with thinning white hair and a florid nose. Coulter continued.

"Now, if you would look at the centre aisle and count seven rows behind Miss Raymonde. Examine the man sitting in the first seat on the right."

It was Harry Stiles!

"But there's no way that can be him. He was dead by then, Norton said so," exclaimed O'Flanahan.

"...That can only mean one thing. We are looking at the Shadow-Killer," I added.

Coulter nodded.

"Now you get it. If Stiles is dead, that must be the Shadow-Killer. Let me see if I can't zoom in on his face..."

The video image jumped forward, giving us a grainy face, out of focus. Coulter continued fiddling with his controls off-screen and the image clarified enough for us to make out a few more details.

"Look at that nose. And the hair. It's damn near perfect. What do you think, Briar?" asked O'Flanahan. "...He did a pretty good job on his disguise, eh?"

"Yes...Yes, he did, O'Flanahan... he did an excellent job in fact..." agreed Briar, while the images vanished and the faces of my three friends returned. Briar seemed annoyed at O'Flanahan's comment.

Who could blame him, really? O'Flanahan was annoying.

"This confirms Norton's story, that the Shadow-Killer took Stiles' place on the plane, probably following Paul after prodding him with the gruesome murder of his parents," continued Briar. "But where could he be now, if that were true? You don't think you've seen him, have you, Paul?"

"No, not at all... How would I know anyway? The Shadow-Killer is obviously great at disguises. The only person I've seen is Norton" I replied.

"Yes... That is what I've been wondering about. I've been doing some research of my own. I checked into Inspector Norton's history. It seems he's had a chequered past. Since the death of his sister, he has claimed to be on the trail of the elusive Shadow-Killer, doing most of the detective work on his own time. It seems his superiors don't necessarily share his belief in the existence of this killer. Furthermore, my contacts inform me that Inspector Norton has just been suspended for dereliction of duty. He seems to have gone missing after your parents' murders."

"What are you trying to say Briar?" asked O'Flanahan in a dubious tone. "That you think Norton is the Shadow-Killer?"

"It is a possibility that must be considered... His behaviour with Paul has been most odd and he *was* in Ottawa at the time of the murders. You must admit that is quite a coincidence."

"Damn it all Briar, the man's a cop, not a killer... Heck, the killer even murdered Norton's sister..." argued O'Flanahan, never one to let go.

"... Unless Norton killed her too. What if that was his first murder and he's been killing ever since, unable to face what he did?"

"Come on guys, this is going nowhere. Maybe Norton *is* the Shadow-Killer but how would we know? We're not cops. We should look at facts, not theories..." Coulter stated, injecting a note of reason in the argument.

"Coulter is right. Although Norton doesn't exactly inspire confidence, right now, we are under pressure to come up with some answers and we've got to do it before someone else shoots at us," I said.

"You know, Paul, when we started, we had one sentence at the bottom of a forgotten little book. Now we seem to have almost too much information," Briar said. "The strangest thing in our possession must be the letter from Adolf Hitler. No matter which way we look at it, it's real. The letter's contents have also presented us with a new question: what could Hitler have come across, in architecture or art, which would have led him to Etretat? I believe it has to be the one common point, the fort of Frefosse. That is why I have been attempting to deepen my knowledge about the archaeological history of the area."

Briar had been busy.

"Unfortunately, most of my research was stymied by a curious lack of information. This void made me suspicious and I asked Coulter to look into it. He came up with some disturbing information that he will share with us in a few moments. However, my own efforts were not totally in vain. I did discover a few items of interest. The first is that there was not one fort in Etretat but two. On the other side of Etretat, on the Amont cliff, there is an ancient church. Behind that church are ruins, the remains of a Roman garrison. These ruins are of the same period as those from the fort of Frefosse. It is also the location of almost all the remaining underground tunnels of Etretat," he said, his explanation sounding like a scholarly presentation. Not finished, he added:

"The problem was that Romans never built two forts in one town. It was too expensive. Someone with a personal interest pushed for the building of the fort of Frefosse and I felt it had to be smugglers or pirates. You see, whoever built the fort really wanted to hide that cave opening, if cave there was. The question was why hide it? What benefit could such a cave have for anyone when hidden? Then it came to me: what if it had a secret opening to the sea?"

Briar was making sense. He continued:

"What if there was a hidden harbour with a passage through the cave to the fort above? A whole community of smugglers could live inside the cave with no one knowing. They would have access to the channel to smuggle goods and a fort to defend the loot. I remembered that pirates and smugglers often had secret signs, to identify themselves to others. One of the most interesting of such signs, is this one..."

Briar's face vanished, replaced by a photo of a crude symbol, carved in rock: a triangle above a rectangle, both inside a circle.

I could not stop myself from exclaiming:

"We've seen those symbols before... on that drawing of Frefosse's dungeon."

"Correct. Move to the head of the class, Mr Sirenne. We *have* seen them before but so have others. This sign was carved in many ancient caves in the cliffs along the English Channel. To date, no one has ever explained their presence, although many of the carvings have been dated to a period near 50 AD. There is the distinct possibility that our Mr Hitler might have come across this symbol in his research and that he was able to understand what he was looking for. He did not know where it was but he might have suspected *what* it was: a secret den, a cave full of pirated treasure. It took Leblanc's Hollow Needle to point out a likely location: beneath the fort of Frefosse!" Briar finished.

An excited Coulter took Briar's silence as his cue and launched into an extension of Briar's theory:

"... Hitler might have been looking for a very specific thing: those geometric symbols. We cannot forget that someone inscribed those very same symbols on a drawing of the fort, a drawing which was deliberately hidden... However, this is not the most alarming information. Allow me to jump back to the other point made by Briar, the absence of local archaeological records. It was odd to have so little information and Briar suspected something might be going on. He emailed me, asking me to check into it. I began working on a program right away. It wasn't long before I had enough data coming in to analyse it. When I had enough data, a pattern appeared. Let me show you..."

His face was replaced by a graph. I was becoming adept at navigating the road while looking directly through a large, transparent screen.

"It's really a very simple analysis. My search program collected information on the net about research done in general in the country of France. From that, I created a graph that showed the average amount of information available for any given geographical area. Of course, I adjusted the graph for population density, economic factors, etc. Once I had obtained that, I derived the amount of information available about Etretat and compared it to the general graph..."

A new graph appeared in red over the previous one. It was markedly different, showing a much lower curve than the other did.

"... I compared the results with several other local areas. Eventually I had to accept that there was something anomalous about research information concerning Etretat. I refined the parameters of my data and came up with this..."

The graphs disappeared, replaced by another drawing showing several peaks and some noticeable drops.

"... This graph reveals the specific areas of 'negative' research that are causing these anomalous results. For example, there is no lack of recent economic or touristic information about Etretat. However, geological information relating to the Etretat area is conspicuously absent. Its history also contains noticeable periods lacking any information whatsoever."

Coulter's face came back on the screen and he continued:

"A quick check showed yet another unexpected result. The reason for these anomalous results was that the research was missing!"

Everyone erupted in a clamour. After we calmed down, he explained his conclusion.

"When you look at the information we have about a given topic, it is easy for us to forget that much of this research was conducted in the past, perhaps hundreds of years ago. Up to the late 1980's, this information existed only in forgotten books, slowly rotting away in museums. If someone were to plan it properly, during the early part of the twentieth century in particular, one could completely eliminate information about a given subject..."

O'Flanahan interrupted him instantly:

"I published a small book about that."

Coulter ignored O'Flanahan and continued.

"... Anyway, I began by looking for periods in time when the documents themselves might have begun disappearing. Eventually, this led me to a certain Professor Biermann. I'm sure none of you know who he is. That is because he disappeared shortly after the end of the First World War. I believe this is when The 'Etretat Brain Drain' started..."

"What started?" I asked.

"Sorry guys, I just couldn't resist saying it. However, that's what it was: a brain drain. Over a period of about twenty years following the First World War, there were a series of unexplained disappearances all over Europe. It started with experts in one science or another, at first general topics, then gradually, more specifically relating to Etretat. Following the human disappearances, the research itself disappeared from different places, universities, colleges, museums, the list is incredible..."

"I guess Hitler was busy," O'Flanahan said.

Briar snorted and objected.

"Oh, it wasn't Hitler; I can assure you of that. Perhaps Hitler wrote a letter to Leblanc that escaped historical attention but there's precious little else that has escaped our notice. Hitler's life has been sifted through with a fine-tooth comb. We know exactly where he was and when he was there. No, if someone was carrying out a secret agenda to destroy information, it wasn't him."

O'Flanahan didn't skip a beat and added:

"That's excellent. That means that there's more than one person involved. That spells 'conspiracy', if you ask me."

"It does seem more likely that Hitler directed and another acted in his behalf... perhaps a hired killer working in the shadows," Briar agreed.

That sounded like the killer after us right now but it couldn't be. These events happened over eighty years ago. If our Shadow-Killer was the same man, he would be positively geriatric by now.

"I think they were obtaining information about Etretat and hiding the trail at the same time," Coulter added. O'Flanahan jumped in excitedly:

"That's it. You've hit the nail on the head. Someone, Hitler and his hired help probably, completely eradicated information about what lay beneath the fort of Frefosse. Beginning with the fort's destruction in 1911 onward, a concerted effort was made to hide the existence of the caves of Etretat. This is a totally new conspiracy theory and the best part is that it could be true! I am in seventh heaven," he exclaimed, grinning from ear to ear.

"Leblanc must have known about it," concluded Coulter, "He must have. I wonder what his role was in all this."

I wondered the same thing: what had Leblanc been up to?

***

I pulled into the driveway and turned off the engine. Thankfully, the Porsche had survived the trip. The brakes had vibrated and we heard some rattles here and there. Apart from that, it had been a good ride. Our differences had been ironed out during the voyage. In particular, Raymonde had made it clear that she expected some techno-glasses rules about privacy.

We had arrived in Perpignan about two hours ago. After renting a motel room, where we both showered and ate a small meal, we had headed off to visit the final residence of Maurice Leblanc.

Our glasses were on, we were recording and everyone was online.

I knocked at the door. For a moment, we heard nothing, then a series of sounds, which got closer and closer, before clarifying into distinct words: *"I'm coming. Just hold on, I'll be right there"*. Finally, the door opened, revealing an older, dishevelled woman with a spot of flour on her left cheek. Seeing us standing there, her face broke into a wide smile and she welcomed us into the front room, which had been converted into a reception area. We introduced ourselves.

As soon as the woman heard Raymonde's last name, she grew animated.

"Oh my Lord. Are you related to Maurice Leblanc the writer?" she asked, her right hand held tight against her chest.

"I am his great-granddaughter," Raymonde answered.

"That's unbelievable," the woman tittered, "Did you know that he stayed here? In the rooms upstairs on the second floor?..." the woman leaned forward and whispered conspiratorially: "They say he died in the room... but we're not supposed to mention that to our guests," she stood back up and returned to a normal tone of voice "Would you like to see the rooms? We charge five Euros... but I guess in your case, I could make an exception, you being family and all... Only two Euros."

I wasn't sure if Raymonde was insulted or complimented by that. I paid the landlady and we were ushered up the stairs by the overly talkative old woman. She opened the door and gave us a few minutes alone in the room. The moment the door was closed, Raymonde headed towards the fireplace. She stayed very quiet, looking at an overstuffed easy chair placed in front of it.

"This is where my great-grandfather sat, when he told that ditty to Maman, sitting on his knee. He was right here. I can almost feel him..."

She fell silent for a few moments, sitting down in the big chair, perhaps to be closer to him. After a short while, she dabbed her eyes with the edge of her sleeve and glanced around the room. Her gaze settled on a small table. She bent down a little and peered under it.

"There's something there. Something is hidden behind that table, on the wall."

Coulter got on it right away.

"I'm enhancing it. Yes, I can see some scratches in the paint. They are deep. Perhaps one of you could move the table. Then we could get a better view of them."

I pulled the table away from the wall, revealing the scratches in their entirety. They had been painted over but the scratches were deep enough to have remained visible. Enhanced by our glasses, we could see two short lines of words:

'Reach a yarn many ought not discover
Last isolation near dawn of narrative'

"What does that nonsense mean?" O'Flanahan said, sounding frustrated. "What a stupid clue to leave behind."

We put the table back in place and looked around the room for a while longer, finding nothing else. We thanked the woman for her help and headed back to our motel room. Once there, Raymonde and I sat down, our online friends still with us. Coulter displayed a still image of the text on the screen.

"First off, let's put it in the context of Leblanc, instead of complaining like O'Flanahan. What if he were trying to leave a message?... Something that would make sense only if you knew what you were looking for. That first line seems fairly clear to me. I think it means: 'if you want to find a story that many people shouldn't know about'..."

"I would agree with your interpretation, Fabian," Briar added right away.

"Thank you so much, Mr Briar," returned Coulter and Raymonde laughed. "... The second line is a bit more difficult. The first line implies that directions to the story are forthcoming in the second line..."

O'Flanahan butted right in, as usual.

"Perhaps you should let an expert try his hand at this. Let's look at those words a bit closer: *'last isolation, near dawn of narrative'* Most of it is obvious but the word 'isolation' is throwing me for a curve. Doesn't it mean to hold the heat in or something?"

Briar, irritated by O'Flanahan's interpretation, instantly corrected:

"No, not insulation!... Isolation. It's a totally different word."

Coulter smiled, enjoying O'Flanahan's discomfiture. Briar tried to get back to the point:

"Isolation means to separate something or someone from the rest of the group. So last isolation might mean... last separation?... No that doesn't sound quite right... Wait, maybe it means to retire or to die... Last retirement?... Final retirement near dawn of narrative? Whose retirement?"

"I might have an idea about that..." Coulter said. "Raymonde, when your mother talked about coming here to Perpignan, she said that some of Leblanc's friend might be living here. Many people ran to Perpignan while escaping from the Germans. Leblanc was not the first to come here, nor was he the last. Earlier, I obtained the registry of people living in Etretat during the twenties, thirties and forties. What if I compared it to Perpignan's registry of the same period, to see if there are any names in common? Let me try that."

We waited while his computer collated the results.

"What's this? Hey guys, guess whose name just popped up?" Coulter asked.

I tried to come up with a name but failed. Briar came to my rescue.

"I think I have an answer to that. It's... Wait... Is it Raymond Lindon?"

Coulter looked stunned.

"Why yes it is. How in the world did you guess that?"

"I was puzzled about the word 'isolation' in Leblanc's second sentence. If he meant retirement, why didn't he say retirement? Leblanc was deliberately trying to make it difficult to understand but I felt there was something more to it than that. The whole thing seemed contrived as if Leblanc was trying to fit a message into some type of formula. I thought about a book I had previously mentioned to Paul, which said Leblanc's books were full of codes. I wondered what type of code could apply here. Going back to the word 'Isolation', I wondered if, maybe, he used that word because of a particular letter in the word. So I started playing with simple codes, my first attempt being to look at the first letter of each word... and that, my friends, gives you R.A.Y.M.O.N.D. on the first line and L.I.N.D.O.N. on the second," Briar glibly explained. I was impressed.

That was quick thinking.

So now, we had two sources of information, both implicating Raymond Lindon. Coulter gathered online information about this intriguing man. Remembering that Lindon had been mayor of Etretat during the Second World War, we were surprised to learn that he had also been Jewish. Because of this, he had been forced to assign a deputy mayor during the Nazi invasion and had moved to Perpignan for the period. After the war had ended, he had returned to Etretat and resumed his post. He continued as mayor for many years, eventually retiring to a small place called Ambrumesy.

"I know Ambrumesy. It is there that the Hollow Needle story begins... in the Castle of Ambrumesy!" exclaimed Raymonde excitedly.

Her words brought everything into sharp relief for me:

"Lindon retired near the beginning of the story that began everything. It's directly connected to the Hollow Needle. That's what the second line means. We have to go to Ambrumesy and visit Lindon's final home. That is where we will discover what we seek."

"It's just like the little ditty. The end and the beginning come together once again. It's so ingenious. Only someone who already knew exactly what they were looking for could figure out that message. It was meant for us. My great-grandfather left us a message after all. We must heed it," Raymonde exclaimed. I realized it could have been me speaking.

In fact, I could have said the exact same words.

***

Ambrumesy was difficult to find. It was so small, that it wasn't indicated on the regular maps. The GPS finally located it near Dieppe. It was a real place. It had a real castle and the ruins of an abbey. Once a home to monks, it was destroyed after the Revolution. The castle had since been repaired and returned to its former glory.

We planned the most direct route there and got on the road early next morning. Driving quietly and enjoying each other's company, we arrived at the Castle of Ambrumesy, late in the evening, when the sun was beginning to set. We both felt certain that something was waiting here and neither of us would leave until we found it.

Coulter had confirmed that Raymond Lindon had purchased the castle in the 1950's. Before his death, he had set up a trust fund to protect the castle and keep it in a good state of repair. It could be no coincidence. Lindon's castle was directly related to the clue left in Perpignan by Leblanc.

The two men had been working together.

The castle was now a museum and tourist attraction. No one lived in it, except for a grounds keeper. It was closed by the time we arrived, so Raymonde and I walked the gardens paths, looking around for anything out of the ordinary. I had thought to call my friends but Raymonde prevented me.

"No, Paul, this moment should be only for the two of us. Our great-grandfathers planned this for us. Their efforts deserve respect and privacy."

"No O'Flanahan nonsense."

"Yes. Just us."

We walked in silence, holding hands and looking around.

It was fitting that Raymonde saw it first:

"That fountain! It's in the story. And that chapel, over there, hidden in the castle's shadows, it's in the Hollow Needle story. Come on, let's go look."

She ran around the large circular fountain and followed a circuitous gravel path through a maze of short hedges. I ran after her, joining her when she reached the ancient chapel. Considering its age, it was in excellent condition. We entered the main chamber and walked down the middle aisle, between two rows of stone pews. The altar was ornate, with decorative carvings covering its entire surface. There were two rooms adjoining the main chamber, one on each side of the altar. We entered the first to find a small baptismal pool and a confessional area. The other room was a small mausoleum, with plaques imbedded into the three walls, each bearing a name and date, none of which I recognised. In the centre of the room was an elaborately carved sarcophagus.

It drew my attention right away. I searched for a name plaque but could find none, which I thought curious. I examined the coffin's carvings finding them to be rather generic in topic. The only exception was on the back face of the coffin's base, where I found a circular image carved into the stone: a snake eating its tail. I asked Raymonde to come look at it.

"If anything defines the phrase 'the end and the beginning', this would be it."

She shook her head in agreement and added

"Remember what Maman's ditty said..."

"The beginning and the end, follow the circle, it bends. The end and the beginning, the answer in the connecting," I quoted from memory.

"Perhaps it is intended to help us figure this out. It suggests we 'follow the circle'. Let's try that..." Raymonde suggested.

She reached out with her hand and touched the snake carving. Hesitatingly, she slid her index finger along the edge of the circle in a clockwise direction. She pulled her finger back with a start.

"It moved!"

"What? No way."

"I tell you, it moved."

"Try it again."

She replaced her finger on the edge of the circle and began the sliding motion around the stone circle again. We noticed that the entire circle of stone was oscillating slightly with each rotation of her hand. She applied more pressure, sliding her finger along the back of the carved snake. Abruptly, the whole circle moved inward a half inch. This gave me an idea.

"I think it's like a loose screw in a big hole. Your oscillations are making it jump its grooves. Slide your fingers in the other direction, counter-clockwise, then push it and let it go."

She looked at me baffled but I motioned her on.

"Go ahead. Try it. It will make sense when you do it," I explained.

The first time she did it, her timing was wrong and the circle did nothing but oscillate. With the second attempt, her timing was perfect. The disk oscillated and popped back out a centimetre, now flush with the surface of the coffin base again.

"YES! I knew it. That's it, do it again."

She slid her finger around, pressing and letting go and it popped out again. She got excited and went faster but lost the rhythm. She had to slow down and do it more carefully. It popped out more and more until, finally, a rock cylinder sprang out and fell to the floor, followed by a thick, coiled spring. We looked in the exposed hole but there was nothing else. I picked up the cylinder. It was heavy although not as heavy as I would have expected for its size. It was about forty-five centimetres long and almost twenty-five centimetres in diameter. After a brief examination, I determined that the cylinder's bottom was made of two pieces of stone: an external circular edge and a plug in the middle.

"I think this thing is hollow."

I lifted it up and shook it. Something slid around inside.

I heard the crunch of footsteps on the path outside the chapel. Ducking down behind the coffin base, I peeked out from the top, keeping my head low. A man was approaching the chapel, walking slowly, looking at everything carefully. It was Norton. He had a pistol in his hand. He stopped at the chapel's entrance briefly before entering cautiously.

Dropping back down, I whispered hurriedly to Raymonde.

"Stay low. We'll try to sneak out when he goes to check the other room."

She whispered back.

"What if he comes in here first?"

"It's a fifty-fifty chance. I hope the odds are in our favour for once. Shhh, he's coming."

Norton had to know we were here. Our car was in the castle's parking lot. My question was how had he known we were here in the first place? I had no answers and we were running out of time.

Luck was with us. Norton walked into the other room, the baptismal chamber. It was now or never.

Picking up the rock cylinder, we sneaked out as fast as possible, sliding along the wall. Norton reached the back of the baptismal chamber and turned around, looking me straight in the eyes. We broke into a run, Raymonde passing me while I lumbered on, the heavy stone cylinder slowing me down.

A shot rang out behind me and a chunk of stone broke off the fountain.

"Stop where you are. My next shot will not miss."

We both froze in our tracks.

"Wise choice. I am an excellent shot. Now turn around, both of you."

I did what he asked, still holding the stone cylinder in my arms. Norton, twenty yards away, was approaching calmly, his pistol held straight towards me, a smug look on his face.

"How did you find us so quickly?"

"I placed a GPS tracking device in the boot of your car, you idiot. You can't get away from me that easily. Who do you think you are? James Bond? HA! You make me laugh, Sirenne. You're so pathetic, so gullible. I knew you were lying to me, right from the start. I just had to follow you until it was time to reel you in... Well, that time has come. Give me that cylinder!"

I began walking towards him. He jerked his pistol in my direction, cautioning me.

"Slowly now, this pistol has a hair trigger."

I had one chance and I wasn't going to blow it, not this time. I made it seem as if I was having trouble holding on to the cylinder, exaggerating its weight. By the time I reached him, I had it looking as if it was almost slipping out of my arms. I jostled it, appearing to be trying to lift it up, while, in fact, allowing it to slip out of my hands.

"Watch out, you fool!" screamed Norton.

By then it was far too late for him to stop me. I gave the cylinder an extra push and it dropped right out of my hands, falling heavily onto its target.

Norton's left foot!

Norton let go a bellow of pain, forgetting everything else for a single moment, the moment I had been waiting for.

I slapped at his right hand, sending the pistol flying. Then, bringing my hand back and balling it into a tight fist, I hit him with the hardest roundhouse I could muster, putting all my anger and frustration over the murders into it. My rigid fist hit his screaming jaw like a brick. Norton flew back, his body flopping loosely against a hedge behind him. Knocked unconscious, he slid down to the ground, his swollen foot pinned beneath the stone cylinder.

Raymonde rushed to my side, her eyes wide.

"That was incredible, Paul. Are you all right?... Is he all right?"

"I damn well hope not!" I exclaimed, trying to slow my racing heart. I had never been that scared. "Just a second here..."

I lifted the cylinder from his foot, straightening out the man's leg. The foot looked swollen. I asked Raymonde to remove his shoe while I searched him. I found his wallet, which I kept just to give the guy more trouble. I retrieved his pistol and found two spare clips in his jacket pocket. I also found a pair of handcuffs, so I handcuffed his hands behind his back, throwing the key in the fountain.

"His foot is very bad. I think the cylinder might have broken something," Raymonde noted, adding, "I know some nursing. If I could wrap it, it might be okay. But we need some bandages."

"Let's use his pants to wrap it up."

No wallet, no pants, no gun. Broken foot and no key for the handcuffs. Not a good day for Norton.

When it was done, Norton's bandaged foot looked more like a soccer ball than a foot. He would have a lot of trouble walking with that. I didn't know if I was doing the right thing, leaving him alive but I still had trouble believing he was the Shadow-Killer, no matter what Briar said. Even if he was, I wasn't a killer.

Picking up the stone cylinder, Raymonde and I returned to the Porsche. Looking around, I finally spotted the GPS tracking device Norton had placed in my tire well. I threw it on the ground, crushing it with the heel of my shoe. Noticing Norton's car, I went over to it and popped the hood. I reached in and yanked out the distributor cap wires, tossing them over the hedge as an extra precaution, anything to slow him down.

We took off as fast as we dared, considering the state of the Porsche, and headed back to Etretat, which was no more than an hour distant. We were laughing, trying to shake off the adrenaline rush.

Pulling in to the familiar parking lot, we both heaved a sigh of relief at being back home. Mrs Leblanc welcomed us with open arms, hugging us both warmly. We updated her on the recent events while we ate a small meal. She gave me a stern look when she learned of the 'misunderstanding' about the special glasses and looked horrified when we told her of Norton's attack.

Our meal done, Raymonde and I headed up to her room. I briefly contacted my friends, informing them about what had happened. Briar was shocked that we had not done more to restrain Norton, whom he still considered the Shadow-Killer.

Raymonde came to my defence. We had left the man in a physically weakened condition, with no money, no identification, no weapon and a disabled vehicle. If he had become a rogue Interpol agent, he would also have to avoid the local police. Norton was not going to bother us, not for a long while. Coulter recorded a video of the cylinder, planning to spend a sleepless night figuring out how to open it. We bid our goodbyes to our online friends and disconnected.

I placed the cylinder on the nightstand and lay down in bed next to an exhausted Raymonde. We held each other and simply lay there until we fell asleep.

When I woke up next morning, the cylinder was gone!

CHAPTER 9

The Secret in the Office

I woke up Raymonde and pointed toward the bed stand. I felt sick with worry and consternation. Where did it go? Who took it? She went to stand up but I held her back.

"No, don't get up yet. Let's just lie here and think about things for a second. I know we're both a bit panicky about the cylinder's disappearance but I think that this situation requires a little reflection before we act," I suggested to her.

She lay back down, nodding in agreement, her exposed bosom distracting me pleasantly while she settled back into place. She noticed where I was looking and, covering herself up with her blanket, smacked me lightly. Laughing a little, she added:

"Keep your eyes on the business at hand!"

I laughed along with her and gave her a kiss, then became serious again:

"Listen, Raymonde, let's look at this step by step. The cylinder is gone, so someone must have taken it. It can't be Norton, there's no way he could have been sneaking around, not with his broken foot. The Killer hasn't shown his face, unless of course, the killer *is* Norton. It has to be the Vallin brothers..."

"But how did they get in? The outside doors were locked. We heard no noise. How did they know we were here, that we had the cylinder? To get that cylinder, they had to come right in here, right into my room..." she stated, her eyes wide and her nostrils flared as she realised that her privacy had been violated.

"I know, I know, try and keep calm. Let's go back to figuring it out and see where that gets us. Right, so... let's look at the room itself. How did they get in and how did they get out? First, the door. It is the most obvious way in. Did they use it?"

We both looked in the door's direction. From our position on the bed, we could see the key, still in its lock. I distinctly remembered double-locking it the night before.

"What about the window?" I continued.

Our heads swivelled in unison, looking at the window, slightly open, allowing a bit of cool air to waft through. Beyond it was a screen. It would have made too much noise to come in through there.

"Then, where could they have come from?" questioned Raymonde, consternation evident in her face.

We silently looked around the room, searching for the slightest clue. I noticed our glasses on the small table by the window and remembered how special they actually were.

"Raymonde, could you get up carefully and get my glasses?... Oh, could you also close the drapes?" I asked her.

She got up on the left side, opposite the bed stand that had held the cylinder. Tip-toeing past the round table, she picked up both pairs of glasses. Sliding the drapes closed, she jumped back in bed, pulling up the covers, slightly chilled by the morning air. She put on her glasses, handing the other pair to me. She looked quite funny, with her wild morning hair and her cool glasses, making me think of a French Janis Joplin. Keeping that observation to myself, I slipped my glasses on.

"Switch them to infrared mode."

"How do you do that?"

I showed her the little toggle. She pushed it on and the small screen changed instantly to a monochromatic greenish hue.

"I didn't know they could do that... Well, I guess they're not just expensive toys after all... Hey, what's that on the screen?" she asked pointing at the rug between the bed and the window.

"That's the heat signature of your feet..." I explained. "...The infrared mode allows us to look at heat instead of normal light. That's why I asked you to close the drapes. Heat signatures hang around much longer than most people would believe but it can be erased by other heat sources, like the morning sun. If we turn the gain up on the infrared mode to maximum, we might be able to detect the footsteps of the person who stole the cylinder. That might reveal how this invader came in to our room."

Raymonde looked suitably impressed.

I looked at the bed stand area, allowing the glasses' infra-red camera to absorb as much heat as possible. Slowly, small red smears appeared in the rug near the bed stand, irregular shapes, too formless to be shoes. Raymonde, looking through her glasses, noted:

"Maybe they walked around in socks."

"That may be right."

I turned my head slowly to the left, following the footsteps. They headed to the wall facing us, vanishing right through it.

"Where did they go?" she asked.

"Whoever it was stopped moving for a second... right there... and stood still. The heat signature of those particular footsteps is quite bright, compared to the others... Looks like only one person. He must have been looking around the room at first... He walked around the bed, came right up to the stand. Cylinder in hand, he returned to the wall, leaving a second set of prints," I surmised aloud.

"How could he have gone through the wall?" she asked.

"There simply has to be a hidden opening. There is no choice," I stated flatly. She looked disbelievingly at me for a moment, until the logic of what I had said sank in.

"It makes sense, really. If there was ever going to be a hidden passage, it would be here, in this house, once owned by the creator of Arsene Lupin, whose adventures held countless hidden passages. How fitting..." her voice trailed off momentarily, after which she came back to the point. "... So if it's there, how do we open it?"

"We push the button, of course."

"The button? What button?"

I stood up and walked to the wall, avoiding the fading footsteps, and pressed on a section of plaster moulding. It clicked back instantly and a panel of the wall suddenly swung away, revealing a dark, narrow corridor. Dust was everywhere. It seemed to have been recently disturbed.

"Wait a minute. I heard that button 'click' as clear as day. There was no way he could have pressed that and not woken us. We would have heard it," she objected.

"He didn't need to use it. He opened the panel from behind, the sound of that mechanism being muffled by the wall. After entering, he left the panel open. That way, he was able to retreat in complete silence..." I answered.

"... If he didn't press it, there can't have been any heat left on the button from his finger. How did you know it was there?" she asked, baffled.

"I knew it had to be in here somewhere. I felt that there was a chance that the button might actually be *colder* than the rest of the room. Cold air insinuates itself in every crack. I thought there might be more cracks around a secret mechanism. All I had to do was look around for cold spots. I found several but only one near the wall where the footsteps disappeared. It had to be our button."

I was realising that my mind was still sharp. My father's training had become habit over the years until it was second nature for me. Perhaps we had a chance of solving this puzzle after all.

"So, what should we do now?" Raymonde asked.

"Well, let's follow the footsteps, find out where they lead. We might catch the Vallin brothers in the tunnel," I urged.

She shook her head, not agreeing with me, a slight smile on her face.

"Don't you think we should get dressed first?" she asked with a touch of sarcasm.

I had overlooked that small detail in all the excitement.

"I guess you are right. Clothes might be appropriate at this point."

"Anyway, they are long gone. I am sure they did not come here recently. Otherwise, the heat of their footsteps would be glowing more than they are," she argued.

She had me there. Her comment gave me an idea.

"You're right about more than you know. Let's shower quickly, contact the team and plan our next step. You go first; I've got something I want to do."

She stood up from the bed, peering into the secret corridor for a second, then turned around, approaching me, seeming incredibly beautiful and happy at the same time. Looking deep into my eyes, she kissed me, going into the washroom and leaving me to my own devices.

My infrared devices!

I started by recording the track of the footprints on the rug. Putting on a pair of socks, I stood briefly on the rug, next to the faded marks. Stepping away, I recorded the new footsteps. The heat signature they left behind were a much more brilliant hue than the nearly faded footsteps of our intruder. I noted the exact time of the recording.

Leaving my equipment on the bed, I joined Raymonde when she came out of the shower. I 'helped' to dry her, and then had my own shower. Getting dressed, I noted that forty-five minutes had passed. I picked up my glasses again and recorded all the footprints one final time. Raymonde looked at me curiously.

"What are you doing?"

"Your comment about the faded footprints made me think that perhaps we could figure out when they *did* come into your room. With the recordings I just did, we should be able to come up with a fairly good estimate. I'll get Coulter to crunch the numbers. He's good at that sort of thing."

I activated the glasses' regular viewing mode, and simply waited, knowing Coulter's monitoring program would alert him. It took only a few minutes for him to connect. Raymonde slipped her glasses on and joined us.

"Good morning Paul, Raymonde. How was your night?" he asked routinely.

Upset by my answer, Coulter could not believe that we had let the cylinder slip through our fingers so easily. However, even he had to admit that there was no way we could have anticipated this. We had taken all the precautions we could think of. I did have to admit that we had underestimated the Vallin brothers.

Coulter might have been upset at the loss of the cylinder but he was happy to learn about the entrance to the secret corridor. I explained about the infrared recordings that I had done in order to calculate the intruder's time of entry. He downloaded the video files from my notebook and worked on it while we talked. Within a few minutes, he had an answer.

"Although there is a margin of error, it's within an acceptable percentage. I would say that your visitor entered at approximately 3:00 AM."

Briar and O'Flanahan signed on, both looking bleary-eyed. We updated them while we prepared to enter the secret passageway. Raymonde had found a small flashlight with fresh batteries. I brought my laptop since the wireless signal from the glasses, strong as it was, would not reach as far as we expected to go. Our online friends were anxious to get started even if it was very early for them and they were still tired.

I entered the corridor first. I was careful not to stir up the dust. Raymonde followed just behind me. I angled my body sideways and walked along slowly for about three metres. Aiming the flashlight in front of me, I saw a descending staircase. It was exceedingly narrow and steep. Here too, the dust had been recently disturbed, no doubt by our unwelcome nocturnal visitor.

Reaching the bottom of the staircase, the corridor ended about two metres in front of us, making it seem like we had reached a dead end. Looking around at the walls, I noticed an odd mechanism with a large toggle. Pushing it up, I heard a muted 'thunk' and a part of the wall cracked open, exposing a hidden door. Filled with trepidation, I pushed it open and stepped into Maurice Leblanc's office!

Our grand exploratory adventure had taken us a total of ten metres and ended one floor below Raymonde's room.

A SELECTION FROM THE WEISSMULLER MANUSCRIPT

The First Four Days

The invasion of Etretat began on the 13th of June 1940, at 11:30 AM. Our tanks led the way, going down each principal road into the small town. Several platoons of infantry followed the Panzers under my command. This was the crucial stage, where our plans finally became reality.

We had expected strong opposition from the French during our takeover but it failed to materialize. Instead we found a town in disarray. Shortly before our arrival, more than fifteen hundred Etretatais had fled the town in panic, only to be rebuffed in their escape attempt at the crossing of the Seine River, where our planes decimated them. There remained little governmental activity and the local economy had been driven into collapse.

Due to the lack of organized resistance, the first invasion phase was completed ahead of schedule. We were in control before the townspeople could utter a single protest. Our second phase could begin.

One platoon was dispatched to begin a house-by-house search, in order to accomplish several goals. The first was to conduct a thorough census of the local population, in order to ascertain the exact number of able-bodied men. The second goal was to seize all available supplies. The third was to instill fear in every single person in the valley. The men were instructed to be brutal and to react strongly to any hint of resistance.

The men found a cache of wine bottles almost immediately and the search degenerated into a destructive, boisterous party. I didn't mind. The drunker they got, the more frightened the villagers would be. They deserved it anyway. We wouldn't be fought off, not like before. I had foreseen every eventuality, every possible nuance of this invasion, anticipating all of its details before the Brown Shirts began their first patrol.

A second platoon headed to the top of the Aval cliff, setting up camp and preparing to dig out the ancient foundation of the Fort of Frefosse, while a third took possession of the main houses that were of interest to us: the Lindon and

Leblanc villas. Once these buildings were secured, a thorough search was undertaken to locate the hidden tunnels we suspected were there.

The deputy mayor, Rene Tonnetot, accompanied by several councilors, stood in front of the City Hall, nervously waiting to greet the person in charge. They were the only persons to venture out of their homes. We selected the White Rocks hotel as our temporary base, where we began organizing the infrastructure necessary for our next phase.

I was baffled by the lack of resistance. The census team reported that no weapons cache had been found and few able-bodied men remained. If there had been members of the French Resistance in this village at one time, they were not here now. I felt cheated. I had been looking forward to this moment for so long. All we found were women and children. Leblanc had run off like the coward he was, not even having the courage to fight to protect his most treasured possession.

The Resistance had made a deadly mistake in choosing to run. They had left behind their two most valuable assets. That which we sought and their women and children! The Resistance had already lost this battle, no matter what they did. For now, I would leave them alone. I had bigger quarry on my mind. I would have to ignore my eagerness to meet them again. My real goal was to seize that which Leblanc had held for more than thirty years.

By the end of the first day, all takeover phases had been carried out with a minimum of casualties among the soldiers. I finished the evening by drinking some champagne and terrorizing the deputy mayor. It was an entertaining enough activity, watching him jump from foot to foot, his face blanching in fear. I knew he was a puppet for the absent Lindon. However, the deputy mayor, Lindon and Leblanc were all powerless to prevent me from finding the secret they had hidden for decades. This time, it was our turn.

On the second day, the men began the search in earnest. Digging was already well underway on top of the Aval cliff. I was informed we would soon break through into the buried Frefosse dungeon. Also, much headway had been made in the Leblanc villa. A secret passageway had been found connecting a bedroom with his office. The men were positive that they would find another passageway soon. Following the recommendations of the census team's report, I had two men brought to me for questioning. They had been selected as the most likely to have information concerning the local plans for resistance. Despite the severity of my questioning, neither of these men admitted a single thing. We buried them behind the ancient church, a good end to a satisfying day.

The third day found me in a less than pleasant mood. The search of both villas had revealed nothing. My men were apparently not up to the task of solving the challenges facing them. During early afternoon, I went out to Leblanc's home, basing my choice on the prior discovery of one hidden passageway.

It took me a mere six hours to find the second tunnel. Once in the tunnel, it took less than two hours for us to reach the caves. This coincided with the breakthrough into Frefosse's ancient dungeon on the other side. Within a few hours more, we had opened a wide tunnel on top of the Aval cliff, giving us complete access to what lay beyond.

The caves were finally ours!

The fourth day was to be our last 'official' day in Etretat. Using an incident that was developing in the distant Havre, we pretended to leave. In fact, only empty vehicles left Etretat, my men and I safely ensconced inside the caves. Another *Kommandant* had already been selected, one ignorant of the existence of the caves. He had orders to impose complete control over the region. We would be free to act.

We hid the entrance to Frefosse's dungeon by concealing it underneath a hastily poured bunker. Its floor could be lowered by a hydraulic system, allowing us to completely camouflage the entrance into the caves. The Leblanc tunnel would continue being used as a secondary access until it was no longer necessary.

Now the most important phase of the project could begin. This is where my planning would prove truly valuable. We would not stop until these caves were transformed into a veritable fortress, unlike any other in the world, from which we could carry out our plans of world domination.

Matt Chatelain

CHAPTER 10

The Tunnels

I was sitting down in Leblanc's antique desk chair. Mrs Leblanc had just joined us and was examining the open panel in the wall. I had been looking around the room, trying to solve the riddle facing us. We knew that the secret passageway led here. We also knew that the Vallin brothers would have been able to escape through Leblanc's office door, along the hallway and out the front door. However, while that was the obvious route, I felt that they hadn't gone that way.

"Paul, I think I may have something," said Briar. He was looking carefully at the image of Leblanc's office, which he was receiving through my glasses. "Could you move back against the wall in front of the desk and slowly pan the room."

I did what he asked.

"Perfect. Tell me what you see. Describe it, my boy," he ordered.

"Well, I see a desk, behind that, a chair, then a low cabinet with a built-in bookshelf above that..."

"But what about *above* the bookshelf? What do you see there? Tell me that!" he emphasized, getting excited, his shiny head bouncing around animatedly.

"I see a... a large rectangle... inside that, a triangle... and inside that, a circle," I screamed this last, not believing it. It had been there all the time, right in plain view.

Another Leblanc masterpiece.

"Bravo, my boy, Bravo!" Briar added, screaming along with me. He caught himself quickly and calmed down, straightening out his jacket.

We examined the bookshelf more closely. Leblanc had purchased this house in 1917. He might very well have renovated it back then, with a few special additions to the plans. He often claimed weakness and illness, spending much of his time in bed, resting. What if, instead, he had a hidden exit, allowing him to escape without being seen, not even by his wife? What then?

I returned to the desk chair, in the perfect place to think. I had always said that I was an armchair detective. I thought of my father training me to organize my thoughts, preparing me for a moment like this one. Feeling his presence strongly, I reviewed the facts I held. I believed the secret entrance was the library unit itself.

Three observations led me to this conclusion. The first was that I had compared the layout of Leblanc's office to the other rooms around it. There wasn't enough room behind the walls for a hidden passage anywhere else. The three geometric symbols made up my second observation, thanks to Briar. Leblanc always put his clues in plain sight in his stories. I was sure he had done the same in his private office. He had placed these designs here, on purpose, to scream at the world: 'it is here, the door is here!'

My third and final observation was that our midnight visitors had travelled through a dusty corridor. Upstairs, the carpet had hidden the traces of dust. Down here, on the varnished wooden floor, dust was much more visible. By simply turning my chair around and looking down, I could see dusty footprints between the bedroom passageway and the bookcase. An attempt to clean up had been made. It had not been thorough enough. Enough of it remained to note two different foot sizes, confirming that *both* Vallin brothers had invaded the house. One had likely remained in the office, keeping a vigil, while the other had gone up to Raymonde's bedroom.

Therefore, logically, the door was right in front of me. Mrs Leblanc was opening cabinets and moving objects at random, trying to trigger the door's mechanism by chance. She would not succeed. It was not a book, because that would be too easy to trigger. There would be no switch, no button. There could be no accidental opening of this doorway.

Yet, it had to be something easily accessible. Knowing Leblanc, I also believed that the opening mechanism would require a logical approach to figure out. A general examination of the library brought to my attention four little rectangles, one on each of the four bookshelf columns. They seemed to jar with the rest of the library unit, as if they were imposed on it, not part of the original design. There was also a shelf missing. Why was it missing?

I stood up.

It was time to start walking.

"Raymonde, could you look through the panel in the wall and check the passage door upstairs and tell me if it's still open."

She checked and nodded in the affirmative.

"Okay. Could you please go up and close it, then come back down and close the panel entrance into this room..."

She did what I asked while I busied myself with the removal of books from selected shelves.

"I think Paul's figured something out," Coulter said.

Raymonde joined me as I approached the bookcase on the left side. I opened the left glass door and removed the last few books from the second shelf, putting them down on the desk. Having exposed the second shelf, I lifted it up. It came off strangely, having been nestled on the left side inside a curious spring-loaded notch unlike the support strip on the other side. I removed the shelf from the notch and heard a faint 'thunk', the sound emanating from inside the walls somewhere.

I was sure I was on the right track now.

Bringing the shelf, I walked to the glass door on the right side and opened it. I examined inside the unit on the right wall, just above the books, looking for the indentation I was convinced had to be there. It had been painted over but I eventually located its edge. With an apologetic look at Mrs Leblanc, I hit the indentation hard with the palm of my hand. The paint let go and the indentation moved inward, revealing a second narrow spring-loaded notch. I pushed the shelf into the indentation and dropped the other side down on a support strip. It seated itself firmly and a deep 'thunk' was heard, much louder than the previous one. I closed all three cabinet glass doors again, feeling them lock much more securely than before. We were all holding our breath in anticipation. I reached for the cabinet handle on the right and pulled on it.

Nothing happened!

While I wondered what I had missed, my eyes fell upon one of the books behind the locked cabinet doors, on the top shelf. It was The Hollow Needle, an identical copy to the two already in my possession. Unfortunately, the cabinet doors would not open again, probably not until after I had activated the mechanism to access the hidden entrance. I would have to examine the book later, when we came back. I returned my attention to the challenge facing us.

"Mrs Leblanc, would you mind closing the office door? It would probably be best if you closed it from the inside."

The door closed with a solid 'thunk'.

"Try opening it again."

She tried but it was impossible.

"Excellent. Now let me have another go at this."

I reached for the cabinet glass door one more time and pulled on its handle. At first, I thought nothing was happening but after a few moments, I detected movement! Excited, I pulled on the handle harder. The entire library pulled out of the wall, accompanied by a hiss of escaping air. It was nothing more than a very thick, very wide door. The low cabinet in front of it had gotten lower, dropping into the floor, while the library opened on its massive hinges. The lower cabinet settled into a new position, becoming a handy step to walk up to the newly exposed passage.

I moved away from the doorway. Raymonde and her mother ran up and peered into the inky blackness of the tunnel beyond, congratulating me all the while. Coulter was the first to ask me how I had done it.

"Oh no. I'm not wasting a half hour explaining things. I'll explain it on the way. It's time for us to go exploring," I stated with finality.

Past the library 'doorway', there was a set of stairs descending into the darkness. Aiming the flashlight around and seeing nothing dangerous, I stepped down slowly, Raymonde following close behind me. We had packed a few supplies and brought a coil of rope, just in case. The glasses were recording and my three friends were glued to their monitors. Mrs Leblanc decided to stay behind, planning to remain in the office until our return.

After about seven metres, the stairs ended, leading us to a straight brick corridor, featureless except for some ancient electrical wires attached to the wall at regular intervals. The wires had been cut near the entrance, suggesting that they had been connected to an outside power source at some point in the past. I saw an extremely old light bulb in a ceramic socket and noticed more bulbs hanging from the wires in the distance.

"Paul, do me a favour and examine that light bulb more closely. Let's see if we can learn more about who placed them here..." Coulter asked.

I lifted the light bulb up, as requested.

"Okay. now turn it over carefully. Sometimes they have some information printed on them."

"There are words here. It's in German... That would mean that Germans were here, in this tunnel. When would they have had the chance? Would you know, Briar?" wondered O'Flanahan aloud. Briar answered with an easy explanation.

"There can only be one time. The Germans invaded Etretat in 1940. They took over Leblanc's house immediately following their arrival. They would have been able to search this house from top to bottom. It could not have held back its secrets for long."

"It must have been heart-rending for Leblanc to run away from this incredible home, knowing that the German army was coming to steal what he had kept hidden all these years," Raymonde commented.

This was no longer a clever theory that we had spun around a coffee table. Something definable and concrete had taken place here. Unfortunately, Leblanc had taken whatever he knew to his grave. Nothing about this had leaked to the rest of the world since his death.

No, I was wrong about that. Some people knew. The Shadow-Killer knew. He had thought nothing of killing my father in order to prod me into action. Hitler also knew, as early as 1911. Hitler and another man, someone who had been going around killing people, stealing the same key information we were desperately trying to collect today.

It truly *was* a conspiracy!

O'Flanahan had been right. My biggest problem was that I could not fathom how Leblanc and Hitler were connected. I could not accept that Leblanc would ever have *allied* himself with that monster. In fact, Leblanc had run from the Germans in 1939. This demonstrated that he was not their ally but rather their *enemy*.

O'Flanahan's voice interrupted my thoughts.

"Say, are you going to explain how you solved the trick of the secret door in Leblanc's office or what?"

While we walked down the featureless brick tunnel, I explained how I had figured out the way in. I had suspected that the library unit was the door after Briar's comment and had become convinced that the four small rectangles were the key to that door:

"It began with the impression of a straight line that wasn't there. Three of the four rectangles and the two shelves connected the first three columns, making a straight line across them. However, there, the line was broken because there was no shelf to connect to the final square, on the right side of the cabinet. It made the library look lopsided. It was only when I transposed the position of the shelf from the left to the right with the concept of *open* and *closed* that I understood Leblanc's game. In other words, the left shelf of the library represented the secret door in Leblanc's bedroom upstairs. The middle shelf represented the office itself and the right shelf represented the secret doorway leading out of the office. To continue from the office to the hidden passageway, one would have to replace the missing shelf on the right. A quick look informed me that there was no spare shelf sitting around for us to use. I continued my comparison a step further. Perhaps, I had to take the left shelf, the one representing the upstairs passageway, and move it to the right side to complete the line. This might mean that only one door could be open at a time. That's why I asked Raymonde to close the door upstairs, and asked Mrs Leblanc to close the office door. With both doors closed and both shelves in the right position, the hidden passageway mechanism was unlocked, allowing me to open the tunnel door," I concluded.

"I can't believe you came up with that. I'm officially impressed," Coulter admitted.

"I'll second that," O'Flanahan said gruffly.

We reached a section where our modern tunnel connected with a much older tunnel carved out of the bedrock. Water pooled around our feet, soaking our shoes. We had not thought to bring rubber boots.

"Maybe that's why the Vallin were walking around in socks. They came in rubber boots and took them off to avoid leaving wet tracks all over," Raymonde suggested.

The older tunnel ended suddenly in a T-junction. The wires turned to the left, heading towards the Aval cliff and the caves we sought. We didn't know where the other side went, except of course, that it headed in the direction of the Amont cliff. Everyone wanted to follow the wires and go find the caves.

As we headed down the dark tunnel on our left, countless noises echoing around us, Briar returned to a previous topic:

"I have done more research into this Norton-as-the-killer issue..."

O'Flanahan interrupted him instantly.

"You've been thinking Norton was the Shadow-Killer for a while now. I just don't see why it has to be him..."

"... Because he's the one after us, I mean after you, Paul... and Raymonde, as well, I would guess. Norton's actions at the Chapel did nothing to make him look innocent. You must admit that... I mean the man shot at both of you. Once he had the cylinder in his possession, who knows what he would have done," Briar retorted.

"He might have done nothing, Briar, being just a cop tracking a killer and coming across an unexpected clue in the form of that cylinder..." O'Flanahan snapped back.

Both had good arguments. I had a tendency to lean in O'Flanahan's corner. Norton might be unhinged but he didn't come across as a killer. Briar spoke up again.

"The real point, O'Flanahan, is that I have done some research on Norton and come up with disturbing information. My contact has told me that I am not the first to suspect Norton of killing his sister. He was investigated but the charges were dropped due to insufficient evidence against him. He saw shadows everywhere... shadow-killers... and he found them, or at least, he claimed he had found them. Many doubted the unsolved murders he collected for his list were connected. His work suffered as his obsession with the 'Shadow-Killer' grew. Then, another inspector from Interpol accused him of being the killer of several of the unsolved murders from his list. Unfortunately, that inspector was conveniently killed in an accident before he could reveal his evidence. Unfortunately, the circumstantial evidence against Norton was not enough to hold up in a court of law without the dead inspector's information, so the case was dropped. Norton was eventually re-instated but warned to steer clear of his mad theories. When he pulled some strings to check on your parent's murder and started talking about the killer again, Interpol became seriously uneasy. After that Harry Stiles murder happened, Interpol stopped hesitating and shut Norton down... or at least they tried to... He took off before they could apprehend him. There is, at this very moment, a warrant for his arrest across the whole of Europe... I tell you, Norton is the killer. I am sure of it."

This was certainly worrisome information... and convincing. Briar might be right after all.

By this point, Raymonde and I had walked about a hundred and fifty metres towards the Aval cliff. We were encountering increasing amounts of rubble and broken chunks of rock. Everyone hoped the caves wouldn't be much further.

The rubble deepened until it eventually filled up the entire tunnel. The wires disappeared into the pile of broken rocks and stones.

"This mess has been here for a long time. It looks like the collapse may have been caused by an explosion of some force," informed Coulter.

"The tunnel was blown up *after* the Germans had been here. Look... Those wires continue through the rubble. They used this tunnel then blew it up when they were done with it," observed O'Flanahan.

We couldn't keep going towards the caves, frustrating as that was, so we headed back the other way.

"This tunnel was built by hand, using stone axes and other similar tools. I've seen the marks before. Digging tunnels through stone is hard work, even soft chalk like this. This is a long tunnel. Someone must have felt it was worth the effort..." stated Briar.

"Could Romans have dug this tunnel?" wondered Coulter.

"Absolutely. Romans were here in 50 BC, they had the tools, the skills and the work force. They would have needed a whole lot of men, let me tell you. This is a very long tunnel."

Raymonde and I were now walking knee-deep in freezing water and it was getting deeper. The further we travelled along the tunnel, the worse the reception for the glasses became. We managed to say good-bye to our friends before completely losing our connection to the Internet.

* * *

We had been wading through deep water for a while and we were shivering from the cold. Luckily, the water grew shallower until, thankfully, we were past it. We took a short break to warm up. I took my pants off and wrung them dry. I was shaking with the cold, feeling numbed by it, as was Raymonde. Chilled or not, she still had enough energy to comment on my appearance while I stood, shivering in my underwear.

Also shivering, she followed my example and removed her sopping pants, squeezing them free of excess water, while cleverly avoiding a sarcastic retort from me. We rubbed each other briskly to get the blood flowing again. Our shaking stopped, banished by our increasingly stimulating rubbing.

A short while later, our shivering taken care of, we dressed, our clothes sufficiently dry. We continued our march along the tunnel leading towards the Amont cliff. My senses sharpened in the gloom and I was able to pick out details in the rock, here and there. I perceived everything with increasing clarity. I felt that I did not need the flashlight at all. I could not explain what I was perceiving.

It was definitely a strange occurrence and I mentioned it to Raymonde while we walked along, our footsteps adding their own echoing beat to the sound of water drops in the distance. She surprised me by saying that she was experiencing the same thing and suggested we turn off the flashlight.

At first, it felt like we were in complete darkness. Once our eyes adjusted, we found that we could see everything clearly. The walls and roof of the tunnel were emanating a dim light, an incredibly faint yellow glow, so weak that the flashlight had overwhelmed it. Neither of us could come up with a satisfactory explanation for the strange luminosity. We continued in silence, enjoying the odd experience while it lasted. After some distance, we were obliged to turn the flashlight back on when the glow faded to nothing.

We arrived at a dead end, the tunnel stopping abruptly, as if work on it had been abandoned. Baffled, Raymonde and I retraced our steps. We found a small room a few metres before the end of the tunnel. It, too, had been hand carved, the walls still showing ancient tool marks. It was empty, except for a few rotten shelves. We returned to the end of the tunnel, lacking any other choice.

To our relief, we uncovered a narrow cleft in the rock on the left, cleverly hidden in the folds of the tunnel walls. It led us to a door made of a single block of stone. A lever released a catch, allowing us to open it. We walked out into a bigger tunnel, this one lined in long bricks, much older than those in the tunnel near the Leblanc residence. Bricks like these had to be from the later Roman period. I recorded everything for future analysis. We decided to travel along the right side of the tunnel. After a short distance, we encountered a locked gate, beyond which we saw an overgrown glade.

Unable to exit, we retraced our footsteps. Reaching the camouflaged door, we continued. In the dark tunnel, the faint sounds of pounding surf reverberated. Soon after, we arrived at the end of the tunnel. We were standing at the edge of a hole in the Amont cliff, about ten metres above the ground. Below us, exposed by the retreating tide, was a short strip of sand connecting us to the main beach.

I uncoiled the rope, glad to have brought it. I looped the rope around an outcropping, dropping both ends down to the beach below. I could tell that we were not the first to come here. There were signs of rope wear right where I had just placed mine. The Vallin brothers had probably come through here twelve hours ago, when the tide was out. The timing was right.

I climbed down first, getting to the bottom quickly. I held the rope tight while Raymonde went carefully over the ledge and made her way down the cliff. She dropped down the last few feet into my waiting arms. After a brief kiss, we separated and I pulled at one of the hanging rope ends until it slipped off the outcropping and fell at my feet. I coiled it, hung it on my shoulder, picked up both our pack-sacks and headed off to Etretat's main beach, Raymonde and I holding hands.

***

It was late afternoon when we reached Etretat from the beach. Raymonde called her mother using my cell phone, letting her know that we were all right. We took a taxi back to the Villa Leblanc. Mrs Leblanc greeted us, inviting us to her private rooms, where we talked while having an afternoon snack.

"So, in the end, this was just a wild goose chase?" Mrs Leblanc stated. "Simply a few forgotten tunnels that go to the channel."

"Not so, Mrs Leblanc. These tunnels have told us much already. For example, we know that Romans built some of them. Those tunnels have probably been in existence for more than two thousand years. Additionally their existence confirms that the caves are real, even though we have not found them yet. That is no little thing to know. We have also learned that the Germans found and used these tunnels, later destroying the section connecting them to the caves. This confirms the link to Hitler. His involvement is no longer a mere letter in Leblanc's office," I explained.

"I have used that letter for many years in the display in Grand-Papa's office. I had found it folded with the final papers and books from his estate. I never knew it was so important, otherwise I would not have left it on display," Mrs Leblanc informed.

"Be happy that you did, because it is what caused us to continue this search. Without that crucial link, we would not have understood the true scale of the mysteries confronting us," I said.

Her comment about Leblanc had reminded me of the book I had seen in the office.

"Mrs Leblanc, when you went through your grandfather's papers, did you come across a copy of The Hollow Needle?"

She nodded her head:

"Why, yes I did. An old copy, signed by him. I have kept it in his office, all these years. It was left to his son, Patrice Leblanc, my father. He died during the Second World War…"

Another piece of the puzzle clicked into place. I now understood why I was here, hot on the trail of a family mystery, while the Leblanc family was not. The person to whom the mystery had been intended to be revealed, Leblanc's son, had died before he even knew of its existence.

"Could we take a look at that book?" I asked her, my excitement translating into newfound energy.

We followed her into Leblanc's office. I took the time to put on my glasses and activate them. Coulter came online, soon followed by Briar. I updated them on the end of our tunnel adventure and about our present search. By then, Mrs Leblanc had opened the cabinet doors and pulled out her copy, handing it to me. Briar exclaimed:

"Good gosh, my boy, it's absolutely identical to the other two."

I opened the book to the printing history, finding the same legend. It was number one of a limited printing of four and one.

"So the other one is not a forgery. They are all identified as number one," commented Coulter.

"Our great-grandfathers had a hidden purpose in printing these books, a purpose we have not yet revealed..." I said.

Mrs Leblanc had been shaking her head at these recent revelations.

"Paul, what is bothering me about this the most, and please don't take this the wrong way, is that you are here in the first place. I cannot understand how you come to be here, led to this place by your great-grandfather. Who was he that he knew about all this?"

The Great Hunt was leading me into increasingly personal territory. It was becoming a search for my own origins. Briar was the next to speak:

"My boy, I have also been asking myself these questions. Your great-grandfather, Paul Sirenne, must once have been in France. I am convinced of that. He had to have been in Etretat at some point. Yet, for an as-yet unexplained reason, he left and relocated to Canada, opening that bookstore of his..."

"He was also very, very rich!" I added. "We know little about his past but I suspect my inherited wealth comes from long ago. The Sirennes did not leave France for reasons of poverty."

I had been riffling through the book in my hands while I spoke. Inspired by a sudden thought, I opened it to the back.

There, facing me, were the same white stitches. Could it be? I bent down, looking closer at them. My examination revealed what I instinctively knew was there. A hidden flap carefully concealed by fake stitches.

"Let me get my tools and see if anything is in it."

Before I could move, Mrs Leblanc had opened the desk drawer, pulling out a pair of tweezers and handing them to me. I got to work, playing with the edge, until I had loosened the thin layer of leather binding. Pulling the flap up, I revealed a piece of folded paper. Trying to stop the trembling in my fingers, I reached in with the tweezers and pulled it out.

Unfolding it gingerly, I read it aloud:

Patrice:

If you have found this note, then you have taken the first step towards regaining your heritage. Time and events have overtaken me. I have not been able to tell you everything. There is much more to know. You know what has been found, I have told you that much. You must look further, to discover what is really there.

When the time is right, your son's son must find a bookstore owner named Paul Sirenne, in Ottawa, Canada. With his help, what we have hidden will be revealed. Do not fail me, do not fail Etretat.

Your Father,
Maurice Leblanc

PS: A real story ends near Etretat
Lost until Patrice infers new ideas subtly
Your friend
Paul Sirenne

My legs collapsing beneath me, I dropped heavily into the desk chair. O'Flanahan had just signed on and the others were talking excitedly. My head was buzzing and I felt dizzy. This note connected the Leblancs and the Sirennes together, telling us to go and find each other. Once again, I was being forced to accept that I was part of a pact spanning generations.

"What is going on?" I exclaimed.

"Perhaps it might help if we knew more about events in Etretat during the Second World War. What happened there? The revelations from this note are also muddying the Vallin waters. Let's not forget that we need to find out how they knew of these tunnels. If we knew that, it might help us piece together a bit more of the puzzle," Briar suggested.

"Would it help to talk to someone who was there?" sprung Mrs Leblanc.

"Do you know of someone?"

"Yes, I do. He is quite old now but, from what I hear, still has his wits about him. I was very young when I ran away with Grand-Papa. When I was old enough to grow curious about such things, I researched the past of this place, to find out what had gone on in our house after we were forced to abandon it. Eventually, I was led to '*Bequilles*', a local man who had been active in the Resistance during the Second World War. He was a cripple, walking around on crutches, and had not been accepted for regular service. However, he found other ways to be helpful. Having been in the Resistance, he was witness to many things. If you tell him I sent you, he might share what he knows..." she said, writing down the old man's address.

We decided to use the next few hours to go see this 'Bequilles' fellow. Perhaps our visit with him would provide us with useful information when I confronted the Vallins later on.

Matt Chatelain

CHAPTER 11
Bequilles' Story

I parked the Porsche in front of an old house converted into apartments. This was the address given to us by Mrs Leblanc. I was wearing my glasses and they were in recording mode. The man's apartment was on the ground floor. There was no answer when we rang. A snooping landlord came out to tell us that his tenant had gone out for a bite to eat when Bequilles returned, surprising all of us in the hallway.

His old frame rested heavily on two worn crutches. He was looking at us with tired eyes, unsure about what we might want. His entire demeanour changed when we mentioned our names and who had sent us here. He grew attentive and a spark scintillated in his deep, black eyes, barely visible underneath a pair of incredibly thick eyebrows.

"I'll not have us standing out in the hallway like a gang of troublesome youngsters," he invited, unlocking the last door on the right. "Besides, I've been walking for almost thirty minutes. My old bones have had it for the day."

We entered into the small apartment. There was clutter everywhere. He led us around various piles of newspapers and magazines, to a small dining table. Once we were seated, he reached into a nearby cupboard, pulling out a bottle of wine, along with three glasses that were more or less clean. Uncorking the bottle, he poured an equal amount in each glass. Lifting his glass up in the air, he called a toast.

"To Victoire Leblanc, who lost so much and endured so much more."

It made both of us reflect on her tribulations, sixty years ago. After a brief moment, Bequilles spoke up.

"Last time I saw Victoire, we talked about some things that happened a long while ago. Most folks around these parts might prefer to let those things be. But she sent you to me and I can't have you wasting all that time coming here for nothing. So go on, ask your questions."

Raymonde and I looked at each other. Right to the point. I liked him already!

"Sir, Raymonde and I are on a search for historical information. We have come up with some unexpected knowledge that has connected Leblanc's old villa with the Germans in World War 2. We found ourselves wondering about what was going on in Etretat back then. Mrs Leblanc felt that you were the best man to tell us about that period."

Looking at me with his deep-set eyes for a moment, he asked.

"These things you want to know, why do you want to know them?"

"Raymonde and I met at the Villa Leblanc. We were both looking for the same thing, although neither of us knew it at the time. Raymonde's interest comes from her mother, who got it from her grandfather, Maurice Leblanc. Mine comes from my father, who gave me Leblanc's book along with a strange message, when I was nine. Our search has united us in a way that we could never have anticipated... We know something happened here long ago and it revolves around what Leblanc did in 1911. We discovered that the Germans were mixed up in it and we know that there are people around right now trying to stop us from finding out more. We want to learn as much as we can about this mystery, before it is too late."

Bequilles sat in silence for a while, still thinking. Finally, he spoke:

"There have been secrets in Etretat for a long time, it seems. I myself have been party to those secrets, something I hesitate to admit to strangers. But, you may be the very people who are meant to hold this knowledge. Who knows? I wasn't part of the inner circle back then, so I wasn't made aware of everything. The war being what it was, some lines got blurred and I learned a bit more than I was supposed to, I guess. I always had a tendency to keep my mouth shut and my eyes and ears open.

"It was bad, this war and Etretat got hit pretty hard... But our little village fared better than some others, so there was little use complaining... I was already working for the Resistance. Lucien Duperoux himself had asked me to join. He knew about my skills with the radio. He had also seen me win a race with my crutches. He knew I could move fast when I needed to, something the Germans would never believe. I always acted stupid and slow around them. They might beat me but they would never suspect me.

"If I were to choose a place to start my story, it would be when Obersleutenant Weissmuller arrived. It was June the 13th, 1940. I'll never forget that day, the day everything changed. One tank drove right up the Henry V Avenue and shot at a large pile of garbage. Can't imagine what they were thinking it was. That's about the only funny thing that happened that day. The Germans had itchy trigger fingers and some people got shot for simply being there. It was terrible... and it got worse. Over the next four days, they ransacked the entire town, terrorizing everyone, breaking into every home, taking whatever they wanted and destroying the rest.

"Our real mayor back then, Raymond Lindon, had left before the Germans arrived, since he was Jewish. He went into hiding and he was good at that. He was an integral part of the local Resistance and had his hands in a lot of things, from what I'd heard. He came right back, as soon as the war ended and took up his post as if he had never left.

"Leblanc was gone by then, never to return... Anyway, Tonnetot, the deputy mayor, was summoned to meet a man in the middle of the night. That man was Obersleutenant Weissmuller. He was sitting in a bed, smoking our cigars and drinking our champagne. He threatened Tonnetot with death should any of his men be harmed and then sent him on his way. Four days later, Weissmuller was gone, called away to squelch a nest of resistance in Dieppe. On the 17th of June, another Kommandant arrived and took over control of the area..."

Bequilles refilled his empty wine glass, reflecting a bit.

"I've had a long time to think about what happened back then. Over the years I came up with a theory that might explain the few facts that I do have. You see, although Weissmuller and his men drove off four days after they got here, apparently never to return, I think they never left!..."

He paused dramatically before resuming.

"I did a lot of things during those four years. Most of it was simple stuff. There was food to bring to those that needed it and that was mostly everybody. We had to hide what we did have, because the Germans kept taking everything. We got pretty tricky along the way and bamboozled them a fair few times... but not all the time! Sometimes, we would get caught. Like what happened to me. I was caught with coal I shouldn't have had, which, back then, was a pretty bad thing. I played dumb as always. They took me to see the Kommandant. He was busy talking with another man, who was giving him a serious dressing down. I only saw that other man for a minute but I would put my hand in the fire and swear that it was Obersleutenant Weissmuller, a man supposed to be gone more than six months before.

"I began suspecting something right then. Whenever there was talk going around, I would listen, always trying to piece more of it together. Everyone in the resistance knew that something strange was going on. Unexplained murders, many of them downright gruesome, convoys in the night, all sorts of things. The first thing I added to my theory was the growing list of new Kommandants.

Germans were a pretty organised lot. I mean they had to be, considering what they were trying to do. I would have thought that when a Kommandant was in place, he would stay there. It would have been the most efficient thing to do. I even checked in other towns and found that it was pretty much the rule. Yet, every six months, a new Kommandant and his troops would roll in. It made no sense... Then, there were the trucks..."

"Trucks?" Raymonde asked, captivated by his story.

"Yes. Lots and lots of trucks. Almost every night, you could hear their rumble. Most times the noise came from the Aval side... And the patrols. At night, the patrols seemed to double. You couldn't go wandering the countryside on a whim, no sir. It was our biggest problem. The Resistance had a lot of trouble getting out there to find out what was going on. I know, from seeing a manifest one very lucky time, that some of those trucks were bringing cement. Tons of cement. Later, there were explosions in the channel. For almost six months, they went on. But things got real interesting when we noticed the duplicate German patrols."

"Duplicate patrols? What do you mean by that?" I asked.

He grinned with a toothless smile.

"It sure threw us for a loop when we figured it out. When the first unexpected patrol came by, we blamed the lookout who had worked on the timetable. But when it started happening again and again, we realised that something entirely different was going on. It didn't happen all the time which made it doubly difficult to catch but, one day, we were lucky. We were able to follow the surprise patrol to a small glade, near the Dungeon, a local restaurant. Soldiers were being dropped off. They entered the wooded glade and never came out. It became clear that this was happening regularly enough. By our count, over one hundred men had entered that glade and vanished during a period of twelve days. To add to the mystery, we were pretty sure that it wasn't the locals Germans either. It seemed likely that the local Germans knew of these other soldiers, I mean, how could they not? But they never paid them the slightest notice.

"This is how we became aware that there was a large company of Germans roaming around that no one really knew about. Two separate groups of Germans, one hidden and the other brought here strictly to deal with the daily tasks, left in the dark about the activities of the first group. It explained why the Kommandants kept changing.

"Eventually, the local leader of the Resistance decided to sneak into that glade to discover what had been going on with the disappearing men. We had all heard the fishermen's tales about secret tunnels and such. Perhaps there was some truth to them. One day, our leader got his chance. Although guarded, the glade had a slight dip in its centre, which he used to crawl past unseen. Seeing a soldier entering a narrow hole in the west side of the glade, he followed him and found himself in a long tunnel, which led him to the beach, on the Amont side. The soldier was nowhere to be seen..."

Raymonde and I knew that tunnel. We had glimpsed the glade through the locked iron gate. Bequilles continued:

"It mystified us. The tunnel on the beach ended at least eight metres in the air, its original access destroyed long ago by the tide. The Germans could not be going there. There had to be another way out. So he searched and searched, only to be nearly caught by four soldiers who came out of the tunnel wall, literally out of nowhere. He dropped to the ground, hiding in the shadows. After they were gone, he examined the spot where they had come out of the wall. He found a trigger brick that opened a hidden door, leading to another tunnel. But more Germans were coming and he had to get out of there. He almost got caught, jumping out into the Channel from the end of the tunnel, the Germans hot on his tail. They must have thought he'd drowned, which he almost did. They beefed up their security around the glade after that. It only was much later that he got the chance to go back, near the end of the war. The Germans were in a panic by then. He returned to the second hidden tunnel and following it, eventually found himself at a crossroad. One way was blocked by a new rock fall. The other led to Leblanc's house."

Bequilles emptied the last dregs of the bottle of wine into his glass.

"That's almost all I know. After the Germans left, there was one more thing that happened. I heard this from a woman who lived out on the *Petit Valaine* Road. She woke up in the night, hearing faint screams and machine gun fire. It went on for a while, followed by sporadic firing, then one final shot. Searches were made the next day but nothing was ever found."

He stopped talking, lost in his memories. I had one question that remained and it was burning my lips.

"The Resistance leader who found those tunnels? What was his name?"

"His name? He was called Vallin, Gerard Vallin."

There was our connection. This was how the Vallin brothers knew of the tunnel. Their father had been in the Resistance.

"Why did you, or he, never tell anyone of the tunnels?"

Bequilles' eyes narrowed.

"That's a good question. Yes sir, it is. Vallin told me about it as quick as he could, the first time around, and told many others, although most didn't believe him. The second time he went in, he only told me. That's because someone else was there when he was doing the telling. Tonnetot. As soon as he heard Vallin, he jumped on both of us right quick. Told us right there and then that we weren't to ever tell anyone else about it. No one was to know about the Secret. That's what he called it: 'The Secret', like it was something big and important. He said that Etretat was hiding something very special and that some of us had the duty to protect it. So, I haven't breathed a word about them until this very day, no Sir, not to anyone," he explained

"So why did you tell us?" Raymonde asked him.

His eyes twinkled a bit.

"I'm not sure. There are many reasons, I guess. I'm not long for this world..." he stopped, seeing our concerned looks, "...Oohh, there's no use denying it, I can feel it coming. I'm thinking this might be the last chance I get to pass on this knowledge that's been in my head all these years, never breathing a word of it. It feels good to let it out. But it's not just that, it's you two as well. Let me try to explain: when Tonnetot told us what he did, he let on more than he intended. I always knew that Tonnetot only stepped in as deputy mayor because Lindon asked him to. I think that when Tonnetot spoke, he was repeating what he was told to say by Lindon. He wasn't surprised about the tunnels. He was more worried about us telling anyone about them, than about what the Germans had been up to. One thing I knew for sure, about Tonnetot, was that he was dead loyal to Etretat. What he was telling us was for the good of Etretat, of that I was positive. Today, when you came in here, when you explained your reasons for being here, I realised that maybe you were here for the good of Etretat. I thought this story long dead but you two are bringing it back to life," he paused, pointing a trembling finger at Raymonde, " You are from the very family that began all this so long ago. You are directly involved in this... Secret... as Tonnetot called it. And you, Mr Sirenne, I believe that you are very special indeed. I am very surprised to finally meet you. I never thought the day would come when I heard your name. No, it is right for both of you to find out about your heritage. I suspect that what is hidden here, whatever it is, has been left here for you to find. Call me an old fool but that is what I believe and that is why I told you. There has to be a purpose to it all."

I shook his hand warmly, thanking him for his trust and Raymonde hugged him tightly. He remained sitting at the kitchen table when we left, looking at his empty glass of wine.

***

It was now late in the afternoon and we still had much to do, or at least I did. We sat down at the restaurant table by the window, having a quick bite. Mrs Leblanc had joined us and Briar was online, as was Coulter. O'Flanahan couldn't make it, so we were recording our conversation. I summarised what we had learned.

"Well, we found out how the Vallins got to us and that is no little thing. Bequilles gave us a few additional clues. Such as Obersleutenant Weissmuller, who was likely involved in some secretive activities. Plus there were odd explosions in the water, trucks in the night, loads of cement, use of hidden tunnels, double patrols, the list goes on..."

I stopped and sipped some coffee. Briar took the opportunity to jump in.

"I'll check into this Weissmuller fellow. I'll contact my friend in Nuremberg. Maybe we can flesh out his character a bit more. We already know that Hitler was involved as early as 1911 and that someone else was working with him, killing people and destroying information about Etretat. This lasted through the First World War and for decades after that... Now it seems they did much more than that. At the first opportunity, at the very beginning of World War 2, they invaded Etretat, marched directly into Leblanc's home and used his hidden tunnel to access the caves. They even built their first bunker right over the fort of Frefosse's site. Could it be that Hitler built a war machine just to take over the Etretat caves? I know it sounds preposterous..." he theorized.

Hearing it put that way, this 'conspiracy' was taking on a more insidious tone. Could Hitler's incredible rush to power have been motivated by his discoveries in Etretat? What about his rise into politics? Hitler devoted his life to these goals. It could not simply be a feint to hide his interest in Etretat. However, the caves could have been a root cause, a hidden motivation for the whole thing.

We would never know, unless we took the next step.

"We have to go after that rock cylinder and deal with the Vallin brothers. No matter what the Germans did in the 1940's, the answer is here, now, and the Vallins stole that answer from us. We still aren't sure about the nature of their involvement but their acts so far haven't seemed very friendly. Let's not forget that they have lived here all their lives. That's a lot of time for research and investigation," I explained.

"So what are we going to do?" Coulter asked.

"I'm going to go visit them right after supper. I'll be going alone... They won't be expecting me. We'll have ourselves a little chat. I'm sure that we will be able to 'resolve' things," I explained.

Raymonde looked a bit miffed.

"There is no way you are leaving me behind. I want to talk to those rascals myself," she said angrily.

"Raymonde, I know you want to come but I can't let you. This is something I have to do on my own. You'll be along anyway. I'll have my glasses on..." I explained.

"I don't care about the stupid glasses. I care about you and I don't want you hurt. They almost killed us, if you remember! What if that killer Norton comes back?" she said, tears in her eyes. I got up and hugged her.

"What? Hobbling on one foot? No, he's out of the picture for a while yet. Listen, Raymonde, I came here to solve a mystery and found you instead. All our search has done is to place both of us at risk. I can't stand that. It's time to end this danger and it's up to me to do it..."

I had never felt like this. It seemed as if my feet were on the ground for the first time in my life.

"... Very well... You can go... but I want you to be careful," she hugged me again, holding me tight. "... Or you'll have to answer to me."

CHAPTER 12

The Vallin Brothers

I pulled out the pistol I had taken from Norton. The weight surprised me. It certainly was a big thing and looked fearsome enough. I held it gingerly, trying to figure out its main mechanisms. I found the safety catch soon enough, ensuring that it was flipped on. I slipped it into the small packsack I was bringing with me.

After saying my good-byes to Raymonde and Mrs Leblanc, I got into the Porsche, directions in hand. Events were forcing me to act impulsively, going simply on gut instinct. I didn't know what to be more surprised at: what I was about to do, or the fact that I was doing it!

I parked far from the Vallin house, not wanting to be seen. According to Mrs Leblanc, it had been home to the Vallin family for almost one hundred and twenty-five years. Old Man Vallin himself had lived there. Approaching the house, I activated the glasses. Everybody connected in, wishing me good luck. I asked them to keep quiet and to avoid turning on their cameras. I didn't want to be interrupted at a crucial moment.

The sun hadn't set yet but the shadows were getting long. I used them to my advantage, getting on my knees and crawling along a row of bushes bordering their property. Reaching the end, I saw their house. It was a one-floor affair, simple enough and poorly maintained. Their lawn hadn't been cut in months. I wasn't complaining. It made sneaking around much easier. Approaching the house and noticing an open window, I slowly raised my head to look inside.

They were both right there, the rock cylinder between them. One had a hammer and the other held a chisel. They were arguing with each other, their nerves frayed. Apparently, they had been at this process for a while and were having little success. Preoccupied as they were, there was a good chance that I could surprise them. I pulled the gun out from the packsack and managed to stop myself from shaking.

"Be careful, my boy. Don't do anything careless."

Briar's comment jolted me out of my concentration.

"Let him do it in peace, for Pete's sake, Briar," whispered O'Flanahan.

From my vantage point, I saw that the front door of their house was a two-part affair with the top separate from the bottom. Deciding on a course of action,

I quietly crawled along the side of the house and reached the door after a few minutes.

I tried the lower knob, which thankfully was unlocked. I remembered my last attempt at unlocking a door. I pulled it open slowly, leaving the top closed, while listening to their ongoing argument. Soon I had the door open wide enough to position myself in the middle of the entrance, crouching on my knees.

It was time.

"Freeze, you two. Stop what you are doing and don't move. I have a gun aimed directly at both of you."

The sudden sound of my loud voice petrified them, freezing them in place.

"Excellent, my boy, you've got them now," Briar jumped in again.

"Hey, man will you please be quiet. This is the best part," Coulter shot back.

"What do you want Mister?" the small Vallin asked, his voice shaking and nervous.

"You know what I want," I answered. "It's right between the two of you. You stole it from us, remember?"

"You have no right to that rock thing. It belongs to us, to Etretat."

What were they talking about?

"No you are wrong about that. I am positive that cylinder was specifically intended for us," I stated, shaking the gun. "... No matter who is right, although we are, you broke into our home and you stole it from us. You also followed us, tried to run us off the road, shot at us and listened in on our conversations..." I listed with increasing volume. "None of these acts are those of honest people. Before anything goes further, we will take back what is ours," I finished, feeling flush with emotions.

I moved forward into the house, intent on reaching the cylinder. My foot hit something and I reacted instinctively, looking down at a pair of old dirty boots. I had taken my attention off the two for a single moment but it was enough! The small Vallin vaulted over the couch, trying to get at a knife, planted in a wooden beam on the other side of the room. I aimed at the knife and pulled the trigger.

The gun went 'Click!'

The safety was still on!

I desperately scrambled to find the safety that had been obvious moments before. The big Vallin jumped to the corner where a double-barrelled shotgun was leaning. He grabbed it, cocking it and lifting it to his shoulders, all in one smooth move.

Safety finally off, I swung my gun in the smaller Vallin's face and he froze in fear. I tried to point my gun towards his brother. Before I could bring it to bear on the big Vallin, he had managed to aim his shotgun directly at my chest. His finger was on the trigger and it was tightening!

"Nobody move. I have a gun on all of you," a familiar voice rang out, strong and clear.

Mrs Leblanc!

For a moment, everybody froze. My adrenaline was really kicking in, my senses at their peak level. Everything had slowed down to a crawl. Mrs Leblanc was standing outside. I saw her through the window, where I had first spied on the Vallin Brothers. For a brief second I wondered how she had gotten here. She held a rifle of some sort. Behind her, I could make out someone else. Raymonde, a look of concern on her face. The smaller Vallin had slid to a stop, a metre from me. He was looking tense, ready for anything.

The bigger one, still holding the shotgun, was turning toward Mrs Leblanc.

In a moment of clarity, I knew that he would shoot her. There was no stopping it. The shotgun blast might kill both her and Raymonde. Even if Mrs Leblanc shot him, he would still shoot in reflex. They would all be killed.

I frantically launched myself at the big Vallin, propelling my body directly at his chest, both of my hands reaching for his shotgun. He was about two hundred centimetres tall and probably near a hundred and twenty kilos. A big man, much taller than me. I was overweight. I hoped that would be enough.

I slammed into him hard. My right hand managed to seize the barrel of the shotgun and I jerked it down fast. It discharged thunderously, blowing a hole into the floor. The big Vallin fell back hard, hitting his head on the corner of the fireplace mantle, knocking himself out cold. My ears buzzing, I rolled off him, wrenching the shotgun out of his limp hands and throwing it in a far corner.

I heard a noise, turning around to see the other Vallin moving again. Before he could do anything, another booming shot rang out and a dish rack exploded into smithereens.

"*Enough.* No more fighting. This has gone far enough," screamed Mrs Leblanc at the top of her lungs. The big Vallin was down on the ground, out for the count, and the small Vallin was cowering in fear in the corner.

"Incredible, my boy. Absolutely incredible," Briar said, the pride obvious in his voice. "I knew you had it in you. Always did."

***

We were sitting around the kitchen table. The big Vallin, named Ives, was lying on the couch, holding an ice-filled rag to the swelling on the back of his head. Jacques Vallin, the smaller one, was sitting at a kitchen chair, his hands tied behind his back. He appeared sullen and unhappy. Mrs Leblanc seemed to be holding up well. She had reserves of strength I had not suspected.

As soon as she had shot her rifle into the air, everyone had stopped fighting. Raymonde had run right in and hugged me, explaining in chopped sentences about her mother worrying, getting the rifle from over the mantelpiece and calling a taxi. Mrs Leblanc stayed exactly where she was, her rifle at the ready, until I found some rope and tied the protesting Jacques Vallin. Then I helped Ives Vallin onto the couch. He was slowly coming around from the glancing blow. Big as he was, he seemed rather gentle.

It was time to get down to business. Now that we had the Vallin Brothers where we wanted them, we would be able to get some answers.

"All right. It's apparent that everyone's upset. You two don't trust us and we don't trust you, perhaps because you followed us and shot at us, among other things. Earlier, you said that the rock cylinder belonged to you and to Etretat. I absolutely know that it was intended for us, not you. That tells me that you don't have a clue what we are doing and why we are doing it..." I began.

Jacques Vallin interrupted, speaking in a slightly remorseful tone.

"We didn't shoot at you... I mean we DID... but we didn't mean to. The truck was running so bad and had already overheated. We had just managed to get some water in the radiator when you took off. You had that fast sports car and you were going just fast enough to stay ahead, like you were taunting us or something. I felt pretty mad, knowing we were going to lose you and I pulled out the gun while I pushed the gas pedal to the floor. I never wanted to fire at you. I don't know what I was going to do, really. That was when the engine just plain blew. Popped a cylinder right through the block. The explosion scared the heck out of me. My finger tightened by reflex and the damn gun went off. By then, the truck was barely moving. We were coasting along without any power when you just took off like a rocket and went right over the side of the road. I had never seen anything like that before. You had to have nerves of steel, Mister. Anyway, I braked like mad, jumped out of the truck and ran right to the edge of the cliff to see if you were all right, Brother right behind me. We got there just in time to see you skim over the river and drive right up to the road, smooth as silk..." he jabbered, getting excited in the retelling.

I didn't remember it like that. It had been more like 'barely getting out alive' after 'losing control of the car'. His brother spoke up, interrupting Jacques.

"... Yeah, then you got out of the car and just waved at us, calm as can be. That took some guts, Mister..."

"... Hey, I was telling the story..." Jacques shot back.

"You never let me speak. Here I am, hurt, my head all busted up, and I can't even say a few words?" Ives retorted, apparently following a familiar refrain. Jacques was getting ready to throw back some other quip. I spoke before he did.

"So you didn't shoot at us on purpose. Fine! What about following us, all over the place?..." I asked.

"... Yes, all over the place, right into our bedroom, while we were sleeping, what about that?" interrupted an angry Raymonde, pointing her finger at the smaller of the two Vallin, her whole body invested in the gesture.

Jacques hung his head down in shame.

"I'm sorry, Miss. It's wasn't like that, really it wasn't, although I sure can't figure out how you knew exactly what I was doing, because you were sleeping all through... I went in, no idea what I was looking for, just looking around, real quiet like..." Raymonde's eyes flashed. Ives kept going, talking faster and more nervously, "It took me just a second to spot the rock thing on the other side of the bed. I figured that had to be something important. We didn't mean no harm. We just had to take it from you."

"Why?" I asked simply.

"Yes, why indeed? A key question my boy. There's more to this than meets the eye," Briar added in my ear. I had almost forgotten about my friends. The three were still rooted to their computers back home. They didn't even get commercial breaks for this show. For all their annoyance, I was glad that they had come along for the ride.

It was the big guy who answered.

"Because we had to. It was our duty to Father. We keep guard for Etretat."

"That's right, Brother, We keep guard for Etretat. When you came in to the Mairie for those records, Mister, you sure got me spooked. No one had asked for those papers, not in a real long time. I had to follow you to find out what you were up to. When I heard you talk about the fort of Frefosse, the next morning at breakfast, I knew you were right in the middle of it, because that's where our great-grandfather was killed. So we had to keep following you..." he explained.

I kept getting more confused. What they were saying made sense, when seen from their perspective. Were we that wrong about the Vallin Brothers? Perhaps this situation could be resolved more peaceably than I had originally thought.

"What if I told you that the things we are looking for, like that cylinder of rock, were hidden by my great-grandfather and by Raymonde's great-grandfather? We also know that your great-grandfather was involved with this mystery. Perhaps what you are doing, this 'keeping on guard for Etretat', is related to the same affair. Maybe, somehow, we could work together instead of fighting each other," I suggested, taking a chance.

Both of them mulled over my words.

"Maybe you're right, Mister. Maybe we are looking for the same thing," Ives said, sitting up and carefully holding his head.

"What is this duty you speak of? What is it you guard?" asked Raymonde.

Jacques looked sheepish, admitting with a slight smile:

"We sure don't know, Miss, and that's a fact. We know it's something big and it has to be kept secret. Our father gave us this duty and we intend to stand by it."

Ives was nodding his head in agreement.

"We've kept at it all these years, just like we promised. It's hard keeping a secret when you don't know what you're supposed to be keeping. We've been trying to figure things out but it's been pretty slow going... Say, you folks wouldn't be willing to untie Brother's hands, would you? I can see they're getting all blue. He won't do nothing. I'm the strong one but I won't do anything either."

Jacques' hands were indeed blue from lack of circulation. Raymonde untied his hands and he rubbed his wrists in relief for a few moments. This done, he grabbed a bottle of red wine from the kitchen counter and some glasses. While he poured, he talked.

"I just have to have a drink. Tonight has been too exciting, even for around these parts," he said. I had to agree with him. Mrs Leblanc did not accept any wine, looking a little tired. Raymonde and I each accepted a small glass.

"Somehow, this mystery is linked directly to all our families, even mine, far away in Canada. This secret was intended to be re-discovered by us for a reason. We don't know what that reason is yet... Perhaps it is lying there, inside that rock cylinder. I suggest that we join efforts. I will even offer you a salary, if you need it or want it. As a team, we can help each other. God knows we could use the help... Although I must warn you, in all conscience, that there is some danger to this. Others are trying to solve this mystery and they don't seem to mind killing people." I finished, hoping that I had said it properly. Raymonde placed her hand on my shoulder, letting me know she was right there with me. Mrs Leblanc did nothing, because she was sleeping, sitting upright in her chair. Perhaps it was time to finish up. Jacques Vallin answered my question.

"Mister, it's true that these ladies are Etretatais through-and-through. We don't know you but you seem to be a fair man, willing to give us a chance. We've been at this quite a while but we never got anywhere as far as you. Maybe you could do the thinking and we could do the helping..." he agreed. His brother interrupted him yet again.

"...Yeah, we're good with helping. We know everyone in these parts. If you need something, you tell us, and we'll get it. If I can ever find out what father was talking about all those years, it'll be the happiest day of my life... and Mister Sirenne, I want to say how sorry I am about the shotgun and what happened... Everything moved so fast, I didn't have a chance to think. I'm so glad you hit me and stopped me from shooting that nice old lady..."

He was honestly remorseful. I went over and offered my hand to him. He stood up slowly, wincing at the pain from his head. He reached his full height, literally towering over me. I couldn't believe I had knocked him down. He was huge. He smiled and held out his hand.

"Friends?" he asked.

"Friends!" I affirmed.

His powerful handshake left my hand numb. I did the same with Jacques, who completed our handshake by raising his hand to his chest, holding the outside fingers and his thumb out while folding in the two inner ones. He was immediately copied by his brother. It must have been a family gesture reserved for solemn occasions. He looked very serious when he spoke.

"I'll work with you, Mister. I know you'll keep the secret. And I'll be there to help, I swear. As for a salary, I wouldn't say no, money being a bit rare for Brother and me these days. "

Instead of enemies, we now had a stronger group working together. I had forgotten about O'Flanahan, who interrupted this eventful moment with his stubborn comment.

"Well, I don't swear an oath to keep quiet. Not a chance. No way. This conspiracy is the biggest thing since the Roswell UFO crash. There is no way I'm not going to publish a book about it, so there."

I would deal with him later. I reached up and turned off the glasses. Walking over to Mrs Leblanc, I gently shook her shoulder, waking her up.

"It's time to go home, Mrs Leblanc. Everything is sorted. We can sleep soundly in our beds tonight, thanks to you."

I asked the Vallin brothers to bring the rock cylinder to the Villa Leblanc the next day, when we would try to open it. They were surprised and pleased by my trust. Seeing their faces, I knew it had been the right thing to do. Raymonde helped her mother outside and Jacques ran up the road to get my Porsche. While we waited for Jacques' return, I held Raymonde's hand and looked at the stars. She whispered in my ear.

"You were so brave, saving my mother... and me, I guess... I can't believe you jumped that big Vallin... but you did and you saved us... and before that with Norton... You were there when it counted... I love you, Paul Sirenne."

Suddenly, the stars looked much brighter.

***

I was moving along at great speed. The sounds I heard around me were strange, muted.

I was dreaming again!

I opened my eyes to find myself underwater, slicing through it at great speed without any physical effort. Inexplicably, I found that I had no problem breathing. I saw fish darting away from me in the deepening waters. I kept going deeper until I could hardly see anything at all. Another type of sight took over. Everything became clearer without being brighter. I could see every rock sharply defined on the rapidly approaching sandy bottom. There was no ambient light. I didn't think I was using my eyes.

I veered at the last minute, following the seabed. Rock cliffs appeared on my left. I turned and went down a side canyon, then another one. The cliffs flew by at a rapid pace on both sides of me, closing in. There was a dead end in front of me. In a flash it was gone, replaced by a giant owl, his monstrous beak open. He was going to cut me in half if I didn't stop moving forward. I saw a yellowish light in his eyes, a light I had seen before. His beak kept getting closer and closer.

I woke up screaming, covered in sweat. Raymonde was shaking me, a concerned look on her face. I felt disoriented as the vivid, surrealistic dream faded away.

"What was that all about, Paul?

"It was a dream... A very strange dream..."

The strangeness of these lucid dreams kept haunting me. I could not refute that the first dream had been prophetic, presaging the moment when Raymonde and I entered that bunker. If this second dream was predicting the future in the same fashion, then I would soon be encountering a giant undersea owl with glowing eyes that would bite me to death.

I was not getting something.

Exhausted from the day and from the ordeal in my dream, I lay back down next to Raymonde and fell into a deep slumber.

***

Raymonde and I had breakfast in bed the next morning. We had decided to keep the dreams between us for the time being, not knowing exactly how to explain them. Mrs Leblanc had slept in, overwrought by the recent events. We were both worried about her. She had insisted that she was fine, or would be, once she'd had some rest.

Since the start we had been spinning theories. Some of them had begun to unravel. For example, we now knew that the Vallins brothers were not villains. Instead, they were somewhat like us, trying to discover their heritage.

If Old Man Vallin was a loyal Etretatais, just like his great-grandsons, eager to protect Tonnetot's 'Secret', then we had to re-evaluate his reasons for blowing up the fort of Frefosse. I had thought an enemy of Leblanc had paid Old Man Vallin to destroy it. Now I was not so sure. Of course, we couldn't forget that we would soon add the rock cylinder's content to our growing resources. Whatever it held had to be important enough to warrant the precautions taken to hide it in the first place.

We were up and showered by ten in the morning, heading down to the restaurant, my jet lag finally abated. Waking up next to Raymonde these past few days had begun to make me realize how difficult it would be to leave her side when I returned home to Canada. We had been acting and thinking almost as one since the beginning of this adventure and I could not imagine being apart from her.

From where I sat in the restaurant, I was able to see the two Vallins arrive in their beat-up old truck. I could hardly fail to notice that they had dressed in their Sunday best, trying to make a better impression. Ives Vallin was proudly carrying the rock cylinder. I activated my glasses, knowing that 'the team' would want a recording of this conversation. Coulter had anticipated our meeting and signed on immediately, despite the early hour for him.

Mrs Leblanc joined us in timely fashion while we shook the hands of the Vallins, each of us wearing a nervous smile, still uncomfortable about last night's events. I introduced both of them to Coulter, by letting them wear my glasses for a few moments. This display of technology seemed to impress them more than any other thing. They couldn't believe that I was connecting to someone in Canada, while we sat here in France.

After a serving of coffee for some and tea for others, we began discussing pertinent topics:

"Before we try to open that mysterious cylinder, I would very much like to hear about how you came to be doing this Duty of yours?" I asked.

Jacques Vallin, apparently getting the honours from his brother, started his explanation:

"I guess you know that our great-grandfather, Old Man Vallin, was murdered at the destroyed fort of Frefosse? Yes? Well, what you may not know is that, Jean Vallin, his son and our grandfather, found a gold coin in an old cigar box hidden under Old Man Vallin's mattress. Where did he get that coin? Who gave it to him? More importantly: were there more coins? There were few clues at the scene of the murder itself. Old Man Vallin had been beaten up real bad before he was thrown into the rocks to die. But he didn't die right away. No sir, our great-grandfather was tough. He managed to hang on long enough to leave us a sign. He placed his hand on his chest like this..." Jacques Vallin paused for a moment, lifting his hand to his chest and repeating the gesture that I had seen him do the night before. "... Which is our family's way of saying: 'we swear loyalty.' So we know that, in his last moments, it was important for him to show that he had stayed loyal to someone. We just didn't know who that someone might be. All we had was that gold coin..."

"... And the money, Brother, don't forget about the money..." Ives said.

Jacques gestured his brother to keep quiet.

"I wasn't going to forget about the money, I was just getting to it and you didn't give me the time... There was about a thousand francs in the cigar box, which back then was a lot. Several times after that, when we were in deep financial troubles, an envelope would appear in the mailbox, filled with money, always just enough to put us back on our feet..."

"How long did that go on?" I asked.

"Well, the last envelope came about 1938. This is all from what my father told me, you understand, so I'm not really sure about the details. But I am sure about the coin, because we still have it, although not with us today..." Jacques started.

"... Because we didn't know that you'd want to see it. Through thick and thin, we never sold it..." Ives finished. Jacques kept going, giving his brother a sidelong glance.

"Anyway, Grandfather and Old Man Vallin had never gotten along, mainly because Grandfather had always been greedy. Not as moral as us, he was..." Jacques explained.

"No Sir, not as moral," added Ives.

"... But he was very curious about the gold coin. He tried for a long time to discover where it had come from. At first, he asked around town but people around here had nothing to say about it. So he went further afield, finally going on a few trips to Paris. He made friends with a pawnbroker who had ears to the ground. One day, Grandfather received a note from that pawnbroker, telling him that someone had just sold more of those coins. Old coins they were, from the early twelve hundred's. Unfortunately, the description of the man who had sold the coins was too vague to help: a well dressed man, slightly taller than average, and a bit thin. That was it, nothing more. Over the years, more gold was sold but there was never enough information to figure out exactly who was doing the selling. It happened so infrequently that any plans to catch him were doomed to failure," Jacques paused to gulp some tea, regretting it because it was still too hot, and then, resumed speaking, this time more carefully as if his tongue were scalded.

"In 1934, something different happened. By then, Father was living on his own. Him and Grandfather didn't get along much either but they did share some interest in the gold coin, although not for the same reasons. Father really wanted to find out what had happened to Old Man Vallin, that was all. Grandfather was just greedy..."

"Tell them about 1937... You're getting sidetracked," Ives prodded.

"I will, Brother, enough already. In 1937, the Vallin family was having some serious bad times. Taxes were owing on the house again and Grandfather had done a few deals too many that had gone sour. One day, an envelope was waiting in the mailbox, nothing written on it, but with plenty of cash inside. In fact, there was enough to pay the back taxes and the bad debts that were outstanding, with about two hundred francs left over for some food and clothes. That money put the Vallins back on their feet. At the very same time, Grandfather got another note from the pawnbroker. Checking on the dates for everything, they confirmed that the gold had been sold about three days before the money was dropped in our mailbox. Of course, a lot more gold was sold than the money we got. Grandfather and Father were both convinced that the coins were connected to whoever was giving us the money... And that person had to be living around here, or at least keeping tabs on us, because otherwise, how would they know about what troubles we were in, to the exact franc?..."

His conclusions were valid. Whoever had helped them had a reason to do so. Could that reason be guilt over the death of Old Man Vallin? An act of retribution? It certainly seemed possible. Jacques went on with his fascinating story:

"Jean Vallin, Grandfather, never found out any more than that. It was Father who figured out the rest. He was smart our father..."

"Very smart, not like me..." added Ives.

"You're smart in your own ways, Brother. Look at what you can do with cars. It's like magic. Anyway, Father was the one who really put things together. It took him a long time though. When the Germans invaded France, he was mad through and through. He wanted to fight them but there was no way he was going to leave Etretat and go die in some God-forsaken trench like all the others. He stayed here and joined the Resistance. He ended up doing so much around here that people never forgot about him. Some even still nod to us, when we pass them on the street, just because we're his children..."

"... Not many of them do that nowadays but some still do, that's true enough..." confirmed Ives Vallin.

"... We weren't around yet, because he had us when he was in his sixties... Anyway, he took risks he might not have taken if he'd had family around, that's for sure. He loved Etretat and he wasn't going to do nothing and see it destroyed. He could always be found putting his nose in places where it didn't belong... We all knew the Old Man Vallin story about the accidental destruction of the fort was made up. The courts had swept it all under the rug rather quickly, giving Old Man Vallin a mere slap on the wrist... and nobody suffered from the blowing up of that fort... It spelled the beginning of the good years for Etretat. No Sir, all of Father's reasoning told him that someone in Etretat had *paid* Old Man Vallin to blow up the fort. Maybe paid the whole town to keep quiet. The question was who? If he could find that out, Father might get one step closer to figuring out who had killed Old Man Vallin. Unfortunately, if anyone knew, they weren't talking..."

Jacques' story was far more than fascinating. It was revelatory! When my friends and I had originally found out about the fort's destruction, we had always assumed that someone against Etretat had done it. Later, Hitler's appearance in our theories had provided a convenient contender for the position. Now we knew that a local Etretatais had ordered Old Man Vallin to blow it up. Its destruction had been meant as an act of protection, rather than one of destruction. If the fort led to the caves, someone around here had tried to prevent others from getting into them.

Jacques started talking again:

"During the war, Father kept his eyes sharp and his ears open. He managed to figure out some pretty interesting things. He told us about the Ghost Germans..." he explained.

"Yeah, the Ghost Germans. I really like this part, go on, Brother, tell them..." Ives added, getting excited.

"Father became aware that, hidden somewhere in Etretat, there was an entire platoon of Germans. You never really saw them, you never talked to them but they were there. He was sure that their leader was someone called Weissmuller. Bequilles, his good friend, told him that. The Ghost Germans were bringing in trucks filled with things, almost every night. Father managed to figure out that they were unloading most of those trucks on top of the Aval cliff, right into the bunker which was built over the ancient location of the Fort of Frefosse. There were always a lot of guards around that bunker and it was absolutely impossible to get anywhere near it. There had to be a secret entrance to some underground lair under that bunker. There was not enough room for them to keep bringing things into that bunker and never bring anything out! When Father finally managed to get into it, right after the Germans had left, he found a freshly poured concrete floor, with all traces of hidden entrances completely gone. The Ghost Germans vanished after that, as if they had never been.

"When Father told his superiors about the tunnels, Tonnetot, the deputy mayor was there. From what Father said, the temperature dropped in the room as soon as he mentioned the word 'tunnels'. It was as if no one wanted to hear about it. Tonnetot wasted no time in ordering Father to shut up. Tonnetot told him that the tunnels were part of a big secret, one that had to be kept quiet. He said there was a group of people in Etretat who had the task of keeping an eye out on things, calling them 'The Net', led by Raymond Lindon. When Father asked what the secret was, he was told that very few people knew exactly what it was. It was safer that way. Tonnetot did tell him he was sure that when Old Man Vallin had blown up the fort, he had acted out of loyalty to Etretat and to the Net. He had faced the consequences silently and willingly and had been killed by an unknown enemy trying to steal the Secret. So Father got the answers he had sought and found himself a new purpose in life: to keep a watchful eye on Etretat and to keep the Secret safe. When we were old enough, he swore us to secrecy and told us about the Net, giving us the same task. Unfortunately, it was not enough for us. We still wanted to know who had killed Old Man Vallin," Jacques finished.

We had learned something new: at some point in the past, around Leblanc's time, there had been a secret organisation, 'The Net', who had the task of keeping the caves safe. Of even more relevance, we had just learned that Raymond Lindon was its leader. O'Flanahan and Briar chose this moment to connect up. I gave them a brief rundown of the latest news.

"Absolutely phenomenal, my boy. I cannot believe how much you have learned in such a short time. Unfortunately, I have some rather disturbing news for you, Paul. Are you sitting down?" asked Briar, with an odd tone in his voice.

"Yes, I am. What's up, Jonathan?" I asked.

"Perhaps you could put this on speaker, so that everyone may hear at the same time. It's too shocking to say it more than once. I can hardly believe it myself," Briar added.

Opening my laptop, I connected the audio feed coming from Briar to the speakers. Briar's voice came on, sounding a bit tinny, with occasional noises in the background, maybe cars, his face close to his laptop's built-in monitor. On both sides of his image, I saw displays of my other two friends, sitting in their respective homes.

"Paul, I'm sorry to be so mysterious but I think that we have reached a turning point. We have managed to confirm that this is no wild goose chase. However, we were still left with one massive question, perhaps the most important one: what was the link between your two families, the Sirennes in Canada and the Leblancs in France? We knew there was a connection but we were unable to pinpoint exactly what it was. Well, I have figured it out…"

"Come on, Briar, stop patting yourself on the back and just tell us…" interrupted O'Flanahan.

Ignoring him, Briar continued:

"When you found that copy of the Hollow Needle in Leblanc's library, you gave me the clue we needed, Paul. The note hidden in the back cover of that book held a message for Leblanc's son. The note in your book also held a note, this one intended for you. My attention was attracted by the Post-Scriptum in both notes because they were almost identical. Your note said:

> *A real story ends near Etretat,*
> *Lost until Paul infers new ideas subtly.*
> *You ought understand responsibility,*
> *Necessarily after moiling Etretat,*
> > *Your father,*
> > *Paul Sirenne.*

In Leblanc's copy, it said:

> *A real story ends near Etretat,*
> *Lost until Patrice infers new ideas subtly*
> > *Your friend*
> > *Paul Sirenne"*

"The Post-Scriptum in each note differed subtly from the other. Your father's PS had the extra two lines about responsibility and said 'Your father' instead of 'Your friend' in Leblanc's copy. Also, the name Paul was substituted for Patrice. My question was: why was it different?"

I remembered reading those lines. It seemed as if it had happened ages ago.

"Something about the wording seemed… awkward. We had come across the same type of awkward wording before…" continued Briar. Raymonde, catching on to what Briar was implying, interrupted:

"... When we were in Perpignan, in Grand-Papa's last apartment, the scratched words on the wall..." she recollected.

"Quite right my dear, the scratched words on the wall. The words in Leblanc's latest note were just as awkward. So I asked myself if, possibly, they could also hold a code? If you remember, breaking the code of the first one gave us the name Raymond Lindon. Why don't you try and figure out what this code gives us."

I began assembling the message by collecting the first letter of each word the way we had done before. I couldn't believe what I decoded, couldn't accept it:

"*ARSENE LUPIN IS YOUR NAME.* What is that saying? That my great-grandfather was Arsene Lupin?... It can't be, Lupin is not even real..." I argued, amidst the excited voices of my friends.

"I thought the same thing, my boy. However, if you were to examine your own name, the one that your family ensured you kept through all these generations, you will discover that it is an exact anagram of Arsene Lupin. The letters that make up the name Arsene Lupin are the same letters that make up your name. Arsene Lupin used this trick repeatedly in Leblanc's stories. While I cannot explain it, you are apparently the descendant of Arsene Lupin, a fictitious character created by Leblanc, a character who has just become very real indeed!" he finished.

"This is too much, Briar," exclaimed O'Flanahan. "How could a fictitious character be Paul's ancestor?"

"There is only one possible answer to that. Arsene Lupin must be real," reasoned Briar.

"Hold on there..." I objected. "There is no way that those stories about Lupin are real."

Raymonde looked at me in sympathy while Briar answered me.

"You are correct, of course, Paul. Total invention, exactly like the Hollow Needle story, right? That does not mean that Arsene Lupin himself cannot have been a real person. I have read a few articles regarding this topic. It seems that some people have long thought that Lupin was based on a real person. Many names were examined, like Marius Jacob, for example. None was ever determined to be a perfect match. It is likely that the real Lupin is not exactly like the fictional one..."

"Gee, that should make him really easy to find," noted O'Flanahan, a tinge of sarcasm tainting his voice.

"... And let's not forget that Raymond Lindon wrote the book: 'The Secret of the Kings of France, or the Real Identity of Arsene Lupin'. Lindon obviously thought Lupin was real..." Coulter added.

Briar added another point:

"Paul, this investigation has uncovered far more than we expected and it is hitting very close to home, I'm afraid. We have not even opened the rock cylinder yet. Who knows what further revelations it may contain? If we were to stop now, we would avoid further discoveries that might be too painful for you to deal with..."

"I appreciate your concerned words but I can no more stop this than I can stop breathing. True, I am shocked by what our efforts have uncovered. However, we cannot forget that these clues were hidden, not to be lost forever but to be re-discovered when the time was right. Our ancestors spent a great amount of effort preparing this and I am sure they did it for what they felt were valid reasons. I cannot turn away, no matters my fears or concerns. The Great Hunt will continue to its inevitable end, whatever it may be," I stated, my voice trembling slightly.

"Well said, Paul," Coulter added.

"You have voiced what I felt in my heart, Paul. I am so glad to hear you say it, to know that you feel as I do..." Raymonde added, holding my hand tightly in hers, enhancing the growing bond between us. However, certain implications of the sentence 'Arsene Lupin is your name' had left me shaken to my core.

"This revelation is attempting to rewrite my very identity and I feel impelled to repudiate it... It makes me question who I am, by revealing that my ancestor was someone else than I had thought. I am not different. I am not that man from long ago, a Lupin, if he even exists. I am Paul Sirenne. That is my name. Perhaps they used this trick to convince me I was truly involved. The letters of my great-grandfather's name may have been an anagram of Arsene Lupin but I am not that man. I never was and I never will be."

Mrs Leblanc moved closer to me and gave me a light hug in sympathy.

"Of course you're not, Paul. We know that. At least now you know you're not related to the Leblanc family, which would not have been good, considering your affection for my daughter."

She had a point.

Her levity steadied me a bit and I calmed down.

"Well, if you're done spouting all about these grandiose issues, why don't you stop talking, pick up that cylinder and open it so we can get on with it!" O'Flanahan blasted impatiently.

Ives got up, lifting the cylinder and cradling it in his massive arms.

"Where should I put it?" he asked.

We certainly could not work in the restaurant. I suggested that we head out into the garden, where we could set up a table to work in the fresh air and in relative privacy.

***

Mrs Leblanc had draped a thick cloth over a folding card table obtained from the Villa Leblanc's basement. Ives Vallin carefully placed the cylinder in the centre of the small table, next to my laptop computer. Everyone was looking at the thick stone tube, trying to figure out how to open it.

Coulter started explaining his progress:

"I've had a bit of time to look at the pictures of the cylinder. I enhanced each image of the object and I believe that it is indeed hollow. One notable characteristic along the shaft is a single thin line carved around its centre. The cylinder itself is made of two separate pieces of stone expertly fitted together. Here, at this end, opposite the snake carving, you can see a stone plug in the centre. What still escapes me is the method used to insert and secure this plug..."

"Why don't you just admit you don't know how to open it, Coulter..." said O'Flanahan.

"Wait, wait, I have an idea. Are the plug and the cylinder made of the same type of stone?" Briar asked.

I examined the cylinder end, using the magnifying power of my glasses to zoom in on the rock itself. When enlarged, it was apparent that they were made of different stone. Briar grew excited:

"Yes, I think I'm right. That plug looks like it is made of slate. The cylinder seems to be made of basaltic granite. If we heated..." Briar was interrupted by Ives Vallin, who was jumping up and down in glee, a big smile on his face:

"I have an idea too, I have an idea. I can't believe it but I have one. A good one, for once, Brother, can I try it, please can I?" he jabbered on, hopping from foot to foot in impatience. Most of us were sitting back in surprise at Ives' display of exuberance and I, for one, had trouble stopping a smile from appearing on my face. Jacques answered his brother seriously, looking slightly stern, almost as a father would look.

"I don't know, Brother, It's not my decision to make. You should ask Mr Sirenne."

The big Vallin turned his imploring face towards me and removed his beret. He held it in his hands, which he clasped together in supplication.

"Mr Sirenne, I just need a little thing from the truck. It'll only take a minute, can I go get it? I know it'll work, I just know it."

I could not refuse him. I nodded my assent and he took off running. No sooner was he gone that Briar re-asserted himself, trying to explain his idea:

"Gentlemen, just a moment, let's not be too hasty. I believe I truly have it. The plug is made of slate. If heated, slate will fragment and crack whereas basaltic granite will not. You could place the plug over a controlled source of heat, like a propane torch or some such device. The plug should eventually crack into smaller and smaller pieces. That would..."

"Briar, your idea is completely ridiculous. There's a journal in there, made of old, dry paper. Wouldn't all that heat burn the journal along with the plug? Seems like a bad idea to me," O'Flanahan argued. Before Briar could voice a single objection, Ives Vallin returned, breathing hard, his hair wildly out of place from his race to the truck. Without consulting a single one of us, he reached out with his left hand, lifted the stone cylinder and overturned it in one single powerful move, laying it down on its side. Jacques, knowing his brother's moods, tried asking a question but Ives beat him to the punch:

"Watch this!" he exclaimed.

Before we could stop him, he lifted a long-handled five-kilo hammer up into the air with his right hand, handling it as if it were a toothpick. I heard Mrs Leblanc's sharp intake of a breath when she realised what he was going to do. Briar screamed in my ear:

"Wait, stop, we can burn..."

He was too late. Ives Vallin was past the point of listening.

I barely had time to grab the laptop, looking on in helpless amazement as the hammer came down with incredible speed, smashing the cylinder right in the middle, a perfect hit! The poor card table used to support the cylinder was simply not able to deal with this massive blow and collapsed in two, crashing to the ground and taking the cylinder with it.

Each of us sat there, stunned, the dust settling from the tremendous impact. Jacques Vallin was the first to recover, jumping up in rage and smacking his brother on the head while at the top of one of his jumps, completely forgetting about his brother's previous head injury. Ives clasped his head in pain while Jacques screamed at him.

"You idiot. I keep telling you... Wait until we've talked about things before acting, Brother, you have to wait..."

"No, Hold on there, Jacques, you're being unfair. Look at the cylinder..." Raymonde said.

There, in the wreck of the card table, lay the cylinder, broken into two equal pieces, an ancient sheaf of papers, wrapped in oilcloth, spilling out of it. Ives' face broke into a wide smile and he exclaimed:

"See, See, Brother, I was right after all..."

Setting the laptop down on an empty chair, I walked over to Ives and gave him a light slap on the back.

"Good job, Ives, good job!"

He beamed at me, overjoyed. I bent down and gently pulled the sheaf of papers from the hollow chamber inside the broken cylinder. It was roughly rolled up, tied with rotting string. Opening it carefully, I revealed a neat, clean handwriting.

Leblanc's Journal!

***

Another round of coffee and tea had been served. Ives had the chance to explain what had motivated him to do what he did. He spoke slowly, trying to say it properly.

"It was the shape, that's what it was. When Brother was speaking, I was looking at the cylinder again and it made me think of a spool. It looked thick at both ends and thinner along the middle. My eyes were drawn to the middle of the cylinder. It was even narrower there, with a neat line circling the whole cylinder. I thought to myself that if I was to hit it in the middle with my best hammer, it should crack right along that line. It almost looked like it was made to crack there."

It seemed obvious in hindsight. The cylinder had been meant to be broken. We had over-complicated the whole thing, especially Briar. His explanation finished, Ives contented himself by eating several cookies and drinking the rest of his tea. There was a slight tension in the air, everyone wondering what we should do next.

"Well, it hardly seems possible but the thing we set out to find is finally in front of us: Leblanc's journal. Who knows what it will tell us. If you are willing, I will read his journal out loud. Let's discover what he wanted us to learn."

Matt Chatelain

MY FINAL STORY

By Maurice Leblanc

Patrice:

I have just left my beloved Etretat. All its wonders and its secrets, gone, just like that. I am sure I will never see it again. This is a one way trip. Always has been, I would venture to say. Somehow, I think that my trip has been somewhat more adventurous than most. Overall, I would have preferred a calmer life.

I can only hope that, when this horrendous burden is finally exposed, my peers will judge me more favourably than I have judged myself. By this point in time, I have done everything I can, everything in my power, to put things right. I probably will never know if my trap will work, if the monster will fall for so vain a ploy but I must believe in its success. The alternative is unthinkable.

I am writing this journal, this confession, my son, hoping that, by presenting my view, by telling you how events unfolded, I can finally explain my shortcomings through these meagre words. Normally a story like this would start at the beginning but for you to have found this text, certain things must already be known. Therefore, the starting point of my adventure has to be the day when I received the letter. If you will allow me, I will relate to you the events, which have led me, step by step, to this very moment, forced to run away from my beloved home in fear and desperation.

ERGO

The Letter and the Man Who Wrote It.

The letter was in German, which was intriguing, because the author, Hister, had to know that I was not fluent in German, making the letter an arrogant act. By pure coincidence, I had recently finished working with Germany to publish my latest novel. As a result, I had become acquainted with the language sufficiently to translate the letter.

He wanted to meet in order to discuss certain things about my book, The Hollow Needle. His letter stated that he had found archaeological evidence telling him there was something more to my novel than the fiction I had presented. Many are the times that I have cursed myself for writing that story. If I had known, back then, the truth behind Etretat's legends, I would never have drawn attention to it in so obvious a fashion. In my defence, what I had done in The Hollow Needle was the exact same process I used in my previous book and all the others since. No other person had ever noticed what I built into the stories.

Hister was the only one.

However, for the letter to arrive at the exact time when my own research was finally giving me some results, now that was a wonder. It was this coincidence which drove me to reply, to send him a letter, not to accept his query but to refuse it, which I did in no uncertain terms, given the rudimentary grasp I had of his language.

He must have felt that my negative response was too strong, that I was hiding something. It is the only possibility I can see which would explain why he came after I sent my refusal. Up to this point I had pursued my research in absolute secrecy, hiding my activities with feigned illness. While people thought I was convalescing in bed, I was wandering through the hillsides, in search of the secret Cochet had alluded to.

I only met the priest Cochet once. What a meeting it was. There was no mistaking our similar minds, the connection immediate. I was very young, full of energy, feeling like the world was mine to seize. He was an older, more introspective man. The wisdom of those years had enabled his search for the hidden Jewel in Etretat, the tunnels. I had previously known about them but had not realised their true significance. We discussed the excavations and his discoveries, in particular the ones he kept hidden from everybody. He knew that his time was limited on this earthly plane and he desperately needed a successor to carry on his search, someone equal to the task, capable of life-long secrecy. His friends, Monseigneur Billard, Father Gelis and Father Boudet each suggested to me that this research was not a waste of time. Rather the opposite, in fact.

That meeting, so long ago, seeded a purpose in me. It kept growing until it blossomed into an obsession. Eventually, I convinced myself to write a fictional story around it and, in my folly, included the Fort of Frefosse. After long reflection, I have realised that it was inevitable that it be mentioned but, by attracting attention to it, I had put in motion events that soon would involve the entire world.

For it was the fort that was the key, of this I was certain.

I had recently gone visiting the Royal Library to examine ancient documents concerning the Fort of Frefosse. It was there that I found the plans for the fort, presented to Francis the First by Guillaume Bude. It was there that I saw the original overview of the dungeon, that I understood the geometric symbols on the walls. I drew them on the plan, circle, rectangle, triangle. So simple.

On the crux of my discovery, I made the decision to hide this drawing. I could not bring myself to destroy it, so placed it in a file full of similar architectural drawings, hiding it in plain sight, my favourite trick. I returned home in exultation, to be confronted by Johann Hister's letter, threatening to expose everything I had worked so long to find.

That was my state of mind when I sent my response. Due to my strong emotions, I wrote quickly, reacting harshly, instead of using the usual caution and care. That was my mistake and I admit it here freely, Patrice. There is no denying it. Because, he came:

He arrived, one early morning while I was measuring the fort from the outside, calculating its original size to discover the exact position of the dungeon. A noise startled me. I turned to find a young man looking at me. Although being slight physically, he exuded an arrogant confidence. I felt instantly repelled by him.

Nodding perfunctorily to the stranger, I started walking away, acting like I was done with my work and leaving. He stopped me with a sudden hand gesture and spoke haltingly, in badly accented French:

"I am Johann Hister. Sorry to have come. But must talk."

The intensity in his eyes was one I had not seen in a long time, not since I had met Cochet. Unlike Cochet, I distrusted this Johann Hister. His being here at this specific time made me distinctly uncomfortable. I had kept my own counsel to that point and still believed that was my best, and only, course of action. I reacted angrily, screaming, gesturing at him to leave. He tried to talk again. I remained obstinate, ignoring his attempts. He grew red-faced, letting go a jet of injurious German insults. In his outburst, I saw a gleam of such cold hatred, such malevolence, that I felt afraid that he would do me physical harm. I braced myself for such an assault but it never came. Instead, he calmed himself and left without another word, glaring at me until he turned away. I stopped my work for the day and returned home.

I had been unnerved by the timing of Hister's appearance because I now was convinced that I had found the entranceway of the cave, if cave there was! It was in the dungeon, of this I was positive. Not in the dungeon of today, however. That one was nothing but a converted wine cellar, yet another false trail. My research had determined that the real dungeon was no longer accessible from the fort, its entrance having been bricked up long ago.

There was an exterior door accessing the servant's quarters from the courtyard. This door led to an extremely curious feature: a sudden turn in the corridor, the purpose of which was not evident from the building's architecture. A closer examination had revealed that expert brickwork had been done at this turning point in the corridor.

I was convinced that this was the lost access way to the ancient dungeon. Ignoring my concerns about Johann Hister, I returned the next day with some tools, determined to get out of sight before prying eyes could notice my presence. Earlier that year, I had rented the fort through a third party, an expensive thing to do at the time but necessary to keep things quiet.

A pickaxe served me well to remove the bricks. Within four hours, I broke through the thick wall and flashed my lantern through the hole, seeing a long dusty hallway. I redoubled my energy and soon cleared a hole big enough to crawl through to the other side. Carrying a small shovel, my lantern, and a spare candle in my back pocket, I headed along the dark, echoing hallway.

It was utterly devoid of any feature, solidly built of large stone blocks. Dust caked the floor, making me cough. I walked slowly along the corridor. I saw an oddly-shaped doorway on my right. It led to an ascending staircase, extremely narrow, its upper landing lost in the darkness. Its odd, oblique construction implied that it was a secret passage, probably leading to a camouflaged entrance in some room upstairs. An alternate access point might explain the bricked-up corridor. Someone had wanted to hide the dungeon access while retaining a way in.

Returning to the corridor, I continued my way to the end, where I found a slightly curving, descending staircase, much older than the other one. Its steps, carved from the bedrock, were deeply worn. Descending past the foundations of the fort, I saw various rock strata in the ceiling above my head, with a layer of crumbly stone in the centre. Rock dust littered the floor, evidence of continuing disintegration. SUM

Reaching the bottom of the staircase, I entered a round room. There was little evidence of it ever being a dungeon. More of a storeroom, perhaps. It was large and circular, ten metres in diameter, with five columns supporting the vaulted ceiling. The columns dissected the room, placed like the five points of a star.

Using the small shovel as a broom, I carefully swept the dust into a corner. Standing back, I examined the columns, looking for the geometric symbols. I saw the circle first, carved at head height in the column to the left of the entrance. The one opposite that, to the right of the entrance, bore a rectangle. Bringing my eyes back to the left again, I saw a triangle on the next column. Exactly as anticipated.

The final two columns had geometric designs, instead of simple symbols. One had a rectangle lying down inside a triangle. The last column, opposite the dungeon's entrance, had three triangles next to each other, the middle one slightly elevated above the other two. It was a code.

Solving the Riddle

The original Roman fort had once been much bigger and heavily fortified. During the Francis years, its shape had been refined, due to Francis' burgeoning interest in architecture. At the time, the fort's original location had seemed to be a most curious choice. I had gone to Rome to search for documents concerning this, which had led me to the crypts of the Vatican itself. Through special dispensation, I was allowed to peruse ancient Roman letters and Documents. I found a document in which approval for a fort was being requested. This letter was from a *legatus legionis* named Manius Stertinius Gallicus, the man in charge of the local garrison. Using this information as a starting point, I came to believe that another element had been involved: smugglers!

While exploring the town of Etretat, I had come across a corner stone on one of the oldest buildings, which was obtained from the fort after a change in its layout. To my surprise and great interest, I had noticed three geometrical shapes roughly carved into the stone. A circle with a rectangle and triangle inside. To the untrained eye, it looked like a childish drawing of a house.

However, previous research had convinced me that this had been a smuggler's sign. Located at the Fort of Frefosse, it had shown the way to the secret entrance of a smuggler's lair unlike any other in history. At long last, I had a theory that made sense. In addition, through Cochet, I knew that secret tunnels ran through the cliffs. What more proof did I need?

Returning my attention to the columns, I played with possible combinations of the geometrical shapes, hoping to find a way to unlock the hidden doorway I felt had to be there. Visualizing the three basic shapes, I tried to fit them into this room. The circle was easy, because the room itself was circular. I noticed that the columns were oddly positioned, not equidistant from each other. Perhaps they had some other, less obvious purpose.

Connecting four of the columns with straight, imaginary lines, I visualised a simple rectangle. I mentally added a triangle above the rectangle, with the fifth column as its top point, exactly the design I had seen carved on the corner stone. The resulting triangle, short and long, outlined an area on the floor.

This was exactly the same triangle shape as the one on the fourth column. Visualizing a smaller rectangle inside the triangle, I realised that this would create three smaller triangles, with one above the other two, the same design shown on the fifth column. Looking closer at the dungeon floor, I saw thin lines duplicating this design, unnoticed before, hidden in the complex tile patterns. That was the clue I needed. I rolled a large heavy barrel onto the triangle to my right and stood on the left one.

There was an audible 'CLICK' the moment my weight pressed down on the second triangle. I noticed that the fifth column had moved *into* the wall. Reaching out, I pushed on it. It swung in, smoothly and silently. It was not a column; it was a door! Lupin would have been proud of me. My excitement could not have been more intense. After all these years, I had finally found the entrance to the caves beneath the fort of Frefosse.

I heard an odd sound behind me, something like a choked cough. Covering my lantern, I stood still in the dark, listening for the slightest noise. After several minutes of total silence, I relaxed my vigilance and walked through the doorway now revealed in front of me. Another curving staircase met my eyes. I descended, my footsteps echoing hollowly around me. I soon reached bottom, a natural stone landing. Raising the lantern, I illuminated a large chamber in front of me, with openings in the distance, leading to other caves. I noticed a clutter of broken amphorae in one corner. Further to my right, a long hallway headed off into the darkness. I wandered along this impressive corridor for about ten metres when a bright gleam caught my eye, a reflection of light from something in a dark patch on the right side.

I quickly ascertained that I was looking at a narrow opening in the wall. Squeezing in, I found myself in a small room, about three metres square. There was a crack in the far wall of the cave. The bright gleam had come from there. I walked over to it but stopped when I heard a noise behind me. Turning my head,

I saw something indistinct heading towards me. I managed to dodge the oncoming object slightly but received a staggering blow nonetheless. I fell to the ground hard, a cloud of dust all around me, my eyesight fading in and out, barely able to comprehend what was happening.

Although everything was a blur and fading fast, I recognised Hister's slight silhouette in the light cast by my lantern, holding my shovel high in the air over his head. His illuminated face held a terrible rictus of hatred. He hit me again, after which, I knew no more!

The Treachery of Johann Hister

I woke in the dark. My head was pounding terribly and I was choking from the thick dust. Dazed as I was, I knew that I had been the victim of foul play. Hister had hit me from behind. Judging by the feel of the large gash on my head, he had probably thought me dead or dying. I certainly felt near death. The air was stuffy and hot, lacking oxygen.

I could see nothing around me. I felt around for the lantern but found nothing. Growing panicky, I hyperventilated briefly until I remembered the spare candle I had stuffed in my back pocket. Finding it, I fished around my jacket pocket for the small packet of matches I always kept there.

I felt such thankfulness for that small spark of flame that it could hardly be believed. I quickly put it to the wick of the candle and light sprang forth, although not as brightly as I had hoped, lacking sufficient air for a proper flame. I noted right away that the crack in the wall, the crack with the bright gleam from before, was now a large gaping hole. I could see a stone recess. It had been hidden in the wall by a cleverly applied coat of painted plaster on a fitted wooden frame. Over the centuries, the plaster had dried out, falling away in places, revealing the natural recess behind it. Something had been hidden in it.

It was now gone, surely stolen by that murderous Hister. Looking at the recess more closely, I found a small sack in the deepest part of the narrow shelf. Pulling it out, the rotten cloth ripped, spilling out a handful of gold coins. I had been fooled by a thief and nearly killed.

With a sigh and a groan, I stood up and walked unsteadily out of the small chamber I was in, my legs feeling like bars of Indian rubber. I headed back toward the entrance staircase, breathing heavily in the stuffy air, protecting the tiny, naked candle flame with my hand. I reached the column door quickly but found it closed. No matter the amount of pulling and prodding, I simply could not get it open again. If I were to get out, this would not be the way. Feeling desperate, I returned to the great cave below.

I knew my candle would not last forever and I had no other. My pounding head and a weak feeling in my limbs told me that I had other things to worry about. Looking around, I saw several openings into a maze of other caverns. I realised how easy it would be to get lost in here. Looking at the ground, I found a white rock. Scratching on the wall with it left a white mark, providing me with a method to mark my passage.

I entered the first cave to my left but left it right away, as it had no other exits. I saw rotting bags on the ground, spilling ancient grain. I saw items laying about, a small casket, wine bottles, rum, statues. None of it meant anything to me. All I could think of was freedom. How quickly my opinion had changed. For my entire life, I had yearned to find this place. Now my every thought was to leave.

I heard the sound of water on my right and could smell it, salty and damp, giving me hope that a way to the channel could be found. I followed the smell, noting that the floor was worn by the passage of countless feet. The size of the cave complex was incredible. Each cave seemed to have its own treasures to reveal. After a long way down, I arrived at an underground lake. The brackish water suggested that it might have an opening to the channel, although I could not see one. Feeling increasingly unwell, I staggered back the way I came. I noticed that the worn steps in the ground forked into two separate trails. Choosing the left one, I found myself in a round tunnel lined with ancient bricks.

It was too late to turn back; I had to go this way. It was my only chance. My senses were fading in and out. I found myself walking through water, then wading through it. My candle was growing dim and I was feeling dizzy, having to rest every few steps. I arrived at a dead end and I truly despaired. Refusing to accept defeat, I kept going, pushing myself beyond my limits.

I finally noticed on the left, a narrow tunnel hidden in the shadows. I could barely fit in it. I walked to its end finding a stone doorway. Large stone pins held it in place. I could see a bar sticking out from the wall next to the stone door. Playing with the bar with my waning strength, I was able to push it upwards. The door opened outwards and I slid myself through its narrow opening.

I knew where I was: this was one of the cliff tunnels mentioned by Cochet, located under the Amont Cliff. I could make out a faint dot of light at its end. The timing could not be better because both my candle and I were on our last legs. Unfortunately, my tribulations were not over. When I arrived at the end, I found myself about seven metres in the air. The cliff had eroded away, removing the last few metres of tunnel. There was no choice but to hang down and let myself fall.

I fell badly, twisting my ankle and knocking myself out on the rocks below. When I came to, I was in the house of Old Man Vallin.

By writing down these words, I have reminded myself of the turmoil of those times, so long ago. The intervening years had softened the impact of those events. I have tried so much to understand if I made the right choices back then. While I cannot fault any specific decision I made, it seemed to all go astray, no matter what I did. Painful as it may be to retrace my footsteps, I must continue, for this was just the beginning. My adventures were far from over.

An Unexpected Friendship

I was lying on a cot, when I woke up, covered by an old smelly blanket. There was something covering the left side of my head. It felt tightly wrapped and my head was throbbing. My ordeal suddenly came back into awareness. I sat up on the bed and a strong wave of dizziness hit me. I felt a hand on my shoulder, steadying me, and, in that way, became aware that I was not alone in the room.

Sitting in a tattered chair next to the cot, was an old man, his face wrinkled and covered with a three-day-old beard. I smelled the sour odour of whisky coming from him. When his face broke into a concerned smile, I understood that he meant me no harm. He explained that he had been combing the beach, looking for odds and ends, when I had fallen onto the rocks about sixty metres away from him. Recognising me, he had dragged me to his cart and placed me in the back, covering me with a few potato sacks to keep me warm. He brought me back to his home and tended to my wounds. I had been unconscious for more than a day.

While I rested, he told me about himself. He admitted being a poacher but he was still a proud man with strong morals having fallen on hard times. I asked him why he had not simply returned me home. He replied that he had seen me often, sneaking about the hills and cliffs of Etretat, when common talk said I was supposedly sick at home. Suspecting I wanted to keep my activities under wraps, he had kept my accident quiet. It took me another day of resting before I was able to summon enough strength to return home. I had rented the usual villa and I was sure that my wife would be worried about my unexplained absence.

Surprisingly, during these few days of rest, a strong friendship had been forged between Old Man Vallin and I. It was as unlikely a friendship as it was timely.

I had shared my discovery with him, knowing instinctively that he could be trusted. I desperately needed a friend and help in dealing with this terrible turn of events. I had discovered the secret of Etretat only to inadvertently reveal it to a thief and would-be murderer, Johann Hister. He had already plundered some of the cave's treasures and I was convinced that he would come back for more, particularly since he thought me dead.

The more time passed, the more I grew concerned about the implications of my discovery. This cave held incredible treasures, many of them historical in nature. It belonged to the whole country. Premature release of its discovery would attract treasure hunters of the worst sort. I need only refer to Hister for proof of this assertion. Whatever the caves contained would vanish in the night. France would be robbed of its heritage before it even learned of it.

Hister had planned to assault me long before I had entered the cave. He had followed me, waiting for the best moment to catch me unaware. Luckily, his vicious blows had not killed me. However, my personal fate paled into insignificance when compared to the fact that a murderous thief now knew the way into the caves.

It was my responsibility, my duty, to right this wrong. Old Man Vallin understood my feelings exactly and swore to help me. I arranged to meet him in a few days in order to return to the fort. In the meantime, Vallin contacted some of his friends, those that could be trusted, to keep an eye out for any suspicious strangers about town. If Hister were still in the area, he would be found and dealt with.

Vallin arrived at the fort, a shotgun cradled in his arms. He considered the situation as serious as I did. Walking into the servant's corridor, I found all evidence of my previous presence completely erased. The wall had been rebuilt; there was no sign of the wheelbarrow or of my tools. Hister had taken his time before vanishing into the night. He must have thought me truly dead.

We broke through the wall easily since I knew exactly where to hit. Soon after, Old Man Vallin and I arrived in the dungeon. To my relief, the column opened as before. With the stronger light from the miner's hat, it was easy to see why I had been unable to open the door when stuck inside the caves. I had been looking in the wrong place. The lack of light from my candle had prevented me from noticing the long rods of stone above the doorway that were used as locks.

I have long felt foolish for having been so close to the way out, yet not finding it. Of course, had I done so, it is likely that I would have encountered Hister bricking the wall back up. In my weakened state, I would not have stood a chance against him.

We noticed an inexplicable slight glowing of the walls when a small draft of fresh air entered into the sealed room but it faded when we closed the door behind us. I was not sure what to think of the phenomena. It was a transient one and we had other things on our minds.

Without a word, we went down the curving staircase, reaching the main chamber and headed into the impressive long hallway. Entering into the small chamber again, I found my shovel on the ground, noting a dark stain on its edge. There was a large pool of drying blood on the ground... my blood... It had been a close thing for me.

Leaving the chamber, we saw paintings on the wall, high up and to the left side. They were magnificent prehistoric drawings of animals, with groups of hunters dancing around them. We saw evidence of ancient fires in another corner, surrounded by piles of flint flakes.

Everywhere I looked, I saw evidence of Roman presence. There were column supports that shored up weaker parts of the cave roof. I saw niches, carved at regular intervals into the tunnel walls, which must have held skeletons at some point. Stone block stairs had been installed in many areas where the cave floor fell away too sharply.

It seemed to me, from the geological features of the cave, that water had been the engineer of this complex. However, the sheer multitude of interconnected caves implied that a latticework of cracks must have existed before any water got in here.

There was much evidence of previous occupation. French workers had been here, confirming Francis' discovery of the caves during his renovations of the fort. He must have been the one who ordered the sealing up of the dungeon access. We found one large chamber that had been transformed into a grand reception hall, with tapestries hanging on every wall. The floor was worn smooth and hard. Two incredibly large chandeliers hung from ancient chains. At the end of the room, a large chair was positioned on a raised platform, looking like a throne. Everything was highly ornate, certainly intended to receive royalty.

Going on, we followed the tunnel that had led me to the large body of brackish water. With the brighter light of our miner's hat, we were finally able to appreciate the true size of this particular cave. It was big enough to hold a small lake. Looking at the roof of the cave, we saw a dip in the northern direction that might continue on to form a large tunnel to the open sea. However, no light came from that direction. Whatever had existed before was now collapsed. We retraced our steps and came upon the second trail where I had changed direction. I had been in a bad state when I last staggered through here and had missed much of what was around me, my concern being survival rather than discovery.

We undertook the journey, our eyes alert. About halfway through, deep under Etretat, a tunnel forked away to the right. We ignored it for the moment, continuing on and reaching the small cave I remembered, carved into the side of the tunnel. Its entrance was cleverly positioned, which might explain why I had such trouble locating it in the first place. Stored inside, we found our first real treasure.

A corner of the small room had a collapsed, plaster-covered cache similar to the one plundered by Hister, only this one was still stuffed full of rotting leather bags, each holding either precious stones or gold and silver coins. A heavy, hinged box, forced into the narrowest part of the crevice, held various gold objects, looking like the spoils of theft or perhaps piracy. A smaller box held a variety of ancient gold rings. Our excitement was palpable.

After a small discussion, I filled our food basket with as many leather sacks as I could carry. Before leaving the small cave, I reiterated what might happen to Etretat if it were ever known what riches lay hidden here. Upon hearing this, Old Man Vallin spit in his hand and then shook mine. While looking straight into my eyes, he held up his other hand, folding in his two middle fingers, leaving the outside ones extended. He held it against his chest, waiting for me to do the same. Then, we swore a solemn oath to secrecy.

We would use these riches to help protect the caves, no matter the cost. Vallin took a single coin to remind him of his oath. He was to receive further payment later on. We left the room and followed the tunnel to its end, where the stone door lay in wait. I had been frantic for sunlight when I had arrived here before. This time, we went the other way to see where it might lead us.

After a long walk along the dark tunnel, we found ourselves going uphill until we reached the end of the tunnel, exiting into a small wooded glade. Seeing a building nearby, I recognised the restaurant known as 'the Dungeon', a name that seemed to fly in the face of coincidence. We had travelled an incredibly long way, coming out on the other side of Etretat.

Our travels had also left us with a fantastic revelation: we now had another way into the caves!

A Decision is Reached

Later that evening, we reviewed that day's discoveries. We were stunned by the size of the cave system and by the magnitude of what lay hidden there. I was also singularly conscious of the fact that there was another man out there who knew of the caves. Although I hoped that I had seen the last of Hister, deep down I knew he would return.

It was Vallin who came up with the most logical solution. He noted that we were the only ones who knew of the *second* entrance to the caves. Even if someone were able to find their way into the tunnel in the glade, they would never find the hidden doorway that led under Etretat. He reasoned that, if we were to destroy the original entrance, Hister would never be able to find his way in again.

It was a good suggestion but could we be so bold? To destroy the Fort of Frefosse, a veritable landmark in Etretat? Somehow, from this idea arose a daring plan. Since this action could not be hidden, it would be done in plain sight. Vallin had a working knowledge of explosives and knew where to place them to ensure the complete obliteration of the dungeon. He felt confident that he could come up with a sufficiently convincing cover story, given his existing reputation. I told him that I would remain in the background, using my influence and our newfound funds to protect him from the legal repercussions of his actions. We were in agreement.

That is how we arrived at the inconceivable but necessary decision of blowing up the fort of Frefosse. All through this journal, I have tried to show you how each decision led to the other, linking into an inevitable chain of events. We had no other choice!

A Friend is Contacted

It took a few weeks to lay the background, with Old Man Vallin pestering the local militia. As for myself, I had decided to enlist the help of yet another in our plans. I had long thought about this step because this would involve someone who already had a dangerous reputation. I sent a message along the usual route, through Raymond Lindon, asking A.L. to come and meet me, on the following evening.

Now, I know what you're thinking, Patrice, so let me put a few things to rest. Yes, my character was based on a real person. He is not much like my creation in real life but he is a man of high intellect and of immense resources. Because of his desire for anonymity, I will not name him, even here. I will simply refer to him as A.L.

He arrived on time, using the small gate door to which only he had the key. We went back many years and had shared more than one adventure together. In the course of our time spent together, we had cemented an odd friendship, considering our differing viewpoints. After the usual small talk and tea, I explained why I had asked him here. The look on his face was priceless when I revealed my investigation, the danger I had been in, and then, my discoveries. He laughed in delight when I explained how I had solved the mechanism of the dungeon door.

However, he became thoughtful when I explained our planned solution, the destruction of the fort itself. He thought deeply for a while then nodded, agreeing with our solution.

He directed me to contact Raymond Lindon again and to engage his services. We both knew we could trust Lindon and he was perfectly placed to assist us with the repercussions of Vallin's plan. Although young, Lindon was already a serious and capable man. Accustomed to money and high society since his early years, due to his affiliations with A.L., Lindon had chosen to devote himself to legal studies. Gifted with a keen intellect, Lindon already had many connections to men of power and the maturity to know when to use these connections.

The next morning, I went to see Lindon. He had already been briefed about the situation. A.L. certainly acted fast. Lindon examined our plans and drafted a more complete version of events. He revealed that he knew of a company anxious to purchase the fort property in order to open a golf resort. It was an impossible request because Etretat's inhabitants would never acquiesce to the fort's removal. Anticipating the fallout from our plans, once the fort was destroyed, Lindon felt that he could obtain economic and public support from them, which would help smooth over the problems for Vallin.

I was impressed by Lindon. I needed an ally with such skills and retained him as my advisor on the spot. He became my friend and my right hand man in a secret battle that was to last for more than thirty years.

The Die is Cast

Inevitably, a date was set. I was jittery throughout that fateful day and, when it finally happened, it was more of a relief than anything else. Many thought there had been an earthquake until the news of the explosion reached them. The incident flooded the local papers and Old Man Vallin had a pretty rough time at first. He bore it well, with honour... and silence.

Lindon was in the background throughout it all. He hired the lawyer who defended Vallin, providing solid evidence supporting the accidental nature of the fort's destruction. It did not hurt that Lindon knew the judge personally and had met with him privately the previous evening.

It took only a week to find Vallin innocent of wrongdoing. He received a mild slap on the hands and was sent on his way. Rumours abounded but, with the judgement passed, little could be done to change it. Events returned to normal. It was the calm before the storm.

Murder is Done

It happened on a Friday evening, late in the night. A horrible scream was heard by Mr Lanoix around midnight. The state of Vallin's body, when he was found, was frightful. He had been severely beaten, tortured for hours before his death. He was thrown, barely alive, down into the massive jumble of stones, all that remained of the fort of Frefosse, left to die, stuck between two jagged boulders.

Lindon was able to view the body discreetly. He noticed that Old Man Vallin's last act was to clench his hand against his chest, with the two middle fingers folded in. That act could have but one meaning for me. He had died without revealing the existence of the second entrance. It also meant that someone had tried to get him to reveal that information before killing him. There could only be one such man.

This is when I first felt the weight of the enormous burden of guilt, which I have shouldered since. We had decided together to blow up the fort but it was Vallin who had been the one to take the blame. Now, because of that decision, he was dead!

Vallin had left behind a son, Georges, who knew nothing of his father's recent actions. After a brief talk with Lindon, we decided to keep the son in the dark. In the succeeding years, I kept tabs on his family and arranged to have money anonymously mailed to them, to help them out during difficult financial times. It was the least my conscience would allow me to do.

After Vallin's death, both Lindon and I kept close counsel indeed. We felt besieged by an invisible villain, looking for a way to get at us and through us, to the treasure and the caves. Because of this, Lindon had contacted many friends and created a string of watchers, all around Etretat. No stranger could enter into Etretat without being seen. It was through this growing 'net' that we learned of Hister's next foray into our territory.

World War 1 had begun by then and I was often called away to fulfill the growing obligations of my chosen public profession. Lindon was also growing in fame but it was of a different sort. His was found in the court of law. I had long since moved my wife from Etretat to Paris, choosing to use the Villa primarily as a summer residence. Nevertheless, I often found myself returning there alone, to conduct more research into the caves.

War is Declared

It was during one of these visits that Hister attacked us. I would always take the precaution of informing Lindon when I arrived in town and he would contact the Net, placing them at the highest alert.

I was at my summer villa, sitting in the office, when I heard a knock at the door. Three large men confronted me, men I knew to be employed by Lindon. They were apologetic for the late hour but something was going on. A motorcycle had been heard in the distance. Following that, two men wearing German uniforms were seen, prowling past the homes in the north. They were staying off the main roads but had been seen nonetheless.

I armed myself and lay down in wait with my companions. My nerves were stretched to the breaking point. Violence had never been my cup of tea, yet here

I was, being thrust into the thick of it. I had no one else to blame, it was all of my own doing. At two in the morning, I heard some shots far away in the distance then, later, more shots followed by screams. Following that, I heard the faint sounds of a motorcycle leaving the area at high speed.

Lindon was at my door the next morning, a sombre look on his face. Two of our men had been killed. The attackers had come prepared. They were skilful and had been well armed. From the description of the assailants, one had probably been Hister and the other, an unknown, taller man.

We compensated the families monetarily but it was not enough for my conscience. My burden of guilt continued to grow. Although our country was in a state of war, there was another war going on, a hidden one, between Hister and myself. Both sides had funds, coming from the same source, the caves. Hister's funds may have been stolen but the wealth was real nonetheless.

This first attack had likely been intended merely as a foray. They came, found us prepared and were repulsed. However, they had killed and escaped unharmed. They now knew we were waiting for them. They also had to know that I was still alive and that Hister's cover-up of his crime had failed.

The first strike of this hidden war had been his letter to me. Hister had always intended to take whatever it was that he found, by force or treachery. He knew what he was looking for and he was not going to stop until he got it. The only problem was that I was standing in his way.

Like me, Hister had chosen to conceal the existence of the caves. We were engaged in a war to the death, hidden in the shadows. Those who helped me, carefully recruited by Lindon, believed in what they were doing, protecting their land from these invaders. Over the succeeding years, this group of people, 'The Net', took pride in their heritage. They would die protecting it, protecting me.

It was becoming apparent, with each subsequent visit that the caves held much more than treasure. Theses caves had been occupied for thousands of years. They had been used for ancient ceremonies and for ritual sacrifice. I had barely begun to plumb the depths of the caves. They went on for tremendous distances, deep into the bedrock. It seemed like each new cave we found was filled with yet more mysterious relics. They had to be protected!

The Net Suffers a Blow

Hister's second attack, a full year later, was nothing like the first one. He came on the sly again, accompanied by the same man as before. They moved silently through the night, a stormy one, easy to hide in. They killed with knives and without conscience. They had come prepared, having identified several members of the Net, brutally killing them and their entire families. Their grisly task completed, they invaded my Villa unnoticed, made their way to my room, stabbing my sleeping body three times in the chest.

However, it was not me. It was another member of the Net, Claude Gislain, who was of my size and appearance. I had thought the precaution excessive when Lindon suggested it. Hister left the Villa, convinced that he had succeeded in his goals. They were careless only for a single moment upon exiting, a sudden lightning strike revealing them to the neighbour's watchful eye.

A general alarm was sounded. Every road was blocked and the two murderous fiends were trapped in the Etretat Valley. Horrified by what they had done, we wanted revenge. Everyone was up and part of the chase, a large group searching the valley, house by house. Etretat was now truly at war!

We felt sure they were trapped but our enemies had anticipated our every move. Abandoning all attempts at subtlety, using a machine gun, they mowed down several men blocking a road, making a run for the weakest part of our line. Once they were past the crest of the valley, they were gone, leaving a veritable massacre behind.

They had killed more than thirty people that night. We held a meeting with everyone involved and it was agreed, once again, to keep the event a secret, despite our sorrow and horror at the unexpected carnage of our loved ones. The bodies were buried, the deaths listed as accidents, or from natural causes. Every house was cleaned up and Etretat returned to its defensive position, licking its wounds, determined to win out in the end.

The interlopers had done some surveillance before attacking. Their attacks had been too precise, too specific. They knew exactly where and who everyone was. Only Lindon's thoroughness had saved me. Hister's first foray had also taught us. I'm sure that his face was crestfallen when he learned that I was still alive and unharmed after stabbing me three times.

Much time had passed between attacks. Perhaps this was because it was difficult for Hister to get here. When the Germans made further inroads into France, dispatch riders were used to bring crucial information from command to outpost. I had learned that some of these dispatch riders were travelling near here. If Hister was a German soldier, his furtive attacks might have been carried out under the cover of genuine orders.

I became convinced that this was the truth of it. After all, he had been in uniform during his second foray. Hister was using the Great War as cover for his own personal twisted plans, trying to sneak back in here and take possession of the caves and their loot. He had enlisted a helper, as I had, but his was a most deadly helper. Whereas I employed farmers and fishermen, Hister's assistant was a trained killer.

Because of these two attacks, Etretat separated itself from the rest of France, becoming a country unto itself, alert for any attack, protecting its own, ever vigilant. The words 'The Net' never had more meaning than during those days. On the surface, to all others, Etretat was a quiet little fishing village, with healthy tourism, a peaceful resort, the exact opposite of what lay hidden below.

Hister's third and final foray was an equal measure of success and failure. By that point, The Net had refined its methods, using affiliations with other groups, such as the Abbey, to provide advance notice. Because of their preparations, Hister's invasion attempt was detected from the very first moment. A contingent of well armed men was alerted within minutes. Before Hister and his cohort had penetrated more than a hundred metres into the valley, the Net was already closing in on them. Our enemies, sharp as ever, retreated immediately, knowing the game was up. Several volleys of shots followed them on their way out and at least one found its mark, wounding Hister in the leg!

There was a celebration in Etretat that night. We were jubilant. In the morning, we were back at our posts, waiting for the next attack.

That attack took decades to come and was the most horrible thing ever perpetrated by a single man in the history of the world!

Caves, Tunnels and Destiny

I continued my exploration of the caves, converting more treasure into a growing fund. A.L. was my partner more than once in these cave expeditions and we both made good use of what we found. The more we found, the more convinced we were that the caves must remain unknown to the world at large. Some knowledge ought never be revealed to the world.

Despite the passage of many quiet years, I remained convinced that, one day, Hister would return. I could not explain his long absence. Perhaps life itself had gotten in his way. Perhaps his goals had changed. However, in my heart, I knew he would return here to claim what he felt was his heritage.

While he might have coveted the caves, they were in *my* possession. I had hidden the way in and he was effectively locked out of Etretat, thanks to the Net. It was a responsibility I took seriously. I purchased the Villa I loved so much and began construction of a concealed tunnel of my own, connecting it with an ancient access tunnel under Etretat. It was an ambitious project but some of the work had already been done long ago.

We had discovered, during our original explorations, that the long tunnel connecting the two cliffs together had a branch heading east, in the general direction of my Villa. It went for a distance of almost two hundred metres. Digging had stopped at that point. Ancient tools were found abandoned at the termination point. We found the reason for the abandoned tools, in a grim discovery of several skeletons, apparently killed in the tunnels thousands of years ago.

Whatever the reason for the tunnel, it saved us weeks of work, allowing us to begin and finish the remaining section of the tunnel in less than three months. Once completed, I could enter the tunnel and access the caves from the safety of my villa. Workers were sworn to silence and the existence of the new tunnel remained largely unknown.

More than ever, I felt that the caves were truly a burden, a curse that would never release me from its clutches. I was held in thrall by them as much as Hister was. The only difference was that I was not motivated by selfish greed the way Hister seemed to be. I came to realise that men of destiny are not those who go out and take what they want, riding roughshod over their victims. No, true destiny is foisted on the average man, *despite* what he wants. He finds himself the plaything of fate, without having had any such intent.

I had not found the caves by accident. They had chosen me. It was up to me to decide what must be done with them. The choice I ended up making altered the course of world history while Hister marched on to *his* destiny, equally controlled by the caves.

A while has passed since my last entry. Victoire and Angelique are safe. They will be cared for, no matter what happens to me. I have arranged it. As for me, Patrice, I know now that it is the end. I fell ill on the way to Perpignan and my old body is telling me it's too tired to fight off the disease. I know I will succumb.

However, I have done what I had to do and few men get that chance. My only regret is the time I never spent with you.

The Monster is Revealed

I settled into my new home and life regained a normality of sorts. I continued my investigation of the caves and wrote my books. In the back of my mind, I could not forget Hister. I knew that the calm was but a temporary period while Hister prepared his forces for another onslaught. During the twenties, I did not learn anything more about him but in the 1930's, I saw a picture of him in the papers. His true name, Adolf Hitler was finally revealed. I read about him in horror. He had somehow managed to convince an entire nation to follow his insane leadership. He had fooled all his fellow countrymen.

I suddenly knew, beyond the shadow of any doubt, that Hister wanted it all. He wanted the caves, Etretat, France, and the world with it. Nothing would stop him. He was working day and night to build an army to come and take what he felt was his. He would return here with ten thousand men, if he felt he needed them.

If no one did what had to be done to stop him, he would never be stopped. If he took the caves, the world would be his. I was the only one who truly understood what he really wanted.

The only good thing was that if he wanted the caves, he would have to come here to get them.

It gave me a chance, a single opportunity to trap him. It was with these thoughts that I sent for A.L. to come and give me his advice, one final time.

A Visit in the Night:

It was nearing midnight when I heard the creak of the door in the garden. I had just stoked the fire in my room and it was getting cozy. He came in silently. I shook his hand, noting the weariness in his eyes. Age was encroaching on us all. I handed him a glass of cognac, explaining my problem.

"You see, A.L., if my enemy is truly Adolf Hitler, Chancellor of the Third Reich, as I am sure he is, I must somehow defeat him without ever getting the opportunity to meet him in person. The man is completely unapproachable!... and he is building a war machine, one which I am convinced he plans to use to come back here. I am the only one who knows he must be stopped, who has a chance of stopping him. I must not fail but how can I succeed, when I face the might of an entire country?" I finished, worried by the desperateness of my situation.

Pointing at me with his cigar, he spoke quietly, the fire snapping and crackling in the background.

"I too, have followed Hitler's career, becoming concerned about his politics. Things have been so unsettled in Europe since the Great War. Germany in particular, has been grumbling more and more loudly, upset by the severity of its reparations payments. Hitler has stepped into power at an auspicious moment. His Brownshirts, and now his Blackshirts, can be seen as nothing more than the beginning of a massive army. His speeches seed unrest and attempt to place the German over everyone else. The Master Race indeed. It is a ludicrous viewpoint, without any real substance, basing itself on reworked history and false myths... but it must not be taken lightly. He seems intent on fomenting trouble. Big trouble."

His words struck a chord within me. I thought about Hitler and his speeches:

"A. L., now that I think about it, there is something wrong with the intensity of his speeches. He is so very sure of himself, impossibly so, as if he believed the lies he was spouting..."

"... You are on to something... What makes a man push himself so, to go after anything he wants, willing to justify any action to achieve his goals?" A.L. wondered.

"He is a maniac... a megalomaniac, seeking power and control by any means believing it to be his right," I answered him, giving myself the very clue I needed to fashion a solution to my problem.

"Yes, a megalomaniac, exactly my thinking. That is how you will trap your man, my dear Leblanc. By using this weakness against him."

I clinked my glass with his and downed my remaining cognac in a single gulp, already planning how I was going to build this trap.

A.L left, after a quiet good-bye, contented in the thought that he had provided me the impetus I needed to get out of my brown study and attend to my most important task: destroying Adolf Hitler.

Of these things, I can speak no more. Hitler is still out there and his spies may yet discover this journal.

I have spent years readying my trap, spending much of the riches found in the caves in preparation. To my sorrow, this has meant that I had to leave investigating the knowledge buried in the caves for another. I had hoped that it would be you, Patrice. Lately, I am not so sure. I have received disturbing news about your safety... so I have made arrangements with A.L., for an alternate person to reclaim Etretat's heritage. You know of whom I speak.

Ever since I entered those caves, I have felt a great purpose controlling my decisions and directing my every move. My personal desires and feelings have been utterly inconsequential. Everything life has taught me has confirmed how little I really know about the caves, about their purpose for being here. For they have a purpose, of that there can be no doubt.

This much I do know: I have prepared the caves for another. I can only hope that it will be you, Patrice, my beloved son. So allow me to believe that you will survive, that the information I have been given about you is wrong. There are so many things I have left unsaid, waiting too long to speak. Now you may be gone and I will surely be gone soon. There is no more time. Only this journal can speak for me.

Allow me to apologise one final time for all the things that I was not as a father and for the things I was forced to do in my life. I can only hope that you see fit to forgive me and to reciprocate the love that is in my heart for you, outshining all that can be found there.

Good-bye, my son, my Patrice.
Your loving father
Maurice Leblanc

PS: ERGO 5-8-1, 10-8-2, 22-1-8, 27-4-4,, 40-5-1, 60-1-5, 49-2-4,, 71-9-1, 75-13-2, 33-6-2, 97-1-6,, 92-2-1, 31-1-2, 61-1-2, 73-14-4, 18-3-1,,, 100-13-2, 90-6-4, 29-1-5, 88-2-4,, 24-2-1, 66-2-2, 62-4-3,, 30-6-1, 14-5-2, 94-3-4,, 69-5-1, 31-7-9, 87-6-6, 20-1-1,, 78-2-1, 57-2-1, 48-6-6, 25-2-3, 95-2-1,,, 98-3-1, 12-1-2, 50-3-3, 91-1-2, 7-1-1,, 38-9-1, 89-1-3, 19-2-1, 41-5-1,, 54-1-4, 45-2-2, 55-1-7,, 82-6-4, 16-1-2, 53-6-3, 8-2-6, 42-1-2, 93-6-2,, 32-6-6, 23-3-2, 64-3-2, 59-9-4,,, SUM : 1P-K4,P-K4, 2 Kt-KB3 Kt-QB3, 3 P-Q4 KtxP, 4 KtxKt PxKt, 5 B-QB4 B-B4, 6 P-QB3 Q-K2, 7 O-O Q-K4, 8 P-KB4 PxPch, 9 K-R1 PxP

Matt Chatelain

CHAPTER 13
Maximillian Bauer

"Well, that's it," I finished, accepting a glass of cold water from Raymonde. I noticed the silence around me. Each person here, and my friends online, had been deeply affected by the contents of the journal.

Mrs Leblanc was crying copiously. The two Vallin Brothers were each bearing a different expression. Ives appeared somewhat bemused and Jacques looked upset. He was biting his lips, trying to restrain himself from bursting out.

They were also looking at me, expecting me to say something. Before I could utter a single word, however, O'Flanahan tactlessly jumped in:

"I can't wait to publish this!"

"O'Flanahan, I'm sure you will agree that discretion is of extreme importance at this point. If Leblanc kept this secret for nearly one hundred years, then surely we can assume that he had a valid reason for doing so. I expect everyone to respect his decision for the time being..."

"Well, I for one do not respect this Leblanc," exclaimed Jacques Vallin, his trembling voice betraying a deep anger.

Mrs Leblanc burst into tears again. Vallin's face instantly mollified when he realized what his harsh words had done. Wrestling his emotions into control, he tried to explain why he was so upset.

"All our lives, our only goal, Brother and me, has been to discover what happened to our great-grandfather. My father before me and his father before him have each spent their lives trying to learn who killed Old Man Vallin and why. Now, after a century, we discover that the reason for all these efforts is that Mr Leblanc simply *chose* not to explain to my grandfather what had transpired. Had he spoken but once, none of this would have happened, none of our lives would have been so wasted... just wasted..." he finished, his tremulous voice trailing off. I felt sympathy for him.

"Jacques, I recognise that you feel genuinely hurt. However, imagine Leblanc's difficulty in deciding whether the cause of Old Man Vallin's murder should be revealed. He understood only too well the impact of his silence because he tried to correct this necessary wrong by anonymously providing your family with funds when you needed them the most. It's easy to see why he wrote his journal as a confession. His choices came at such a heavy price. This can only speak more on the need to maintain silence until we comprehend what is now in our hands..." I explained.

Jacques' expression softened until he nodded in agreement, hesitantly at first, then firmly, his brother joining him.

"Well said, my boy," stated Briar. "I will support you one hundred percent in this. Discretion is called for, extreme discretion. There is more here than meets the eye. The fewer who know about it the better..."

"That's not all," Coulter added. "Leblanc's journal, while explaining many things, leaves almost as many questions as it answers," he said. On the laptop screen, O'Flanahan was nodding his head vigorously in agreement with Coulter.

"My first question would be: what trap did he set for Hitler?" I wondered aloud.

Mrs Leblanc, barely composed, added her own question.

"I'm wondering if we might head inside for a short rest? This afternoon has simply been too emotional for me."

Everyone agreed with Mrs Leblanc. I suspected we were all equally drained by this incredible series of revelations.

***

A few hours later, I was sitting in my room, getting up from a short rest that had done me a world of good. Raymonde had gone out to run a few errands for her mother. I did not have any such tasks, so I was free to sit and reflect on Leblanc's journal. It was so sad the way things had turned out for him. Here was a man who had solved the most amazing historical mystery of his time and then found himself in the fight of his life, literally forced to contend with the direct and horrific attention of the most dangerous man in the twentieth century.

Despite all that, Leblanc's revelations were nothing less than astounding.

He had found the caves hidden within the Aval cliff and he had discovered treasure. He also alluded to unrevealed knowledge buried in their depths. In the fight of his life against a lurking Hitler and company, Leblanc committed himself to protecting the caves at any cost. Apparently, most of the town had been in on the protection, although only a few had known about the caves specifically.

A beeping sound from my laptop drew my attention. Three windows popped up on the screen, displaying my friends. Behind Coulter, I could see discarded cups of coffee and a few pizza boxes. Behind O'Flanahan, I saw the usual mess of his office. Briar seemed to be outside. I could see a building in the background but couldn't make it out. No matter where they were, these guys had been reviewing the journal non-stop since they had signed off with me. Now they were coming back with their conclusions. I had to admit that I welcomed their call.

"Ah, Paul, my boy, there you are. Thank God, Coulter understands all this techno-wizardry. Being far away like this is quite limiting, you know. I am becoming somewhat frustrated with it..." Briar explained, "I assume you have been thinking about the journal?"

"I have been thinking of nothing else. Its revelations seem to fly in the face of history. We now have to accept that Hitler came back to Etretat several times, with murder and theft on his mind, although, in the end, he failed to gain his objective. Leblanc even claims that Hitler was wounded..." I said.

"I knew that you would wonder about that, because, frankly, that is what I thought. Like minds and all that. Anyway, we've come up with a theory," Briar responded.

"Go on, I'm listening,"

"If Leblanc's journal is accurate, its facts would inevitably have to fit with what we know of Hitler's life. This may actually be the case. For example, we can now confirm that the specific encounters related in the journal fit quite nicely within the First World War period of Hitler's life. Hitler volunteered repeatedly to be a courier, delivering important messages to German outposts, deep within France. On certain missions, he travelled within thirty kilometres of Etretat... Another fact is that Hitler was seen wearing a German uniform by members of the Net. Better yet, Hitler *was* wounded during the First World War, an injury that won him a prestigious award. Perhaps, the true reason for this injury was not what the world was led to believe..." he continued. Coulter interrupted him, eager to add his piece:

"... And, thanks to Leblanc, we now know that there *was* another man with Hitler in Etretat, a trained assassin. Did he become a convenient witness, explaining away Hitler's mysterious wound? Were other witnesses coerced into supporting Hitler's altered version?"

"... So, you're implying that Hitler used his official missions as a cover, during which he returned to Etretat. That begs the question: If Hitler was willing to join the army in order to sneak back into Etretat, what would he be willing to do following that failure?" I replied.

"By that, do you mean to ask if Hitler would have been bold and treacherous enough to lead an entire country astray, to raise an army to conquer Etretat, as Leblanc attests in his journal?" Briar retorted.

"Yes, that is exactly what I am asking. I think that Hitler's entire life, ever since he entered into those caves, was devoted to returning there, to the exclusion of all else, a true obsession. The only thing I can't understand is why he never went back later, when he so obviously could have. His army took Etretat over in 1940... Yet, you all know your history as well as I do, and it is clear that Hitler never returned to Etretat. We even know where he died, in that Berlin bunker in 1945... So why didn't Hitler escape to those caves if that had been his goal in the first place?" I asked.

"I think I have an answer to that particular question, Paul..." affirmed O'Flanahan. "... Have any of you ever heard of Maximillian Bauer?" he asked innocently.

"I hope this isn't another conspiracy theory, O'Flanahan" flatly objected Briar, preventing me from saying the same thing.

O'Flanahan, instead of looking flustered, looked smug.

"In the world of conspiracies, my friends, some are so far-fetched that they barely register on the conspiracy scale. Others are supported by mountains of facts. However, there are a few that get placed in a very special pile. If you were to look in that pile, every conspiracy that confronted you would sound preposterous on the surface but the more you thought about it, the more you would realize that only your *viewpoint* prevented it from being true. Well, the top story in that pile would be the strange case of Maximillian Bauer... So I repeat to you: have any of you heard of him?" he finished.

None of us had. O'Flanahan explained what he knew:

"In the month of February1939, a small book was published by the Macaulay Press that bore the title: 'The Strange Death of Adolf Hitler'. The author remained anonymous, afraid of persecution. He claimed to have been entrusted this document by Maximillian Bauer. Following a dangerous and circuitous route, our Mr Anonymous managed to escape from Germany and find his way to the United States. He translated the document into English and submitted it for publication. Of course, it didn't matter to the editors whether the story was true or not, just so long as it caused a furor," O'Flanahan began "... And a furor it did cause, of that there can be no doubt."

"Stop beating around the bush, O'Flanahan and tell us about it, for Pete's sake..." ranted Coulter.

"I'm getting to it, just calm down. It seems that Maximillian Bauer was born with the unlucky fate of looking exactly like Adolf Hitler. He not only looked like Hitler, he could *talk* like Hitler. He had his *Voice!* "

"Are you telling us that this guy was Hitler's exact double?" asked Coulter.

"Now you're getting it. To the public, the two were one and the same. However, if we are to believe the book, behind the scenes, all was not well. Because of his special position, Bauer was uniquely placed to observe the events leading up to the Second World War. He witnessed the in-fighting between Hitler's henchmen, Boormann, Von Arnheim, Goebbels and the others. There were many conspiracies to unseat Hitler. There was a third problem. Hitler himself was sick. He was also becoming more paranoid, thinking danger to be everywhere. He was probably right. As time went on, Bauer did most of the public appearances and speeches with Hitler directing behind the scenes... Now, you must remember that this book was published in 1939 and had been smuggled out of Germany before the war had even begun. Every small detail noted in his book has been verified by independent investigations over the years. The conveniently anonymous author *had* to have been present to know what happened in those private chambers. The secret love affairs, the illegal activities, it's all there. Were it not for those little details, this book would not be credible. With them, it becomes very, very plausible..."

"Well, it is known that Hitler had doubles. That is no big secret..." scoffed Briar.

"True, but the big secret revealed in the book is that Hitler, the real Hitler, died before 1939, from a combination of ill health and poison. It was his double who carried on and finished the war. It was his double who died in the bunker."

It was possible that our version of these events was correct after all.

"What happened to the author?" asked Briar.

"The author disappeared in December 1938, just before the first publication of the book. He was never heard from again, never claiming a single penny of his royalties. A year and a half later, Etretat was invaded by the Nazis," O'Flanahan clarified.

"What if the author was a *complete* fake?" I said, getting the attention of all three. "... What if the reason he was anonymous was that his own background would not hold up to scrutiny if it were investigated? If the author was Hitler's henchman, this Weissmuller perhaps, then the whole Bauer story could be a plant, with just enough facts to make it believable. Once Hitler had taken the caves of Etretat, Maximilian Bauer took his place, allowing Hitler to vanish into the caves without anyone noticing... Of course, we still don't understand why Hitler was so fascinated by the caves..."

"... As was Leblanc, let us not forget..." added Briar.

"Yes, exactly like Leblanc, in fact. Obsessed with the caves. So much so that Hitler subjugated an entire country in order to regain his objective! Let's assume that the book about Bauer was part of that plan, seeded with half-truths to 'prove' that Hitler had died. This false conclusion could end any burgeoning investigation into Hitler's whereabouts, further protecting the caves. Once Etretat was invaded, with Weissmuller in charge, Hitler had no further interest in remaining in Germany. The minute the caves were ready, he abandoned Germany, leaving his double behind."

"Well, I'm glad someone has figured out why I thought it was important to talk about that book," asserted O'Flanahan, looking to be congratulated. I didn't hesitate:

"You were right to bring it to our attention. If anything, it strengthens our version of the facts. Now that I think of it, after the beginning of World War Two, Hitler's behaviour was the opposite of what you would expect of a leader. Instead of making *more* appearances everywhere, he reduced the number of public speeches. He never changed his appearance, always presenting the exact same look. This all supports the fact that a double was in his place, simply repeating what he had been taught. Perhaps, in the end, Germany *failed* because the real Hitler was no longer at its helm directing the war, replaced by an imitator skilled only in deception. It would have become a fatal weakness for the Nazi regime..."

"... It suddenly seems quite possible that we have much more to thank Maurice Leblanc for than we imagined at first. Perhaps his trap succeeded, leaving a Nazi War machine decapitated when it was at the height of its power. Bauer tried to keep it going but ultimately failed, being a mimic rather than the military genius that Hitler was," said Briar.

"It also implies something else," added O'Flanahan. "If that book was indeed a plant and was published before the Second World War started, then its author had to be aware of the plan to invade Etretat. Publishing the book was a premeditated act, *anticipating* the act of invasion. Hitler and the author were in cahoots with each other. It had to be Weissmuller."

Trust O'Flanahan to come up with something that twisty.

I sat back in my chair, looking at my friends' faces on the computer monitor, overwhelmed yet again at how this story kept evolving into something unexpected. I was reminded of Leblanc's final comment in his journal:

'I have felt a great purpose, controlling my decisions and directing my every move. This much I know: I have prepared the way for another.'

Something deeper was going on, something still hidden from us. Both men, Leblanc and Hitler had been changed forever by their encounter with the caves. Diametrically opposed, they seemed to represent the forces of good and evil in their time. Whatever had happened in those caves had *polarized* these two men, setting into motion a string of events, which had led directly to my presence here, a full century later.

I made my decision. If we were going to find our answers, there was only one place for us to look.

"Gentlemen, I think it's time that we think about going into the caves!"

***

After disconnecting with my friends, before Raymonde returned, I decided to do some advance scouting by returning to the Aval cliff. Arriving at the Golf Club parking, I got out of my car and headed down the path, putting on my glasses and turning them on. A moment later, Coulter signed on.

"Hey, Paul. Where are you now?"

"Hi, Fabian. I'm on top of the cliff near the bunker. It's right over there..." I turned my head in its direction while I walked nearer. "... Where are the other guys?"

"O'Flanahan's off hunting some other clues about something. He was mumbling when he signed off so I missed most of it. I don't know where Briar is. I haven't seen him in a while but admittedly he's been incredibly busy doing research. He sure has come up with the goods on a pile of stuff, hasn't he?" Coulter said, drinking from a thermos cup and sitting back in his chair, fascinated by my cam video of the bunker.

"You're telling me. I'm glad I brought him in on this. He has a lot of resources," I replied.

"Me too but what is the deal between him and O'Flanahan?"

"Beats me. However, let's admit it, O'Flanahan can be irritating at the best of times."

"You got that right," Coulter laughed, nodding his head in agreement. "Why did you ask him along if he's so irritating?"

I walked into the bunker looking around. Finding nothing new, I went back outside.

"... I know he's quirky but I can't help that. From the first day I met him, I knew I could trust him. No matter his antics, this guy will be there when you need him. Besides, he knows the oddest stuff. He really seems to be in his element with all these Hitler conspiracies. What do you think of him?"

"Oh, Paul, you know me. I'm easy going. I think both guys have different viewpoints and that has to be a good thing. As for me, I'm just along for the ride..." he broke off, laughing a bit more "... But seriously, you have to watch yourself... and you don't just have yourself to think of anymore... There's Raymonde... and her mom... and the Vallin brothers. These people are all counting on you."

"I'm beginning to realise that, Fabian but, come on, you've got to give me a break. I've only been in France a few days... I'm doing my best to catch up..."

"I know. You've done pretty well, if you ask me... except for last night when you forgot to take the safety off your gun. I thought you were a goner."

I laughed at the memory but there was a serious edge to his comment. I knew I was learning. Would I learn fast enough? I couldn't always be lucky. Reaching the edge of the cliff, I looked down, seeing the Needle below, waves crashing all around it.

"Wow! Look at that. Man, that's a sight, Paul. What are you doing up here anyway?"

"I've been thinking about the way to get into those caves. If what we've learnt is true, that bunker is right over the Frefosse dungeon entrance into those caves. We've also surmised that an ancient entrance once existed at sea level... but not at the sea level of today. A much lower level, from more than two thousand years ago..."

"I get it. You think we have to go underwater to find our way in."

"Yes. I want you to check into that. Find out what equipment we might need, who's got it and how much it is. Then use my account, make a deal and get it here fast. Along with that, let's try to pin down some data to back up our approach, just to make absolutely sure..."

"You seem pretty committed already..."

"Let me just say that I've had a hunch..."

And a dream!

"Why don't you just stop right where you are, Sirenne. I've got a gun!"

I froze for a moment. Coulter began talking at a rapid-fire pace in my ear.

"Is that Norton? It is, isn't it? Oh, man, this is bad... What are we going to do?... What are *you* going to do?... Wait, wait, I've got it... I'm on it, Paul. I'm calling Raymonde right now... NO... I'm calling the Vallin Brothers. They're closer... and meaner..."

"Norton! What a surprise... How's your foot?" I spoke up, saying anything to keep the dangerous man off balance.

"... It's still ringing at the Vallin... WAIT, someone's picking up..." Coulter's voice faded off into the background.

"It *hurts*, what do you think? You almost broke it, you cretin. I should kill you right here, Sirenne, you bother me so much. But I'm not going to, not now, not yet. Because I want some *answers*, damn it. Now turn around slow and easy. Don't make a single, stupid move."

I could see the pistol he was holding, a small stubby thing, probably a back up. I had forgotten to search his car. Another mistake! Norton held the pistol low, trying to avoid attention from the few tourists in the distance. I had a plan but I had to get it right.

I had brought my pistol too.

Unfortunately, it was behind my back, stuck in my pants, underneath my jacket, exactly the spot where Norton was looking. Pretending to obey him, I turned my body slowly. At the same time, keeping all movement hidden behind my body, I frantically slid my hand inside my jacket. With incredible relief, I felt my palm grasp the pistol.

Part one of the plan was over.

"Keep your hands in view," Norton warned too late.

Time for part two!

I slid my hand back, pulling the pistol out of my pants without a hitch, flipping the safety catch at the same time. It was now or never. In a single gesture, I jerked my gun out, aiming it directly at Norton's head, catching him completely unaware. Surprised, he froze for a moment, allowing me to take several steps, narrowing the distance between us.

"The Vallins are on the way, Paul. Five minutes tops and they'll be here... Oh no, what are you doing?... You've got your gun!... Why didn't you say that?" Coulter stammered. "... Hey, don't get *closer* to the guy..."

"Shut up and get me a map of this place..." I whispered.

"What?" he questioned, not understanding what I meant.

"Find me a way out of here... Get me a MAP..." I shot back, out of time.

His face brightened.

"Ohh, I got it. One 3D map of the cliff front coming up - it'll take a few secs, sorry..."

Norton was stuck in an awkward position, with his arm down, his gun held at waist height. He had put his shoes back on and was using a branch as a cane. He spoke angrily.

"I keep underestimating you... So, good for you, you got a pistol on me and I've got a pistol on you..." he started.

My plan was to do something I knew he could not. I was going to run! Unfortunately, in order to do this, I had to get closer to him, because I was on a projection of the cliff and he was blocking my way.

Norton continued talking while I kept walking closer, my left arm held out stiffly, holding the pistol aimed right at his face. The few tourists in the distance hadn't noticed anything yet but it was just a matter of time.

"... That doesn't change a thing. We might shoot each other but I want some answers from you and I am going to get them, no matter what... "

"... What questions?" I retorted, stalling.

"What does H.N. mean? Answer that, for starters," he screamed at me.

"Don't you know?" I shot back.

"God damn it, stop it with these games. It's always games, all the time. Just tell me, I beg you..." his face contorted, looking almost ready to cry for a moment, then flashing into a twisted rage, then back to tears.

"That guy is *not* stable..." Coulter whispered, looking at his watch. "Three more minutes and the Vallin brothers will be there. Just hold on Paul, you're doing great so far. That was fast thinking with the gun... Can't believe you did that... Here's the 3D map you asked for..."

I scanned it rapidly, orienting myself while Coulter rotated it into position. I immediately found what I needed: a way down those precipitous cliffs! It was on my right about thirty yards away, the second dip in the cliff past the Needle. Unlike the first dip, the second one didn't stop, going all the way down to a disused metal staircase. Norton began speaking again, his voice going up and down in volume. He was losing it.

"First, it was my sister, Helena... then it was my friend Henri Nadeau... then all the others, all the same and they were all blaming me. But they didn't understand. It was all a game and I was stuck in it. It wasn't me... They were wrong... I just can't *prove* it... and now HE stole my file, everything I had on him..." he broke out into frenzied laughter but stopped himself, continuing his incomprehensible ramble. "... And this time, the first time ever, I caught him ... *I saw him*... the Shadow-Killer... he was leaving with my file under his arm... I saw him in the mirror, the door was open... and he... he was *me*, he was me, ha-ha, he was me, can you believe it? Ha-ha-ha, what a perfect trick."

He broke down into another crazy laugh and his head fell down to his chest, taking his eyes off me, lost in his insane thoughts.

The moment his eyes dropped, I took off running, knowing exactly where I was going thanks to Coulter's map. I had never broken any speed records before but, at that moment, I felt as if I were moving like a train, barrelling non-stop across the landscape, increasing my momentum and distance with every second. His pistol's barrel was too short for any type of accuracy. If he wanted to shoot me, he would have to catch me and I wasn't planning to give him the chance!

Coulter kept scrolling the map on the screen, showing me exactly where I had to go, cheering me on all the while. I heard Norton yelling and risked a single glance backwards. He was hobbling after me at a decent pace, using his cane to lop forward, his pistol waving around with every step.

He looked angry.

I heard some car doors slam and more screaming in the distance. The Vallin brothers were in the parking lot, running all out toward Norton. They were both brandishing bats and waving them madly. I kept running, aiming directly for the cleft. I headed down, mostly sliding on one foot, dangerously out of control. Norton was closer behind me than I would've liked.

"Watch it, you're going to lose it, you're going to lose it... No... You're fine, doing good, now be careful, here's the stairs..." Coulter yammered on in my ear, keeping up a running commentary. I had to slide to a desperate stop right above the rusty steps. They were clogged with silt and sand that had come down from the cleft. I saw signs warning tourists off and bars blocking the staircase. Coulter screamed:

"Just go for it, Norton's right behind you."

Incredibly, Norton was sliding down the cleft on his good foot, using his branch to balance himself. He was coming down fast, still holding his gun, determined to catch me.

I scrambled over the bars and dropped my feet down on the railing of the narrow staircase, pushing myself off in desperation and sliding down the railing at a precipitous pace. A mound of dirt blocked the bottom of the staircase and I jumped off, landing in the soft sand below. Not stopping for a second, I ran along the beach in the Needle's direction. Norton, seeing me get away, shot at me once but his bullet missed me. He bellowed in frustration, following me down the stairs, getting angrier by the minute. A glance upwards showed me the Vallins just starting to come down the steep slope of the cleft, still screaming at Norton. The hunter was about to become the hunted. I redoubled my speed and neared the Needle, intent on rejoining Etretat's main beach beyond the arch.

Unfortunately, by this time of the day, the tide was coming back in and the area around the arch was already flooded. I didn't hesitate for a second and jumped in the channel water. I knew it was cold but I felt nothing, the adrenaline numbing the shock. Norton, letting go another bellow of frustration, shot once more at me, uselessly, still too far away.

I resisted the idea of shooting back. I just couldn't convince myself to do it. Coulter had other concerns:

"Try not to get the glasses wet, they *are* waterproof but I'll probably lose reception and I don't want to miss a second of this."

"I'll try not to, Fabian. I am trying to get away, you know," I answered back, too breathless to sound sarcastic. Wading in to my neck, I started swimming, trying to keep ahead of the undercurrent.

"You gotta turn your head back. I want to see how close the Vallin brothers are... Christ, go, man, go. Norton's about to shoot again," Coulter shouted.

I heard Norton ranting behind me, his words reaching me faintly.

"You just won't listen... well, I'll *make* you listen..."

That didn't sound good!

I dove underwater, soaking the glasses and losing Coulter, just as Norton emptied his gun at me. He was close enough by now that he might actually hit me. I heard the shots and felt a wallop in my shoulder.

I was hit.

Right away, I knew it wasn't that bad. I had been underwater and the bullet had been robbed of most of its momentum. I might be sore but I wasn't dead!

With renewed vigour, I kicked with my legs, propelling myself forward a fair distance, coming back up to the surface. I desperately turned myself around to face the beach, lifting my gun above the water in defence.

I had nothing to shoot at.

I fell back into the water, my glasses miraculously still glued to my face. Norton had been forced to jump into the water in an attempt to escape the approaching Vallin Brothers. He was swimming towards me in earnest, his face contorting in agony every time he moved his damaged foot through the water. Soon, he was sinking more than swimming. It was easy for me to outdistance him in his debilitated condition and I pulled away.

A look of intense frustration appeared on his face. Unfortunately, his body was completely worn out and his foot was hurting him tremendously. I swam a big circle around him, heading back towards the shore. By this time, the Vallin brothers had reached the water and waded in knee deep. They helped me out of the water and I turned around, looking for Norton.

I finally spotted him. He was in trouble. He had to kick constantly with his legs to stay afloat and his foot was causing him agony. He was sinking under the heavy waves, unable to keep his head above the water any longer. I had an impulse to try to save him in spite of all he had done but I was too exhausted. Ives Vallin headed off into the waters valiantly in my stead but Norton went under long before he could reach him.

He never resurfaced.

Matt Chatelain

A SELECTION FROM THE WEISSMULLER MANUSCRIPT

Meeting Hitler

I first met Hitler while in Vienna in 1908. All I knew of him at that time was that he painted for food and lodging money. Several years later, he renewed contact, intent on involving me in a new scheme of his.

At first, I was not very interested. I couldn't imagine what such a man could have to offer me. I also tended to work alone. However, something had changed about him. This Hitler was different. He was now brimming with energy, his eyes glowing with conviction.

Slowly, over supper, he exposed the most incredible discovery: a complex of caves hidden near a small town in France. He hesitatingly admitted to killing a man, named Leblanc, in the caves. He also spoke of gold and jewels, some of which he had taken.

He admitted to feeling guilty about his murder in the caves for several days following it but the guilt was eventually replaced by a growing sense of rightness: he had been justified to take ownership of the caves, said he, they were his by right of conquest. He had begun dreaming about what he could do with such a lair at his disposal. His perspective had kept evolving until he had perceived a path laid out in front of him, revealed to him by Destiny itself. The caves were his to take and use.

He had felt confident that the caves were his because he had bricked up the entrance and left the body of Leblanc entombed in them. No one would ever find him. Then the impossible had happened. Leblanc was seen returning home. He was not dead and had somehow escaped from the caves. The problem was that Hitler was convinced he had killed the man. There was something going on in there, something he desperately wanted to investigate.

I wasn't sure about his claims. It was hard to kill a man, particularly if you didn't know what you were doing. I still didn't know why he was admitting all these things to me. Hitler wasn't done with his explanation.

Baffled by Leblanc's return to life, Hitler had returned to the town, hoping to finish the job. Upon his arrival there, he was horrified to discover that the fort with the entrance into the caves had been destroyed. His plans to kill Leblanc had to be put on hold until he figured out a new way in. Learning about the involvement of another local man, named Vallin, Hitler took him prisoner.

He tortured the man for several hours but, either the man was a true drunken idiot, or he was devoted to his cause, because he never spoke a word. Frustrated, Hitler took the man to the destroyed fort and threw him into the hole, leaving him there to die. Returning to Vienna, Hitler knew his plans had now been forced to become much more complex. He could no longer take control of the caves, having lost the way in. Worse yet, Leblanc had free access to them, stealing the gold Hitler believed to be his by right. Leblanc was also free to explore the deeper mysteries of the caves. Hitler was convinced that these mysteries were more important than all the gold in the world.

No matter what his wild claims were, the inner energy animating him was strong. This was a man not easily thwarted once he set himself upon a path. I still didn't know why he was talking to me. I didn't have long to wonder when he launched into a different type of history: my own.

Apparently, he had been impressed by me, during the time we had spent together. He had felt something was different about me. In that, he was, of course, absolutely correct. Then he amazed me, by talking about a particular incident that had happened while I was still in school.

For the first time in many years, my heart jumped and I almost felt worry. Hitler had somehow uncovered the one event in my past where I had made the slightest of mistakes in my experiments. With this dangerous information in his hands, I wondered if perhaps Hitler himself ought not participate in one of my experiments. I had been thinking of a new approach lately. However, these interesting thoughts were banished when he pulled out a thick folder from a paper bag, handing it to me, saying it was a gift.

Opening it, I found that it held three complete copies of the file concerning the incident. They were the ones I had not been able to remove from the school's records. At the time, I was not gifted enough to succeed in this necessary task. Hitler had gone back and done what I should have done myself.

I had finally met a kindred spirit. One with whom I could share my thoughts. Unlike me, he had purpose. I was wandering through life, trying to understand why I felt so disconnected from the rest of the world. Here was a man who was telling me that it did not have to be like that. If I joined him in his quest, acting as his lieutenant, I would be able to continue my experiments but this time I would have a reason for them. The thought appealed to me mightily.

His timing perfect, he pulled out a small leather purse, full of gold coins, handing it to me. At that very moment, I decided to do it. I would join him and with me at his side, we could not fail.

***

We left Vienna to find a place we could use as a home base. During that trip, Hitler revealed his deeper thoughts and ambitions. This was no mere whim. Although he was obsessed about the caves, he had other aspirations, political ones. They were still nebulous, unclear but, somehow, he knew the greatness he was destined to achieve. He had chosen me with care, after reviewing all those he had encountered, knowing that he needed help of a special nature.

He admitted that he had always noticed something special about me. The thought bothered me, because I had believed that my outer shell, the 'skin' that others saw, had become smooth enough to escape detection. He calmed my concerns by stating that he himself was different. He spent much time indicating the exact points which had alerted him, helping me greatly in designing a better 'skin' for myself.

He revealed what he expected me to do and I grew more and more amazed. It was as if he had read my mind and selected a task designed specifically for me. He wanted me to start by becoming completely invisible. No one was to be left alive that might know my true nature. I was to refine the art of camouflage, until it was a science, until I could hide myself in the 'skin' of others quickly and easily, learning to hide in plain view.

Once that was done, I was to begin my assigned task. Hitler wanted me to investigate absolutely everything about the caves and the town surrounding it. He wanted me to achieve two things at the same time. First, I was to assemble all available information about the caves into a coherent format, and, second, I was to erase the caves from recorded history. Such a task appealed to me immediately. It would provide me with the freedom I needed to continue my experiments. I could explore putting on different 'skins', learning to become anyone and then vanish, fooling everyone.

Matt Chatelain

As for those I encountered with the information I sought, they were to be eliminated. This final requirement was the most incredible, the most wonderful. Hitler understood my love of experiments. Now he had provided me with a format in which I could continue them. With structure, the experiments had deeper meaning.

Both his goals and mine could be served at the same time. I truly did not care about the caves. I only cared about the opportunity he presented me with, to follow my life's ambition, this time structured with exquisite planning.

From past experience, I knew that structure was the only thing which kept me from prison. Without the care taken to perfect my 'skins', without the extreme attention to detail, I would be arrested before I could even begin.

As for Hitler's claims, I would reserve my judgment. His wilder statements did not truly matter. Who was I to say whether his beliefs were justified or not? I was happy doing his bidding, as long as it continued to fit with my own goals.

***

We parted ways soon after. He would contact me by sending messages to our home base. In the meantime, I had much to do. He was adamant about my achieving complete invisibility, so I determined that the best way to begin this would be to return to the neighborhoods of my past and eliminate every remaining shred of evidence concerning my existence. In being absolutely thorough, I would achieve true invisibility. This series of exercises would double as training for my future investigations.

The first exercise I selected was the eradication of my family. I knew that they were aware of some of my animal experiments. If I 'killed' myself along with them, anyone investigating my trail would come to an abrupt end. Using my father's birthday as a reason to get us all together, I prepared the end of my beginning. In the morning, I selected a man of similar build to mine, knocking him out shortly after he left his home. Tying and gagging him securely, I lay him down in the woodshed behind my house, covering his body with a tarp and a few planks of wood.

The evening went as planned. My family arrived early and we ate the meal my mother had brought. They all enjoyed the cake I had prepared. Shortly after ingestion, I noted the oncoming of the cramps, caused by the large quantity of strychnine I had added to the cake's recipe. I put the 'concerned' look on my face and pretended to help. It didn't take long before they were unable to move, due to the increasing severity of the cramping. I allowed myself to relax and removed all masks from my face, allowing my true interest to show.

After drawing the drapes, I brought all of their cramping bodies into the living room to watch them die together. I had to tie their hands and muffle their screams with napkins stuffed in their mouths. I watched while the strychnine-induced spasms increased, until the slightest noise would send them into paroxysms of pain. I gazed deep into their eyes to try and see what they were seeing, what they were feeling. Once more I failed in my effort. The bodies collapsed and I saw no evidence of souls leaving. Just bodies.

I felt satisfied that my plan had worked. I resolved not to use strychnine again. It was too slow a poison to be useful in quick experiments. I went out to the woodshed to retrieve the bound man, still hidden under the tarp. His eyes were wild when I lifted him over my shoulder and carried him into the house. I dropped him down next to the rest of my family. Seeing them, he wriggled as hard as he could, perhaps getting an inkling of what was waiting for him.

I ignored him for the time being while I busied myself removing the bindings from my dead family. I staged their bodies around the dining table, as if we had all been sitting together after a wonderful meal but something had happened and each had tried to unsuccessfully escape. My mind flashed back to our meal and my mouth salivated. I would miss my mother's cooking.

I positioned my father on the ground, his left arm reaching for the door. My mother was placed at the table. My two brothers lay behind her, lying on the floor, tangled, as if they had tripped over each other in their haste to leave the room. Finally, all the bodies were arranged in exactly the right position.

I picked up a large pillow from the couch and sat down on top of the bound man, straddling his chest. He was looking at me desperately, unable to utter a single sound, his eyes darting left and right frantically, trying to find some way out of his situation. I realized that if I used the pillow, I would be unable to see his eyes while he died so I put it down. He took this to mean that he was getting a reprieve and relief appeared in his eyes. Whatever it was disappeared when I lay myself flat on top of his body, my eyes centimeters away from his. Using an extended index finger from both hands, I slowly moved in on his face from each side, coming closer and closer to his nose. He could see it happening and he redoubled in his efforts, trying to throw me off, to spit out his gag. I moved my legs, locking myself over him, and brought both index fingers against his flaring nostrils, pushing them hard together.

His air supply cut off, he fought wildly but I kept my position, using whatever force necessary to keep his nostrils shut tight. He would get no further reprieve. This was the moment I had chosen for him to die, the moment of my experiment. It happened suddenly. One moment, he was fighting, the next he was gone. Nothing left him. Whatever souls were, if they existed, they were not physical.

I sat up and untied him, placing him near 'his' mother as if he had been trying to save her, a loyal son to the end. I grabbed two kerosene lanterns and threw the first on the middle of the dining table. A huge wall of flame exploded, engulfing my mother instantly, the fire spreading rapidly. Before exiting out the back door, I threw the second lantern near my two brothers, giving the impression that they had dropped it by accident while they ran like the cowards that they were. Both fires joined, consuming the living room and my family.

I walked away from the house, already planning the next step in the process of making myself invisible.

My classmates and teachers! They all had to go.

CHAPTER 14
A Surprise from my Friends

I was resting, my shoulder still sore from its encounter with a bullet. Raymonde brought supper with her and no new information. She confirmed that no one had seen Norton, nor had his body been found. He had vanished. Coulter had dug up some of Norton's high school records. He had been captain of the swimming team and had once been considered for the Olympics. His survival was a distinct possibility.

I was still not sure what to make of Norton's attack. Why was he after me and not the Shadow-Killer? Why was he so stuck on the letters 'HN'? Everything had happened so fast. The man had seemed demented, speaking in circles.

I was still troubled by his disappearance. Had I been responsible somehow? Perhaps I should have told him what he wanted to know. If I had gone down that route, things might have turned out far worse. Norton was not listening to me anyway. His ramble had made sense only to him.

Raymonde's hand on my shoulder pulled me out of my reverie.

"I still can't believe what happened this afternoon. When I looked at the video that Coulter sent me, I was amazed by what you did. That was incredibly brave..."

I knew it had been fear that had made me fleet of foot. Bravery had little to do with it. Had I been in my right mind, I would never have contemplated such a reckless course of action. I had trouble believing I had done it. Hugging her after she sat down on the bed, I explained how I felt:

"These last few days have been a whirlwind, as if time were being compressed. We are on a roller-coaster of a ride, with death, danger and mystery all around. After reading the Leblanc journal, when I saw your mother crying so hard, I didn't know what to say to you. I'm worried that you might be upset with me for bringing such turmoil to your mother's life, to your life."

Her arms tightened around me, her eyes shining with warmth.

"Paul, my mother's tears were good tears. To finally know what really happened back then, to be able to lay those ghosts to rest. I don't regret a single instant of what has happened since you arrived here. These are things we were meant to go through, I can feel it. Besides, it allowed us to find each other."

"Well, thank God for that, then" I said and she smiled. "I talked to my friends online this afternoon..."

"Uh-oh, I know what that means. Our adventures aren't over, are they?"

"Uhm, no, not yet," I answered. I summarized the Maximillian Bauer story and then explained our plan.

"All along through the Great Hunt, we have always found just enough facts to point the way to where we should go next. Leblanc's journal gave me the final few pieces I needed to figure out where we had to go this time. Did Hitler return to the caves? Was he trapped and killed there, the way Leblanc intended? There is only one way to get the answers: by entering the caves."

"But you don't know how to get in. The Germans blocked all the entrances," she argued.

"No, I don't think they did. I think there is a chance that we can find a way in. We'll talk more about that in the morning, when Briar and the others connect back on," I said, refusing to explain further. It was no longer time to talk about the caves.

It was time for bed!

***

Next morning found me frustrated. We had gotten up early, showered, and eaten. Since then, I had been trying to connect with my friends. I had run through our last conversation, confirming to myself that they had definitely set a contact time of 10:00 AM. It was now 10:35 AM and I could not get them to answer, no matter what I did.

Raymonde was of absolutely no help, trying to tickle me whenever I brought the topic up. There was a knock at the door. It was the maid:

"There is a phone call for Mr Sirenne. The front desk said that you'll have to go down to the restaurant to pick it up," she informed us.

"Fine, thank you. I'll be down presently."

"Thank you sir, I'll tell them," she said, leaving quickly. Them?

"It must be them. Perhaps the Internet is down. Are you coming down with me?..." I asked Raymonde.

"Paul, I wouldn't miss this for the world," she answered mysteriously.

Reaching the small restaurant room and, seeing 'our' table, where a phone had been placed, I sat down, picking it up.

"Yes, this is Paul Sirenne. There's a call for me?

"Just a second, Sir, I'll connect you."

I heard a few clicks and pops then an unmistakable voice blasted over the phone:

"Paul, thank God it's you. It's O'Flanahan, old buddy..."

"I know who you are, Liam, what is this all about? Where have you been?..." I tried to say but he interrupted me right away:

"There's no time for that, me boy, I just need you to do a wee favour for me, is all," he begged, his Irish accent overwhelming the phone's tiny speaker.

"A favour? You've got to be kidding, right?" I answered.

"Please, it's such a small thing. I was wondering if you could settle an argument I was having with Coulter. Could you turn your head about seventy-five degrees to the right?" he asked. That request sounded very familiar. I did what he asked and turned my head to the right.

I was looking at a table where three men were sitting. One of them was facing me directly, holding up a cell phone. It was O'Flanahan. The other two turned around. It was Coulter and Briar. My jaw dropped open in surprise. I turned to look at Raymonde, her face half-covered by her hand while she tried to hide her smile. Mrs Leblanc was peeking in from the restaurant entrance, also laughing. Had they all been in on it?

I started laughing finally. They had done it well; I had to admit it. I walked over to my friends and sat down in the fourth chair, trying to look unflappable.

"Coffees all around? I believe it's my round this time, gentlemen."

***

Apparently, the distance had been bothering all three of them. The events in Etretat were occurring with ever-increasing speed and there they were, sitting around at home, looking at their computers. A unanimous decision had been reached to do what they knew had to be done. Coulter had managed to find two seats on a red-eye flight for himself and O'Flanahan while Briar had organized another flight on his own. They had met in the Paris International Airport.

"My dear boy, sorry for springing this on you in this manner but, really, there was no way any of us could stay away from Etretat for one more second, grading of papers be damned," exclaimed Briar.

A pot of coffee sat on the table, three quarters empty. Mrs Leblanc had joined us, hugging everybody. Introductions over, I got back on topic.

"Yesterday, before all the excitement, I said to all of you that it was time to go find the caves. If you think back on Leblanc's journal, you may remember the section when he had wandered into a very big cave with a large body of brackish water. Brackish water would mean that there must be some sort of opening to the English Channel. I wondered if, at some point in the past, that opening might have been larger. The fort of Frefosse once had another entrance, a hidden port, giving access to the open sea for the smugglers. This ancient beach entrance would have been covered by silt and debris more than a thousand years ago. However, the Germans might have re-opened this hidden entrance, an entrance that would be more than three hundred metres out to sea and perhaps just as deep, an explanation for all the blasting Bequilles mentioned, " I concluded.

"I don't know why I didn't think of that before. You must be right... But why make an opening below sea level?... Unless it was designed for submarine access..." theorized O'Flanahan aloud.

"Yes, I think so. With a sub, Hitler could have come here unseen at any time. And it is going to be our way in," I affirmed.

"If there really were such an opening, why wouldn't it have been found yet?" Briar asked.

"It is a concern that the Germans would also have had. Perhaps they found some way of dealing with that," I suggested.

"Paul, none of us are deep sea divers. How do you expect us to go down there?" worried Raymonde, a concern supported by most of the others.

"Coulter's looking into that... Before we even think of going into the water, however, we might be able to use our resources to pinpoint the area where we should search," I explained. Coulter popped open his laptop and began typing. Within seconds, he pushed his laptop to the centre of the table, a smug look on his face:

"Take a look at this."

We examined a digital display of Etretat's underwater topography. The exposed seabed was a series of frozen, undulating waves radiating away from the coastline, looking like spokes on a wheel. The spokes seemed to be radiating from a central point: the Aval cliff and the Needle.

"Where did you get this? This is great!" O'Flanahan exclaimed.

"This program allows you to look at any underwater area of the world, using digitized satellite imagery. It's not usually available for public use but I found us a special pass. " he explained.

"Do you guys see the same pattern that I'm seeing?" I asked, pointing at the image. "There certainly would be room for a sub in those chasms between the radiating spokes. Look at that one in the centre. It's perfectly lined up with the cliff."

Coulter pressed a few keys and added.

"At this scale, the chasm depth would be... uh, just a sec... about one hundred metres. I tried comparing rock density to reveal an opening but nothing stood out. If there's an entrance down there, it's well camouflaged."

"Everything points to it being in that central furrow. The others are simply too far. When we go looking, that's where were going," I affirmed.

I just had to hope that Coulter came up with something to get us there.

***

Raymonde got out of the Porsche and walked up to the front door, knocking on it. Jacques Vallin opened, calling out loudly to his brother who was in the old garage next to the house.

"I'm so sorry for what I said yesterday," Jacques apologised. "I don't know what came over me. I felt like my whole life had been ripped away from me... But I've had a bit of time to think it over... I can see how Mr Leblanc never had any choice. He did the best he could to help those who got hurt. Our family just got caught in the middle..."

Ives walked in, his face breaking into a smile when he saw us.

"You two have had a rough time of it, it's true enough. You've got to realise that there's no need to worry about the past like that anymore. The present seems exciting enough, wouldn't you say? I think we've figured out a way to get into the caves but we're going to need your local connections: is there a boat we could rent, something big and seaworthy?" I asked them.

"I know a fellow who's got a real wide boat on those pontoons. It's pretty big and fast and he knows how to keep quiet too," Ives suggested.

"Are you talking about Languenoc's boat?" asked Jacques.

"You know I am, Brother."

"We can go see him right away and have a talk with him," Jacques said, getting up. "Don't you worry, Mr Paul, we'll get you your boat... just like we agreed... You do the thinking and we'll do what we can to get you what you need..."

We decided to meet on the beach at 8:00 AM next morning, hopefully giving Coulter enough time to get organized. His last text message had said that he had found something and was working hard to get it here. Arriving back at the Villa Leblanc, Raymonde and I found the other two, Briar and O'Flanahan in the restaurant, still arguing. We joined them.

As I sat down, I received a second call from Coulter, who informed me that the package was on its way. He still had much work to do to secure the second part of our plan. It was crucial if we wanted to reach the caves. I wished him good luck. It was a big undertaking, especially in such little time.

O'Flanahan spoke up, bothered by something.

"Listen, Paul, Raymonde, I know I've been ranting a lot about publishing this thing. I'm sure you understand why... We have uncovered a whopping conspiracy and it's my business to publish that type of stuff. This is pure gold. The biggest conspiracy of them all, right here in our hands... and nobody knows a thing about it. It's unbearable! "

"I know this is an issue for you, Liam. From the beginning, the Great Hunt has been teaching us the need for caution. We have uncovered evidence of an incredible battle, fought entirely in the shadows. What is this battle about? Can it really be just about some caves? Something about the whole thing doesn't fit. I can't express it in words but I can tell you this: we have not uncovered the real story yet..." I said.

Briar added:

"I've felt a bit of this myself. It's as if we are out of control. The events keep drawing us further and further into the unknown."

Raymonde was nodding her head in agreement.

"I've felt like that too. Every day has brought more complexity. What does it mean? Where is it leading us?" she asked in earnest.

"It's leading us to the caves. That's obvious. When those caves were last entered, the entire world was affected. Hitler and Leblanc's lives were irrevocably altered. It is this thought that cautions me. We truly do not yet know what we are dealing with. It *behooves* us to move forward carefully, with due consideration. To answer your original question, Liam, I think that discretion is not an option, it's a *requirement*. There's something in those caves. I can feel it. I don't know what it is but it's there. Until we find out what it is, we must keep it absolutely quiet!"

"I concur wholeheartedly!" supported Briar.

***

The morning found us on Etretat's main beach with the Vallin brothers. A fishing boat was pulled up on the shore. Mrs Leblanc had declined joining us, her aging body simply not up to the rigours of the task awaiting us. O'Flanahan appeared distinctly greenish when he stepped into the boat.

"Is this the stable boat you were talking about?"

"No, Mr Paul, it isn't. Languenoc's ship is much too big to come this close to the shore. We arranged for a local fisherman to take us out." replied Jacques Vallin.

I clambered into the boat, followed by the others. Ives jumped in deftly after giving the boat a strong, hard push. The pilot started the motor and we headed out to the channel. The boat was bobbing and weaving madly. We huddled together in the middle of the boat, avoiding the waves as much as possible. O'Flanahan was holding on for dear life.

"I can't fathom how anyone could earn a living doing something as dangerous as this," he exclaimed. "It's almost enough to take my mind off Leblanc's journal."

"Nothing could succeed in my case. I've done nothing but read and re-read his journal, this last day," Briar admitted, wiping the sea spray from his face. "There are a few passages that seem more worthy of note than others..."

"...Like what, Briar?" asked O'Flanahan.

"In particular, the section where he mentions that he contacted Raymond Lindon to reach A.L. Why Lindon?..." Briar started.

"... Yeah, that's a good one, all right. I noticed one of my own: It was near the beginning when Leblanc met Father Cochet. He mentioned a couple of other names that are rather curious. In particular, Father Boudet... If these names lead us where I suspect they will, our little conspiracy just connected to a whole family of conspiracies we haven't even considered yet," added O'Flanahan.

"That's all well and good, O'Flanahan but my concern about Lindon may be important to us, unlike these vague conspiracies of yours... Our attention has been hovering around Raymond Lindon for a while now. He became Leblanc's lieutenant, helping him through thick and thin. He was in charge of the Net, no small thing there, and now we know he was Leblanc's go-between for contacting A.L. So, again, why Lindon? He continued playing a role after the war, by purchasing Ambrumesy castle and hiding the stone cylinder there. There can be no question. He was an integral part of Leblanc's plans, Paul, and he deserves more attention. We should investigate his past more closely and see what we can uncover," Briar concluded.

"I'm much more curious about that group of numbers at the end of his journal," Coulter added. "They are obviously a code. I think that his whole journal is off-kilter, as if the words were concealing a deeper meaning. Perhaps those numbers are the key. But that's not all. Since O'Flanahan mentioned Maximillian Bauer, I haven't been able to keep the story out of my mind. I did some research and eventually managed to find a single faded picture of the anonymous author of the Bauer book. I compared it to a fuzzy picture of Weissmuller I managed to ferret out from a book about Etretat and the Second World War. The two pictures seem to be a close match. Bauer may be Weissmuller after all. I am now trying to find pictures of Hitler during the First World War. Perhaps I can find one with our elusive Weissmuller standing nearby..."

"Hey, we're going the wrong way. The Needle is over there. I don't want to have to suffer through this torture any more than necessary, for Pete's sake," exclaimed O'Flanahan.

Jacques took a moment to clarify the situation.

"We're just going to meet Captain Languenoc."

"Look, there it is. I can see it," Raymonde exclaimed

As we rounded a bend, Languenoc's ship was finally revealed. It was an impressive sight. Two incredibly large pontoons anchored a massive platform. Near the rear of the platform, a series of structures were erected, with a second level featuring the bridge of the ship. I could not see any form of propulsion but it was moving along at a good clip.

"Thank God, look at how stable it is," stated O'Flanahan.

The fishing boat swerved smartly, positioning itself next to the nearest pontoon, where I noticed a mooring post and some metal steps. A large man, wearing a deep blue, woollen shirt and a captain's hat, waited for us while we climbed aboard.

"Welcome to my ship, the 'Helen'. Named after my ex-wife, may we never encounter her in person. I am Captain Languenoc."

"This is quite a vessel, Captain. My name is Paul Sirenne..."

"Glad to finally meet you, Mr Sirenne. Jacques told me all about you. Thanks for the comment about Helen. I built her myself, not another one like her... And she never talks back..." he answered, an easy smile complimenting his rugged features.

"How come it's so stable?" wondered Coulter.

"There are two more pontoons below the ones you can see, well below the waves on the surfaces. I can control how much ballast is in them. Gives us instant mass and almost complete stability. I have four massive water jets powered by that generator over there. They control the motion of the boat in any direction, giving me the ability to really speed or to stay exactly where I want."

"We'll I'm impressed," Coulter added. "Did our package arrive in time?"

"A helicopter dropped it off ten minutes before we left port this morning. Good timing on your part, Mr Coulter. Follow my man there, he'll show you where it is, while I tend to things here. I'll have you where you want to go in about twenty minutes."

Curious about the mysterious package, everyone followed Coulter. A large crate was facing us, with the words 'Oceanographic Institute of France' stamped on the side. We made quick work of opening it, using a couple of crowbars left for that purpose by our Captain. Our host had thought of almost everything.

"Anyone want some coffee? It's freshly brewed!"

No, I was wrong: he had thought of everything after all!

***

"People, let me present to you 'Calvin the Third'," stated Coulter, sounding as if he were showing us a newborn baby. The pride apparent in his voice, he continued: "Calvin here is the latest development in remote-controlled underwater camera technology. From this console, we can control *and* watch Calvin's descent, while sitting comfortably on the surface. Additionally, we can record everything on a DVD for later analysis. All we have to do is drop Calvin over the side and we can begin our exploration."

"I've had a hunch about this for a long while. It's time to see if I'm right!" I exclaimed.

It was more than a hunch... it was a dream.

Matt Chatelain

EXCERPT FROM THE WEISSMULLER MANUSCRIPT

Fighting the Net

After six months of construction, the infrastructure of our underground complex is well established. I have driven the men hard but it has paid good dividends. The power station will soon be brought online. The main connecting tunnels have all been cleared and stabilized. We have mapped out most of the upper level caves and will be starting on the lower levels within one month.

We have found many curious things in the caves, the most intriguing being a fast-growing fungus, unique to these caves, which has fascinating bio-luminescent properties. It was quite dark when we originally entered into the caves but when we pumped fresh air into them, the fungus began emitting more and more light until there was no need to use our electrical lamps.

While the refurbishing of the caves is going well, the situation above ground is another matter. When we arrived and completed our takeover of Etretat, I had felt quite elated by the apparent cowardice of the French Resistance. Now, it is clear that I was mistaken. I have become convinced that a large component of the local population is actively fighting against us. They even have a name for themselves, the 'Net'.

They are being clever about it. It is mostly a war of passive resistance. At first, there were some apparently innocent incidents. Vehicles broke down, gas leaks were found, fires broke out. After a month of these incidents, I increased security and severely punished any man linked to the problems. It became obvious that these were not acts of carelessness but rather sabotage.

The Resistance had chosen to fight a battle of attrition. I had to admit it was an effective approach, having developed the process to an art form myself. Admittedly, I was irritated when the same tactics were used against me.

However, acts of sabotage were only the beginning. The attacks quickly grew more aggressive. The *Maquis*, an extremist section of the French Resistance, made its deadly appearance, attacking vehicles all over the countryside. During these attacks, my men were killed, the vehicle stolen, leaving little evidence behind. No one ever heard or saw anything. Rarely, we would find hastily buried bodies, deep in the undergrowth. Usually, those bodies were mutilated, showing evidence of torture. Too much violence for the Maquis. As a result, I suspected the Net.

Within several months, what had first appeared to be an irritating mosquito had changed into a murderous jackal snapping at our heels. I had to remain completely focused on the development of the cave complex yet my attention was being bifurcated by the savagery of the attacks against us.

My Weissmuller 'skin' came with an increasing amount of responsibility. Demands on my time were severe. I could no longer easily return to the shadows which I yearned for. No matter the intensity of these cravings, I found fewer and fewer occasions to carry out my experiments. I enjoyed the fear that my men had of me and the thought of controlling others held a powerful appeal but these pleasures were not enough to drown out the call for experiments.

The murderous acts of the Maquis incensed me, challenging me to my core. I knew the Maquis felt safe in the covertness of their actions. They believed that their power lay in the fact that I did not know who they were. They were wrong. I could turn their very invisibility into their Achilles' Heel, since I could *also* carry out torture and murder. I did not even need to be as specific as them, as long as the blame fell directly upon the Maquis and, subsequently, the Net.

I would retaliate personally, choosing a new victim with every death of my men, with every act of sabotage against us. My retaliation would bring fear and horror into the Maquis' heart and blame for the Net.

I began going out during the night, alone, draped in the shadows I so loved. I would choose a victim at random, performing experiments reminiscent of the tortures wrought upon my men by the Maquis. I would always leave a small propaganda leaflet, bearing the 'Croix de Lorraine', the French Resistance symbol.

Over time, rumors spread and locals began viewing the Maquis with disfavor, attributing the horrible deaths to them. The fear eventually extended into members of their own ranks, distrust spreading deep into the Net. They did not know who was doing the killing, thus were powerless to fight against it, foisting upon them the very feelings of helplessness they wished to force upon me.

With every succeeding tactical experiment, I found the intensity of my cravings diminishing, my inner calm returning. I reveled in my dual role for many months. I felt released from the Maquis' manipulations, confident that my approach was sufficient to reduce their attacks against us.

Carrying out these nocturnal activities was satisfying for me but they were also very draining. My solution was to go out and perform a batch of experiments once a week, leaving me with six full days to devote to the continuing expansion of the cave complex.

One of the rooms fascinated me in particular. My research indicated that Francis the First was likely to have been the architect of this hidden chamber, which had been converted into a fabulously wealthy throne room. I knew Hitler would be impressed by it.

***

I was also frustrated by the disappearance of Leblanc and Lindon. They had both vanished well before I had neared their small town. I was convinced that they were still acting against us. Unfortunately, I had priorities to attend to and could not look for them, no matter their strategic importance. There was nothing that they could do against us now, in any case. The stronghold was ours.

As the war progressed, I formulated secondary plans to further destabilize the local Resistance movement, by striking directly at key personnel. A few collaborators, blended into the local army, worked the locals and returned some specific results. The name Vallin surfaced, a name I remembered from stories Hitler had told me. However, this Vallin was careful and we got few chances to trap him. Then, during a covert observation of his activities, I uncovered the familiar name of Leblanc.

Quick research informed me that I was dealing with the son of Maurice Leblanc himself. He had joined the Resistance movement and was involved in planning many missions. I began preparing a very special experiment for him, one that would send a message directly into his scheming father's heart. Maurice Leblanc would learn the error of his ways. I would be his teacher and the lesson would be difficult.

During the period of the Maquis-inspired experiments, I perceived a different *excitement* than I had during my previous experiments. Over time, I realized that when I carried out a dual-purposed experiment, my satisfaction with the entire process literally doubled. The addition of this secondary purpose to my experiments was revelatory to me.

When I had performed my first experiments under Hitler's new guidelines, I had felt a similar increase in satisfaction. Recently, with my tactical approach to the Maquis situation, I found that increasing the level of purpose seemed to enhance the experiments themselves in a way I could hardly explain.

When I tried combining my basic desire for experiments with both military purpose *and* revenge on Leblanc's son, my attention and eagerness nearly tripled in intensity. I became infused with energy, my planning reaching heights of complexity I had never previously imagined possible. I felt as if I were floating above everyone, my control absolute.

I had begun my experiments in order to understand the purpose of life. My first approach had been to determine the presence of souls. Now I knew that I had been looking in the wrong place. The crescendo of my experiment was not its culmination. Souls didn't matter. Nothing mattered. It was only my *approach* that mattered. It was all about method and purpose!

I had finally found the way to proceed, the path I was looking for, and I embraced it without reserve. Safe in the caves, I planned and planned. Maurice Leblanc's son would pay for his father's sins. Retribution would be at hand. I would carry out Hitler's orders. I would build my fortress.

I would establish my true superiority over all the others.

I had found Purpose!

CHAPTER 15
The Secret in the Depths

Captain Languenoc had provided us with a cabin, away from the wind and salt spray, which could damage the electronic equipment. Calvin had been lowered over the side, the portable antenna had been erected and we had retreated to the relative comfort of the small room. Our eyes were glued to the monitor while Calvin's cameras revealed the depths of the channel waters, controlled by an already adept Coulter:

"Don't forget that there's been more than sixty years since anyone's been down there, if anyone was ever down there, of course."

"There's something there, I'm sure of it," asserted O'Flanahan.

"I'm with Mr O'Flanahan. I think this is terribly exciting, don't you, Maman?" asked Raymonde.

For a moment, I thought I had taken leave of my senses. Had she just addressed her mother, who was this very moment, sitting down at the Villa Leblanc? The answer came when Mrs Leblanc's voice emanated from a tiny speaker, located on Coulter's laptop:

"Yes Raymonde, I can see everything perfectly well. This is wonderful. It is just as if I were there with you. These glasses are incredible. Thank Mr Coulter for arranging this."

I noticed for the first time that Raymonde was wearing her special glasses. Mine were nowhere to be seen.

"I re-routed the signal from Raymonde's glasses, through my laptop, to your glasses, Paul," Coulter explained.

"Look, there's the bottom now."

Our eyes returned to the monitor. Coulter went on, manipulating Calvin's controls all the while.

"These cameras are so highly advanced they don't need any light to see. We are using a combination of sophisticated radar waves emitted from two sides of Calvin... We're coming up to the edge of the trench now. If we continue along this path we will reach its end within a few minutes... We should be coming up to a bend on our right."

The screen indeed revealed a slow bend in the trench wall, leading into a side canyon of some depth. Leaving nothing to chance, remembering my dream, I suggested:

"Go into there, Fabian."

Calvin headed down the side canyon. It was about twenty metres wide and formed a deep cut into the trench walls. Suddenly the cameras grew confused in the centre of the screen, becoming blurry.

"Let me switch to regular lights for this area. There's something reflective in the centre."

There was a shift in the monitor's image, which clarified, showing us the end of the side canyon. The steep side walls of the trench closed in rapidly to a sharp line about twenty-five metres in front of us.

"Why is the radar having so much trouble?" asked Briar.

"Over there, see those nodules? They could be natural magnetite. The compass is flying all over the place. If the magnetic fields surrounding those natural deposits were strong enough, they would probably cause disruptions to most equipment. Sound waves could be similarly affected by odd compositions of the bedrock, or by certain reflective shapes. There's nothing here. This is a dead end. Let's go back and continue on the original route," Coulter suggested.

Calvin turned around and travelled at a steady speed until it returned to the main trench. Heading down to its end, the cameras revealed that something had been going on in the depths after all. The view-screen showed an increasing quantity of rubble. Rock falls were apparent. The trench walls had suffered explosive damage at some point in the past.

I kept looking for a giant underwater owl.

Calvin floated upward, following the wall of rubble. Soon it reached an area that had definitely been cleared away and flattened. At the back of the flattened plateau was an area where a tunnel might have been located but another rock fall completely covered it.

"Look at that," exclaimed Briar.

I saw what he had noticed. Partially obscured by rubble, there was a faint, slightly curved line traversing the cliff wall. Below the line, the stone looked greyer than normal and far smoother than it should be.

"What is it?" wondered Coulter.

"It looks like the edge of a circular entrance, don't you think?" suggested Briar.

"Is it big enough for a submarine?"

"It's possible, Raymonde. Very good eyes, Briar!" I said. "... Unfortunately, if there had ever been an opening there, it has been sealed up, either by the forces of man or nature. No matter the cause, we will have to accept that there is no way into the caves to be found here."

Our common disappointment left a palpable atmosphere in the cabin. Coulter guided Calvin carefully up along the natural cleft created by the massive trench walls and we looked with sharp eyes but found nothing else. The rocks covering the ancient opening had eclipsed our best chance.

I found that I could not let go. My second dream had to be right! The first one had been prophetic about the bunker and about Raymonde. I had to keep trying.

"Fabian, why don't we go back to that side canyon? All those strange readings have left me a bit curious..." I suggested

"Yeah. Why not? Since we're here..." added O'Flanahan.

"I was thinking about going back there anyway," Coulter agreed. "I didn't like that weird stuff with the cameras and the compass. We have about another hour of onboard power for Calvin. There's no umbilical with this baby. It's all wireless, can you believe that? There, we're back at the bottom now. I'll turn around and go back the way we came."

Slowly, we returned to the side canyon. It curved in to our left, revealing the odd clumps of magnetite on each side of the jagged canyon walls.

"Why is this side canyon so clean while the other one is full of debris? You would expect it to be... Well, isn't that strange..."

"What is it, Coulter?" asked Briar.

"Sorry... it's just that... Just a second, let me do something..."

He directed Calvin to slide sideways while keeping the cameras directly on the cleft formed by the joining of the two side canyon walls.

"Look at the cleft. There is something very strange about it. It seems to be following us..."

"Not following us, my boy, it's changing perspective! Will you look at that," exclaimed Briar.

As Calvin travelled sideways, the cleft did indeed seem to be constantly re-adjusting itself to remain in the exact centre of our field of vision. There could only be one explanation.

The cleft was not real.

"Fabian, make Calvin head directly into the cleft. Aim it right at the centre."

Coulter complained about crashing expensive equipment into rock walls but did what I asked. We watched the monitors intently while Calvin moved forward, inexorably getting closer to the rock wall. Then, something exceedingly strange happened. The cleft became stretched out, the image distorted.

"Huh... Paul, I'm losing Calvin's signal, something's going on down there."

"Keep going, push the motors to the max and power up all the sensors on that thing."

"But it'll crash, Paul"

"I don't care. Just ram it. Do it."

Coulter unwillingly aimed it for the wavering cleft. At the exact point when it should have smashed into the stone cleft, everything went crazy on the monitor. The image warped bizarrely on both sides, stressing the centre point until it completely split apart. Calvin's cameras were becoming wobbly when they briefly flashed on odd, giant, silvery disks, one on the left and the other on the right.

"I'm losing Calvin. I can't hold it..." screamed Coulter in a fit of panic.

Calvin was in an uncontrolled spiralling descent. The monitor screen wavered as the camera signal weakened. Just before Calvin's signal failed completely, the cameras whirled around one last time, giving us a single view of a long tunnel heading into the cliff.

**

Calvin's command centre had been turned off, useless now, with the loss of the deep-sea camera. Coffees had been refilled and Coulter was preparing his computer to do an analysis of the amazing footage we had obtained.

"... There, everybody gather round. I'm going to replay the last moments at half speed."

The screen brightened for a moment then the image coalesced into a view of the seabed floor. We approached the side canyon 'end', which we now knew was a disguised passage. What had been done to cast such a convincing illusion of a rock wall? One thing we were sure of: there was a way in!

"Did you see those strange owl eyes? What do you think those were?" asked Raymonde, her words giving me a start. She was right! The silvery disks had looked like giant owl eyes.

My dream.

"Hold on, we're getting to that point. There... the weird stuff is about to start. Let me slow it right down to frame by frame. Here we go..." Coulter ran his fingers over the keyboard, presenting a still image of the two canyon walls meeting abruptly in front of us, forming the cleft.

"Now, Calvin is going to start moving sideways. That was when we noticed that bizarre 'change of perspective'," informed Coulter.

"Look, there it goes," stated Briar, "the perspective jumps with each frame. It's as if the meeting point of the two canyon walls is re-adjusting itself constantly to our changing point of view..."

"Each side wall seems to be stretching or compressing, depending on where we are. The end result is that the cleft is always right in front of us," O'Flanahan added.

"It's got to be an illusion of some sort," affirmed Coulter. A voice spoke up from his speaker. I had forgotten in all the excitement that Mrs Leblanc was still with us, looking at everything through Raymonde's glasses.

"Paul, I've seen something like that before... That strange effect of always having the same point exactly in your centre of vision... I'm not sure if that information can be helpful to you..."

"Anything could be useful at this point, Mrs Leblanc," I replied.

"It's just a small area downstairs, in a corner, near the front desk of the Villa Leblanc. I had mirrors installed in the corner and placed some plants in front of it. It made the corner look so much bigger. I noticed that whenever you looked right in the corner, you couldn't see your face. It was always hidden by the joining point of the two mirrors, the cleft. You could bend your head this way or that..."

"... Changing your perspective..." added Briar thoughtfully.

"Yes, that's right, Mr Briar. The corner seemed to shift with you, matching your every move..." she finished.

"... Maybe those disks are mirrors," theorized Coulter.

O'Flanahan made a desultory gesture, commenting:

"Mirrors? You can't be serious. Look in front of you. We are seeing a three dimensional image..."

"Hold on, O'Flanahan" I objected, "Remember what happened after this? Coulter, fast-forward the video a bit..."

Once again, we witnessed a strange flattening of the image, during the underwater camera's final, calamitous approach toward the canyon wall.

"... Freeze it for a second, would you Coulter? Now, O'Flanahan, look at what is happening here: all cleft details are becoming grainier and stretched out. This supports Mrs Leblanc's comparison to a mirror. However, I don't think these are regular mirrors. Move ahead a bit more, Coulter."

As the video showed Calvin nearing what should have been a massive rock wall, a line suddenly appeared in the centre of the screen.

"This is where I lost control of Calvin," remembered Coulter.

"It's also when we saw those huge owl eyes," added Raymonde.

"I don't think they were eyes..." I predicted. "Move the images forward until we see them again."

Coulter complied quickly, curious to see them revealed. The line grew wider and wider, until the canyon walls were completely gone. By then, Calvin was rotating uncontrollably in a wide circle, falling to the seabed. The images swirled slowly until the first eye came into view. Coulter froze the image.

"Will you look at that," exclaimed Raymonde "It does look like a giant owl eye but it's a mirror, isn't it?"

I nodded my head.

"Yes... I believe that we are looking at a concave mirror, built on an inconceivable scale, able to project an incredibly large image... When I was younger, a friend showed me a magic trick. It was a small, black conical pyramid with an open top where a penny floated. Try as you might, you could not touch that penny. Your fingers would just float through it because, in fact, the penny wasn't there. It was sitting below, in the bottom of a bowl-shaped mirror. Because of its concave shape, you saw the penny's reflection floating in front of the mirror surface, not behind it," I explained.

"Look, Calvin's rotated around and there's another of those 'owl eye' mirrors, exactly opposite the first one. This one is a bit clearer. We can see more details... Gosh, it's huge... What's that shape in the middle there?" wondered Coulter.

"I think it's a miniature side canyon wall. The mirrors collect that image and reflect it, hugely magnified, in front there, behind Calvin's position. The two mirrors act in concert projecting an illusion of rock walls in the center. That's why the centre kept shifting. We were looking at two projected images," I added.

"Hey, check that out," Coulter exclaimed, freezing the image again and jabbing his finger at a corner of the monitor. "Look at that. The whole wall is covered with small pocks. That explains everything..."

"What are you talking about, Coulter" badgered O'Flanahan.

"Well, Calvin's deep sea camera worked with sound waves. When we went into the side canyon and looked at the end, the signals got all messed up..."

"I remember that. You had to switch to regular lights," added Briar, joining in.

"That's right. I couldn't explain why that was happening before but now I can. Whoever built this place covered the walls with small concave indentations. Any sound wave hitting those pocks would be sent careening in some side direction and the signal would be lost. It's brilliant. They knew about radar and came up with this natural defence against detection. That magnetite was probably planted too!"

"That's how this place stayed hidden for so long," mentioned Briar, "They certainly planned well..."

"Look, there's the tunnel," pointed Raymonde.

There it was, on the screen. The tunnel I had known we would find. There had been no doubt in my mind; it simply had to be there. I noticed a large arch over the entrance to the tunnel, looking like an owl's beak. The dream was complete!

We had found the way in.

Now, all we needed was to obtain some convenient transportation to get us physically down there, part two of our plan.

"Coulter, we need to talk to Captain Languenoc."

***

The Captain was heading back to a point off Etretat's beach. We would use his ship as a base of operations. He had assured me that the second item Coulter had ordered could be docked easily on the left pontoon. Coulter informed me that he had been successful in its rental and that, given the amount of money he had thrown at the owners, the item should be here within a few days. Languenoc would contact us when it arrived. We decided to head back to shore. Jacques Vallin made a quick phone call, using O'Flanahan's cell phone.

"The fishing boat is on its way back. Should be here soon."

"I can't wait," said O'Flanahan, his voice laced with sarcasm.

As we approached the beach, it seemed to me that it was much busier than when we left. I didn't like it. Something about it didn't feel right. I looked at the two Vallin Brothers.

"Keep a sharp eye out."

"Yes Sir, Mr Paul."

The fishing boat hit the bottom gently, carried in by the fading crest of a wave. The Vallins jumped out first, Ives holding the boat steady, while Jacques looked around like a hawk. I helped Raymonde out. There was a tension in the air, as if an electrical storm was about to break. Both Briar and O'Flanahan stayed close to me while Coulter jumped out, each of them feeling the same apprehension.

Something was going to happen.

I scanned around frantically, trying to find anything out of the ordinary. Suddenly a man stepped out from the crowd, limping badly. Norton! He was still holding the stubby little pistol, aimed straight in our direction, his face contorted in a rictus of rage.

Briar stood next to me on my left, looking tense and concerned, O'Flanahan on my right. Raymonde and Coulter were behind me to one side. Before any of us could do anything, Norton aimed his pistol, seeming ready to shoot. He was mumbling something to himself. I couldn't hear what he was saying. A woman screamed, seeing Norton's levelled pistol. He jumped at the sound, his face jittery, and the crowd began to run away from him in panic.

At the very moment he jumped, distracted by the woman's cry, a blur of metal shot towards Norton from my left, planting itself right into his gun arm with a solid '*thock*. Norton screamed in pain, dropping the pistol into the sand.

Jacques Vallin had thrown a knife! He was holding another one, looking ready for anything.

Norton grabbed his arm, his screams turning to whimpers while he bent down desperately to pick up his pistol. Before he could reach it, Ives Vallin's big, meaty hand clamped down on the inspector's ravaged arm, grabbing his shoulder with the other one, lifting the man bodily off the ground and shaking him mightily. Norton looked completely done in.

Most tourists had run away but a large group of men remained, forming a tight circle around us, perhaps curious to see what would happen next.

Ives lowered Norton as we approached cautiously. The long knife was still sticking out of his right arm, blood dripping from the wound. He was barely conscious. I stopped in front of him, Briar standing next to me. Norton looked up and began laughing again. It was a pitiful sound.

"You again... I know you now... I was wrong earlier when I said that it was me in the mirror... he-he-he... I know that now... I figured it out... You almost had me fooled... It wasn't me, it was YOU!"

Listening to him speaking in circles, I finally became convinced that Norton was the Shadow-Killer. It had to be him. It was as if he had two personalities, one forever chasing the other. Whoever got in his way became the Shadow-Killer to him. No wonder so many of his friends had been killed.

Having spoken those few words with a failing, gasping breath, Norton collapsed weakly in Ives Vallin's arms. Surprising us all, in a frenetic move, his left hand shot out, grasping the knife stuck in his right arm. He wrenched it out in a desperate jerk, blood spurting out from his wound, trailing after the knife. He twisted himself out of Ives' loosened grip and jerked his body up, suddenly bringing himself to a standing position. Using his last reserves of energy, he stabbed at me with the bloody blade.

He might even have succeeded in his attempt but Briar, the ever-alert Briar, jumped in front of me, his hand jabbing out in a frantic attempt to stop the oncoming blow. Norton swerved the knife and it twisted past Briar's outstretched arm, aiming directly at his chest, instead of mine. The knife slid closer and Briar twisted himself around in a rapid sideways move, barely avoiding injury. His left hand managed to grasp the stabbing knife by the handle, squeezing Norton's hand underneath his own in a grip of iron. In a sudden, adrenaline-infused move, Briar jerked the bloody knife out from his ripped shirt, Norton's arm trailing after it, his hand pinned inside Briar's tense grip.

For a moment, everything froze!

Briar was standing to my left and in front of me, his right arm held high, the blood-covered knife reaching the top of its arc. I glimpsed a light of anger and rage still burning in Norton's eyes. I could feel Raymonde's hand on the small of my back and saw O'Flanahan standing to my right, his eyes open and alert.

Time clicked back in and the knife flashed, impelled with tremendous force, as Briar twisted it back down and under, slicing directly into Norton's abdomen, slamming it up, straight into his heart! The flame of life faded from Norton's eyes and, after one final breath, he fell limply to the ground, taking the Shadow-Killer's secrets with him as he died.

Briar released the knife in horror.

"My God, what have I done? It all happened so fast... First he tried to stab you, Paul, then I stopped him, he stabbed, I twirled, he missed... Then I... I stabbed him... I couldn't stop myself... I'm sorry... so sorry..."

Raymonde went to him and patted his back in sympathy. I was glad Briar had escaped serious injury. I had thought him finished when he was stabbed. He had moved so very fast! So had the Vallins. Everybody had, while I had stood around, doing absolutely nothing! I had been frozen.

"He was crazy, Briar, nothing could have stopped him. It would have happened sooner or later. At least now, it's over," O'Flanahan said, trying to provide some support. I felt thankful for Briar's action but, in my heart, I still felt that some other path could have been taken to resolve this. Now, a man was dead because of me, even if it was the Shadow-Killer. Perhaps if I had told him what he had wanted to know, things would have turned out differently.

I was to have no time for second-guessing myself because no sooner had Norton's lifeless body collapsed on the beach that our problems worsened. The circle of discontented men around us had grown to an alarming number. Now with Norton's death, the men became downright unruly and the circle tightened around us. Some of them were holding improvised weapons, branches, clubs and shotguns.

"This doesn't look good. You'd better handle this, Paul," O'Flanahan said, supportive as ever. "I'll be right next to you."

Jacques Vallin stood protectively to my right while Ives towered over my left shoulder, looking tense, ready for anything. I hoped it wouldn't be necessary. The crowd was suddenly upon us, several shotguns aimed at our feet. They looked determined.

"We think it's time for you to leave. You are bringing too much attention to this place," blustered a thickset man near me. While he spoke, his shotgun inched up towards my chest, adding a serious threat to his words. Before I could make a single move, Ives Vallin suddenly bellowed at the crowd:

"No one is going to threaten Mr Paul. No one, do you hear? Or you'll have to deal with me... and you all know me and what I can do," He roared, looking at the thickset man and the others behind him, completely ignoring the shotgun. A knife, thrown with incredible accuracy, planted itself into the sand, inches from the thickset man's feet.

"... And me. You all know me and I know all of you," Jacques said. The cowed, thickset man shifted his feet and retreated back into the anonymity of the crowd, his gun almost slipping from his trembling hands. The crowd had taken a step back, not expecting the aggressive reaction of the Vallin brothers. I used the lull to try to take control of the situation instead of being buffeted by it. I would not remain frozen again.

"I think it's time to calm down a bit and talk this out. Is there one of you who could step forward and talk for you? A bit of civility could lead us much further than threats and violence, don't you think?" I said loudly. Many of them looked away, unwilling to meet my gaze. Another man stepped out from the group.

"I'll talk."

He was a tall man, thin, with piercing blue eyes and an incredibly bushy moustache. Many of the others nodded in agreement, willing to let him speak for them.

"Very well. My name is..."

"We don't care who you are. You're just like all the others. We've dealt with your type before. You've been snooping around since you arrived. We've been watching all of you. We're used to the regular tourists, even the Lupin fanatics, but when you had that chase yesterday, we knew it was time to get you to move on. With what we've just seen, a murder this time, on our very beach, we know it's time for you to go. We'll deal with the body. No police. Just pack your bags and leave... and never come back."

They were watching us? I had to find out more.

"Why do you want us to move on? Why are we a threat to you?" I shot back. Looking at the others, who were milling around in indecision, the man explained:

"We don't like strangers who snoop too much. This is our town. You come here and try to stir up trouble. You could destroy everything we have here. We want you to leave."

Well, that was plain enough! However, it didn't explain much, sounding more like dogma than anything. Familiar dogma!

"You said you were watching us. How long have you been watching people?" I pushed a bit more.

"Since long before you were born, mister. This is our town and we intend to protect it," he answered, as if by rote.

This was starting to make sense to me, in a strange sort of way. I decided to take a gamble:

"Do you remember when you started protecting your town like this?" I asked, looking around at each of them "Do any of you? Or are you doing what your parents told you had to be done: to protect your town?... to keep the Secret?... Do you remember what started all this, what started the *Net*?"

A murmur swept through the crowd. They hadn't expected for me to know about them. Their reaction proved that I was on the right track.

"You're what's left of the Net aren't you? Doing what your parents did? Not knowing why it had to be done, just that you had to be on the lookout? That's it, isn't it?"

"How do you know all this, Mister? How do you know about us?"

Looking back at the crowd, I spoke quietly:

"Allow me to introduce Raymonde Leblanc, Maurice Leblanc's great-granddaughter. Some of you may not remember her. She has been living in British Columbia for a while. The reason your Net was created was to protect Maurice Leblanc, her great-grandfather. I suspect that, over time, you may have forgotten this. So, let me remind you that your parents, and their parents before them, swore to protect Etretat's big secret. The Leblanc family held that secret. You are here to protect *her*."

My latest statement was a revelation to them. Their mood changed when they realized that we might not be a danger to them, that, in fact, we might be the original reason for the existence of the Net. Still, the man with the moustache resisted:

"How do we know you're saying the truth, Mister?"

"What if *I* said it was the truth? Would you believe me, you bunch of idiots?"

The thin, wheezing voice had come from the edge of the beach, barely audible, where a taxi had stopped, disgorging a determined-looking Mrs Leblanc and an older man, a man with two crutches.

Bequilles!

"That's right, you all know who I am and what I did in the war, so don't you go questioning me. I know these people and I know why they're here. You idiots couldn't even realize that you're not here to kick them out, you're here to *protect* them. It is a bit my fault because there is something that I have told none of you, never thinking the time would actually come: That man there, standing next to Miss Leblanc, that's Paul Sirenne! Long, long ago, I was told by Raymond Lindon himself that a man of that name would be coming one day and that, on that day, purpose would return to our town. Well, he is right there in front of you. What a reception you've given him I must say. I'm too tired and too old for all this nonsense. I'm going home."

Without another word, exhausted by his efforts, Bequilles returned to the waiting taxi, heading back to his small apartment. His task was done, thanks to Mrs Leblanc. I saw that she was removing her glasses. She had techno-seen what was happening and had done the one thing she could to help us: to get Bequilles. Her timing could not have been better.

His words prodded a question within me. How could he have known about me, before I was even born?

By the time Mrs Leblanc had made her way to the dock, the crowd's mood had changed completely. People were moving off the beach, letting us pass by to join Mrs Leblanc. I saw several men converge on Norton's body, including the Vallin Brothers. O'Flanahan accompanied the group, eager to be part of a developing conspiracy. Within moments, the crowd had dispersed, as if nothing had taken place.

The man with the moustache walked along with us.

"We're really sorry, Mr Sirenne, Miss Leblanc. We just didn't know. We've been watching for so long, we lost track of the most important things. We won't make that mistake again. You can count on us. You do what you have to. We'll keep an eye out for you."

Many members of the Net had followed us, an avid curiosity evident in them, yet another unexpected development. Unexpected but it made sense. If the Net had been as organised as Leblanc's journal said it was, there was reason to expect that it would have remained active to this day, a hundred years after its inception. These loyal Etretatais had been given an incredible sense of purpose, to protect something so important that it could never be revealed. It would have set them apart from everyone else around them, like a 'country unto itself', as Leblanc had said.

My head began spinning with the enormity of it all: a single event, distant by a century, was still affecting thousands, perhaps millions of people today. I was awed by the power of that event. I returned in my mind to the moment when Leblanc and Hitler entered into those caves. It was as if that moment had sent ripples out into time, affecting everyone in its path, right up to today, culminating in Norton's death moments ago. A strong shudder of discomfort ran up my spine. I understood all too clearly that the responsibility for these caves was being thrust directly into *my* hands. Even though I had not yet set foot in those caves, I was already irrevocably connected to them.

A band of sweat broke on my brow and I felt faint, thinking of Norton's blood, Leblanc, Hitler, the caves, and Bequilles with my name on his lips.

"Paul, are you all right?" Raymonde asked, noticing my change in demeanour.

I felt like I was spinning, my head whirling, buffeted by the events, everything overtaking me, my life spiralling out of control.

"I need to sit down. I seem to... to have lost my bearings for a moment," I said. My thoughts continued unravelling in my head and I felt increasingly dizzy.

"Don't worry, I've got you, Mr Paul," Ives said, his strong arm giving me a support I suddenly needed.

With Raymonde on one side and Ives Vallin on the other, I was led to a beach chair, proffered by a concerned man nearby. I sat down and immediately closed my eyes, trying to slow the insane spinning in my head.

"Here's some water," Raymonde said, sliding a water bottle in my left palm. I put it on my forehead for a moment, just lying there and savouring its coolness. I uncapped the water bottle and took a long drink, keeping my eyes closed, regaining a bit of perspective. For a moment, I had felt completely overwhelmed by the reality of my developing situation. The tide was retreating and my feet had found bottom, if only just. I opened my eyes again, adjusting to the sunlight.

More than thirty people surrounded me, everyone looking at me in concern,. My friends were nearest, members of the Net in the background. In the distance, a man with a black bag was running towards us. The amount of concern threatened to overwhelm me yet again and I closed my eyes for another moment.

Realising this was no answer, I steeled myself and re-opened them.

"How are you feeling, Paul? You're scaring me," Raymonde asked, her voice thick with emotion.

"I'm okay, I think, Raymonde. I just need a bit of quiet," I answered, my voice shaky.

"Make way for the Doctor! The Doctor is here," I heard a voice say in the crowd, which parted, allowing the man with the black back to approach.

"There's no need for all this fuss, really," I objected weakly, only to be tut-tutted by the doctor.

"Why don't you let me be the judge of that, young man? Hmm? Move back everybody. Give him some room, he looks like he needs fresh air."

As he spoke, his hands flew all over me, checking my pulse, temperature, eyes, ears, heart, nothing escaped.

"You seem to be suffering from mild shock, young man. Everything should be fine after a good rest. Would you like a tranquiliser?"

"... Uhm, no, I don't think so but thank you. There's no need to go to all this trouble," I argued again.

"Listen, young man: if I took the trouble of coming here this fast, you can certainly take the trouble of following my orders. You get some rest. Let things sort themselves for a while."

The doctor gave my shoulder a quick pat and stood up, snapping his black bag shut.

"It's all over folks. He's fine. He'll be up and around in no time."

***

I was lying down in Raymonde's bed, resting as ordered. My friends had stayed around for a while but had eventually opted for the restaurant downstairs. Everyone felt slightly uncomfortable around everyone else, especially around Briar. These last events had been too much. Raymonde entered the room.

"Are you up for some company?" she asked.

"Sure. I'm feeling much better now," I answered. "I'm so sorry about what happened. I didn't mean to scare anybody."

"I know. It's okay," she said, sitting down next to me.

"... It all happened so fast... Norton attacked us and he... died... and the Net confronted us... and finally Bequilles mentioned my name... then, after it all, I was standing there, my thoughts rolling around Leblanc and Hitler going into those caves. That's what started it, I think. That single event has caused a huge impact on the entire world and nobody even knows! It now seems likely that Hitler's actions in World War 2 might be directly related to his coming to these caves. My entire family's history, my father's murder, is all due to Leblanc and his plans to leave a heritage. A killer is now dead because of us... My name is not even my name, it's Lupin. Bequilles said my arrival was foretold decades before I was even born. Everything around me... even you... it's all connected to these caves. And now it was *my* life that was being affected by these caves. I felt like I had nothing to hold on to, nothing that was mine. It was all for the caves."

"You seemed ready to faint. You got so pale."

"My head was spinning. It just wouldn't stop. The final blow was Norton's death. I realised, with inescapable clarity, that the responsibility of this incredible secret was being placed directly into my hands. Why me? Why did they prepare all this, Leblanc, Lindon, Lupin? What were they doing and why was it so important that I return?"

"You've got to give it some time, Paul. At least we know that it's over! The Shadow-Killer is dead. We are free of his manipulations. You can lay your family to rest, their deaths avenged. As for these other events, with Leblanc and the others, all that happened a long time ago. Nothing is happening today. It's all over and done with. Whatever has happened, has happened. We are just finding out about it but the story itself is finished."

"Is it, Raymonde? It doesn't feel finished. It feels vibrant and alive. You are right about one thing though: Leblanc, Hitler, Lindon, Lupin, they're all gone. However, I can feel their influence on everything that surrounds us. Although they are gone, their ideas, their thoughts have lived on after their death and the direct result is that I have been *brought* here, to uncover the mysteries they have left for me."

She was right and so was I. The past was gone but it was also still with us, appearing between the cracks here and there, directing our movements, its ideas still alive and powerful, undiminished by the passage of time. I lay there, reflecting when Raymonde leaned over and gave me a hug.

It became longer, until she stretched out next to me and we fell asleep in each other's arms.

***

A knock on the door woke us up. A glance at the bedside clock told me it was almost suppertime. I felt grounded again after the much-needed rest. My shoulder was better, almost back to normal. Raymonde, stretched her back and got up, opening the door.

Mrs Leblanc was standing there, holding two steaming plates.

"I thought you two might be hungry. Everyone else has eaten and retired to their rooms. No one felt much like speaking anyway."

"Come in, Maman. Thanks!" Raymonde exclaimed, taking the two plates from her mother, keeping the plate with bigger portions and handing the other one to me. I sat down with both of them at the small table nook. For a while, no one spoke. We both picked at our plates, too excited to be hungry. Giving up, I sat back, looking at Mrs Leblanc, while Raymonde resolutely tried to finish her plate. Something had been bothering me about Raymonde's mother for a while now.

"Mrs Leblanc, I have something I would like to ask you. I think it might be a bit forward on my part but I simply must ask..." I stopped, hesitating, not exactly sure how to proceed.

"Paul?" asked Raymonde, wondering what this was all about.

"It's all right, Raymonde," Mrs Leblanc said, "I know where he's going with this. Go ahead, Paul, ask your question."

"I've been thinking about the role you've played in our discoveries. For example: You were there, just in time, to save me, when I was in the Vallin's house... The comments you made about Leblanc's journal that started us off on our chase to Perpignan... You knew, by heart, the address of the place in Perpignan, where you and Maurice Leblanc stayed... The ditty which helped us find Maurice Leblanc's journal... Sending us to Bequilles to get key information about the events in the Second World War... Even having Hitler's letter displayed prominently in Maurice Leblanc's office and bringing me there to see it... Almost everything we have achieved here has been due to your timely intervention. Today, your timing was so perfect, when you arrived with Bequilles in tow... whose admission about my name intimated that he knew more than he said when we visited him..."

"Just ask your question, Paul," Mrs Leblanc prodded.

"... Very well. You seem to know much more than you have let on. Do you?"

"Of course I do, Paul. I am the grand-daughter of Maurice Leblanc. How could I not? Surely that must have been obvious to you for a while now..." she admitted, her stance completely different. Her back seemed straighter, her voice sure and confident.

"Maman?" queried Raymonde, baffled by her mother's words.

"Yes, my dear, it's true! After Grand-Papa's death, friends of the family, part of the Net, brought me up. Raymond Lindon also played a role in my upbringing. When the time was right, he gave me some letters from Grand-Papa. They revealed many things about what he had prepared. The letters told me that Paul would come and that I should be ready to help him find answers... Raymonde, I was going to tell you about all this, on your thirty-fifth birthday as arranged. When Paul arrived six months early, everything happened so quickly that I had no opportunity to sit down with you and explain..."

Now, it was Raymonde's turn to be in shock. Mrs Leblanc's revelations were not done yet:

"I'm so sorry, Raymonde but Grand-papa was very clear on certain points. I had to wait until a specific time before I could tell you everything."

"Everything, Maman? Is there more to tell?" Raymonde asked, almost afraid to hear the answer.

"Grand-papa left us more than a few letters. He also left us a trust, a very large trust, with over one hundred million Francs. This money was entrusted to me, in order to prepare for your return and for Paul's. So now, following Grand-papa's wishes, this trust will be passed on to you, my daughter, so that you may help Paul finish what was started so long ago."

"And what is that, Mrs Leblanc?" I wondered aloud.

"Why, to reclaim your heritage, our combined heritage, Paul. My ancestors and yours have conspired to prepare the way for you. Now, you have only to reach out and it will be yours. For a long while now, Bequilles and I have been the only ones to know the truth. The Net had been allowed to lay dormant, another part of Grand-papa's plans, waiting for the day of your arrival. I was prepared for all these things. Nothing could have prepared me for you two ending up in love with each other."

Having said that, she stood up, looking at us tenderly:

"I couldn't be prouder of both of you."

With tears in her eyes, after a brief hug and kiss, she left the room. I looked at Raymonde.

"You know what this means, don't you?"

"No, what, Paul?"

"We're both multi-millionaires now."

She smiled a bit, then laughed, realizing I was right.

***

Arriving downstairs early next morning, I felt I was back to my old self. Entering the restaurant with Raymonde, I found Jonathan Briar and Mrs Leblanc. The others were nowhere to be seen. Briar, noticing us, stood up, concern still evident on his face.

"Good morning to both of you. I am glad to see you up and around, Paul."

"I am feeling much better. How about you?" I added.

"I am fine. I thought I might be bothered about what... what I did to Norton but I am not. I rid the world of a monster and that has to be a good thing."

We sat down and the waitress took our breakfast order. Briar continued.

"Physically, I was very lucky. I escaped with only a few scratches, having swerved with the knife, thank god. Last night I was in shock about everything but this morning, I feel somewhat calmer. Reason tells me that Norton would have stopped at nothing to get at you. Taking that into account, I know that the memory will still be with me for a long while."

I wasn't sure if I understood what he was feeling but he was right about one thing: with Norton gone, the danger was past.

"Where are the other two?" I asked, curious.

"Captain Languenoc called for Coulter. He had some news about whatever it is we are waiting for and needed some help smoothing things over for a speedy delivery," Briar explained. Coulter was excellent at 'smoothing difficulties'. Briar continued: "O'Flanahan went down to the beach, with plans to walk around and get the feel of the place."

Breakfast arrived and we ate. I stuck to coffee, not feeling hungry. I didn't think that Coulter would succeed in his endeavours today but there was a fair chance tomorrow morning might bring better luck. Briar was looking at me with a pensive look in his eyes. Seeing that I was not eating, he leaned over to me:

"Paul, would you be up to a walk in that wonderful garden out back? I have a few things I would like to share with you. It shouldn't take more than a few minutes."

"Certainly. I'll take my cup of coffee with me, if that's okay, Mrs Leblanc? I'll be right back."

"Take your time, Paul. I'll sit here with Maman," added Raymonde.

Briar and I made our way to the back doorway. Stepping down the stone stairs, we walked along the brick path.

"My boy, you had me quite worried yesterday..." Briar started.

"I'm sorry about that, I don't know what came over me," I returned, abashed by all the sympathy.

"The thing is, Paul, I think you know exactly what happened. That is why I asked you to come out here with me. We've known each other for more than ten years, so I guess it's no secret to you that I've come to look upon you almost as the son I've never had. This means so much more to me, now that your real father is gone... That's why I found yesterday so painful to watch... My boy, I must speak frankly..."

"Go ahead, Jonathan. I know you mean well. Hey, you just risked your life to save mine," I replied.

"All these things which have been happening to you are putting an unexpected, perhaps even unwanted, load on your shoulders. You cannot understand how this comes to be and you cannot accept that you are being singled out," Briar continued, his finger pointing directly at me in emphasis.

His words struck deep into my heart. It was as if he were there with me, feeling the same burden.

"I have lived many years longer than you and have travelled all over the world during that time. Experience has taught me much. You have stayed mostly at home, surrounded by your books, always living as if in a cave. I have always thought it so sad how you seem to have missed most of life. I think that yesterday, the shock you felt was a necessary step for you, Paul..."

Briar continued, as we sat down on a stone bench.

"... A step you had to take. Your breakdown yesterday is, I believe, the direct result of you refusing to face up to the things that are happening. You stood still, while Norton attacked you, refusing to protect yourself. Had I not been there, you might well have died!... It is time for you to stop being afraid, to stop being the 'armchair detective' and to accept that, in the real world, events *have* conspired to place you in the exact centre of things. If you keep trying to refuse what *is*, you will drive yourself mad. Life is asking you to step up to the plate and it is time to go at bat. What are you going to do? Close your eyes and look away? Or are you going to *grasp* what is in front of you for all it's worth?... In so doing, you may just discover what life has in store for you," Briar finished.

His words made sense: all my life, I had been getting ready for this moment. I felt my fear slipping away from me in realization, in acceptance that this *was* what I had been preparing for. Briar was right!

It was time to step up to the plate.

I still didn't know why it was intended for me but I would no longer shy away from what I had to do. I would follow the Great Hunt through to the end. If this was to be my challenge in life, then so be it!

"Thank you, Jonathan, thank you," I spoke, fervent emotions choking my voice.

I stood up, followed by Briar, noticing that Raymonde had come out of the Villa Leblanc and was running towards us, a note in her hand.

"Paul, you won't believe this. A representative has invited us to a meeting from the Net. They want to know what's going on."

"What? When?"

"Mid-afternoon. They're going to send someone to pick us up in an hour."

***

Coming in with Briar, we met up with O'Flanahan, just returning from his expedition, looking excited. Sitting down at Raymonde's table in the restaurant, I called Coulter, informing him of the upcoming meeting with the Net.

"Good gosh, Paul, that's crazy. We haven't been here two days and already the cat's out of the bag. What are we going to tell them?" he wondered.

"I don't know. I don't want to lie to them, though. Let me think about it. I'll come up with something."

"Well, I'm still wrapping things up here. We had a few glitches. I had to field a lot of questions. It got kind of expensive. I won't make it for that meeting. The good news is that I think we should be ready tomorrow."

"Great. I knew I could count on you."

Snapping the cell phone shut, I noticed that O'Flanahan seemed saddened that Coulter wouldn't be joining us. He looked like a little boy, bursting with news, hardly able to contain himself.

"This morning, I went down to the beach and checked out a bunch of those touristy features. I saw that mysterious door in the cliff and the oyster beds. On the way back, I met up with Ives and Jacques Vallin and we decided to share a bottle of wine..." no surprise there, I thought, "... Along the way, we started talking about the coin that Old Man Vallin had left in the cigar box hidden under his mattress, you remember?..." he asked, looking particularly at me for confirmation that I did, indeed, remember. Seeing my nod, he continued:

"Well, one thing led to another, we ended up at their place, where we found another bottle of wine... and the coin, of course. Well, I examined that coin, let me tell you. They wouldn't let me bring it back with me but I made a pencil rubbing of both sides so I could show you..." he pulled a tattered translucent sheet of onion paper out of his right trouser pocket and laid it on the table. "...There... Now if you look at the date on this side of the coin, you'll note that it says 1306. If you know your coins, you'll know that these coins were minted by Edward the Second, who was then King of England. I've been wondering a wee bit, if this coin couldn't possibly provide us with proof that Cartier did steal some gold in Canada, English gold, and left a trap for those who buried it? Couldn't that just be possible? Couldn't it, Paul?" he goaded.

O'Flanahan was insufferable. He was throwing his beloved Oak Island farce in my face again, using whatever was conveniently at hand. It was unfortunate that the gold coin *did* fit in nicely with his theory, making it irritatingly harder to refute.

"Liam. What can I say? Yes, I must agree with you that a gold coin minted in 1306..." I began but he interrupted me.

"... An English coin..."

Raymonde tried to suppress a smile and Briar looked up at the ceiling in exasperation.

"...Yes, an *English* coin minted in 1306 might be construed to fit into a contrived theory about Oak Island... IF you could prove that the English had buried it there. I'm sorry, Liam, but it's still so weak that it hardly holds up. While the gold coin does nothing to hurt your theory, there is simply not enough there to support it," I finished.

He shook his head, his lower jaw sticking out, making him resemble even more the bulldog he made me think of. He was getting ready to bark a counter-argument but Raymonde beat him to the punch, laughter obvious in her voice:

"Mr O'Flanahan, I have enjoyed listening to your theory. Perhaps we could talk about it again later? Right now, I think we have to prepare ourselves. It is nearing mid-afternoon. The Net will be here to pick us up soon."

I finished my coffee and got up.

"Sorry O'Flanahan, this will have to wait. I've got to get ready. I'm not even sure what to expect. I'm just going to have to play it by ear."

"Well, I hope you can play a good tune, my boy," Briar added, pointedly.

"So do I, Jonathan, so do I!"

CHAPTER 16

A Meeting with the Net

A procession of three vehicles arrived, exactly on time. A well-dressed chauffeur stepped out of a Rolls Royce and opened the rear door next to us.

"Mr Sirenne, Miss Leblanc. Welcome. Would you both be so kind as to step into my vehicle? The others will follow in the remaining cars," he informed us.

The procession was soon under way. We headed out of town, instead of towards Etretat. After several circuitous turns, the driver stopped on the side of a non-descript dirt road. I noted that two other cars were already parked in front of ours. They were empty. The driver hurried around the Rolls Royce and opened the side door.

Stepping out after Raymonde, I noticed a trail heading off into the woods.

"If you would follow me."

The trail was well maintained, having recently been shored up in many places. We arrived at a small clearing. Near the far end, a small group of people waited for us. A short, pudgy man smiled widely when we approached. He held out his thick hand to me.

I shook it, surprised by the steel in his grip. He was literally bubbling with enthusiasm.

"Mr Sirenne. I am so pleased to finally meet you. Thank you for accepting our invitation. I am Adrien Tonnetot, Mayor of Etretat, This is our treasurer, Mr Louis Joseph, and that is my good friend, Alain Boisvert. We are the... uhm... the ad-hoc committee elected to represent the Net. We brought you here, in this out of the way glade, to show you this..." Mayor Tonnetot said, pulling back the branches of a large bush, revealing a narrow, marble slab. The slab bore a long list of names at its centre. Each had died on the same day, in 1916. The list had a simple heading:

'You will be avenged!'

Without any further clue, I knew that we were looking at the list of names of those killed by Hitler and his cohort, Weissmuller, during their second treacherous foray into Etretat.

"This stone was found about ten years ago. It had somehow been completely forgotten. Who placed it here? More importantly, why? No one seemed to know. It cannot be coincidence that these people died on the same night. This is part of what has alerted us and re-awakened the Net, sleeping for so long. Our parents never explained what happened in the past to any of us but they did tell us that, when the time came, we would be called upon to help. Until then, we had to stay on guard," the mayor explained.

He remained quiet for a moment, looking at the stone slab.

"Yesterday, when Bequilles revealed that you were the one we had waited for, most of us were convinced that this was the time to bring the Net back to life. After meeting to discuss this issue, most of our members expressed the desire, no, the *need* for answers. Our history demands it. That is why I called this meeting and I must thank you for agreeing to attend. I felt it best to discuss these issues privately with you for now. Later, I will inform the Net Members about the topics we have discussed... These people who elected me, my friends, have been waiting for this moment a very long time. Since our birth, we have been indoctrinated in a society of our ancestors' making, prepared by them for a purpose we never understood: to wait for you and to help you after that. Now that you are finally here, Mr Paul Sirenne, after all these years, not one of us can wait a single moment longer. We need to re-discover our purpose."

His earnest words filled me with amazement. The entire town had been recruited into the Net. Now, these people were looking at me, not only to help them understand the cause of what had brought them here but also to lead them. This was an incredible responsibility. It made me flash back vividly to my father's words on the note in the back of The Hollow Needle:

'A real story ends near Etretat,
Lost until Paul infers new ideas subtly.
You ought understand responsibility,
Necessarily after moiling Etretat'

Could this be the anticipated responsibility to which he was referring? That word 'moiling' was certainly indicative. It meant to dig, to move dirt, to mess things around. These words had been selected to hold many meanings, relevant to this moment. The more I dug, the more responsibility I would find.

The mayor continued:

"... Our parents all told us the same story... that some things were best left forgotten and that time had to pass before Etretat could regain its glory. They also told us that a day would come when our heritage would return to us. Until then, we kept quiet because of our shared oath. Silence Above All! We were all made to swear to it on our fifteenth birthday. When we grew older, each of us was taught more of our role but never enough for any of us to truly understand the original cause for the existence of the Net. We all know how much we already owe Maurice Leblanc and Raymond Lindon, the creators of the Net. Every Net member, every family in Etretat was helped financially in some way by them. Loans, no-interest mortgages or outright donations of cash, there was no limit to their incredible generosity. The survival of our town, in this century, is due solely to them. We cannot ignore what these men have done for us in the past..."

Listening to him, I realized once again the impact these few men had on so many. The Net members owed everything they had to the caves, to the riches within and to the moral men who had created the Net. Briar's words came back to me, reminding me of my nascent role as a leader of men, a role I had never expected to play.

Now, it was up to me to do the right thing.

"I cannot express how much I am affected by your revelations," I replied. "I am just as indebted to Leblanc and Lindon as every one of you. My presence here is a direct result of my great-grandfather preparing the way for me, using clues and codes. Just like each of you, I was placed on the trail of a forgotten mystery, a secret of incredible proportions... and as you have seen, a dangerous one, even today... However, we have not completely solved this puzzle yet, I am sorry to say. In the past, Maurice Leblanc shared nothing of what he knew with the Net members. Today, the conditions requiring this are long gone and the original people concerned are dead. Time has healed many wounds. I think that it is time to break with tradition and share our knowledge with you and the Net. We are all involved," I stated, making my decision.

It felt right!

No more games, no more deceit, not with these people. If I was ever going to unravel this mystery, I would need all the help I could get. An entire group was ready to give me that help. All I had to do was to trust them, to give them the answers they had been seeking all their lives:

"In 1911, Maurice Leblanc found a secret in Etretat, so incredible that it had to be kept out of public hands. He was not the only one on the trail of what he knew. There was another, a man so heinous that Maurice Leblanc decided that he must do whatever possible to stop him... Your ancestors banded together to help protect Leblanc and Etretat but the cost was high..." Stopping for a moment, I lowered the tone of my voice and spoke respectfully: "... I know what happened to the people named in the list inscribed on your mysterious stone: They were killed by the man Maurice Leblanc was fighting, probably one of the most dangerous men in the world... Adolf Hitler!"

The Mayor's eyes widened. I continued:

"Leblanc appealed to his friends, to Old Man Vallin, to Raymond Lindon and in turn, to all of your grand-parents. A Net was formed, a group of people protecting something they did not know much about. Leblanc hatched a trap for Hitler that would take many years to unfold. Once sprung, decades would have to pass to give the world time to forget. So Leblanc prepared for the future, when it would be safe, the monster dead and forgotten. Your parents were part of that plan, as were mine, far away in Canada. Now, together, we will re-discover what has lain hidden in your midst, waiting until the time was right... Unfortunately, the path is not a simple one to follow. Our only chance to be successful in our search is to work together!... I have been called here, to Etretat to do this very thing... So, let us seize this moment and regain what our fathers have left for us. The Net must return to full and active duty, our ancestors must be honoured..."

The Mayor's face was beaming at my words and he grabbed my hand, pumping it effusively while he exclaimed:

"I think I can speak for all of the Net when I say: We Accept! We accept most proudly and eagerly. The Net has returned, with Paul Sirenne at the helm! With you in place, there will be nothing we cannot achieve."

***

I was flying in a great big circle.

I was dreaming again.

I opened my eyes to find myself floating over Etretat, high in the air, moving in a great lazy circle around the Aval cliff and the Needle. It was night yet I could see clearly. A yellow light illuminated everything, emanating from the inside of the cliff, growing brighter by the second. The source of the light was so bright that it shone right through the rock.

As I flew around the cliff, I saw a swastika, lit from within by the overpowering light. I flew several times around it in total silence, my eyes glued on the symbol of so much hatred and so much pain. I rotated around it, seeing it from both front and back. Something about the opposite images drew my attention but the light interfered, growing in brightness. The light continued increasing in intensity until it blotted everything out. An odd, repeating, strident noise began intruding through the blinding light.

Slowly I became aware that my eyes were open and that I was looking directly at the sun, peeking through the shades of Raymonde's bedroom window. I averted my burning eyes, annoyed by the racket next to my ears.

The phone was ringing.

It was Captain Languenoc. Our package had arrived and they were getting it ready. It was time to go. We were soon dressed and fed, anxious to get back to Languenoc's ship.

Except for O'Flanahan, perhaps.

To our surprise, we found a much better boat waiting for us, surrounded by a large crowd of new friends. The Mayor had been true to his word and all Net Members were keeping a watchful eye, making sure we were left in peace to find the answers so many were looking for.

It was a much more stable and speedy trip out to the Helen. I was wearing my glasses again, recording for later analysis. Coulter and I had managed to stay quiet about what we had obtained and the others were understandably very curious. Upon arrival, Captain Languenoc led us to the other side of the platform, where a large, bright orange, oblong vehicle was floating in the water, tethered solidly to the pontoon.

"Gentlemen, allow me to present to you the Argos, a sixteen passenger electric submarine," proudly intoned Coulter. "It has the ability to go to a depth of one hundred metres, which is perfect for us. The owners agreed to rent it for a few weeks for four hundred thousand dollars. If we like it, we can consider that a down payment. Isn't she beautiful?... And simple to drive, too. You should see the controls."

"It's fully charged and ready to go, Mr Sirenne," informed Captain Languenoc.

With his help, we crossed the hinged gangplank stretched between the Helen and the Argos. I was the second to step onto the submarine deck, wobbling slowly in the calm waters. I ascended the small ladder, stepped onto the top of the conning tower and went down the open hatch. Inside, I was confronted by a spacious area, with two rows of seven seats. There were two more seats at the front. Large viewing ports allowed each passenger to look at their underwater surroundings comfortably.

Coulter ran to the front, seating himself in the Pilot's chair.

"Paul, sit up here with me. You can take the Captain's chair."

Raymonde seated herself right behind me and I sat down in the luxurious chair. A row of screens showed us views from all around the sub. Coulter was already pressing switches and toggles.

"How do you know what to do?" asked Briar, looking over Coulter's shoulder before seating himself.

"I downloaded the manual last night and brushed up on the specifics of this particular submarine. I've done tons of simulated submarine dives before, so I'm already familiar with most of the controls... I'm closing the hatch now..." he explained, pressing another button. A whirring noise began and I turned in time to see the hatch lifting up slowly and locking with a solid clang. My ears popped when the pressure increased and stabilised. "This baby is all automatic, so it's very easy to operate. Okay, everyone put on your seat belts. We're going down!"

I heard a muted whine. Bubbles flowed up both sides of the Argos while it slowly sank down into the channel waters, moving forward at a brisk rate.

"It's so quiet," commented Raymonde. "Look, I can see fish."

We examined the marine life while we continued our descent. I experienced a slight apprehension when the gloom became darkness. Lights flashed on, dispelling my vague feelings for the moment.

"There's the bottom... I've got our position marked, now to set our proper heading ... there... Now the Argos knows where to go."

The Argos was much more powerful than Calvin and we reached the cleft in the underwater canyon walls quickly. Coulter reduced speed, slowing the Argos to a crawl. We headed into the side canyon. The sub's powerful lights exposed the strange optical illusion in front of us once more. Even when I knew it was not really there, it still remained completely convincing. I found myself tensing up while we inched closer, my hands gripping the arms of my chair tightly.

"Thank God, there's the line. I thought we were going to crash," exclaimed O'Flanahan, voicing our common apprehension.

His observation was correct. The two canyon walls had split into two, a dark line appearing where they joined. The line grew wider, revealing the optical illusion for what it was. Halfway through, Coulter slowed the Argos to a complete stop, giving us a chance to examine the huge concave mirrors more closely. They seemed to be made of some type of metal plates, polished to a high sheen. They required no energy, our lights providing the reflection only when needed. Overall, it was a brilliant camouflaging system. Simple and effective.

"There's Calvin!" shouted Coulter, jabbing his finger at a screen in excitement.

Calvin, our lost remote camera, was lying on the seabed floor where it had landed after it lost our controlling signals.

"I had Captain Languenoc attach a magnet to a winch under the sub, thinking about this exact possibility. I think we can recover Calvin. Bear with me for a few moments while I get ready," he explained, his fingers flying over the controls.

The submarine inched forward imperceptibly. Coulter pressed a button and the main view screen switched to a camera below the submarine, illuminating the seabed floor. Calvin was almost directly below us. He was getting closer and closer to the centre of the screen, where red crosshairs had appeared. The moment Calvin lined up with the crosshairs, Coulter pressed another button and a large magnet floated down, wavering from side to side as it descended. Its aim was true and it landed directly onto Calvin's back.

"Contact! I've got him," exclaimed Coulter in glee.

"Enough of this time wasting, Coulter. It's time to go down that tunnel," prodded O'Flanahan.

"Fine. I was just trying to get our deposit back," Coulter shot back. Once the remote camera was nestled safely under the Argos, he activated the propellers, starting us moving towards the hidden tunnel. We could now see that it headed directly under the cliff at a sharp angle. Nothing but a submarine could come here.

"Keep moving forward slowly until we've reached the end of the tunnel. Everyone keep your eyes peeled," I cautioned, not sure what to expect.

The Argos slid forward, exiting the tunnel. Coulter brought the sub to a full stop. We were in the bottom of a large rock depression, shaped like a giant pipe bowl. The sides were close. Coulter filled the ballast tanks with compressed air and we began rising. The sides vanished from view, moving away rapidly, forming a vast chamber.

"The radar's detected something floating above us. It's almost as large as the Argos," informed Coulter.

"Can we surface beside it?" I asked.

"Yes. There's plenty of room. It's like a small lake up there."

While we continued our ascent, the waters became clearer, as if light were coming down from above, which should be impossible in a cave. I mentioned this to the others.

"You're quite correct, my boy. There should be no light here," supported Briar.

By now, it was easy to see the shape Coulter had detected above us with his radar. It was large and cigar-shaped, appearing distinctly like another submarine. Its shape was compact, like ours, and covered in a reflective yellow metal. Its surface had the same indentations we had seen in the camouflaged entrance.

The Argos broke the surface of the calm waters. Coulter turned off most of the submarine systems and opened the outside hatch remotely. The ambient, yellowish light was strong while seeming to have no direct source. It reminded me of the light from my dreams.

"We're here! Time to disembark."

"Me first," O'Flanahan said, running for the opening hatch and lumbering up out of sight.

Soon, we were standing on the Argos' deck, looking around in awe, while we organised our supplies into backpacks. We were in a massive chamber. On the far left side were huge stalagmites surrounded by a small natural landing. On this side, a concrete stairway wound its way upwards, coming from a long dock. The ancient submarine next to us was moored to it.

"Look at that sub. It's all gold!" whispered O'Flanahan, his voice hushed.

It did indeed seem covered entirely in gold. It was sleek and stylish, looking almost feral in its design. Embossed on the conning tower was the Swastika symbol, putting to rest all of our questions about the Nazi involvement with these caves. They had been here and they had left their flagship behind!

The dock was a massive structure stretching on our right for a distance of at least thirty metres. At its end, the concrete staircase climbed along the vaulted walls of the cavern. Far up above, a large concrete structure overlooked the entire cavern. Two gun turrets jutted out, one on each side of the structure.

A deep silence filled the cave, broken only by the occasional drip of water and the lapping of small waves, echoing lightly around us.

"Let's take the gangplank and stretch it across between the two submarines. After that, we should be able to get onto that dock," suggested Jacques Vallin.

We used a mooring line, which we fastened to the Nazi submarine's hatch handle. Once across, we located a metal ladder fastened to the concrete dock. Climbing up, we looked around the dock for a moment then walked to the end and went up the wide staircase. It didn't take long to reach a dizzying height.

Looking down, both of the submarines next to each other reminded me of toys, floating in the translucent water. Light reflected from everywhere, dancing designs all over the walls. We continued the climb, the irrepressible O'Flanahan staying several steps above us. He entered the guard room, after looking at one of the gun turrets, its barrels aiming downward, untouched by human hands in decades.

"There's a doorway in here, guys."

Entering the long, narrow room overlooking the small lake below us, I saw a doorway directly in the centre of the back wall, where O'Flanahan waited for us.

"It certainly is quiet in here," said Raymonde.

"Some systems are still active. I can feel dry, fresh air coming from that doorway. We are more than thirty-five metres over the surface of the water, which means that there are still more than sixty-five metres of chalk cliff above us. Fresh air could not possibly be filtering down into here without help," Coulter mentioned.

I entered the doorway, any trepidation I might have felt easily overwhelmed by my curiosity. Walking along a well-lit corridor, still without any apparent light source, I saw several doorways ahead of us. We stopped briefly at the first two, concluding that the rooms had been intended as barracks. There was an old radio in the corner of one of the rooms. Briar stopped suddenly when he was about to leave the second room, his eyes peering in the corner.

"What's that, over there, in the corner, behind the bed frame?"

Coulter, who was closest, walked over and leaned down, looking at the indistinct shape on the ground. He recoiled in horror, his hand held over his mouth, a scream exploding from him.

"It's a dead man!"

We rushed forward, more to see the body than in sympathy for Coulter. The years had softened the outline of the body, mummified by the dry air.

"There's another one over here."

O'Flanahan had found it hidden behind the desk, by the radio. Mummified, like the first.

"I wonder what happened here?" asked Raymonde, "How did they die?"

"They don't seem to have been wounded. It's like they just dropped where they were standing," observed Briar, bending down to look at the second body.

As he did this, he placed his hand on the wall for support. He pulled it away immediately, in surprise, and then placed it back on the wall, looking dumbfounded.

"What is it, Jonathan?" I asked.

The wall had darkened where his hand had rested, leaving an imprint that was slowly fading. His hand was now glowing faintly. I did as he had. The first contact was a surprise. I could understand why Briar had pulled his hand away suddenly. The wall felt soft and alive, its surface odd and leathery. I had thought it was metal, painted a bright reflective white but it wasn't reflecting light, it was exuding it.

"These walls are bioluminescent," I said.

"Exactly my thoughts, my boy. Whoever built this knew what they were doing."

"Both of these men are curled up in a fetal position. That's why we didn't see them at first," exclaimed O'Flanahan. "Look at the hands. They died clutching their throats. Their mouths are frozen open in a last gasping breath."

"These poor men," observed Raymonde.

"Poor nothing, Miss Leblanc," retorted O'Flanahan. "Look at those uniforms. Those insignia say they were part of the SS. These were very bad people. I don't pity them for one second."

"Still, something happened that caused both of those men to drop to the ground, right where they stood," commented Briar. "I think these men were poisoned or suffocated."

Ives Vallin grew agitated hearing this. His brother mentioned quickly:

"Don't worry, Brother. Whatever happened here, happened very long ago. The danger has passed. Hasn't it, Mr Paul?"

"I'm sure we're fine. It's been over sixty years. I don't know of many poisons which could last that long. Still, we should be careful. This is a warning that not everything is as it appears. This is a more of a tomb than a fortress," I said, shuddering slightly.

"Let's move on. I don't think we can find much more around here," Raymonde suggested, eager to be out of the room.

We returned to the corridor and continued on to its end, arriving at a metal door. A screen in its top half area allowed fresh air to flow freely. Entering, we found ourselves in a large octagonal room, a central hub, with eight passages heading off into different areas of the caves. I heard a faint humming. Rails were imbedded in the floor, heading off in all directions. There was small turntable in the centre of the room from which a rail cart could be sent in any direction. Plaques with symbols above each passageway indicated either their direction or purpose.

One of them was a lightning bolt.

"That's might be leading to a generating station," I inferred.

Raymonde pointed at another plaque:

"Could that one indicate another connecting hub, like this one?" she asked.

It was a symbol, shaped vaguely like an octopus, with eight arms around it. Below it was an arrow aiming upward next to a staircase symbol.

"Yes, another hub, likely one above us," I agreed.

"How big is this place?" exclaimed O'Flanahan.

"We could get lost in here!" realized Briar. "We'd better be careful."

"Don't worry, we won't get lost, added Coulter. "Using an enhanced GPS, I've been logging our movements. I know exactly where we are."

Good old technology! Couldn't leave home without it.

"What does that plaque mean?" asked O'Flanahan, a certain tone in his voice. He was getting excited about something.

"It looks like rows of shelves, to me," helped Briar. "Perhaps that corridor leads to storage areas."

"Let's go there," urged O'Flanahan, with a light in his eyes.

"I'd much rather go up," I said. "I want to try to get to the entrance under the destroyed foundation of the Fort of Frefosse. We might find more answers there."

"Fine. You go up, I'll go over there," O'Flanahan replied.

Sensing an upcoming argument, Raymonde interfered:

"Why don't we take a break here? We can use the time to figure out what to do."

"Sounds good to me, young lady. I'm quite thirsty. Considering all that water below, I find this air very dry," Briar agreed.

Opening our backpacks, Raymonde passed out sandwiches and coffee from a thermos. Wanting neither, I sat down on one of the metal benches lining the walls between the passageways.

"Why do you want to go see those shelves so much?" asked Coulter, giving in to his growing curiosity.

Liam O'Flanahan swallowed his mouthful with a noisy gulp. Wiping his lips with the back of his hand, he stood up and walked to a position where each of us could look at him.

"Guys, you know that I live on conspiracies. It's my bread and butter. This adventure has been like heaven to me but that plaque has to take the cake. If I'm right, that passage will lead us to the answer of one of World War 2's most infamous theft."

Our eyes were locked on O'Flanahan. He did have his moments.

"Throughout the Second World War, the invading Nazis stole countless heirlooms and invaluable pieces of art. As many as one hundred thousand items were stolen. It is well known that the Nazis had convoys bearing gold, silver, art, statues and other valuables, streaming out of all invaded countries to be ferreted in secret underground hiding places. Eisenhower himself went to examine some of the bigger finds after the war. Over the years, many paintings were recovered. Unfortunately, despite the best efforts of the bereft families and other well-intentioned researchers, over twenty thousand items remain unrecovered. Rumours abound of a 'Lost Museum', filled with the largest collection of stolen art in the world. The caves of Etretat would have been perfect for such a hiding place. It is likely that Hitler would have felt secure in bringing the most valuable stolen art to this stronghold. You all remember the stories from Bequilles and from the Vallins, about the constant convoys of trucks. So, just like you, I've been putting two and two together. I think that we are standing at the entrance to that 'Lost Museum'. Hidden below us might be thousands of art pieces, stolen from the Nazis' battered victims."

"... I'd like to find out if he's right, Paul," Raymonde added.

Seeing a similar glint of morbid curiosity reflected in everyone else's eyes, I knew what I had to say.

"All right, O'Flanahan, let's do it! Let's go look at your shelves."

***

We headed down a long sloping corridor, following the rails from the hub. Reaching the bottom, we found a tunnel lined with endless sliding doors, stretching almost as far as our eyes could see. We entered the first room we came to. It was filled to overflowing, heavily obstructed with crates. Managing to squeeze in between the boxes, we made our way to a large shelf system. Every crate was emblazoned by the swastika symbol. My mind flashed back to my dream.

Had it been referring to this?

The shelving structure was massive. There were four levels, one above another, reaching a height of five metres. Hinged glass panels covered individual sections. Opening the first glass panel with a grinding squeak, I exposed a tall, narrow shelf on which rested four large frames. Selecting one at random, I picked up a Rembrandt, a landscape. Seeing another small panel, I reached in further, lifting it up gingerly. Another Rembrandt.

Looking rapidly at other paintings confirmed it. This was indeed the 'Lost Museum', its aisles glutted with the spoils of war. We had finally found a treasure but I wanted none of it. I felt horror instead of awe. How many people had died to fill this room? Our mood had turned sombre, the joviality of the moment completely gone.

"Let's get out of here," O'Flanahan said.

Matt Chatelain

A SELECTION FROM THE WEISSMULLER MANUSCRIPT

Developing the caves

It has taken several years to complete the work in the cave complex. The power plant, developed by captive scientists, is now producing more energy than we will ever need. The illuminating fungus has been trained to grow in all corridors, which are used to provide air for both men and this plant-based light source. A filtering system has been built to control the dust and humidity. The cave mapping has been completed, providing us with a complex of more than seven hundred distinct caves. A rail system has been added which has greatly facilitated the moving of the crates which arrive nightly.

Over the years, I have lost more than fifty of my men through the efforts of the Maquis but I feel satisfied that I have exacted a high price for them. I have also been informed of Maurice Leblanc's death. I can only hope that he learned of his son's demise before dying. Perhaps it even hastened his death. He is now completely powerless against me. As for Lindon, he has vanished. I can feel him moving pawns all around me but never close enough to matter. I know that his puppet, the Vallin descendant, entered the tunnels a few times. He was much too late. The important tunnel had been blocked by then. He can play in there all he wants. He will find nothing.

While my men were the ones who constructed the complex, I was the only one who obtained a complete perspective of the scope of these caves. I designed a three dimensional map which revealed certain oddities in the cave layout. The caves were arrayed in a vast circle, layer upon layer of them, most connected by cracks or tunnels. The central area was solid, filled with an amalgam of rubble, rather than bedrock. We used this area to install our main air shaft and stair system.

Near sea level, we encountered an underground river blocking our way into the lower cave system. We also discovered that the water of this river has bizarre curative properties which could not be explained by analysis. It was used as a potable water source in the fortress, keeping my men in much better health than should have been expected.

It was this vast rubble-filled shaft in the center of the complex which had me baffled. I knew by then, that the caves' creation could neither be explained by natural sedimentary process nor by erosion. Water had been involved, to be sure, but another force had been originally responsible for this intricately woven web of caves. From my prior research, I knew that the only answer possible was the destructive power of a meteorite.

When we dug an exploratory tunnel directly into this central area, we struck a massive object composed of magnetic iron and traces of iridium, about one hundred meters below the cliff surface, confirming the meteorite hypothesis. It had been subjected to high levels of heat, melting its surface perfectly smooth. We dug other exploratory tunnels. If we were heading for the center of the cave complex, we would always encounter the same iron core.

This convinced me that it was a gigantic elongated conical meteorite which had been driven deep into these cliffs. I did not know of any other meteorite which had this shape. The meteorite was too hard to mine easily and we had no need of unprocessed iron, so, after a few tests, we left it alone. The tests confirmed that it had indeed originated from outer space and that its magnetic nature had likely been created during its superheated travel through Earth's magnetic field.

***

The time is nearing when Hitler will arrive to take control of the fortress. His double is ready and travel arrangements are being prepared. Hitler has learnt much since I first met him. Our goals were almost one for a while. However, I have found him strangely distant during his last visits. He has issued orders for me to eliminate my men since they know too much about the caves. The fewer who know about them, the better, he claimed.

I had expected those orders, as I also agree with this decision, but I worry about Hitler's increasing megalomania. Dare I trust his motivations? He believes the caves are his destiny. What role shall I play, now that his plans have reached fruition?

I too have become fascinated by the caves. We found evidence of Roman occupation and of their extermination. We found countless caches of gold and jewels, hidden in various locations in the caves. Several of these caches had been pilfered, probably by Leblanc and his cohorts. I determined that these caches had been created during the period of Francis the First, although I had no explanation for their presence. The gold Hitler had stolen from the caves had come from one such cache.

That did not stop me from reserving several caches for myself. Hitler could have his art and his paintings but I would have my experiments, my purpose, and the gold from the caves.

I have left the massive throne room almost completely intact for Hitler. Behind the giant tapestries, I found ancient burial niches, filled with Neanderthal skeletons. I felt distinctly uncomfortable in that room but it impressed Hitler to no end. I felt sure that this throne room would be a fitting, parting gift, from me to him.

In retrospect, I find that my meeting Hitler has had a beneficial impact on my life, providing me with many lessons. I have also recognized that the caves themselves still have much to teach me and I do not wish to relinquish my control. I believe he is a weak man, no longer able to make the right decisions, to proceed in the right direction.

I do not have this weakness.

I see things far more clearly than he, unhampered by bothersome emotions. I had long thought this to be a flaw but my experiments have proven to me that this lack is no weakness. Rather, it is a strength. It allows me to see into the center of everything. I am free of the rules and the puppet strings which bind all others.

Therefore, because of my strength in this matter, I am no longer Hitler's lieutenant.

He is mine!

I will allow him his final illusion. I will remain in the shadows, the place where I truly belong. From the shadows, I can do whatever I desire, control whomever I choose. I will even kill my men, following his orders. However, if treachery is on Hitler's mind, he will not find me easy prey and retribution will not be far behind!

Matt Chatelain

CHAPTER 17

Final Answers

Having returned to the central hub, we headed for the stairs to the level above us. The stairs were a circular affair, going around a large open shaft. We arrived at a new level, seeing a passageway heading off to another hub in the distance but the staircase kept going up.

"It seems we have found a way to the top, my boy," stated Briar.

We continued our ascension, reaching a new level with every turn around the staircase. Finally, we arrived at the top, finding a grand circular opening. The rails were also present, leading me to believe that the open shaft was once used to lower material to the various levels below. On the other end of the large circular room, on each side of a grandiose entrance, hung two larger-than-life paintings of Adolf Hitler, with his arm raised.

"Guys, hold up for a second..." wheezed O'Flanahan, huffing and puffing, still half a level below us. Everyone gathered round the top of the staircase, waiting for him. O'Flanahan finished his climb, joining us and leaning on the staircase railing for support.

Seeing O'Flanahan struggling made me realize that I felt much better than when I had arrived in Etretat. I had been through so much physical activity these past few days that my muscles had limbered up. I wasn't back in shape by any stretch of the imagination but I no longer felt like a sack of potatoes.

"Should we take a break for you, O'Flanahan?" asked Briar. O'Flanahan's face scrunched up in annoyance.

"No, I don't need a break, thank you very much. I'm fit as a fiddle. I just wouldn't mind a drink is all. I can't reach it in my packsack by myself," he blustered. "There's no way I want to stop now anyway. We've worked this hard to get here and I don't see why we should stop ten metres from our goal."

Coulter handed him a bottle of water while we walked to the overlarge and pretentious doorway. We entered a very tall, sloping hallway, the ever-present rails leading the way. The roof overhead was bedrock and I saw a faint line in the centre.

"I think that we are in the original hallway of the caves. That crack in the ceiling reminds me of Leblanc's words when he entered the main room beyond the entrance in Frefosse's lost dungeon..." I reflected aloud.

We continued along the slowly ascending corridor. It grew wider, giving way to a large natural cave. On my right was a doorway leading to an empty chamber. Further on, I noticed the ruins of a primitive locking mechanism, over an irregularly shaped opening.

"We must be near that bunker, where the fort used to be," noted Raymonde.

"The GPS says we're almost under it," informed Coulter.

Passing through the ancient opening, we came to a solid concrete plug.

"They've blocked the entrance off. They unloaded all the stolen treasure and the supplies needed to build this place, then they sealed it with fresh cement. After that, coming in here would be by submarine only," concluded O'Flanahan.

Retracing our steps led us to another hallway on our right. I walked slowly along its length, reminded of Leblanc's description when he entered this place for the first time, almost one hundred years ago. I thought of the small chamber, where the treacherous Hitler had assaulted him. Looking carefully along the left side, I saw the narrow cleft Leblanc had described. Stopping the group, I squeezed into the dark crevice. The others followed me in. I looked around, my eyes freezing on a dark stain on the ground, still visible through the layer of dust. Sweeping the dust away with my foot, I revealed it.

"That's a lot of blood. No wonder Hitler thought Leblanc was dead," remarked Coulter.

Briar found the exposed crack in the wall where Leblanc had discovered the small sack of gold coins, one of which he had given to Old Man Vallin. Remnants of plaster used to camouflage the crack were still visible. Who could have hidden that gold here and why? Our questions unanswered, we returned to the hallway.

"Leblanc described a large chamber, covered in ancient tapestries, close to here. Let's go find that," I suggested.

"What are you looking for, my boy?" asked Briar.

"I have not forgotten what Leblanc said in his journal. He had sworn to devote all of his efforts in an attempt to create a trap for Hitler. It must be somewhere in this place. Everything we have seen so far suggests to me that his trap was successful. For example, why is that fancy gold submarine still here?... The bunker entrance was filled with concrete and the tunnels under Etretat were sealed by an explosion. So, how did the Nazis leave this place, if they left their submarine behind? I don't think they left. Remember those two dead guards, looking as if they were poisoned or suffocated... In Leblanc's journal, he mentions the room with the tapestries only once but his words gave me the feeling that he thought it important. I have reasoned that his trap must have been something irresistible for Hitler, designed specifically for him. I think we will find our answer in that room."

"Well, what are we waiting for then? Let's go find it," exclaimed O'Flanahan.

Walking along the grand hall, I noticed that, while work had been done to shore up weakened cavern walls, they had left the caves and hallways in their original state, wherever possible. Jacques Vallin pointed ahead of us, where an arched entrance led into a chamber to our left. We slowed our pace, feeling an unexplainable apprehension.

Approaching the door, I saw the first body since seeing those two guards. It was lying near the left side of the entrance. Ives Vallin found two shapes on the right. More guards! They were clutching their throats, poisoned like the others.

I followed Raymonde's gaze, deep into the room.

I was overwhelmed by the incredible splendour confronting me. The cave had been prepared as a King's chamber. Rich tapestries hung on all the walls, woven with gold and silver thread, showing hunting scenes and heroic battles. Suits of armour stood at regular intervals against the wall. Two ornate chandeliers hung from the ceiling. The brilliance of the lower crystals attracted my eye. Stepping closer, I realized that they were diamonds, rubies, emeralds, opals and other precious stones. Doing a quick count, I calculated that each chandelier held more than three hundred precious stones. A veritable fortune was suspended above our heads.

Looking back down, I scanned the rest of the cavernous room. A large stone platform, a metre in height, stood near the furthest wall, a gilded throne in its centre. Our voices hushed, we approached the platform. Bodies were lying all around, mummified where they had fallen. From their positions, it seemed as if they had been assembled around the throne.

"There's something lying by the side of the throne... Hey, look at that," exclaimed O'Flanahan, climbing up the short staircase in front of him.

Another body lay curled up beside the throne. It had been hidden from us by the throne's position. Curiously, one of the man's hands had remained extended, instead of clutching at his throat.

"What's he holding on to?" asked O'Flanahan, besides himself with morbid curiosity.

The man's arm extended and disappeared under the left side of the throne chair, frozen in death. Walking around the throne, I saw an open panel, revealing a hidden chamber below the throne seat itself. Sitting there, still held by the dead man's mummified fingers, was the most exquisite crown I had ever seen. Covered in jewels, intricately carved out of pure gold, it was opulent beyond belief.

"Look at his face... Look at the dead man's face..." stuttered Raymonde, her face blanched.

Looking down, I saw what her keen eye had noticed. There, on the dead man's upper lip, were the remains of a tiny moustache. My eyes swept upwards, seeing the sharp lock of hair going down at an angle.

It was the body of Adolf Hitler!

This was the secret hidden for so long; this was what Etretat had been hiding.

Hitler had fooled everyone. All along, his goal had been to return to these caves, to build an invisible fortress, from which he could continue carrying on his insane plans. He trained a double and then, at the peak of his power, went on a secret trip to Etretat, intent on grasping what he had sought all those years. Instead, he disappeared, never to return. His double, Maximillian Bauer, was forced to step into his shoes permanently. While an excellent mimic, Bauer could not match Hitler's mad strategic genius. From that point on, the war effort was doomed. The Nazi machine was headless; their true leader vanished.

Leblanc was the only one who understood Hitler's master plan. He was the one who had anticipated his moves, like an expert chess master. He had accepted the inevitable and placed his trap exactly where he knew Hitler would end up: inside the Caves of Etretat! Not only this, he had come up with the perfect plan, appealing directly to Hitler's feelings of megalomania. It was a stroke of genius.

He had hidden his trap inside a special niche, waiting for his mouse to figure out the way in. The piece of cheese he used was ideal: the most fabulous crown you could imagine. It would have been irresistible to a man like Hitler, drawing him like a moth to a flame. As soon as he touched that crown, moved it a single centimetre, it would have been too late.

The trap would be sprung!

"Stop that, what do you think you are doing?" Coulter exploded suddenly, looking at O'Flanahan, who was reaching for the crown.

"Don't worry, Coulter. Whatever poison came out of that trap is long gone."

"Well, I wouldn't like to find out if you were wrong. I'd wait, if I were you, at least until we've examined it a bit more."

A glint of caution entered O'Flanahan's eyes and he carefully inched his hand away from the trigger, suddenly seeing it for what it really was. A tempting worm dangling on a very dangerous hook.

"So my great-grandfather succeeded in his goal. He really killed Hitler," stated Raymonde.

"Yes, he actually did it. This entire room was designed with one purpose in mind, to entice Hitler to sit on that throne. Once there, he would have eventually figured out that there was a hidden mechanism on the chair. It would have been a bit complex... Nothing straightforward, I'm sure... something clever, requiring some thought. That would have been the convincing key to the trap. Hitler, filled with the vanity of his immense ego, would not have believed that anyone else could have figured out the mechanism. Then, he found that irresistible, bejewelled crown. He would have instinctively reached out and seized it" I explained.

"But what killed them? How did Mr Leblanc do it?" asked Ives Vallin.

Coulter had bent down near the throne and was looking at it closely. Standing up, he asked if he could borrow my special glasses. Putting them on, he returned to his kneeling position, examining the throne's entire base, using the binocular mode of the glasses as a microscope.

"I'm not sure but it looks as if the plate below the crown is separate from the base of the throne. It could be a pressure switch of some sort. If it were set just right, any movement of that crown could have triggered it."

"A pressure switch? For what?" asked Briar, joining in.

"I don't know yet," Coulter replied

"Might I see those glasses for a moment?" asked Briar.

Receiving them from Coulter, Briar pressed a toggle on the glasses.

"I'm turning on the infrared mode. Infrared can be used to detect hollows or cracks, using the slight temperature differential as a method to perceive what our regular eyes could never hope to notice."

Briar, looking around the whole room, kept coming back to the raised platform beneath the throne.

"As I suspected, there is a hollow chamber beneath this entire platform. The infrared is showing an area shaped like a large rectangle, covering most of the length of this rock platform. Let me calculate its volume..."

He walked along an invisible line, almost reaching the distant wall. He turned at a ninety-degree angle at the last moment, counting footsteps all the while.

"My natural stride measures exactly one metre. Using that base number, I can calculate that the hollow beneath us measures about ten metres by seven metres square and is at least one metre deep. Leblanc must have built this huge platform, expertly camouflaged to look like a natural piece of the bedrock, using the space created to hide his poison chamber and his trap mechanism..."

"That's seventy cubic metres!... That's crazy. How much poison did they need? Depending on the poison, that amount could have been enough to kill an entire country!" said O'Flanahan.

"I'm sure with more investigation we would find some type of vents hidden around this room, perhaps behind the tapestries. If my numbers are right, the poison would have been released in enormous quantities. It does seem like overkill," observed Briar.

"Not if he intended to kill any surviving Nazis, eager to take over the abandoned fortress," I added. "He released so much poison that it would take years to dissipate. By doing that, any subsequent invader would be poisoned upon arrival. Maybe that is why we had to wait so long before our return. "

"Makes sense, Paul," agreed Raymonde. "My great-grandfather could not take any chance. So he turned the caves into a deathtrap, effectively closing them down."

"We should think of getting back," I suggested. "We can return tomorrow and begin a deeper investigation into what happened. There are many questions left unanswered. One thing is certain however. We have finally succeeded in the Great Hunt. We now know what they wanted us to discover: Maurice Leblanc stopped Adolf Hitler, and the Nazi regime with him.

***

Upon returning to the original hub we had encountered, Coulter remarked:
"I still can't believe how fresh the air is."

"You're right. It is surprising that the machinery still works..." added Briar.

"... And that there's still power to run it. I've been wondering what type of power plant could keep working after all these years," Coulter returned.

"Sounds to me like you're asking to go visit the generator room," observed O'Flanahan.

"Yes, I guess I am. We're so close... I'm sure that plaque over the corridor, the one with the lightning bolt, goes directly there... It would only take a few moments."

Our excitement was still running high, so we agreed to go. The generator tunnel led us to a monstrous cavern. There were ten huge boxes in the middle of the cavernous space.

"What are those? Where are the generators?" asked Jacques Vallin, looking around in consternation, like the rest of us.

"I don't know...I'm not sure... Let's get closer..." Coulter muttered, at a loss for words, his mind racing.

"Technology's got his tongue," sniggered O'Flanahan.

Coulter approached the dull-gray metallic cubes, followed by the rest of us. They towered above us, each measuring five meters to a side. Two massive copper bars emerged from each cube and connected to thick cables. These joined together, snaking around the cubes. Coulter ran around, finding a long panel with several meters on it:

"That meter... I think it shows the voltage coming out of that box there... Look at the numbers... I'm fairly certain that... yes... These cubes *are* the generators. Each is putting out... twenty-four volts... at... uhm..." he stopped looking at the panel, his eyes settling on a row of smaller meters below the voltmeters, "...Four thousand amperes... that can't be right..." his eyes roved all over the boxes, coming back to the panel. "No, it's four thousand amperes all right..." Coulter stood back in awe. "... Good gosh, this system is generating almost a million watts of power..."

"How is it generating all that?" asked Briar.

"I'm working on it. Give me another minute."

Coulter walked up to the nearest cube, looking at it closely and then putting his hand on it.

"It's warm... Hey, does anyone have a knife?"

Jacques Vallin, slid a long sharp knife out from a leg holster and passed it, handle first, to Coulter.

Coulter used the tip and scraped a gouge in the surface of the cube.

"Ah-ha! I thought so," he exclaimed, scraping the cube again, this time removing a small amount of metal. Holding it between two fingers and bending it easily, he smiled in satisfaction.

"It's lead. I know what this thing is, although I don't believe it. I think it's a nuclear battery!"

"A nuclear battery? You've got to be kidding," snapped O'Flanahan in disdain. "Those are hoaxes."

"Actually no, not all of them are. The military has developed some working prototypes. They're not very efficient but they do work," Briar remarked "... Looking at this system, they seem to work for a very long time!"

"If they are not efficient, how can they be generating all that power?" asked Raymonde, still mystified.

"I think it's a question of scale," Coulter answered. "Inside that thick lead box shielding us all, lies a very large quantity of some radioactive material, possibly uranium. These radioactive elements emit alpha and beta particles which can be harnessed to generate heat. Hundreds of thousands of thermocouples, two different metal wires welded together, are used to generate electricity from the heat. It can be designed as a closed system and will last as long as the radioactive material continues emitting its particles."

"It's surprising you can figure that out so quickly, my boy. I am convinced you are right. A brilliant analysis," Briar added, with an admiring look in his eyes. "What is that noise I hear in the background, that loud hum?"

"Well it's not coming from the nuclear batteries. They are completely silent. Perhaps there is some machinery nearby..." Coulter replied.

"It sounds like it's louder over there," mentioned Ives Vallin, pointing at a doorway.

"Let's go look," Briar decided, heading off in that direction without waiting for the rest of us.

We ran after him, reaching him when he arrived at the door, a plaque above it bearing an image of a rotating blade.

"Could be the fan room," suggested O'Flanahan.

Opening the door, Briar walked along a hallway. The sound was becoming deafening. We passed a side door, barely giving it a glance. Entering the last room, we found three massive fans in a tall shaft, surrounded by a platform. A nearby wall was covered with electrical panels, thick cables coming out from them and connecting to the large fan motors.

One of the fans had broken down but the other two were still powerful enough to move a huge volume of air. It seemed to be pulling the air from somewhere below this level and pushing it up a shaft that took it to the uppermost level. From there, gravity would cause a trickling down of fresh air in the entire cavern system. Simple and clever. They spared no expense here. This place was built to last. The noise of the fans was overwhelming and we beat a hasty retreat to the corridor.

Retracing our footsteps, Briar stopped at the side door we had previously ignored.

"I wonder what's in here," he asked, opening the door. He stood still for a moment, then moved slowly backwards.

"There's another body in there," he said in a monotone, unable to take his eyes off the gruesome sight.

O'Flanahan rushed forward to look.

"His hands aren't at his throat. He's mummified, though. Hey... Look at that..." he stated, pointing at a small round hole in the man's jacket. "He was shot in the back, whoever he was," O'Flanahan said, turning the mummified body over. "He looks familiar somehow... I know, he reminds me of you, Briar..."

Briar peered closer at the man's face.

"His features are similar, now that you mention it but this is a mummified corpse. I doubt he would have looked the same while alive."

"One thing for sure: he had way more hair than you, pal," O'Flanahan couldn't resist saying.

Miffed, Briar was about to retort but paused, noticing a bulge in the man's dried out leather coat.

"What's that?"

O'Flanahan pulled open the cracked leather flaps of the coat, reaching inside.

"It's a book or something. Let me pull it out."

Working at the dried leather slowly, O'Flanahan gradually removed the old book. He opened the first page.

"Looks like a manuscript of some sort. It's written in German. Nice handwriting. Very neat..." O'Flanahan randomly flipped to the middle, then to the end. "Wait a second, I don't believe it... Guys, this book was signed by Weissmuller. This is his manuscript... Unbelievable."

Who had killed him? What was he doing here? More questions without answers. One deduction was easily made, based on the way he had died. He had been killed before the poison was released in the caves.

Raymonde, noticing another door beyond Weissmuller's body, exclaimed:

"That door has no screen and has a lock. Why would that be?"

The door was tightly sealed and none of us could open it without the key. The quick-witted Jacques Vallin had an idea. He returned to Weissmuller's body and searched his clothes. The result of his search were a Luger... and two keys on a ring!

"This Luger's been fired twice, I think. At least, it's missing two bullets in its clip," Vallin asserted. "Here, try these keys, Mr. Paul."

I caught the keys in mid-air and tried one in the lock. No good. The other fit perfectly. The lock was seized with age but finally gave way under the pressure I exerted. We heard a clunk when the deadbolt released.

The room had been completely airtight. When we opened the door, a ghastly odor was released. Fresh air entered the room, activating the dormant lichen on the wall. The increasing light revealed a horrifying sight, literally from Dante's Hell: the room was filled with corpses, piled one upon another. Decomposition stains covered what floor we could see, leading to a drain. The sealed room had prevented these bodies from mummifying. They had rotted instead. It was overwhelming. There were hundreds of dead bodies here.

"Could these be Weissmuller's men?" questioned O'Flanahan.

Seeing our questioning looks, he explained:

"Sorry guys but I always think in terms of conspiracy. If this place was mine, I might be led to want to kill anyone who might have loose lips and reveal my big secret... For proof, look at those," he added, showing two machine guns near some rotting tarps. Behind both was a dead man, each shot in the head. "He hid machine guns under those tarps, called the men in. The tarps were removed and the shooting began, like fish in a pond. The carnage over, Weissmuller shot the last two men, the executioners..."

"Who shot Weissmuller, if his men were all dead?" continued Raymonde, going along with O'Flanahan's theory.

"I think I know that answer."

All eyes turned on me.

"Adolf Hitler killed him!"

It was the only answer that made sense. The single loose end, after the death of Weissmuller's men, would have been Weissmuller himself, a man privy to all of Hitler's deepest secrets. Once the massacre was over, Hitler would have shot Weissmuller in the back, completing his *own* decades-long plan. A fitting end to Weissmuller, betrayed by a man who had betrayed everyone.

We closed the door silently, heading back out without a word. Returning to the Argos, I reflected on what we had found. These caves had held much suffering. So many dead because of them. The allure of finding riches here, our original goal, had been completely muted by the reality of what lay hidden here. The legacy my father had left me had nothing wonderful about it. It was not about treasure. A burden had been placed on my shoulders, one I truly did not know if I wanted. Like it or not, the Caves of Etretat were now in my hands.

I made a silent vow to all those who had laid out the path to bring me here. I would hold true to their lofty ideals and adopt them as mine. I would discover what mysteries lay hidden in the depths of the caves. With my loyal friends at my side, with Raymonde as my partner and with an entire town ready to do my bidding, it was now up to me to begin the real task, the real challenge.

I remembered, one more time, the coded words my father had given me:

'You ought understand responsibility,
Necessarily after moiling Etretat'

I would assume that responsibility and I would never let go, not until I solved the mystery of the Caves of Etretat!

***

I entered into the private room, stopping at the side of the hospital bed, where Bequilles lay dying. Upon our return from the caves, we were informed that Bequilles had been found on his kitchen floor, stricken by a massive coronary. The doctor had told me that he could go any time. Bequilles' eyes fluttered open, still clear. I saw a faint smile on his lips when he recognized me.

"... Sirenne..."

"Yes, Bequilles, it's me. The doctor told me you didn't have much time left..."

"... S'okay... Time for me to go..." he whispered.

"I brought you a parting gift, if that's okay?" I said.

"....A gift?... Now?..."

"Yes, a gift. Have you ever seen these?"

"... Your glasses?..."

"That's right. These glasses are quite special. Here, let me show you..."

I slipped the glasses onto his nose before he could object. Coulter was waiting online, Raymonde next to him. With tears in her eyes, she explained with this was all about:

"Hello Bequilles. Paul told me you don't have long. We thought you might enjoy watching a bit of a home-made movie, before you pass on. Before we start it, though, I want to say thank you for all your help. We could never have done this without you... Take care and know that we will always remember you."

Raymonde surreptitiously wiped a tear from her cheek, motioning to Coulter and he started the movie. Bequilles was suddenly viewing the inside of our submarine when we were preparing to go down to enter the caves for the first time.

Bequilles realized that he was watching a video taking him into the caves beneath the Aval cliff. The big secret he had protected with his silence all these years was now being revealed. He watched silently, his vital signs slowly fading, his breath wheezing in and out laboriously. I slid my hand into his, letting him know that I was there with him as he left us.

Halfway through the video, his heart had a serious jump and began failing. The doctor came in and stood next to me but he could do no more. Bequilles' hand tightened on mine. He held on to every precious second, until, finally, the face of a dead Adolf Hitler was revealed on the video.

Bequilles' face broke into a big smile.

"... It was worth it after all... My life was not wasted... There was a real Secret!"

"Yes, Bequilles, it was real and you kept it."

My words were wasted. Bequilles could hear no more.

ADDENDUM

A Note about O'Flanahan

Liam O'Flanahan would not allow me to publish this book without including this next section. Despite our many arguments about the subject, O'Flanahan has displayed a single-minded tenaciousness, coming back to this issue repeatedly. I cannot dispute the fact that, in this instance, I have no better theory to offer.

O'Flanahan may be right after all!

Paul Sirenne

Matt Chatelain

A King's Displeasure

By Liam O'Flanahan

"All right, he's been standing out there for three hours. That should be enough. We want everybody out except for you, Bude... Don't give Us that look, you know exactly what part you played in this and so do We."

King Francis the First motioned to his Grand Chamberlain to empty the throne room of all the courtiers and attendants. A muted, polite expression of protest wafted up from the closest Courtiers but Francis was firm. His Chamberlain had been instructed. These were exceedingly private matters and none were to be within hearing distance, except for those concerned.

Jacques Cartier was ushered in, the Grand Chamberlain closing the massive doors behind him. Far away, at the end of the large room, Cartier could see the King, sitting impassively on the throne. He wiped his cold, sweaty palms on his pants and started the long walk to approach the throne.

A few small voices had spoken in his ear; people had been asking questions. Then, last week, two of his men had gone drinking and never returned. Seeing Bude, standing there nervously next to the King, did nothing to assuage Cartier's growing concerns. What if the King knew everything?

He was about to find out. He had run out of red carpet and out of time. He took his place, well below the raised throne, looking up at his stern-faced King, with what he hoped was an innocent face.

"Jacques Cartier, We have summoned you this day, because you have incurred Our Displeasure."

The King paused heavily, leaving the silence laced with accusations.

"My King, what could your lowly servant have done?"

"Don't you play that fawning game with Us. You know very well what you have done."

"Perhaps, your Highness would be willing to provide his servant with the barest of indications as to how one might have acted wrongly?"

"Let Us discuss your trip to the New World. Perhaps that might jar your... failing memories..."

Cartier's face fell. The game was up. The King knew... but how much? Cartier decided to brazen it out. He would not admit anything willingly.

"My trip, Your Majesty? It went perfectly... I'm not sure...."

"So you said in your report to Us. We were very pleased at the time. However, We were not so pleased with the rumors that later came to Our ears. Rumors of a part of the trip not reported... To an island?... What do you have to say about that?... *SPEAK*... instead of standing there with your mouth gaping like a fish."

The anger in the King's voice shot a blast of fear through Cartier's veins.

"Certainly, Your Majesty, your servant did go to several islands that he did not report. Most were too small to mention..."

"We thought that you might have difficulty remembering. That is why We asked Our Royal Investigators to... question... some of the sailors who accompanied you on this voyage that We funded."

The King knew far more than he was saying. He was just leading Cartier on, letting him hang himself. Thinking fast, Cartier decided to admit to something, anything, to steer the story away from the most damning facts.

"Your Servant does remember a particular island, now that your Highness mentions it. We rested there for a short while..."

"About two full months, from what We have heard. A large gap in your report, wouldn't you say? And what led you there?"

"Uhm... uh... we... uh... We were led there by a ship."

"What type of ship? From what country, tell Us that?"

"We... uhm... we followed an English ship, your Majesty... But... but it was a Pirate ship. They had lost all morals..."

"SILENCE."

Cartier stopped blubbering. He had lost control for a moment. Luckily, the King's outburst gave Cartier time to calm down. He had to think this thing out. He kept his eyes low, not trusting himself to look up.

"... Now go on and tell Us what this English ship was doing to make you follow it and exactly why you felt it was not necessary to include it in your supposedly comprehensive report."

Feeling like his entire head was in a vise that he was being forced to tighten himself, Cartier explained his actions, his shifty eyes locked on the ground, trying to unload the blame wherever possible.

"Your servant's intentions were always honorable, Your Majesty. The English ship was sighted in the distance, behaving... uhm... oddly. Further out, barely visible on the horizon, our man in the turret could see smoke, which could only mean a sinking, destroyed ship, implying *Piracy*, your Majesty! We decided to follow the ship from a distance, to find out what they were doing. They landed at an island, where they moored in a small bay. They had obviously been there before, your Highness. We watched them while they unloaded several big caskets and brought them to a tree, after making some complicated measurements from key stones on the island. Once arrived at this tree, they dug down a few feet, removing thick oak planks and exposing a hidden shaft that led deep into the ground. They lowered their caskets down the shaft, using a block and tackle tied to a stout branch of the tree. After they were all done, they covered the shaft again and then, hid all evidence of their presence and left."

"It seems as if your memory has recovered from its sudden bout of amnesia. We wonder how much of what you are telling Us now is really true?

This line of inquiry had to be stopped, before all was revealed.

"Your Highness, please permit your servant to finish explaining. Your Majesty will see that we have acted properly all along..."

"Humphfff, this should be interesting to hear. Very well, you have Our permission to finish."

"Well... We moored our ship and disembarked to look around. Our scouts showed us where the block and tackle had been hidden. Using it, my men exposed the shaft and went down to the bottom, over thirty meters below the island's surface. Once there, the men found many caskets, which were brought back up to the surface, the excitement of the crew turning rapidly into greed. But when they opened the caskets, we... uh... they found only... uhm... cloth, beads, mirrors and... and tin knives. This discovery angered the men, who had been hoping for something more valuable. I had little choice but to allow them to vent their anger, if only to prevent a mutiny, your Majesty..."

"Enough of this prattle. What did you do then, pray tell?"

"My men felt that these English pirates would be... uhm... dangerous on the high seas, where perhaps, we ourselves might come under attack by the immoral heathens, so they decided to lay a trap for them..."

"Your men designed a trap? What type of trap?"

"Well, they dug a few small shafts, to allow a little bit of the seawater to flood the lower chamber where the barrels were found. If the... uh... the English ever returned, they would learn their lesson."

"Why did you not feel it worth mentioning all this in your report?"

"Your Majesty, I did not feel good about allowing my men to lay such a trap, warranted though it may have been. I felt my actions were not above some small amount of reproach. Also, no real harm had been done. If those men never conducted an act of piracy on the open seas again, then, they would suffer no harm. Justice would only come to the wicked."

"In other words, you are almost blameless. Apart from a minor straying, you acted properly all along."

"This is what I have been saying, your Majesty. Your servant has always tried to do the... the best thing for France."

There, that didn't go so badly, Cartier thought. It almost sounded believable to his own ears.

"Your words have almost satisfied Us. There is only one other matter, Cartier and then, you may go."

Upon hearing this, Cartier's heart soared with elation. He had done it. One more question and he was free of this. He felt brave enough to look up at his King, keeping his eyes as straight and clear as was possible.

"Your servant lives but to answer."

"Perfect. Then you will have no problem in telling Us about the gold!"

Cartier's entire body froze.

"The... g-gold... Your Highness? What g-gold?"

"Stop that stuttering. Yes the gold. Gold like this."

Francis the First threw several gold coins at Cartier's feet. Cartier recognized them instantly. He had told his men not to spend their portions until he gave them permission. Obviously, not all had listened. Cartier kept his eyes on the ground, knowing that the King was spearing him with his gaze, demanding an answer. How would he get out of this?

"Your servant now remembers that a few of the caskets, caskets we had not opened until much later, until it was too late to... uh... to return them, did, in fact, have a few pieces of gold in them. I did not think it worthy of mention."

"We noticed that fact. It seems your first trip to the New World has been a disappointment all around. We sent you there to find diamonds, gold and other riches. All you brought back to Us was two Indians, kidnapped Indians no less, and some few bales of moldy fur. Imagine Our surprise, when We hear that Our trusted Captain omitted to mention that he had stolen caskets filled with gold..."

"Hardly filled, your Majesty...."

"BE QUIET AND STOP YOUR LIES. WE WILL HAVE YOUR TONGUE CUT OUT IF WE HEAR ONE MORE LIE. DO YOU UNDERSTAND THAT, 'CAPTAIN' CARTIER?"

Cartier fell to the floor, prostrating himself in supplication, keeping his tongue deep within his tightly shut mouth. Perhaps he had gone too far with that last remark.

"So you followed an English ship to an island, lay in wait while they hid their gold, then stole it from them and lay a trap to drown them if they ever returned. Did We state what happened correctly?"

"Yes, your Majesty, perfectly correctly."

"Excellent. Now tell Us what have you been doing since you returned?"

"Hardly anything, Your Majesty. I have been exhausted from the trip to the New World and have spent my time resting."

"Did you perhaps go for a vacation or two during that resting time?"

"Yes Sire. Seeing the beauty of France always bring such joy to your servant's eyes."

"Yes, well, did you feel any of that joy while visiting Our fort?"

"Your fort, Your Highness?"

"Yes, Our fort. You know very well which fort I speak of: the Fort of Frefosse. The one We have been repairing."

"I did not know it was yours, Your Majesty. It is a lovely fort. I do remember it slightly. I may have passed by it, once or twice."

The King made a face, upon hearing this last evasion. Getting tired of Cartier's constant slithering shiftiness, Francis took a different tact.

"Imagine Our surprise when Our Royal Investigators informed me of a link between you and the College de France's administrator, Guillaume Bude. Perhaps you remember meeting him in passing? When We asked him to present himself in Our Presence to explain this connection, can you imagine what he might have told Us?"

The reason for Bude's presence was finally being revealed. The weak-willed fool had probably admitted everything he knew, eager to maintain his present post. Still Cartier refused to give up everything.

"Your Majesty is clearly all knowing. How could such a lowly servant such I pretend to know what Your Highness knows."

He was good, Francis had to admit but his admiration was easily dampened by the anger he felt at having been duped.

"We learned that you have been made aware of what lies below Frefosse's dungeon, thanks to Bude's loose lips. We have also learned that you entered in the fort, having been seen at least twice, carrying heavy sacks and coming back out without them. We have also learned that our neighbor, England, is extremely upset at the disappearance of several of their vessels, under suspicious circumstances. We believe that YOU HAVE HIDDEN THE GOLD YOU STOLE IN THE CAVES BENEATH THE DUNGEON."

"Your Majesty, I must admit that I did hide some gold in those caves, to keep it safe from my thieving men, but it is hardly anything worth making such a fuss about. I never thought it would cause such trouble. However, Sire, I have memorized the way into the cave and have carefully written it down and put it in a safe place."

"We are amazed at how you constantly manage to change the events to suit you. Do you dare to imply a threat on Our Royal Person with that last sentence?

"No, never Your Majesty. Your servant reveres your Royal Person. It is simply a precaution, in case anyone should do me harm. These are uncertain times, Your Highness."

Cartier's veiled words made the King pause. He knew that knowledge of the caves had to be kept quiet at all cost. Too many skeletons buried in there. Francis understood that the situation had changed. Until he was assured that the caves were safe, he could do Cartier no real harm. Frustrated but used to these cat-and-mouse games, he changed approach immediately.

"We want that gold returned in Our hands."

"Your Majesty, your servant lives but to obey. I would be happy to return to the caves and..."

"Oh no. You will never set foot in those caves again. We do not trust you. Unfortunately, We still have need of you since you are, unfortunately, Our most knowledgeable man, when it comes to the New World. You can draw a map to your hidden gold. Then you will make immediate preparations to leave France. Until then, you will be accompanied by heavy guard, no matter where you should go. We are banishing you to the New World, for the time being. We shall require that you return there and remove this trap of yours. You are to avoid any contact with the English from now on... and the Spanish for that matter. You will return the two kidnapped Indian sons to their father; you will look for, and return with, real gold and real diamonds for the glory of France... AND YOU WILL NEVER SPEAK OF THIS TO ANYONE EVER AGAIN. DO YOU UNDERSTAND?"

"Yes Your Majesty. Thank you for your overwhelming mercy, your Majesty. I will be forever in your debt and will carry out your every bidding from this moment forward. As long as I remain under your protection, the caves will remain our secret!"

"Shut up you worm. We have heard enough of your sniveling. Remove yourself at once from Our Royal Presence."

Cartier beat a hasty retreat, almost tripping over his feet in his anxiousness to leave the throne room. He couldn't believe that he had come out of there with his head still attached. Thank God he had taken a few precautions... In fact, it hadn't turned out too bad.

The King hadn't even asked about the jewels!

He would draw a confusing map for the King and then head back to the New World and kill those English cowards, if he could find them. When he came back, he would sneak into the caves, get his gold and disappear. It should be a piece of cake.

Back in the throne room, the King was fuming.

"Who does he think he is? Trying to blackmail Us indeed! And you, Bude! How could you have helped that odious man?"

"Sire, certainly you just heard him speak. His gilded tongue is adept at ferreting out support in the unlikeliest of persons. One seems to remember that he was the one selected, over so many others, to go to the New World, by none other than Your Majesty...."

"Watch what you say, Bude. You may be the College de France's administrator but We don't need your tongue to have you present your written reports to Us. You would do well to remember that."

Bude gulped heavily, mentally kicking himself for that comment but it had been irresistible. The King had been asking for it. Francis continued in his rant.

"As for that upstart, We shall teach him to hide his gold in Our caves. I want you to instruct Our Royal Engineer to begin drawing up plans to close off the access to the dungeon..."

"Your Majesty, the restoration of the fort has only recently been completed!"

"Be quiet. You will do what We request. Ensure that the hallway leading to the dungeon is permanently sealed and plans prepared to build a secret access to it in Our private chambers. Cartier will never find his way back into those caves. Now get out of here. We don't want to see you for at least a month."

Bude ran out of the throne room almost as fast as Cartier had, moments before him, glad that the King had not uncovered exactly why he had helped Cartier. He would have to melt those gold coins down. He hurried out, intent on carrying out that task without delay.

The End... for now.

THE SIRENNE SAGA

Unknowingly manipulated to become the key in the final phase of a complex conspiracy spanning millennia, Paul Sirenne is led to discover hidden knowledge and gain fantastic new abilities, preparing him for an ultimate confrontation beyond the forces of good and evil.

The Sirenne saga is a four book, epic adventure which follows Sirenne as he seeks the meaning behind everything, his efforts unwittingly causing Armageddon. Inextricably woven into history, the series gradually reveals an alternate perspective on the nature of reality, explaining the why and the how of our existence through Sirenne's evolution.

Delve deeper into the mysteries of Paul Sirenne's story in all four books of Sirenne Saga:

Book One: The Caves of Etretat

In the first novel of the series, Paul Sirenne uncovers a lost family secret, leading him on a historical treasure chase, shortly after his father is found brutally murdered. Assisted by three friends via the internet and hunted by a serial killer, he ends up in touristic Etretat, France, on the trail of a hundred year old mystery, hidden in Maurice Leblanc's book 'The Hollow Needle'. Falling in love with Leblanc's great-granddaughter and running at a breakneck pace, he deals with puzzles, theories, codes and historical mysteries, leading him to believe that Leblanc held a secret war against Adolf Hitler for the control of an incredible complex of caves hidden next to Etretat.

Book Two: The Four Books of Etretat

In the second novel, Sirenne discovers the real reason for the hidden war: the secret of immortality. Becoming an immortal himself, Sirenne learns of the Abbey, a thousand year old organization dedicated to chasing the oldest immortal on earth, known as the Greyman. The Abbey has given Sirenne control of the caves and its secrets, apparently preparing him for a confrontation with the Greyman. Unfortunately, the serial killer who killed Sirenne's father, Weissmuller, has discovered this knowledge before Sirenne. Now an immortal and constantly dogging Sirenne's steps, Weissmuller seems to be playing a game of his own.

Book Three: The One Book of Etretat

In the third novel, the world is in chaos. Countless disasters are occurring everywhere and a pandemic disease is killing all children in the womb. People and countries, desperate for a solution, are demanding Sirenne's immortality cure. Sirenne knows it's not the true answer and is desperately trying to solve the clues laid out by Maurice Leblanc and the Abbey, looking for the One Book. Changed by his immortality, he develops new senses which give him an increasingly different perspective on everything he sees. At the same time, all events seem to be converging on him. Weissmuller, the immortal serial killer is circling closer and closer.

Book Four: The Greyman.

In the fourth and final novel of the series, Sirenne learns that he has been selected to lead the Abbey to the Other, the only being strong enough to defeat the Greyman. Sirenne has mastered electromagnetic flight and the ability to manifest objects and manipulate matter. Weissmuller has revealed himself and an uneasy alliance has been made. The world is falling apart and people are dying by the millions as Sirenne continues trying to understand what is really going on. The unstoppable Greyman is drawing near and an ultimate confrontation seems inevitable. Everything rests on Sirenne's final decision. Will he be able to accept the real answers behind everything?

FOR MORE ON

'THE SIRENNE SAGA'

Check out the Author's website:

www.mattchatelain.com

On his site, you will find background information about the series and about the author's current projects. The site also contains material from previous projects and a bio of the author.

Of particular interest to 'The Caves of Etretat' readers will be an excerpt from Leblanc's original manuscript for those interested in solving his secret code. Otherwise, you will find the answer in book two, 'The Four Books of Etretat'.

Matt Chatelain

Bonus

A Short Excerpt from Book Two:
'The Four Books of Etretat'
Chapter One

Early that morning, Coulter had called me on the wireless intranet that connected all of us together. Raymonde and I had continued wearing our techno-glasses (sunglasses with built-in monitor, cameras, speakers and microphones, all connected wirelessly via an intranet). The lenses were now tinted darkly, because the fungus-produced light in the caves had been increasing in intensity. The techno-glasses' usefulness had been noted and others were obtained so that the main personnel could stay in contact with each other. More were purchased until, eventually, everyone in the caves had a pair. They became a popular tool for Net members, who could connect instantly with each other and consult in real-time while examining streaming video of the discoveries. It speeded up the process to no end. Now people, would just stop working, sit down for a break and have an online discussion about the best way to proceed. As many could be brought into the decision-making process as was necessary. Once done, people would disconnect and continue with their work.

It made for a certain type of hive mentality and private channels were quickly set up to allow for gossip and social activities. Schedules were organized for video broadcasts at certain times and a 'breaking-news' interactive hotline had been set-up, which had received rave reviews. Coulter had designed all intranet systems for simplicity of use and now, the glasses were part of our social lives, most wearing them nearly twenty-four/seven.

Coulter had given me a five minutes heads-up that he wanted to hold an online meeting. He and I were going to meet O'Flanahan physically in a little while and I did not understand the rush. He had sounded serious, telling me to prepare myself for some bad news. He would not say more. I connected online with Raymonde and we talked privately, as I prepared a coffee in our kitchen.

"What do you think he could have to say?" she wondered.

"I don't know. He had that look in his eyes, the one that spells worry and trouble. It can't be good," I replied. "How has your day gone?"

"Fine... Excellent really. I am on my way to you on the first automated electric golf cart to be brought online. They have an onboard computer and can safely carry anyone to any point in the renovated cave areas. They can even recharge themselves. We have just finished bringing in the last of the supplies this morning. So everyone is fairly happy. It figures that Coulter would announce rain on such a good day... Here I am..." she got off her cart, her video showing her approach to a familiar-looking door.

Our own.

I got up, turning off my glasses and opened the main door, finding her standing there, about to enter. I hugged her tightly and we returned to the kitchen, where I served her some coffee. I had made it strong but found it weak and flat. The others signed on and the online meeting got underway.

"What was so important, Coulter?" rasped Liam O'Flanahan. "We're going to meet in a little while anyway."

"Indeed, Coulter, I was in the middle of a meeting with the head of the archeological team. We are just about to begin the first excavations. Despite the convenience of this intranet, it is sometimes a bother," added Jonathan Briar.

"Guys, please, this is difficult enough..." interrupted a nervous Coulter. "... Maybe I should just get to the point. You all remember this video, I hope..."

The glasses' monitor changed to show a still video image, slightly grainy. It was a rearward-looking shot over several passengers sitting in a plane. I remembered it instantly. This was from my first plane flight to Paris, the one where I originally met Raymonde, thanks to O'Flanahan's antics. It was also the one where we had seen Norton, the Shadow-Killer, disguised as Harry Stiles, a man he had killed for his plane ticket. My eyes refocused on the image, picking out the perfectly disguised Norton, as Coulter superimposed a red outline around his face.

"You all know how I like playing with my videos...."

O'Flanahan snickered but Coulter ignored him, remaining focused on what he was telling us.

".... This one image bothered me in particular. It took me a while to figure out what was niggling at me but I finally got it. Let me give you a hint..." the image altered, with the fake Harry Stiles fading suddenly into light grey tones. This allowed me to focus more closely on what was behind Stiles. I could see a row of seats, filled with various people. My eyes were drawn by an odd shape behind and just to the right of Stiles. It was a man sitting in a seat, his body and face mostly hidden by Stiles' outline. Although he was bending his head down, as if deliberately trying to hide himself, something in the curve of the nose and the end of the man's chin struck me as familiar.

I felt my mind revving up, scanning through all the faces I could think of. Only one matched. I mentally superimposed it on the video image and it fit perfectly.

"Norton was on that plane *with* the Shadow-Killer." I spoke up.

"How did you catch on so quickly?" Coulter exclaimed, as he highlighted the Interpol Inspector's outline.

"I just saw it. It was obvious." I said simply.

"Well, you are, as always, correct. Norton *was* on that plane, sitting right behind the man disguised as Harry Stiles, who *had* to be the Shadow-Killer... and if Norton was on that plane with the killer..."

O'Flanahan, jumping to the conspiracy-minded conclusion, interrupted Coulter.

"... Then Norton couldn't be the Shadow-Killer... Ha-ha-ha... I knew it. Briar killed the wrong man..."

Briar's face became apoplectic when he heard this.

"I resent that, O'Flanahan. You're trying to imply that I did the wrong thing, that I killed an innocent man somehow... Well, you couldn't be more wrong and you know it... Killer or not, the man was deranged. You all saw that. He *shot* at Sirenne before and then he attacked him on the beach with a *knife*, intent on killing him. If I hadn't done what I did, Paul would be dead by now. I don't regret what I did, not for a second..."

"Yes, Liam, Jonathan's right," supported Raymonde. " We can't blame him for doing the best he could during difficult times. He made the only decision he was able to..."

Briar jumped back in, not finished.

"... Thank you, Raymonde, but it's not just that... I don't think any of you have thought this through to its inevitable conclusions. Firstly, Sirenne's father warned us of the importance of silence. Perhaps Norton was not the Shadow-Killer but he was dangerous nonetheless and knew something about our caves. He was screaming the letters H and N at every opportunity, pointing his finger at the book, the Hollow Needle. How long would our Great Hunt have lasted then?" Briar added. "Perhaps you all find me heartless but we have proven to ourselves the reality of these caves. I am convinced that keeping them secret is of paramount importance."

"Hey, Briar, you just made me realize something..." O'Flanahan admitted. "When you mentioned about Norton always talking about HN... We always thought that it was connected to Leblanc's Hollow Needle book. But now I'm beginning to wonder if he even knew of the book... Do any of you remember what Norton was screaming at Sirenne, when he attacked him on top of the cliff? Didn't he ask Paul about his sister after mentioning the letters?"

I flashed on the scene in my mind, the image vivid, seeing Norton as he held his gun pointed at me, screaming in the wind. I ran Norton's words in slow motion in my mind, editing out the wind noise.

"... Helena... He called her Helena... Helena Norton... The letters HN!" I whispered.

"You got it, Bucko. But I'm sure he said something else after that..."

"I remember that too... Let me call up the video, I've got it right here," Coulter exclaimed excitedly.

The monitor image jumped to the streaming video recorded by my techno-glasses when I was walking towards the bunker on top of Etretat's Aval cliff, the location of the original fort of Frefosse, where our adventure had begun. The video fast-forwarded and I watched myself running through my paces until it froze as I turned around to face Norton. He held his small gun at waist height. Everyone saw me whip out my gun in a surprise move.

"Man, that was nervy, Paul. I'd forgotten about that," stated an impressed Coulter. He started the video and played back Norton's key words.

"*First, it was my sister, Helena... Then it was my friend Henri Nadeau... Then all the others, all the same and they were all blaming me. But they didn't understand. It was all a game and I was stuck in it. It wasn't me... they were wrong... I just can't PROVE it... And now he stole my file, everything I had on him...*"

He laughed, a bit madly in my opinion but stopped himself and continued his ramble.

"*... And this time, the first time ever, I caught him... I SAW HIM... the Shadow-Killer... he was leaving with my file under his arm and I saw him in the mirror, the door was open... and he... he was ME, he was me, ha-ha, he was me, can you believe it? Ha-ha-ha, what a perfect disguise.*"

When I had heard these words the first time, I had thought them incomprehensible, the ravings of a demented killer. Now, looking at it slightly differently, I understood his words in a completely new way. Everyone spoke up at the same time. O'Flanahan took control, talking louder than everyone, anxious to bring his point home. "... Something had been bugging me about what he said. It wasn't just his sister but his friend Henri Nadeau... another HN. Then Norton says something about all the others and everyone blaming him..."

Coulter sprang into action, his fingers flashing on his keyboard.

"I can check into that. I'll tap into the Interpol files about Norton... There we go..."

He scanned his results with a practiced eye and exclaimed:

"... Wow, it was right there in front of us, all the time. Every one of the murdered victims had the initials HN... Horatio Nolan... Honore Noel... the list goes on and on... Norton's words are making more and more sense all of a sudden."

O'Flanahan continued spinning logical conclusions.

"If Norton was not the killer, then the Shadow-Killer was the one murdering all manner of people around Norton, anyone with the initials HN, driving Norton mad, goading him constantly... When Paul's parents were killed and their bodies twisted into those exact same letters, it was like drawing a moth to the flame. Norton would have run directly towards any murder connected to the letters HN... Perhaps the Hollow Needle never had anything to do with it for him..."

Raymonde exclaimed, struck by another possibility.

"After that, when he talked of seeing the Shadow-Killer reflected in the mirror..."

"... The very thing which made me think that he had two personalities and had finally gone over the deep end..." I added, in tune with Raymonde's thoughts.

"Exactly... We already knew that the Shadow-Killer could disguise himself... What if he disguised himself as Norton and Norton saw *him* in the mirror, not himself?... Then his words would not be those of a multiple personality murderer, but those of a man driven nearly mad by a killer haunting his footsteps for years... The very idea of it is absolutely horrifying. But why was the killer doing this?" she asked.

"Isn't it obvious?... It *was* to drive him mad, to prime him and goad him until he was ready to explode. When Paul's parents were arranged in the shape of those letters, it guaranteed that the murders would be quickly followed by an enraged cop who would pounce on Sirenne... It was a set-up... probably planned by the Shadow-Killer... to lead the crazed Norton directly to Paul's doorstep." O'Flanahan continued.

Hearing this last theory, I exploded.

"O'Flanahan, if that's true, then it also means that the Shadow-Killer began planning this thing fifteen years ago at least, when he killed Norton's sister. That is a scary thought. Not only is he still out there, he has been planning this thing for a very, very long time..."

O'Flanahan nodded his head, looking thoughtful.

"I wonder how old the guy is?..."

"Maybe the killer needed someone for us to blame... to focus on... in order to take our attention off what he was really doing," suggested Briar.

"That sounds exactly right, Briar," supported O'Flanahan.

"Well, it seems that he has succeeded in his attempts." I added. "So far we still don't know who he is, where he is and why he is there in the first place. At least we now know that he *is* out there. We can hopefully begin taking measures to protect ourselves against him."

"*If* we can find him... He certainly seems to live up to his name. He has successfully remained deeply in the shadows and is probably still hiding there now, watching our every move, using us as puppets. The thought is frightening," stated Coulter.

"The only option available to us is to continue our efforts in uncovering the secret of the caves and, through that, we might be able to understand why the killer is prodding us. He knows more than we do about this mystery and is looking for something that he believes only we can provide. Until we find that, there is a fair chance that we will remain safe." I reasoned.

"I agree, Paul. The Shadow-Killer has not attacked any of us personally to date. He did manipulate Norton and is apparently manipulating us now. As long as we keep doing what he wants, he will likely remain in the shadows. It gives us a window of opportunity. Let us seize it and try to find some answers but let's do it faster than he is expecting. Then, he will be in *our* shadow." Briar added, as forceful and focused as ever.

End of Excerpt
See you in Book Two!

www.ingramcontent.com/pod-product-compliance
Lightning Source LLC
Chambersburg PA
CBHW070307260626
47160CB00003B/746